SHE

broadview editions
series editor: L.W. Conolly

SHE

A HISTORY OF ADVENTURE

H. Rider Haggard

edited by Andrew M. Stauffer

broadview editions

FACSIMILE OF THE SHERD OF AMENARTAS

FACSIMILE OF THE REVERSE OF THE SHERD OF AMENARTAS

Library and Archives Canada Cataloguing in Publication

Haggard, H. Rider (Henry Rider), 1856-1925
    She : a history of adventure / H. Rider Haggard ; edited by Andrew M.

Stauffer.

(Broadview editions)
Includes bibliographical references.
ISBN 1-55111-647-2

    I. Stauffer, Andrew M., 1968- II. Title. III. Series.

PR4731.S48 2006   823'.8   C2005-907134-6

Broadview Editions

The Broadview Editions series represents the ever-changing canon of literature by bringing together texts long regarded as classics with valuable lesser-known works.

Advisory editor for this volume: Professor Eugene Benson

Broadview Press Ltd. is an independent, international publishing house, incorporated in 1985. Broadview believes in shared ownership, both with its employees and with the general public; since the year 2000 Broadview shares have traded publicly on the Toronto Venture Exchange under the symbol BDP.

We welcome comments and suggestions regarding any aspect of our publications–please feel free to contact us at the addresses below or at broadview@broadviewpress.com / www.broadviewpress.com

North America
PO Box 1243, Peterborough, Ontario, Canada K9J 7H5
Tel: (705) 743-8990; Fax: (705) 743-8353
email: customerservice@broadviewpress.com
PO Box 1015, 3576 California Road, Orchard Park, NY, USA 14127

UK, Ireland, and continental Europe
NBN Plymbridge
Estover Road
Plymouth PL6 7PY UK
Tel: 44 (0) 1752 202 301
Fax: 44 (0) 1752 202 331
Fax Order Line: 44 (0) 1752 202 333
Customer Service: cservs@nbnplymbridge.com
Orders: orders@nbnplymbridge.com

Australia and New Zealand
UNIREPS, University of New South Wales
Sydney, NSW, 2052
Australia
Tel: 61 2 9664 0999; Fax: 61 2 9664 5420
email: info.press@unsw.edu.au

PRINTED IN CANADA

Contents

Preface

First published in 1886, *She* has always been Rider Haggard's most popular and influential novel, challenged only by *King Solomon's Mines* in this regard. In the character of Ayesha, Haggard created a powerful myth of intertwined imperial and sexual passions: a beautiful, semi-divine, veiled white woman ruling over black Africans in a lost city of the dead. In this way, the novel reflects its historical contexts, including the flowering of archaeology in the Victorian era (particularly with regard to Egyptology and Great Zimbabwe), the expansion of British Empire and "the scramble for Africa" among the European powers, and the Woman Question as it developed in the late Victorian era. Furthermore, Haggard had spent time in South Africa as part of the English imperial administration in the time of the Zulu and Boer Wars, and the novel reflects those immediate experiences. Finally, and perhaps most importantly, *She* is a fascinating, troubling, and intricate novel, written rapidly but with great intensity.

This Broadview edition of *She* is designed to give readers a clearer sense of what it was like to read the novel within its Victorian contexts. It presents the text of the original periodical version (published in the *Graphic*, July 1886–January 1887), and reprints the twelve original illustrations by E.K. Johnson. In addition, it provides background readings including contemporary reviews and selections from Haggard and his contemporaries on issues such as race, gender, archaeology, and empire. This material is accompanied by a critical introduction, a chronology of Haggard's life and work, and a bibliography of suggested readings. Finally, Appendix E traces the major revisions that Haggard made to the novel as he revised it for publication in book form.

In preparing this edition, I have benefited greatly from the work of others who have taken up the task of editing Haggard, especially Norman Etherington, Daniel Karlin, Patrick Brantlinger, and Gerald Monsman, whose editions and introductions are all models of their kind. In addition, I owe a collective debt to my anonymous Broadview readers, who influenced the shape of the edition in many ways. Steve Arata was an invaluable resource in this regard, and he has my gratitude. I would also like to thank Robert Aguirre, Jason Atkin, Erik Gray, Michelle Hawley, Khaled Arafat Kazi, Shawn Malley, Gemma Rodrigues, and Chuck Rzepka for their encouragement of the project and for helpful suggestions as it grew. Cara Norris was particularly indispensable in the final stages, and Michael Hamilton did a terrific job with the images. Thanks also to Julia Gaunce, Barbara and Leonard Conolly, and Don LePan of Broadview Press, who were wonderfully generous with their assistance and support. My greatest debts are to my father, George H. Stauffer, for his ongoing interest in my edition and his much-appreciated readings and suggestions regarding both novel and contextual materials; to my mother, Libby Stauffer, for her continual support and encouragement in all my work; and to my wife, Zahr Said Stauffer, scholar-adventurer from the province of Yaman the Happy, for inspiration, proofreading, and everything else that counts.

Introduction

In February 1886, the 29-year-old Henry Rider Haggard began to write *She: A History of Adventure*, the last and best of his most famous works of fiction. He had penned *King Solomon's Mines* and *Allan Quatermain* the previous year, and although he would continue producing novels for almost four decades (including three sequels to *She*), Haggard was peaking as he filled pages "at white heat, almost without rest" with the story of Ayesha, "She-who-must-be-obeyed" (Haggard, *Days*, 1.245). Like most of his work up to this point, the new novel grew out of the author's first-hand experiences of southern Africa during the eventful years of 1875-81, which saw the British annexation (and later, the retrocession) of the Transvaal, war with the Zulu nation, and the First Boer War. Onto this African material, Haggard was grafting deeply-imagined, almost dream-like narratives and figures, producing novels that combine the evocative specificity of travel writing with the uncanny visions of Gothic romance. With *She*, he triumphed in creating two compelling characters whose contrasts and affinities anchor our interest, and made the novel an instant popular success: Horace Holly, the grizzled Cambridge scholar-turned-explorer, and Ayesha, the beautiful, white-skinned Arab queen who has ruled for centuries in the heart of Africa. Their novel—named for her, but told in his voice—captures the uneasy attraction that late-Victorian Britons felt towards the African continent, which remained for most an imagined land of natives both cruel and sexually alluring; of big and exotic game; of lost cities and archaeological treasures; and of hidden sources of life and fertility, all ringed with dangers and death. Moreover, Ayesha herself becomes a focus of desires and anxieties related to women's power, late in Queen Victoria's reign, when modern ideas about gender equality were being raised in earnest. At times, Haggard's novel seems to have emerged straight out of the Victorian subconscious; Rudyard Kipling once said to its author, "You didn't write *She*, you know; something wrote it through you" (qtd. in Addy, xiv). But *She* is also the work of an author concerned with authenticity and the craft of storytelling; it remains one of the most fascinating novels of the period.

One hardly would have expected Haggard to write such a book. A younger son of a large, minor-gentry English family, he was given a desultory education (he did not attend university) and showed little aptitude for or interest in a career, even failing the army entrance examination.

But when he was nineteen, his father's influence landed him a position as secretary to Sir Henry Bulwer, who had just been appointed lieutenant governor of the Natal, the British territory in present-day South Africa. Once there, Haggard quickly became involved in the imperial politics of the region, joining Sir Theophilus Shepstone, the Secretary for Native Affairs, on a fateful diplomatic mission to the Transvaal, the Dutch republic north of the Natal. In 1877, Shepstone and his officials claimed the republic as part of the British Empire, citing the need to protect the settlers from the ravages of the Zulus, whose kingdom abutted both the English and Dutch territories. Haggard himself read part of the proclamation, and remembered the April morning in Market Square, Pretoria, when he helped to raise the British flag over the Transvaal for the first time. Soon England would be at war with the Zulus, and then with the Boers, who demanded the return of their republic. Meanwhile, Haggard had loved and lost Lily Jackson ("Lilith"), the model for the unattainable, ideal woman featured in many of his novels, including *She*. And he had, in 1880, married Louisa Margitson, a steady and companionable woman for whom one suspects he felt something less than great passion. But Louisa accompanied him back to Africa, giving birth to their first child, Jock, on Haggard's unsuccessful ostrich farm on the Natal-Transvaal border, with the Boer War rumbling close in the background.

It was during this tumultuous period that Haggard began writing, first sending home journalistic accounts of events and his experiences, and then (after returning to England for good) publishing his first book, *Cetywayo and His White Neighbors* (1882). This was a non-fictional account of the Zulu king Cetshwayo and the Anglo-Dutch conflicts of the previous years, a book that, as Norman Etherington puts it, "nailed Haggard's political colors to the mast of the Tory party, which he never deserted" (*Annotated* She, xvi). Soon, after some trial-runs writing fairly predictable novels, Haggard turned his hand to the adventure genre with *King Solomon's Mines*, and realized he had found his strength: putting his African memories—and his powerful imagination—in the service of what we now call the imperial romance. Inspired by Robert Louis Stevenson's *Treasure Island* (1883), *King Solomon's Mines* also begins with the image of a map indicating the path to buried treasure. In Haggard's novel, the diamond mines of King Solomon lie in a barely-charted part of Africa; the map becomes a promissory note for English readers who knew of the diamond fields of South Africa (discovered in the late 1860s), and wanted to believe in the value of colonizing other parts of the subcontinent. Like *She* and *Allan Quatermain*, *King Solomon's*

Mines presents Africa as a rich, mysterious, and dangerous field for English exertion, a place that requires (and rewards) courage, intelligence, honor, and warlike deeds. In short, Haggard wrote his way to fame with fantasies of exploration and violence set on the fringes of the British empire, using his knowledge of Africa to set the stage.

She, however, represents an advance in artistic sophistication, beyond the "boy's book" adventure story and onto more complex ground. Our first clue is the subtitle, "A History of Adventure," which foreshadows the priority Haggard gives to historical records, relics, and narratives in the novel—not in the interest of simple realism, but in a way that keeps questions of authenticity and evidence in constant tension with the plainly fantastic occurrences that comprise the plot. The whole novel is introduced by a fictional editor (a version of Haggard himself), who presents Holly's "wonderful and mysterious" story as a thing upon which "the reader must form his own judgment" (35; 39). Furthermore, the ancient "sherd of Amenartas" stands at the heart of the plot as another "wonderful" written text or narrative that requires interpretation. When the novel was published in book form, Haggard had a "fake" sherd fabricated to the specifications of the story, and had photogravure images of it inserted as a frontispiece (reproduced at the front of this edition); he also greatly augmented the historical transcriptions from the ancient sherd (see Appendix E). In December of 1887, he confessed to his friend H.A. Holden, who helped write the Greek inscriptions on the sherd, that he meant to fool the experts: "I am not without hopes of getting a rise or two out of the antiquarians" (UCLA 418.2.5). Indeed, archaeological desires shape this "history" throughout, from the unwrapping of the sherd to the exploration of Kôr and its mummy-filled catacombs, episodes that evoke the experience of reading the novel itself. As fellow novelist Wilkie Collins wrote to Haggard while in the midst of reading *She*, "I am already adrift in that boat among the swamps of the fatal coast, and for the first time in my life I am longing to make an African Discovery—the discovery of 'She'" (UCLA 418.2.2).

In emphasizing relics, monuments, and tombs in his novel, Haggard was engaging the Victorian fascination with Near Eastern archaeology, particularly in Egypt and Assyria, where Europeans had been uncovering (and appropriating) the records and remains of ancient civilizations since the first half of the century. Thanks to agents such as Giovanni Belzoni (in Egypt) and Austen Henry Layard (in Mesopotamia), the British Museum had amassed its impressive collections of ancient sculptures, bas-reliefs, hieroglyphic inscriptions, and mummies in the years that led up to the publication of *She*. Furthermore, by the 1880s, British archaeological exploration and acquisition in the Near East had given rise to a flourishing popular culture of ancient civilizations, visible in travel narratives and guidebooks, panoramic exhibitions and theatrical displays, private collections of antiquities and public unwrapping of mummies, and a burgeoning tourist industry in Egypt. However, surprisingly little of this had migrated to the English novel prior to *She*. Written soon after the great discovery of royal Egyptian mummies at Deir el-Bahri in 1881 (Appendix B.1-3, 6) and amidst speculation regarding the Great Zimbabwe ruins in Africa (Appendix B.4-5), Haggard's novel was predicated on archaeological curiosity and the contemporary passion for the exotic past. What is more, it represented a romantic, interactive version of the museum experience. The ruins of Kôr are located somewhere in central Africa, but the city was apparently built by a lost white race with affinities to the Egyptians under the pharaohs, including their mummification of the dead; and their presiding ruler lived in ancient Egypt and regularly appears swathed in linen from head to foot. The characters sleep in the catacombs in former burial-rooms decorated with hieroglyphs and reliefs, and they tour the ruins of Kôr under optimal conditions, by moonlight or by lamps filled with mummy-fragments, with no crowds of tourists, guided by a wise and beautiful living relic to sites, untouched for centuries, that pre-date any known civilization by thousands of years. Looking at some of the ancient bas-reliefs, Holly thinks "how envious some antiquarian friends of my own at Cambridge would be if ever I got an opportunity of describing these wonderful remains to them," (139) something which of course he has just done for us, his readers. Our envy feels like curiosity, as Holly travels with continued astonishment through the many occult spaces of the novel—Ayesha's boudoir, the tombs of Kôr, the Temple of Truth, the cave of the Spirit of Life.

As the first of that list indicates, Ayesha (pronounced "ASH-uh") herself is the primary focus of readerly curiosity from the time that her history emerges from the triple-locked, nested boxes of the Vinceys. In a memorable scene, Holly describes his thoughts while he waits anxiously to see the legendary "She-who-must-be-obeyed" for the first time:

> At last the curtain began to move. Who could be behind it?—some naked savage queen, a languishing Oriental beauty, or a nineteenth-century young lady, drinking afternoon tea? I had not the slightest idea, and should not have been astonished at seeing any of the three. I was getting beyond astonishment. (143)

One of Holly's great strengths as a narrator is the ability to recreate such moments of expectation and surprise, as if he himself doesn't know what is going to happen next, and is continually amazed (despite his protestations) when new wonders appear. And yet he maintains a subdued, irreverent sense of humor, remaining all the while alive to the oddity of his story. Here, his three guesses about "She" evoke the tangle of sexual and racial tensions that energize the novel, even as they suggest an unexpected imaginative proximity between Victorian England and this ancient civilization in central Africa. In the event, "She" turns out to be none of these things, or rather an uncanny synthesis of all of them (minus the tea-drinking): Ayesha slowly reveals herself to be a multi-faceted idealization who captivates Holly and Leo—not to mention Haggard himself, who wondered if "any reader of the book" could be "but half as much in love with She as I confess to being" (Appendix A.7). Indeed, the terms of the book suggest that, as the world's wisest and most beautiful woman, Ayesha herself is the ultimate virginal site for exploration and discovery.

Yet "She-who-must-be-obeyed" is anything but a passive, exploitable territory. Her strength emerges not only in her iron-willed rule of the Amahagger, her tenacious love for Kallikrates/Leo, her physical fearless-ness, and her magical powers—but also, more immediately, in the glamor of her conversation. If Ayesha becomes something more than a superla-tive cipher, it is because of the way she interacts with Holly, the only person close to being her intellectual equal in the novel, and the one most alive to her attractions. In Holly's company, Ayesha shows the many moods and tempers of mind that together evoke the synthesis of savage queen, Oriental beauty, and Victorian young lady that Holly had imag-ined. Taken out of context, the sentences that She speaks may or may not be great prose—Haggard has often been criticized for his overblown and awkward rhetoric—but they nevertheless compel because of Ayesha's charisma, as in the extraordinary scene in Chapter XVII when she tempts Holly to admire her beauty and he begs her to marry him:

> For a moment she looked a little surprised, and then she began to laugh, and clap her hands in glee.
>
> "Oh, so soon, oh Holly!" she said. "I wondered how many minutes it would take to bring thee to thy knees. I have not seen a man kneel before me for so many days, and, believe me, to a woman's heart the sight is sweet, ay, wisdom and length of days take not from that dear pleasure which is our sex's only right.

"What wouldst thou?—what wouldst thou? Thou dost not know what thou doest. Have I not told thee that I am not for thee? I love but one, and it is not thee. Ah Holly, for all thy wisdom—and in a way thou art wise—thou art but a fool running after folly. Thou wouldst look into mine eyes—thou wouldst kiss me. Well, if it pleaseth thee, *look*," and she bent herself towards me, and fixed her dark and thrilling orbs upon my own; "ay, and *kiss*, too, if thou wilt, for, thanks be given to the scheme of things, kisses leave no marks, except upon the heart. But if thou dost kiss, I tell thee of a surety thou wilt eat out thy heart with love of me, and die!" (182)

In such scenes, Ayesha's attractions unite beauty with a threatening authority: she appears as Venus Victrix, the conquering goddess of love, to whom Holly compares her when he first sees her unveiled. Yet in this midst of this, she also coquettishly gestures towards feminine vulnerability, calling the pleasure of sexual conquest "our sex's only right." Haggard knew that the success of *She* depended on his ability to make Ayesha an irresistible, eroticized celebrity, an end he furthers by emphasizing both her power and her vulnerability, and using Holly as an adoring reporter, the most flattering of cameras.

Nevertheless, we do see Ayesha's dark side; even Holly calls her beauty "evil" when he first sees her face (153). She pursues her ends with whatever tools she has, including political terror, torture, and murder, mostly deployed against the Amahagger, whom she despises. One Haggard scholar has gone so far as to call her "a Diana in jackboots who preaches materialism in philosophy and fascism in politics" (Etherington, *Rider Haggard*, 47). As with so many of its themes, the novel seems divided in its attitude towards Ayesha's hunger for power and her might-makes-right philosophy. When Holly learns that the queen of the ruins of Kôr has bigger plans for domination, he writes,

The terrible *She* had evidently made up her mind to go to England, and it made me absolutely shudder to think what would be the result of her arrival there.... In the end she would, I had little doubt, assume absolute rule over the British dominions, and probably over the whole earth, and though I was sure that she would speedily make ours the most glorious and prosperous empire that the world has ever seen, it would be at the cost of a terrible sacrifice of life. (232–33)

Is Holly's shudder over Ayesha's imagined "absolute rule" one of dread or anticipation? The reiterated "terrible" seems to indicate the former, and yet the promise of a "glorious and prosperous empire" over the entire world appears to be dangerously attractive to these Englishmen in Ayesha's orbit.

Under the influence of his love for She, Holly goes on to provide two excuses for her selfish behavior, first, that two thousand years of experience might make anyone into a moral relativist, and second, that she did it all for love. Haggard himself called Ayesha's love for Kallikrates her "saving grace and a gate of redemption" (Appendix A.7), something that becomes clearer in the novel's grimmer, duller sequel, *Ayesha: The Return of She* (1905). Indeed, at a basic level, *She* is a love story: Haggard says that when he started writing, "The only clear notion that I had in my head was that of an immortal woman inspired by an immortal love" (*Days*, 1:246). The problem (from our perspective) is Leo Vincey, the object of her passion: he remains a beautiful, empty-headed, flat character who moreover is almost entirely passive, someone hardly worth a two-thousand-year wait. When Haggard's friend Andrew Lang raised this objection precisely, the novelist responded by adding a postscript to the "Editor's" preface, speculating that Ayesha perceived a "spark of greatness" in Leo's soul. Haggard suggests that, like her virtue, his wisdom can only be catalyzed by the other's love, a process cut short (or postponed indefinitely) by the terrifying conclusion in the cave of the Spirit of Life.

The *Graphic* Context

The first readers to encounter Haggard's novel did so in the pages of the *Graphic*, a large folio magazine with lavish illustrations, published weekly in London. Each installment of the novel (except the last) was accompanied by an engraving by E.K. Johnson, and the text was broken up into fifteen segments that did not always correspond to the chapter divisions. For example, the 18 December installment concludes with a cliff-hanger in the midst of chapter twenty-four, with Ayesha summoning Holly across the narrow board to the swinging stone. *Graphic* readers would have waited a week to discover the sequel which the novel presents immediately without so much as a line-break. Furthermore, the last two sections are shorter than the rest, suggesting that a single installment was split in two in order to draw out the publication run. In preserving these divisions and reproducing the Johnson engravings, this edition approximates the contours of the *Graphic* text, bringing readers closer to the original experience of the novel in its serial form.

However, one still misses the incredibly rich context of the *Graphic* itself. Like its contemporary the *Illustrated London News*, the *Graphic* attracted readers with its numerous pictures, large and small, of people and scenes from all corners of the globe, with particular emphasis on the British empire. The volumes in which *She* appears also feature pictorial spreads and articles on Constantinople, Burma, South Africa, Egypt, and India, some of which connect in significant ways to the novel itself. In volume 34, for example, we find an article entitled "Royal Mummies Recently Unbandaged at the Boulak Museum," accompanied by engravings of the withered, ancient faces of the pharaohs Seti I and Ramses II (see Appendix B.2), evoking the mummies of Haggard's Kôr as well as the fictionalized Egyptian past of Ayesha and Kallikrates. Furthermore, other articles in this volume of the *Graphic* deal with the British military occupation of Egypt and conflicts in the Sudan, implicitly relating these archaeological interests to larger imperial concerns (290, 323, 531). Items such "The South African Gold Fields" (98), "A Visit to the Kimberly Diamond Fields, South Africa" (51), and the "Cape Town Illustrated" supplement (Oct. 30, 1886) provide real-life illustrative corollaries for the settings of Haggard's fiction. But one need not single out any particular article or engraving to see that the *Graphic* placed *She* amidst an array of material both exotic and deeply English. One thinks of Holly with things like his "Paysandu" potted meat (77): British commercial products that serve him faithfully in uncharted Africa, and which provide familiar counterpoints to the strangeness of everything else around him. When he takes a little mummified foot from Billali and places it in his "Gladstone" bag, Holly thinks it "a strange combination," (119) and so it is—but no stranger than the juxtapositions of items in the *Graphic*, where advertisements for Gladstone bags and Pear's soap (promising "white and beautiful hands") sit next to engravings of Seti and Ramses, and of native Africans armed with Martini-Henry rifles (e.g., 35:114, 271). Especially in its serial incarnation, *She* is firmly a part of an increasingly global imagination on the part of the English middle-classes; Leo, Holly, and Job at Kôr come to resemble the readers of the London magazine in which they appear, continually confronting, wondering at, and finally assimilating foreignness with their expansive, imperial imaginations.

Race and Empire

In July 1882, Britain had invaded Egypt to suppress a popular uprising led by Urabi Pasha, then the minister of war, who had rallied the public against the growing European influence in Egyptian affairs and against the current ruler, Khedive Tawfiq Pasha. Urabi's Egyptian nationalist movement was crushed by the British at the battle of Tel al-Kebir, and, although Tawfiq's rule was re-established, Britain occupied and essentially controlled Egypt until World War I. These imperial exertions took place amid the so-called "scramble for Africa" by the Western nations, as territories were being claimed and contested by the English, Dutch, French, Germans, Italians, Belgians, Spanish, and Portuguese; the struggle over the Transvaal is an episode that Haggard himself experienced up close. In 1884, the Conference of Berlin was convened so that the Europeans could create a legal framework for administering the colonization of the African continent. *She* therefore emerges out of an historical context supercharged with questions of race and empire in Africa and invokes a particularly British view of the world. At first glance, Holly, Leo, and Job may seem to have little to do with geopolitical negotiations or imperial conquests, but their itinerary and attitudes are best understood in relation to these immediate historical events.

We know that Leo was born in May of 1856 (56), meaning that Holly, Leo, and Job begin their journey in August of 1881 and return "exactly two years from the date of our departure" (279). Although they travel a long way from the "quiet college rooms" and "wind-swayed English elms" of Cambridge, they never leave England entirely behind: the route to Zanzibar would have taken them through territory almost consistently controlled by the British (66). If Haggard's Victorian readers had made the same trip, they would have sailed through the Suez Canal in occupied Egypt, down the Red Sea past the British outpost at Aden in Yemen, past British Somaliland along the Horn of Africa, and from there to British East Africa and the Sultanate of Zanzibar, which would itself be made a protectorate a few years later, in 1890.[1] In this manner, one might say that the imperial reach of Great Britain enables the journey of the novel's protagonists, as do Mahomed and his fellow Arab sailors, who would have been hired at one of these ports of call. Haggard gives us none of this backdrop, however, picking up the

---

[1]   See Thomas Pakenham, *The Scramble for Africa: White Man's Conquest of the Dark Continent from 1876 to 1912* (New York: HarperCollins, 1991) 276ff.

narrative only as the characters enter an unknown East African coast at the fictional rock formation known as the Head of the Ethiopian, an effigy that marks the boundary of the familiar world, and of Ayesha's domain. In a sense, then, a single property line divides the realm of Queen Victoria and that of "She-who-must-be-obeyed," two white queens who rule dark-skinned natives of the African continent.

Like many of his English contemporaries, Haggard proceeds on the assumption that whites are naturally superior to blacks, and that Britain's imperial extensions into Africa are a noble, civilizing enterprise (see Appendix C). In the novel, Ayesha, the ancient citizens of Kôr, and the three Englishmen are all white-skinned, and stand for the forces of civilization, while the darker-skinned Amahagger are aligned with savagery, cannibalism, and superstition—although as subordinates they may demonstrate admirable traits such as bravery or fidelity, as is the case with Billali and Ustane. One can hardly defend *She* from charges of racism to a degree typical of writing of its era. At the same time, the racial politics of the novel are more complex than they first appear: Ayesha is an Arab; Leo precisely resembles (and perhaps is) an ancient Greek; Holly looks like a baboon, an association Victorians typically made with black Africans; the Arabic-speaking Amahagger are light-skinned ("yellowish") with straight hair and "aquiline" features (90); and Ustane may be a reincarnated Egyptian. That is, Haggard seems not to have intended a straight contrast between Anglo-Saxon whites and dark-skinned races. Rather, the novel suggests deeper connections among the races, an ancient genealogy of ethnicities and civilizations in which every character is a hybrid.

Nevertheless, it is true that the novel treats the native Africans as marginal, degenerate figures in this history of grander civilizations that preoccupies both Holly and Ayesha. They imagine a line connecting Kôr, ancient Egypt, Greece, Rome, and England as imperial standard-bearers of human accomplishment, while the Amahagger are simply debased by-products of the march of history, apparently incapable of noble creations or advancement of any kind. In fact, this attitude toward native Africans was reflected in late-Victorian theories regarding the Great Zimbabwe ruins, discovered in the 1860s. European archaeologists immediately assumed that these stone structures and ornaments (located in present-day Zimbabwe, a word that means "houses of stone") must have been created by a lost, "civilized" race, assuming (wrongly) that native Africans would not have been capable of creating them. Haggard himself speculated that the Phoenicians or "some race intimately connected with them" must have built Great Zimbabwe (see Appendix B.4). What's more, he also associates the ruins with Ophir, the ancient Biblical city ruled by the Queen of Sheba, providing a link to Ayesha, the Yemeni queen of Kôr. Haggard's theories are thus connected to his depiction of Kôr as the product of an advanced white culture that has since disappeared (but perhaps migrated north to found ancient Egyptian civilization). The Amahagger (or "people of the rocks") remain as the childlike, brutal remnant of this progression, with no culture of their own other than what they have borrowed (and debased) from the ancient residents of Kôr, in whose tombs they now reside. Their recycled habitat becomes a powerful metaphor of belatedness and degeneration.

The Woman Question

As one might expect of a novel named with a feminine pronoun, *She* also raises issues of gender and sexual politics, particularly in relation to late-Victorian debates regarding women's rights and responsibilities. Referred to generally as "The Woman Question," these debates began in earnest in the 1880s, and involved a wide range of topics, including marriage, property, legal rights, fashion, deportment, education, politics, and literature. The roles for and rights of women in English society had changed radically since the early part of the century, as they joined the workforce in greater numbers, received better and more complete educations, and were given rights to their own property and more power in married relationships. With these changes grew an increasingly vocal and influential women's movement and the predictable conservative reaction, meaning that the image of a powerful female called "She-who-must-be-obeyed" resonated as part of the struggle over the proper political and cultural roles for women. Indeed, a disapproving male writer reviewing Margaret Pember-Devereux's feminist work, *The Ascent of Woman*, in 1897 says ruefully of the author's dedication to "Her that shall be," "'She that shall be' will most probably appear as 'She-who-must-be-obeyed'" (see Appendix D.6). In addition, *She* was published in book form in 1887, the year of Queen Victoria's Golden Jubilee, and Adrienne Munich suggests that Haggard's work "could fittingly be considered an ominous literary monument to Victoria after fifty years of her reign" (198). Certainly it engages the whole question of female political power, and in its representation of a wise, beautiful, tyrannical sorceress and queen, Haggard's novel provided a touchstone for many of the anxieties surrounding the

New Woman in late-Victorian England. As Sandra Gilbert and Susan Gubar describe Ayesha,

> She was neither an angel nor a monster. Rather, *She-who-must-be-obeyed* was an odd blend of the two types—an angelically chaste woman with monstrous powers, a monstrously passionate woman with angelic charms. Just as importantly, however, She was in certain ways an entirely New Woman: the all-knowing, all-powerful ruler of a matriarchal society. (6)

In other ways, however (and perhaps more like Queen Victoria in this regard), Ayesha represents a femininity as old-fashioned as her two thousand years might suggest: her power is tempered by her all-consuming devotion to Kallikrates/Leo, to whom she swears virtuous wifely obedience at the novel's climax, in what she calls the "first most holy hour of completed Womanhood" (254). Furthermore, in her role as seductive *femme fatale*, She is part of a long tradition of male fantasy that includes Homer's Circe, Shakespeare's Cleopatra, and Keats's "La Belle Dame sans Merci." Steven Arata calls her "the veiled woman, that ubiquitous nineteenth-century figure of male desire and anxiety, whose body is Truth but a Truth that blasts" (97). Even the confirmed misogynist Holly is instantly captivated.

Haggard's daughter tells the story that the name "She-who-must-be-obeyed" was taken from "a disreputable rag doll of particularly hideous aspect, with boot-button eyes, hair of black wool and a sinister leer upon its painted face," which Haggard's "unscrupulous nurse" used in order "to frighten him into obedience" (*Cloak*, 28). The anecdote suggests Ayesha's proximity to what Anne McClintock calls the "ominous and inexplicable authority" of women in Haggard's imagination, which "he was compelled to ward ... off with an act of ideological exorcism in *She*" (235-36). Thus, Ayesha's fate at the conclusion of the novel comes as a wishful punishment by Haggard and his fellow readers, a disintegration of the anxiety-producing female power and sexuality that she incarnates. As Haggard himself described it in a letter to the *Spectator*,

> In the insolence of her strength and loveliness, she lifts herself up against the Omnipotent. Therefore, at the appointed time she is swept away by It with every circumstance of "shame and hideous mockery." Vengeance, more heavy because more long-delayed, strikes her in her proudest part—her beauty; and in her lover's very presence she is

made to learn the thing she really is, and what is the end of earthly wisdom and of the loveliness she prized so highly. (Appendix A.7)

Yet as an exorcism, the events in the Cave of Life are more inconclusive than this summary suggests, and the novel's final sentence points to what the sequel, *Ayesha: The Return of She*, makes clear: Haggard wanted to preserve his heroine and the forces she represents. She disappears from the novel, but not from the myth that he was bent on forging; and, while she is more virtuous and less sexual in the later novels, she is also more heartless and powerful. The titles he contemplated for his second novel about her are telling: "The Priestess," "The Oracle," "The Spirit," and "The Goddess." Rather than dispelling her, Haggard turns her into a divinity—which, in the end, perhaps amounts to the same thing.

The Reception and Afterlife of *She*

Victorian readers and critics of *She* responded with what has become a familiar set of praises and complaints: they called the novel haunting, vigorous, and imaginative, but found it filled with "tawdry sentiment" and "bad grammar" (Appendix A.10). One reviewer said that the novel was like reading an account of Dante's Inferno written by a reporter for the *Daily Telegraph*, an observation meant as a "compliment" to its conception and to its style, given the appetites of the reading public (Appendix A.1). Indeed, the early conversation about Haggard's novel focused on whether it was closer to being popular entertainment or literature, a "penny dreadful" (a cheap, sensational book) or a serious work of art. Given Haggard's energetic but often careless writing, many saw (and indeed continue to see) his novels as something less than a literary achievement. For example, the *Blackwood's* reviewer was of the opinion that *She* would work better as a theatrical spectacle: "It might be wrought up into an unparalleled stage effect: but it is rather a failure in pen and ink" (Appendix A.8). The justice of this remark may perhaps be measured by the many movies based on the novel, from George Méliès silent *La Colonne de Feu* (*The Pillar of Fire*) in 1899 to Robert Day's *She* with Ursula Andress in 1965, and beyond.[1] However, none of the film versions is a masterpiece and the novel itself continues to compel readers: since its initial publication, it has never been out of print.

---

[1]   See Ellis, *H. Rider Haggard*, 278, for a list of film versions of *She* through 1978.

Haggard himself addressed the question of literary merit in a slightly arrogant essay entitled "About Fiction," published just after *She* appeared in book form (Appendix A.9). He takes the position that "really good romance writing is perhaps the most difficult art practised by the sons of men," and decries most of the work of his fellow novelists as a "worthless" "crude mass of fiction." Calling contemporary American literature "emasculated," French literature "carnal and filthy," and English literature "namby-pamby nonsense," Haggard recommends a return to the high ideals and imaginative freedoms of "purely romantic fiction" like Swift's *Gulliver's Travels* (1726), Defoe's *Robinson Crusoe* (1719-20), and—one draws the inference—*King Solomon's Mines* and *She*: works that he says appeal "to all time and humanity at large." In this essay, Haggard stakes out a territory of compelling invention and romantic storytelling; he has little to say about the matter of prose style other than praising "the swiftness, and strength, and directness of the great English writers of the past." Again, the adjectives are telling with regard to Haggard's own writing, which often shares these virtues at the expense of grace, care, and subtlety. Predictably, the essay provoked angry reactions from other writers and critics, such as Augustus Moore, who blasts *She* and Haggard for his "lack of imagination and deficiency in constructive power" and states bluntly and rather ill-naturedly, "Mr. Haggard cannot write English at all" (Appendix A.10).

As Daniel Karlin has said, "That Haggard's style is frequently bathetic or clumsy cannot be denied; but the matter is not so easily settled" (xvi). In a passage that seems to be a prime example of the charges against him, Holly finds himself meditating on the contrast between the mortal and the ideal as he tries to fall asleep on "a little oasis of dry in the midst of the miry wilderness":

> so I lay and watched the stars come out by thousands, till all the immense arch of Heaven was strewn with glittering points, and every point a world! Here was a glorious sight by which man might well measure his own insignificance!... Oh, that we could shake loose the prisoned pinions of the soul and soar to that superior point, whence, like to some traveller looking out through space from Darien's giddiest peak, we might gaze with the spirit eyes of noble thoughts deep into Infinity!... Yes ... to have done with the foul and thorny places of the world; and like to those glittering points above me, to sit on high wrapped for ever in the brightness of our better selves,... and lay down our littleness in that wide glory of our

dreams, that invisible but surrounding Good, from which all Truth and Beauty comes! (122–23)

At first glance, this seems to be merely awkward slush; but then the mention of Darien stands out, an allusion to Keats's poem, "On First Looking into Chapman's Homer," in which the poet compares his experience of reading Homer to that of an explorer encountering the Pacific Ocean for the first time, "silent, upon a peak in Darien." Once we note this, the Keatsian frame to Holly's thoughts emerges from the background: his star-gazing wish "to sit on high wrapped for ever in the brightness of our better selves" alludes to the sonnet "Bright Star!" in which Keats desires to be "steadfast" as the star which he addresses, "and so live ever." And the concluding reference to "Truth and Beauty" evokes the famous ending of Keats's "Ode on a Grecian Urn": "'Beauty is truth, truth beauty,'—that is all/Ye know on earth, and all ye need to know." That is, Haggard provides a literary framework for Holly's musings by echoing three Keats poems that concern man's desire for ideality and permanence, with "La Belle Dame sans Merci" looming somewhere ahead. Further, the difficulty of phrases like "the spirit eyes of noble thoughts" help enact Holly's sense of blocked and contorted movement as he strives towards an unreachable philosophical euphony. Then, in a characteristic move, Holly remarks dryly, "I at last managed to get to sleep, a fact for which anybody who reads this narrative, if anybody ever does, may very probably be thankful" (123). The disarming deflation of the passage also goes a long way toward redeeming it, and is typical of the winning contradictions of the narrator's style.

Ultimately however, one thinks of Haggard's plots, episodes, and images as the source of his lasting reputation and influence. Sigmund Freud (born the same year as Haggard) and Carl Jung both admired *She* and integrated the novel into their works on psychoanalysis. Recommending the book to a patient, Freud calls it "a *strange* book, and full of hidden meaning … the eternal feminine, the immortality of our emotions" and Jung sees Ayesha as an example of the anima, the unattainable, ideal woman that men seek.[1] In addition, authors such as Rudyard Kipling, Henry Miller, Graham Greene, J.R.R. Tolkien, and Margaret Atwood have all acknowledged the importance of Haggard's fiction. He has been credited with inventing the "Lost Civilization" novel and the romance of archaeological exploration; even Steven Spielberg's Indiana Jones owes something to

---

[1] For Freud's comments, see *The Interpretation of Dreams*, 452–55.

Holly, the college professor-adventurer seeking relics of an ancient past. In addition, Haggard has inspired a good amount of twentieth-century science fiction, from the work of Edgar Rice Burroughs and C.S. Lewis to Alan Moore's *The League of Extraordinary Gentlemen* (2000). Certainly Ayesha herself has her share of descendents: Brian Aldiss writes in *Trillion Year Spree*, "From Haggard on, crumbling women, priestesses, or empresses—all symbols of women as Untouchable and Unmakeable—fill the pages of many a 'scientific romance'" (139). Like other fictional human monsters of the nineteenth century such as Robert Louis Stevenson's Dr. Jekyll and Mr. Hyde and Bram Stoker's Dracula, Haggard's She has escaped from her eponymous novel to stalk the wider field of culture as a bona fide literary myth. Leading Holly through the mummy-filled catacombs of Kôr, Ayesha exclaims, "to the tomb, and to the forgetfulness that hides the tomb, must we all come at last! Ay, even I who live so long. Even for me, oh Holly, thousands upon thousands of years hence ... a day will dawn whereon I shall die" (179). If such a day is approaching, we have seen no sign of it.

H. Rider Haggard: A Brief Chronology

1856	Born in Norfolk, England (22 June), the sixth son of ten children.
1869–72	Attends Ipswich Grammar School. Fails army entrance examination.
1875	Meets Lily Jackson ("Lilith"), his great love. Passes the foreign office entrance examination, and is appointed as secretary to Sir Henry Bulwer, the lieutenant governor of Natal, South Africa. Arrives in Cape Town in August.
1876–77	Visits Zulu Chief Pagate. Joins Sir Theophilus Shepstone as part of a delegation to the Transvaal, which Britain then annexes from the Boers. Haggard himself raises the Union Jack over the Transvaal for the first time. Appointed Master and Registrar of the High Court of the Transvaal. Begins publishing articles about his African experiences in English periodicals.
1878–79	Hears of Lilith's marriage to another man. British forces attack the Zulus and are crushed at Isandhlwana. Resigns his office with an eye towards ostrich-farming. Visits England and meets Louisa Margitson. Zulus defeated by the British.
1880	Marries Louisa and returns with her to South Africa. First Boer War begins.
1881	Son Jock is born (August). Transvaal is ceded to the Boers. Family returns to England and Haggard studies law.
1882	*Cetywayo and His White Neighbors*, a study of the recent political events in South Africa, making the case for British imperial governance. This is first of over fifty books Haggard would publish in his lifetime. Great Britain takes control of Egypt.
1883	Daughter Agnes born (January).
1884	Daughter Dorothy born (March). Realistic novels *Dawn* and *The Witch's Head*. Admitted to the bar.
1885	*King Solomon's Mines*, his first, hugely successful work of adventure fiction.
1886	*She: A History of Adventure* written in six weeks and then serialized in the *Graphic*.

1887   *She* appears in book form. *Allan Quatermain*, and *Jess*. Tours Egypt.

1888   *Maiwa's Revenge* and *Colonel Quaritch V.G.* Travels to Iceland.

1889   *Cleopatra*, based on his experiences in Egypt. Death of Haggard's mother.

1890   *The World's Desire*, written in collaboration with Andrew Lang.

1891   Travels to Mexico. Son Jock dies (age 9). *Eric Brighteyes*, an Icelandic saga.

1892   Daughter Lilias born (December). *Nada the Lily*, a romance of the Zulus.

1895   Runs for Parliament but loses. Co-edits *The African Review*.

1901–02   Travels around the country, surveying agricultural developments, and publishes *Rural England*. Death of Queen Victoria.

1905   *Ayesha or the Return of She*, the sequel to *She*. Visits America to write a report on the Salvation Army (*Regeneration*, 1910).

1908   *The Ghost Kings*, written in collaboration with Rudyard Kipling.

1912   Begins publishing his Zulu trilogy with *Marie*. *Child of Storm* (1913) and *Finished* (1917) complete the series.

1914   Returns to South Africa; visits the Great Zimbabwe ruins. World War I begins.

1919   Made a Knight Commander of the British Empire.

1920   *The Ancient Allan* and *Smith and the Pharaohs*.

1921   *She and Allan*, a prequel to *She*, with Allan Quatermain as narrator.

1923   *Wisdom's Daughter*, a further prequel to *She*, telling the story of Ayesha and the original Kallikrates.

1925   Dies (14 May) in a London hospital (age 68).

A Note on the Text

Haggard wrote *She*, as he says, "at white heat" in February and March of 1886, and the novel was first published serially, with illustrations by E.K. Johnson, between October 1886 and January 1887 (vols. 34-5) in the *Graphic*, a weekly, large-format London magazine. Just before this serialization concluded (8 January), an American edition published by Harper and Bros. appeared in New York (24 December 1886); it included the Johnson illustrations. This was followed by an English edition published by Longmans, Green, and Co. (1 January 1887). The first illustrated English edition, with drawings by Maurice Greiffenhagen and C.H.M. Kerr, appeared in London in 1888. Haggard continued to revise the novel as later editions appeared (1891 and 1896).[1]

I have chosen to present the *Graphic* version of *She*, a text that has not been reprinted in a modern edition. Haggard himself said that romances like *She* should not be much revised, since "wine of this character loses its bouquet when it is poured from glass to glass" (*Days*, 2:92). Striking differences include a scene (later revised) in which a minor character, Mahomed, is killed when cannibals place a red-hot pot upon his head in preparation for eating him. Also, for the first edition, Haggard added a large amount of material to the description (and transcription) of the sherd of Amenartas in chapter three, and generally bolstered the novel's historical scholarship. The style and grammar of the *Graphic* is more energetic and immediate (if sometimes more flawed), and stands in closer relation to that six week flush of creativity that produced the novel in the first place. In Appendix E, the larger additions and revisions Haggard made for the first English edition have been included, but I have not attempted anything like a complete collation of variants.

Obvious typographical errors and misprints, involving punctuation or minor spelling errors, have been emended. Haggard varies his spelling of "naught" (or "nought"), and I have left these as they originally appeared, despite the inconsistency. Haggard's original notes have been retained in the text and are identified by asterisks and daggers.

---

[1]   See the introduction to *The Annotated* She (xix-xxiii), for the best description of Haggard's revisions to the novel. Etherington's notes (211-38) record variants between the manuscript, *Graphic*, and later book editions.

With the exception of the frontispiece, the illustrations included here are from the *Graphic*; the frontispiece images of the "Sherd of Amenartas" were added in the first English edition.

List of Illustrations

SHE

A HISTORY OF ADVENTURE

"A tall man of about thirty, with the remains of great personal beauty, came hurrying in, staggering beneath the weight of a massive iron box."

INTRODUCTION

In giving to the world the record of what, looked at from that point of view only, is I suppose one of the most wonderful and mysterious adventures ever experienced by mortal men, I feel it incumbent on me to explain what my exact connection with it is. And so I may as well say at once that I am not the narrator but only the editor of this extraordinary history, and then proceed to tell how it found its way into my hands.

Some years ago I, the editor, was staying with a brother at one of the Universities, which for the purposes of this history we will call Cambridge, and was one day much struck with the appearance of two people whom I saw going arm-in-arm down the street. One of these gentlemen was I think, without exception, the handsomest young fellow I have ever set eyes on. He was very tall, very broad, and had a look of power and a grace of bearing that seemed as native to him as it is to a wild stag. In addition his face was almost without flaw—a good face as well as a beautiful one, and when he lifted his hat, which he did just then to a passing lady, I saw that his head was covered with little golden curls growing close to the scalp.

"Good gracious!" I said to my brother, with whom I was walking, "why, that fellow looks like a statue of Apollo[1] come to life. What a splendid man he is."

"Yes," he answered, "he is the handsomest man in the University, and one of the nicest too. They call him 'the Greek god;' but look at the other one, he's Vincey's (that's the god's name) guardian, and supposed to be full of every kind of information. They call him 'Charon.'"[2] I looked, and found the older man quite as interesting in his way as the glorified specimen of humanity at his side. He appeared to be about forty years of age, and was I think as ugly as his companion was handsome. To begin with, he was shortish, rather bow-legged, very deep chested, and with unusually long arms. He had dark hair and small eyes, and the hair grew right down on his forehead, and his whiskers grew right up to his hair, so that there was uncommonly

---

[1] The god of poetry, archery, and sunlight, typically represented as a beautiful young man.
[2] In Greek mythology, the blind, aged boatman who ferries dead souls across the river Styx into Hades.

little of his countenance to be seen. Altogether he reminded me forcibly of a gorilla, and yet there was something very pleasing and genial about the man's eye. I remember saying that I should like to know him.

"All right," answered my brother, "nothing easier. I know Vincey; I'll introduce you," and he did, and for some minutes we stood chatting—about the Zulu people, I think, for I had just returned from the Cape at the time.[1] Presently, however, a stoutish lady, whose name I do not remember, came along the pavement, accompanied by a pretty fair-haired girl, and these two Mr. Vincey, who clearly knew them well, at once joined, and walked off in their company. I remember being rather amused because of the change in the expression of the elder man, whose name I discovered was Holly, when he saw the ladies advancing. He suddenly stopped short in his talk, cast a reproachful look at his companion, and, with an abrupt nod to myself, turned and marched off alone across the street. I heard afterwards that he was popularly supposed to be as much afraid of a woman as most people are of a mad dog, which accounted for his precipitate retreat. I cannot say, however, that young Vincey showed much aversion to feminine society on this occasion. Indeed I remember laughing, and remarking to my brother at the time that he was not the sort of man whom one would care to introduce to the lady one was going to marry, since it is exceedingly probable that the acquaintance would end in a transfer of her affections. He was altogether too good-looking, and, what is more, he had none of that consciousness and conceit about him which usually afflicts handsome men, and makes them deservedly disliked by their fellows.

That evening my visit came to an end, and that was the last I saw or heard of Charon and the Greek god for many a long day. Indeed I have never seen either of them from that hour to this, and do not suppose it likely that I shall. But a month ago I received a letter and two packets, one of manuscript, and on opening the first found that it was signed by "Horace Holly," a name that at the moment was not familiar to me. It ran as follows:—

---

[1] As a young man, Haggard had spent six years in southern Africa, working for the British colonial government; see Introduction.

—— College, Cambridge,
"1st May, 18——.

"My dear Sir,

"You will be surprised, considering the very slight nature of our acquaintance, to get a letter from me. Indeed, I think I had better begin by reminding you that we once met, now some five years ago, when your brother introduced me and my ward Leo Vincey to you in the street at Cambridge. To be brief and come to my business. I have recently read with much interest a book of yours describing a Central African adventure.[1] I take it that this book is partly true, and partly an effort of the imagination. However this may be, it has given me an idea. It happens, how you will see in the accompanying manuscript (which together with the Scarab,[2] the "Royal Son of the Sun," and the original sherd,[3] I am sending to you by hand), that my ward, or rather my adopted son, Leo Vincey and myself have recently passed through a real African adventure, of a nature so much more marvellous than the one which you describe, that to tell the truth I am almost ashamed to submit it to you for fear lest you should disbelieve me. You will see it stated in this manuscript that I, or rather we, had made up our minds not to make this history public during our joint lives. Nor should we alter our determination were it not for a circumstance that has recently arisen. We are, for reasons that you may be able to guess, after perusing this manuscript, going away again, this time to Central Asia, where, if anywhere upon this earth, wisdom is to be found, and anticipate that our sojourn there will be a long one.[4] Possibly we shall not return. Under these altered conditions it has become a question whether we are justified in withholding from the world an account of a phenomenon which we believe to be of unparalleled interest, merely because our private life is involved, or because we are afraid of ridicule and doubt being cast upon our statements. I hold one view about this matter, and Leo holds another, and finally after much discussion, we have come to a compromise, namely, to send the history to you, giving you full leave to publish it if you think fit, the only stipulation being that you shall disguise our real

---

1 A reference to Haggard's previous work of fiction, *King Solomon's Mines* (1885).
2 Short for scarabaeus, a beetle held sacred by the ancient Egyptians, often represented in carved stone talismans and ornaments.
3 A fragment of pottery; a potsherd.
4 Haggard's sequel to *She*, entitled *Ayesha: The Return of She* (1905), takes place in the mountains of Tibet.

names, and as much concerning our identity as is consistent with the maintenance of the *bona fides* of the narrative.

"And now what am I to say further? I really do not know beyond once more repeating that everything described in the accompanying manuscript is exactly as it happened. As regards *She* herself I have nothing to add. Day by day we have greater occasion to regret that we did not better avail ourselves of our opportunities to obtain more information from that marvellous woman. Who was she? How did she first come to the Caves of Kôr, and what was her real religion? We never ascertained, and now alas, we never shall, at least not yet. These and many other questions arise in my mind, but what is the good of asking them now?

"Will you undertake the task? We give you complete freedom, and as a reward you will certainly have the credit of giving to the world the most wonderful history, as distinguished from romance, that its records can show. Read the manuscript (which I have copied out fairly for your benefit), and let me know.

"Believe me,

"Very truly yours,

"L. HORACE HOLLY

"P.S.—Of course, if any profit results from the sale of the writing should you care to undertake it, you can do what you like with it, but if there is a loss I will leave instructions with my lawyers, Messrs. Geoffrey and Jordan, to meet it. We entrust the sherd, the scarab, and the parchment to your keeping till such time as we demand them back again."—L.H.H.

This letter, as may be imagined, astonished me considerably, but when I came to look at the MS., which the pressure of other work prevented me from doing for a fortnight, I was still more astonished, as I think the reader will be also, and at once made up my mind to press on with the matter. I wrote to this effect to Mr. Holly, but a week afterwards received a letter from that gentleman's lawyers, returning my own, with the information that their client and Mr. Leo Vincey had already left this country for Thibet, and they did not at present know their address.

Well, that is all I have to say. Of the history itself the reader must judge. I give it him, with the exception of a very few alterations, made with the object of concealing the identity of the actors from the general public, exactly as it has come to me. Personally I have made up my mind to refrain from comments. At first I was inclined to believe that this history of a woman on whom, clothed in the majesty of her almost endless years, the shadow of Eternity itself lay like the dark wing of Night, was some gigantic allegory of which I could not catch the meaning. Then I thought that it might be a bold attempt to portray the possible results of immortality, grafted on the substance of a mortal who yet drew her strength from the earth, and in whose human bosom passions yet rose and fell and beat as in the undying world around her the winds and the tides rise and fall and beat unceasingly. But as I went on I abandoned that idea also. To me the story seems to bear the stamp of truth upon its face. Its explanation I must leave to others, and with this slight preface which circumstances make necessary, I introduce the world to Ayesha and the Caves of Kôr.

THE EDITOR

P.S.—There is on consideration one circumstance that, after a reperusal of this history, struck me with so much force that I cannot resist calling the attention of the reader to it. He will observe that so far as we are made acquainted with him there is nothing in the character of Leo Vincey which in the opinion of most people would have been likely to attract an intellect so powerful as that of Ayesha. He is not even, at any rate to my view, particularly interesting. Indeed, one might have imagined that Mr. Holly would under ordinary circumstances have easily outstripped him in the favour of *She*. Can it be that extremes meet, and that the very excess and splendour of her mind led her by means of some strange physical reaction to worship at the shrine of matter? Was that ancient Kallikrates nothing but a splendid animal beloved for his Greek beauty? Or is the true explanation what I believe it to be, namely, that Ayesha, seeing further than we can see, perceived the germ and smouldering spark of greatness that lay hid within her lover's soul, and well knew that under the influence of her gift of life, watered by her wisdom, and shone upon with the sunshine of her presence, it would bloom like a flower and flash out like a star, filling the world with fragrance and with light?

Here also I am not able to answer, but must leave the reader to form his own judgment on the materials before him.

I

MY VISITOR

There are some events of which every circumstance and surrounding detail seems to be graven on the memory in such fashion that we cannot forget it, and so it is with the scene that I am about to describe. It rises as clearly before my mind at this moment as though it had happened yesterday.

It was in this very month something over twenty years ago that I, Ludwig Horace Holly, was sitting one night in my rooms at Cambridge, grinding away at some mathematical work, I forget what. I was to go up for my fellowship within a week, and was expected by my tutor and my College generally to distinguish myself. At last, wearied out, I flung my book down, and, going to the mantelpiece, took down a pipe and filled it. There was a candle burning on the mantelpiece, and a long, narrow glass at the back of it; and as I was in the act of lighting the pipe I caught sight of my own countenance in the glass, and paused to reflect. The lighted match burnt away till it scorched my fingers, forcing me to drop it; but still I stood and stared at myself in the glass, and reflected.

"Well," I said aloud, at last, "it is to be hoped that I shall be able to do something with the inside of my head, for I shall certainly never do anything by the help of the outside."

This remark will doubtless strike anybody who reads it as being slightly obscure, but I was in reality alluding to my physical deficiencies. Most men of twenty-two are endowed at any rate with some share of the comeliness of youth, but to me even this was denied. Short, thick-set, and deep-chested almost to deformity, with long sinewy arms, heavy features, deep-set grey eyes, a low brow half overgrown with a mop of thick black hair, like a deserted clearing on which the forest had once more begun to encroach; such was my appearance nearly a quarter of a century ago, and such, with some modification, is it to this day. Like Cain, I was branded[1]—branded by Nature with the stamp of abnormal ugliness, as I was gifted by Nature with iron and abnormal strength and considerable intellectual powers. So ugly was I that the spruce young men of my College, though they were proud enough of my feats of endurance and physical prowess, did not even care to be seen walking

---

[1]   See Genesis 4:15; Cain kills his brother Abel and is both protected and exiled by God's brand or mark upon him.

with me. Was it wonderful that I was misanthropic and sullen? Was it wonderful that I brooded and worked alone, and had no friends—at least, only one? I was set apart by Nature to live alone, and draw comfort from her breast, and hers only. Women hated the sight of me. Only a week before I had heard one call me a "monster" when she thought I was out of hearing, and say that I had converted her to Darwin's theory.[1] Once, indeed, a woman pretended to care for me, and I lavished all the pent-up affection of my nature upon her. Then money that was to have come to me went elsewhere, and she discarded me. I pleaded with her as I have never pleaded with any living creature before or since, for I was caught by her sweet face, and loved her; and in the end by way of answer she took me to the glass, and stood side by side with me, and looked into it.

"Now," she said, "if I am Beauty, who are you?" and I cursed her and fled. That was when I was only twenty.

And so I stood and stared, and felt a sort of grim satisfaction in the sense of my own loneliness; for I had neither father, nor mother, nor brother; and as I did so there came a knock at my door.

I listened before I went to open it, for it was nearly twelve o'clock at night, and I was in no mood to admit any stranger. I had but one friend in the College, or, indeed, in the world—perhaps it was he.

Just then the person outside the door coughed, and I hastened to open it, for I knew the cough.

A tall man of about thirty, with the remains of great personal beauty, came hurrying in, staggering beneath the weight of a massive iron box which he carried by a handle in his right hand. He placed the box upon the table, and then fell into an awful fit of coughing. He coughed and coughed till his face became quite purple, and at last he sank into a chair and began to spit up blood. I poured out some whisky into a tumbler, and gave it to him. He drank it, and seemed better, though his better was very bad indeed.

"Why did you keep me standing there in the cold?" he asked; "you know the draughts are death to me."

"I did not know who it was," I answered. "You are a late visitor."

"Yes; and I verily believe it is my last visit," he answered, with a ghastly attempt at a smile. "I am done for, Holly. I am done for. I do not believe that I shall see to-morrow!"

---

[1]   Charles Darwin's *On the Origin of Species* (1859) advanced the theory that humans are descended from apes.

"Nonsense!" I said. "Let me go for a doctor."

He waved me back imperiously with his hand. "It is sober sense; but I want no doctors. I have studied medicine, and I know all about it. No doctors can help me. My last hour has come! For a year past I have only lived by a miracle. Now listen to me as you never listened to anybody before; for you will not have the opportunity of getting me to repeat my words. We have been friends for two years; now tell me how much do you know about me?"

"I know that you are rich, and have had a fancy to come to College long after the age that most men leave it. I know that you have been married, and that your wife died; and that you have been the best, indeed almost the only, friend I ever had."

"Did you know that I have a son?"

"No."

"I have. He is five years old. He cost me his mother's life, and I have never been able to bear to look upon his face in consequence. Holly, if you will accept the trust, I am going to leave you the boy's sole guardian."

I sprang almost out of my chair. "*Me!*" I said.

"Yes, you. I have not studied you for two years for nothing. I have known for some time that I could not last, and since I realised the fact, I have been searching for some one to whom I could confide the boy and this," and he tapped the iron box. "You are the man, Holly; for, like a rugged tree, you are hard and sound at core. Listen; the boy will be the last survivor of one of the most ancient families in the world, that is, so far as families can be traced. You will laugh at me when I say it, but one day it will be proved to you beyond a doubt, that the founder of the family, my sixty-fifth or sixty-sixth lineal ancestor, was an Egyptian priest of Isis,[1] though he was himself of Grecian extraction, and was called Kallikrates, or the Strong and Beautiful, or, to be still more accurate, the Beautiful in Strength! His father was, I believe, one of the Greek mercenaries raised by Hakor, a Mendesian Prince of the Twenty-ninth Dynasty.[2] In or about the year 339 before Christ, just at the time of the final fall of the Pharaohs, this Kallikrates broke his vows of celibacy, and fled from Egypt with a Princess of Royal blood who had fallen in love with him, and was finally wrecked upon the coast of Africa, somewhere, as I believe, in the neighbourhood of where Delagoa

---

[1]   Ancient Egyptian goddess of fertility, wife and sister of Osiris.
[2]   Also known as Achoris, whose family came from the Egyptian city of Mendes. He ruled Egypt from 393–380 BCE.

Bay[1] now is, or rather to the north of it, he and his wife being saved, and all the remainder of their company destroyed in one way or another. Here they endured great hardships, but were at last entertained by the mighty Queen of a savage people, a white woman of peculiar loveliness, who, under circumstances which I cannot enter into, but which you will one day learn, if you live, from the contents of the box, finally murdered my ancestor, Kallikrates. His wife, however, escaped, how, I know not, to Athens, bearing a child with her, whom she named Tisisthenes, or the Mighty Avenger. Five hundred years or more afterwards, the family migrated to Rome under circumstances of which no trace remains, and here, probably with the idea of preserving the idea of vengeance which we find set out in Tisisthenes, they appear to have pretty regularly assumed the cognomen of Vindex, or Avenger. Here, too, they remained for another five centuries or more, till about 770 A.D., when Charlemagne[2] invaded Lombardy, where they were then settled, whereon the head of the family seems to have attached himself to the great Emperor, and to have returned with him across the Alps, and finally to have settled in Brittany. Six generations later his lineal representative crossed to England in the reign of Edward the Confessor,[3] and in the time of William the Conqueror was advanced to great honour and power. From that time till the present day I can trace my descent without a break. Not that the Vinceys—for that was the final corruption of the name after its bearers took root in English soil—have been particularly distinguished—they never came much to the fore. Sometimes they were soldiers, sometimes merchants, but on the whole they have preserved a dead level of respectability, and a still deader level of mediocrity. From the time of Charles II.[4] till the beginning of the present century they were merchants. About 1790 my grandfather made a considerable fortune out of brewing, and retired. In 1821 he died, and my father succeeded him, and dissipated most of the money. Ten years ago he died also, leaving me a net income of about two thousand a year. Then it was that I undertook an expedition in connection with that," and he pointed to the iron chest, "which ended disastrously enough. On my way back I travelled in the South of

---

[1]   An inlet on the southeastern coast of Africa in Mozambique, in what was then Portuguese East Africa.

[2]   Charles the Great (742–814), king of the Franks, and, after 800, Emperor of the West.

[3]   Saxon king of the English from 1042 until 1066, when William the Conqueror of Normandy defeated him at the Battle of Hastings and became king, reigning until 1087.

[4]   King of England, 1660–85.

Europe, and finally reached Athens. There I met my beloved wife, who might well also have been called the 'Beautiful,' like my old Greek ancestor. There I married her, and there, a year afterwards, she died."

He paused a while, his head sunk upon his hand, and then continued—

"My marriage had diverted me from a project which I cannot enter into now. I have no time, Holly—I have no time! One day, if you accept my trust, you will learn all about it. After my wife's death I turned my mind to it again. But first it was necessary, or, at least, I conceived that it was necessary, that I should attain to a perfect knowledge of Eastern dialects, especially Arabic. It was to facilitate my studies that I came here. Very soon, however, my disease developed itself, and now there is an end of me." And as though to emphasise his words he burst into another terrible fit of coughing.

I gave him some more whisky, and after resting he went on—

"I have never seen my boy, Leo, since he was a tiny baby. I never could see him, but they tell me that he is a quick and handsome child. In this envelope," and he produced a letter from his pocket addressed to myself, "I have jotted down the course I wish followed in the boy's education. It is a somewhat peculiar one. At any rate, I could not entrust it to a stranger. Once more, will you undertake it?"

"I must first know what I am to undertake," I answered.

"You are to undertake to have the boy, Leo, to live with you till he is twenty-five years of age—not to send him to school, remember. On his twenty-fifth birthday your guardianship will end, and you will then, with the keys that I give you now" (and he placed them on the table) "open the iron box, and let him see and read the contents, and say whether or no he is willing to undertake the quest. There is no obligation on him to do so. Now, as regards terms. My present income is two thousand two hundred a year. Half of that income I have secured to you by will for life contingently on your undertaking the guardianship—that is, one thousand a year remuneration to yourself, for you will have to give up your life to it, and one hundred a year to pay for the board of the boy. The rest is to accumulate till Leo is twenty-five, so that there may be a sum in hand should he wish to undertake the quest of which I spoke."

"And suppose I were to die?" I asked.

"Then the boy must become a ward of Chancery and take his chance. Only be careful that the iron chest is passed on to him by your will. Listen, Holly, don't refuse me. Believe me, this is to your advantage. You are not fit to mix with the world—it would only embitter you. In a few weeks you will become a Fellow of your College, and the income that you will derive from that combined with what I have left you will enable you to live a life of learned leisure, alternated with the sport of which you are so fond, such as will exactly suit you."

He paused and looked at me anxiously, but I still hesitated. The charge seemed so very strange.

"For my sake, Holly. We have been good friends, and I have no time to make other arrangements."

"Very well," I said, "I will do it, provided there is nothing in this paper to make me change my mind," and I touched the envelope he had put upon the table by the keys.

"Thank you, Holly, thank you. There is nothing at all. Swear to me by God that you will be a father to the boy, and follow my directions to the letter."

"I swear it," I answered solemnly.

"Very well, remember that perhaps one day I shall ask for the account of your oath, for though I am dead and forgotten, yet I shall live. There is no such thing as death, Holly, only a change, and as you may perhaps learn in time to come, I believe that even here that change could under certain circumstances be indefinitely postponed," and here again he broke into one of his dreadful fits of coughing.

"There," he said, "I must go. You have the chest, and my will will be found among my papers, under the authority of which the child will be handed over to you. You will be well paid, Holly, and I know that you are honest, but if you betray my trust, by Heaven I will haunt you."

I said nothing, being, indeed, too bewildered to speak.

He held up the candle, and looked at his own face in the glass. It had been a beautiful face, but disease had wrecked it. "Food for the worms," he said. "Curious to think that in a few hours I shall be stiff and cold—the journey done, the little game played out. Ah me, Holly! life is not worth the trouble of life, except when one is in love—at least, mine has not been; but the boy Leo's may be if he has the courage and the faith. Good-bye, my friend!" and with a sudden access of tenderness he flung his arm about me and kissed me on the forehead, and then turned to go.

"Look here, Vincey," I said, "if you are as ill as you think you had better let me fetch a doctor."

"No, no," he said earnestly. "Promise me that you won't. I am going to die, and, like a poisoned rat, I wish to die alone."

"I don't believe that you are going to do anything of the sort," I answered. He smiled, and with the word "Remember," on his lips, was gone. As for myself, I sat down and rubbed my eyes, wondering if I had been asleep. As this supposition would not bear investigation I gave it up, and began to think that Vincey must have been drinking. I knew that he was, and had been, very ill, but still it seemed impossible that he could be in such a condition as to be able to know for certain that he would not outlive the night. Had he been so near dissolution surely he would scarcely have been able to walk, and carry a heavy iron box with him. The whole story, on reflection, seemed to me utterly incredible, for I was not then old enough to be aware how many things happen in this world that the common sense of the average man would set down as so improbable as to be absolutely impossible. This is a fact that I have only recently mastered. Was it likely that a man would have a son five years of age whom he had never seen since he was a tiny infant? No. Was it likely that he could foretell his own death so accurately? No. Was it likely that he could trace his pedigree for more than three centuries before Christ, or that he would suddenly confide the absolute guardianship of his child, and leave half his fortune, to a college friend? Most certainly not. Clearly Vincey was either drunk or mad. That being so, what did it mean? and what was in the sealed iron chest?

The whole thing baffled and puzzled me to such an extent that at last I could stand it no longer, and determined to sleep over it. So I jumped up, and having put away into my despatch-box the keys and the letter that Vincey had left and stowed the iron chest in a large portmanteau, I turned in, and was soon fast asleep.

As it seemed to me, I had only been asleep for a few minutes when I was awakened by somebody calling me. I sat up and rubbed my eyes; it was broad daylight—eight o'clock, in fact.

"Why, what is the matter with you, John?" I asked of the gyp[1] who waited on Vincey and myself, "you look as though you had seen a ghost!"

"Yes, sir, and so I have," he answered; "leastways I've seen a corpse, which is worse. I've been in to call Mr. Vincey, as usual, and there he lies stark and dead!"

(*To be continued*)

---

[1]   A servant at Cambridge University (slang).

"At last the lock yielded, and the casket stood open before us."

II

THE YEARS ROLL BY

Of course, poor Vincey's sudden death created a great stir in the College; but, as he was known to be very ill, and a satisfactory doctor's certificate was forthcoming, there was no inquest. They were not so particular about inquests in those days as they are now, indeed, they were generally disliked, as causing a scandal. Under all these circumstances, as I was asked no questions, I did not feel called upon to volunteer any information about our interview of the night of Vincey's decease, beyond saying that he had come into my rooms to see me, as he often did. On the day of the funeral a lawyer came down from London and followed my poor friend's remains to the grave, and then went back with his papers and effects, excepting, of course, the iron chest which had been left in my keeping. For a week after this I heard no more of the matter, and, indeed, my attention was amply occupied in other ways, for I was up for my Fellowship, a fact that had prevented me from attending the funeral, or seeing the lawyer. At last, however, the examination was over, and I came back to my rooms and sank into an easy chair with a happy consciousness that I had got through it very fairly. Soon, however, my thoughts, relieved of the pressure that had crushed them into a single groove during the last few days, turned to the events of the night of poor Vincey's death, and again I asked myself what it all meant, and wondered if I should hear anything more of the matter, and, if I did not, what it would be my duty to do with the curious iron chest. I sat there and thought and thought till I began to grow quite disturbed over the whole occurrence: the mysterious midnight visit, the prophecy of death so shortly to be fulfilled, the solemn oath that I had taken, and which he had called on me to answer for in another world to this. Had the man committed suicide? It looked like it. And what was the quest of which he spoke? The circumstances were almost uncanny, so much so that, though I am by no means nervous, or apt to be alarmed at anything that may seem to cross the bounds of the natural, I grew afraid, and began to wish I had had nothing to do with it. How much more do I wish it now over twenty years afterwards!

As I sat and thought there was a knock at the door, and a letter, in a big blue envelope, was brought in to me. I saw at a glance that it was a lawyer's letter, and an instinct told me that it was connected with my trust. The letter—which I still have—runs thus:—

"Sir,—

"Our client, the late M.L.Vincey, Esq., who died on the 9th instant in —— College, Cambridge, has left behind him a Will, of which you will please find copy enclosed and of which we are the executors. By this Will you will perceive that you take a life-interest in about half of the late Mr.Vincey's property, now invested in Consols,[1] subject to your acceptance of the guardianship of his only son, Leo Vincey, at present an infant, aged five. Had we not ourselves drawn up the document in question in obedience to Mr.Vincey's clear and precise instructions, both personal and written, and had he not then assured us that he had very good reasons for what he was doing, we are bound to tell you that its provisions seem to us of so unusual a nature, that we should have felt bound to call the attention of the Court of Chancery to them, in order that such steps might be taken as seemed desirable to it, either by contesting the capacity of the testator or otherwise, to safeguard the interests of the infant. As it is, knowing that the testator was a gentleman of the highest intelligence and acumen, and that he has absolutely no relations living to whom he could have confided the guardianship of the child, we do not feel justified in taking this course.

"Awaiting such instructions as you please to send us as regards the delivery of the infant and the payment of the proportion of the dividends due to you,

"We remain, Sir,

"Faithfully yours,

"GEOFFREY AND JORDAN."

I put down the letter, and ran my eye through the Will, which appeared, from its utter unintelligibility, to have been drawn on the strictest legal principles. So far as I could discover, however, it exactly bore out what my friend had told me on the night of his death. So it was true after all. I must take the boy. Suddenly I remembered the letter which he had left with the chest. I fetched it and opened it. It only contained such directions as he had already given to me as to opening the chest on Leo's

---

1   Annuity bonds issued by the British government.

twenty-fifth birthday, and laid down the outlines of the boy's education, which was to include Greek, the higher Mathematics, and *Arabic*. At the bottom there was a postscript to the effect that if the boy died under the age of twenty-five, which, however, he did not believe would be the case, I was to open the chest, and act on the information I obtained if I saw fit. If I did not see fit, I was to destroy all the contents. On no account was I to pass them on to a stranger.

As this letter added nothing material to my knowledge, and certainly raised no further objection in my mind to undertaking the task I had promised my dead friend to undertake, there was only one course open to me, namely, to write to Messrs. Geoffrey and Jordan, and express my readiness to enter on the trust, stating that I should be willing to undertake the charge of the lad in ten days' time. This done, I proceeded to the authorities of my College, and, having told them as much of the story as I considered desirable, which was not very much, after considerable difficulty succeeded in persuading them to stretch a point, and, in the event of my having obtained a fellowship, which I was pretty certain I had done, allow me to have the child to live with me. Their consent, however, was only granted on the condition that I vacated my rooms in college, and took lodgings. This I did, and with some difficulty succeeded in obtaining very good apartments quite close to the college gates. The next thing was to find a nurse. And on this point I came to a determination. I would have no woman to lord it over me about the child, and steal his affections from me. The boy was old enough to do without female assistance, so I set to work to hunt up a suitable male attendant. With some difficulty I succeeded in hiring a most respectable round-faced young man, who had been a helper in a hunting-stable, but who said that he was one of a family of seventeen and well-accustomed to the ways of children, and professed himself quite willing to undertake the charge of Master Leo when he arrived. Then, having taken the iron box to town, and with my own hands deposited it at my bankers, I bought some books upon the health and management of children, and read them, first to myself, and then aloud to Job—that was the young man's name—and waited.

At length the child arrived in the charge of an elderly person, who wept bitterly at parting with him, and a beautiful boy he was. Indeed, I do not think that I ever saw such a perfect child before or since. His eyes were grey, his forehead was broad, and his face, even at that early age, clean cut as a cameo, without being pinched or thin. But perhaps his most attractive point was his hair, which was pure gold in colour and tightly curled over his shapely head. He cried a little when his nurse finally tore herself away, and left him with us. Never shall I forget the scene. There he stood, with the sunlight from the window playing upon his golden curls, his fist screwed in one eye, whilst he took us in with the other. I was seated in a chair, and stretched out my hand to him to induce him to come to me, while Job, in the corner, was making a sort of clucking noise, which, arguing from his previous experience, or from the analogy of the hen, he judged would have a soothing effect, and inspire confidence in the youthful mind, and running a wooden horse of peculiar hideousness backwards and forwards in a way that was little short of inane. This went on for some minutes, and then all of a sudden the lad stretched out both his little arms and ran to me.

"I like you," he said: "you is ugly, but you is good."

Ten minutes afterwards he was eating large slices of bread and butter, with every sign of satisfaction; Job wanted to put jam on to them, but I sternly reminded him of the excellent works that we had read, and forbade it.

In a very little while (for, as I expected, I got my fellowship) the boy became the favourite of the whole College—where all orders and regulations to the contrary notwithstanding, he was continually in and out—a sort of chartered libertine, in whose favour all rules were relaxed. The offerings made at his shrine were simply without number, and I had serious difference of opinion with one old resident Fellow, now long dead, who was usually supposed to be the crustiest man in the University, and to abhor the sight of a child. And yet I discovered, when a frequently-recurring fit of sickness had forced Job to keep a strict look-out, that this unprincipled old man was in the habit of enticing the boy to his rooms and there feeding him upon unlimited quantities of brandy-balls, and making him promise to say nothing about it. Job told him that he ought to be ashamed of himself, "at his age, too, when he might have been a grandfather if he had done what was right," by which Job understood had got married, and thence arose the row.

But I have no space to dwell upon those delightful years, upon which memory still fondly hovers. One by one they went by, and as they passed we two grew dearer and yet more dear to each other. Few sons have been loved as I love Leo, and few fathers know the deep and continuous affection that Leo bears to me.

The child grew into the boy, and the boy into the young man, as one by one the remorseless years flew by, and as he grew and increased so did his beauty and the beauty of his mind grow with him. When he was about fifteen they used to call him Beauty about the College, and me they nicknamed the Beast. Beauty and the Beast was what they called us when we went out walking together, as we used to every day. Once Leo attacked a great strapping butcher's-man, twice his size, because he sung it out after us, and thrashed him, too—thrashed him fairly. I walked on and pretended not to see, till the combat got too exciting, when I turned round and cheered him on to victory. It was the chaff of the College at the time, but I could not help it. Then when he was a little older the undergraduates got fresh names for us. They called me Charon, and Leo the Greek god! I will pass over my own appellation with the humble remark that I was never handsome, and did not grow more so as I grew older. As for his, there was no doubt about its fitness. Leo at twenty-one might have stood for a statue of Apollo. I never saw anybody to touch him in looks, or anybody so absolutely unconscious of them. As for his mind, he was brilliant and keen-witted, but not a scholar. He had not the dulness necessary for that result. We followed out his father's instructions as regards his education strictly enough, and on the whole the results, especially so far as the Greek and Arabic went, were satisfactory. I learnt the latter language in order to help to teach it to him, but after five years of it he knew it as well as I did—almost as well as the professor who instructed us both. I always was a great sportsman—it is my one passion—and every autumn we went away somewhere shooting or fishing, sometimes to Scotland, sometimes to Norway, once even to Russia. I am a good shot, but even in this he learnt to excel me. When Leo was eighteen I moved back into my rooms, and entered him at my own College, and at twenty-one he took his degree—a respectable degree, but not a very high one. Then it was that I, for the first time, told him something of his own story, and of the mystery that loomed ahead. Of course he was very curious about it, and of course I explained to him that his curiosity could not be gratified at present. After that, to pass the time away, I suggested that he should get himself called to the Bar; and this he did, reading at Cambridge, and only going up to London to eat his dinners.

I had only one trouble about him, and that was that every young woman who came across him, or, if not every one, nearly so, would insist on falling in love with him. Hence arose difficulties which I need not enter into here, though they were troublesome enough at the time. On the whole, he behaved fairly well; I can't say more than that.

And so the time went by till at last he reached his twenty-fifth birthday, at which date this strange and, in some ways awful, history really begins.

III

THE SHERD OF AMENARTAS

On the day preceding Leo's twenty-fifth birthday we both proceeded to London, and extracted the mysterious chest from the bank where I had deposited it twenty years before. It was, I remember, brought up by the same clerk who had taken it down. He perfectly remembered having hidden it away. Had he not done so, he said, he should have had difficulty in finding it, it was so covered up with cobwebs.

In the evening we returned with our precious burden to Cambridge, and I think that we might both of us have given away all the sleep we got that night and not have been much the poorer. At daybreak Leo arrived in my room in a dressing-gown, and suggested that we should at once proceed to business. I scouted the idea as showing an unworthy curiosity. The chest had waited twenty years I said; it could very well continue to wait until after breakfast. Accordingly at nine—an unusually sharp nine—we breakfasted; and so occupied was I with my own thoughts that I regret to state that I put a piece of bacon into Leo's tea in mistake for a lump of sugar. Job, too, to whom the contagion of excitement had, of course, spread, managed to break the handle off my Sèvres[1] china tea-cup, the identical one I believe that Marat[2] had been drinking from just before he was stabbed in his bath.

At last, however, breakfast was cleared away, and Job, at my request, fetched the chest, and placed it upon the table in a somewhat gingerly fashion, as though he mistrusted it. Then he prepared to leave the room.

"Stop a moment, Job," I said; "If Mr. Leo has no objection, I should prefer to have an independent witness to this business, who can be relied upon to hold his tongue unless he is asked to speak."

"Certainly, Uncle Horace," answered Leo; for I had brought him up to call me uncle—though he varied the appellation somewhat disrespectfully by calling me "old fellow," or even "my avuncular relative."

Job touched his head, not having a hat on.

"Lock the door, Job," I said, "and bring me my despatch-box."

He obeyed, and from the box I took the keys that poor Vincey, Leo's father, had given me on the night of his death. There were three of

---

[1]   Fine porcelain produced in France from the mid-eighteenth century.

[2]   Jean-Paul Marat (1743–93); radical journalist and political leader of the French Revolution, assassinated in his bathtub by Charlotte Corday.

them: the largest a comparatively modern key, the second an exceedingly ancient one, and the third entirely unlike anything of the sort that we had ever seen before, being fashioned apparently from a strip of solid silver, with a bar placed across to serve as a handle, and some nicks cut in the edge of the bar. It was more like a model of some antediluvian railway key than anything else.

"Now are you both ready?" I said, as people do when they are going to fire a mine. There was no answer, so I took the big key, rubbed some salad oil into the wards, and after one or two bad shots, for my hands were shaking, managed to fit it, and shoot the lock. Leo bent over and caught the massive lid in both his hands, and, with an effort, for the hinges had rusted, leaned it back. Its removal revealed another case covered with dust. This we extracted from the iron chest without any difficulty, and removed the accumulated filth of years from it with a clothes-brush.

It was, or appeared to be, of ebony, or some such close-grained black wood, and was bound in every direction with flat bands of iron. Its antiquity must have been extreme, for the dense heavy wood was actually in parts commencing to crumble away from age.

"Now for it," I said, inserting the second key.

Job and Leo bent forward in breathless silence. The key turned, and I flung back the lid, and uttered an exclamation, as did the others, and no wonder, for inside the ebony case was a magnificent silver casket, about twelve inches square by eight high. It appeared to be of Egyptian workmanship, for the four legs were formed of Sphinxes, and the dome-shaped cover was also surmounted by a Sphinx. The casket was of course much tarnished and dinted with age, but otherwise in almost perfect condition.

I drew it out and set it on the table, and then, in the midst of the most perfect silence, I inserted the strange looking silver key, and pressed this way and that until at last the lock yielded, and the casket stood open before us. It was filled to the brim with some brown shredded material, more like vegetable fibre than paper, the nature of which I have never been able to discover. This I carefully removed to the depth of some three inches, when I came to a letter enclosed in an ordinary modern-looking envelope, and addressed in the handwriting of my dead friend Vincey,

"*To my son Leo, should he live to open this casket.*"

I handed the letter to Leo, who glanced at the envelope, and then put it down upon the table, making a motion to me to go on emptying the casket.

The next thing that I came to was a parchment carefully rolled up. I unrolled it, and seeing that it was also in Vincey's handwriting, and headed "Translation of the Uncial Greek Writing[1] on the Potsherd," put it down by the letter. Then followed another ancient roll of parchment, that had become yellow and crinkled with the passage of years. This I also unrolled. It was likewise a translation of the same Greek original, but into black-letter Latin[2] this time, and appeared to me from the style and character to date from the end of the fifteenth, or perhaps the middle of the sixteenth, century. Immediately beneath this roll was something hard and heavy, wrapped up in yellow linen, and reposing upon another layer of the fibrous material. Slowly and carefully we unrolled the linen, exposing to view a very large but undoubtedly ancient potsherd of a dirty yellow colour! This potsherd had in my judgment, once been a part of an ordinary amphora[3] of medium size. For the rest, it measured eleven inches in length by ten in width, was about a quarter of an inch thick, and densely covered on the convex side that lay towards the bottom of the box with writing in the later uncial Greek character, faded here and there, but for the most part perfectly legible, the inscription having evidently been executed with the greatest care, and by means of a reed pen, such as the ancients often used. I must not forget to mention that in some remote age this wonderful fragment had been broken in two, and rejoined by means of cement and eight long rivets. Also there were numerous inscriptions on the inner side, but these were of the most erratic character, and had clearly been made by different hands and in many different ages, and of them I shall have to speak presently.

"Is there anything more?" asked Leo, in a kind of excited whisper.

I groped about, and produced something hard, done up in a little linen bag. Out of the bag we took first a very beautiful miniature done upon ivory, and secondly, a small chocolate-coloured composition *scarabœus*, marked thus:

---

[1] Rounded script somewhere between block letters and cursive, typically found in medieval Greek and Latin manuscripts.

[2] Gothic, heavily-ornamented script used in the medieval period.

[3] Two-handled jar used to carry oil or wine.

symbols which, we have since ascertained, mean "Suten se Rā," which is being translated the "Royal Son of Rā[1] or the Sun." The miniature was a picture of Leo's Greek mother—a lovely, dark-eyed creature. On the back of it was written, in poor Vincey's handwriting, "My beloved wife, died May, 1856."

"That is all," I said.

"Very well," answered Leo, putting down the miniature at which he had been gazing affectionately; "and now let us read the letter," and without further ado he broke the seal, and read aloud as follows:—

"MY SON LEO,—When you open this, if you ever live to do so, you will have attained to manhood, and I shall have been long enough dead to be absolutely forgotten by nearly all who knew me. Yet in reading it remember that I have been, and for anything you know may still be, and that in it, through this link of pen and paper, I stretch out my hand to you across the gulf of death, and my voice speaks to you from the unutterable silence of the grave.[2] Though I am dead, and no memory of me remains in your mind, yet am I with you in this hour that you read. Since your birth to this day I have scarcely seen your face. Forgive me this. Your life supplanted the life of one whom I loved better than women are often loved, and the bitterness of it endureth yet. Had I lived I should in time have conquered this foolish feeling, but I am not destined to live. My sufferings, physical and mental, are more than I can bear, and when such small arrangements as I have to make for your future well-being are completed it is my intention to put a period to them. May God forgive me if I do wrong. At the best I could not live more than another year."

"So he killed himself," I exclaimed. "I thought so."

"And now," Leo went on, without replying, "enough of myself. What has to be said belongs to you who live, not to me, who am dead, and almost as much forgotten as though I had never been. Holly, my friend (to whom, if he will accept the trust, it is my intention to confide you), will have told you something of the extraordinary antiquity of your race. In the contents of this casket you will find sufficient to prove it. The strange legend that you will find inscribed by your remote

---

[1]   The ancient Egyptian god of the sun.
[2]   Alluding to Virgil, *Aeneid*, 6:313.

ancestress upon the potsherd was communicated to me by my father on his deathbed, and took a strong hold upon my imagination. When I was only nineteen years of age I determined, as, to his misfortune, did one of our ancestors about the time of Elizabeth, to investigate its truth. Into all that befell me I cannot enter now. But this I saw with my own eyes. On the coast of Africa, in a hitherto unexplored region, some distance to the north of where the Zambesi falls into the sea,[1] there is a headland, at the extremity of which a peak towers up, shaped like the head of a negro, similar to that of which the writing speaks. I landed there, and learnt from a wandering native who had been cast out by his people because of some crime which he had committed, that far inland are great mountains, shaped like cups, and caves surrounded by measureless swamps. I learnt also that the people there speak a dialect of Arabic, and are ruled over by a *beautiful white woman* who is seldom seen by them, but who is reported to have power over all things living and dead. Two days after I had ascertained this the man died of fever contracted in crossing the swamps, and I was forced by want of provisions and by symptoms of the illness which afterwards prostrated me to take to my dhow[2] again.

"Of the adventures that befell me after this I need not now speak. I was wrecked upon the coast of Madagascar,[3] and rescued some months afterwards by an English ship that brought me to Aden,[4] whence I started for England, intending to prosecute my search as soon as I had made sufficient preparations. On my way I stopped in Greece, and there, for 'Omnia vincit amor,'[5] I met your beloved mother, and married her, and there you were born and she died. Then it was that my last illness seized me, and I returned hither to die. But still I hoped against hope, and set myself to work to learn Arabic, with the intention, should I ever get better, of returning to the coast of Africa, and solving the mystery of which the tradition has lived so many centuries in our family. But I have not got better, and, so far as I am concerned, the story is at an end.

"For you, however, my son, it is not at an end, and to you I hand on these the results of my labour, together with the hereditary proofs of its origin. It is my intention to provide that they shall not be put into your

---

[1]   The Zambezi river flows through southeastern Africa towards Delagoa Bay and the Mozambique channel.

[2]   An Arab or African sailing boat with a single mast and a triangular sail.

[3]   Island off the coast of Mozambique in southeastern Africa.

[4]   Port city in southwestern Yemen; it was under British control from 1839 to 1936.

[5]   "Love conquers all" (Latin).

hands until you have reached an age when you will be able to judge for yourself whether or no you will choose to investigate what, if it is true, must be the greatest mystery in the world, or to put it by as an idle fable, originating in the first place in a woman's disordered brain.

"I do not believe that it is a fable; I believe that if it can only be re-discovered there is a spot where the vital forces of the world visibly exist. Life exists; why therefore should not the means of preserving it indefinitely exist also? But I have no wish to prejudice your mind about the matter. Read and judge for yourself. If you are inclined to under-take the search I have so provided that you will not lack for means. If, on the other hand, you are satisfied that the whole thing is a chimera, then, I adjure you, destroy the potsherd and the writings, and let a cause of troubling be removed from our race for ever. Perhaps that will be wisest. The unknown is generally taken to be terrible, not as the proverb would infer, from the inherent superstition of man, but because it so often is terrible. He who would tamper with the vast and secret forces that animate the world may well fall a victim to them. And if the end were attained, if at last you emerged from the trial ever beautiful and ever young, defying time and evil, and lifted above the natural decay of flesh and intellect, who shall say that the awesome change would prove a happy one? Choose, my son, and may the Power who rules all things, and who says 'thus far shalt thou go, and thus much shalt thou learn,' direct the choice to your own happiness and the happiness of the world, which, in the event of your success, you would one day certainly rule by the pure force of accumulated experience.—Farewell!"

Thus the letter, which was unsigned and undated, abruptly ended.

"What do you make of that, Uncle Holly?" said Leo, with a sort of gasp, as he replaced it on the table. "We have been looking for a mystery, and we certainly seem to have found one."

"What do I make of it? Why, that your poor dear father was off his head, of course," I answered, testily. "I guessed as much that night, twenty years ago, when he came into my room. You see he evidently hurried his own end, poor man. It is absolute balderdash."

"That's it, sir!" said Job, solemnly. Job was a most matter-of-fact spec-imen of a matter-of-fact class.

"Well, let's see what the potsherd has to say, at any rate," said Leo, taking up the translation in his father's writing, and commencing to read:—

"I, Amenartas, of the Royal House of Hakor, a Pharaoh of Egypt, wife of Kallikrates (the Strong and Beautiful or the Beautiful in Strength), a Priest of Isis, whom the gods cherish and the demons obey, being about to die, to my little son Tisisthenes (the Mighty Avenger). I fled with thy father from Egypt in the days of Nekht-nebf,* causing him through love to break the vows that he had vowed. We fled southward, across the waters, and we wandered for twice twelve moons on the coast of Libya (Africa) that looks towards the rising sun, where by a river is a great rock carven like the head of an Ethiopian. Four days on the water from the mouth of a mighty river were we cast away, and some were drowned and some died of sickness. But us wild men took through wastes and marshes, where the sea fowl hid the sky, bearing us ten days' journey till we came to a hollow mountain, where a great city had been and fallen, and where there are caves of which no man hath seen the end; and they brought us to the Queen of the people who place pots upon the heads of strangers, who is a magician having a knowledge of all things, and life and loveliness that does not die. And she cast eyes of love upon thy father, Kallikrates, and would have slain me, and taken him to husband, but he loved me and feared her, and would not. Then did she take us, and lead us by terrible ways, by means of dark magic, to where the great pit is, in the mouth of which the old philosopher lay dead, and showed to us the rolling Pillar of Life that dies not, whereof the voice is as the voice of thunder, and did stand in the flames, and come forth unharmed, and yet more beautiful. Then did she swear to make thy father undying even as she is, if he would but slay me, and give himself to her, for me she could not slay because of the magic of my own people that I have, and that prevailed thus far against her. And he held his hand before his eyes to hide her beauty, and would not. Then in her rage did she smite him by her magic, and he died, but she wept over him, and bore him thence with lamentations, and being afraid, me she sent to the mouth of the great river where the ships come, and I was carried far away on the ships where I gave thee birth, and hither to Athens I came at last after many wanderings. Now I say to thee, my son, Tisisthenes, seek out the woman, and learn the secret of life, and if thou mayest find a way slay her, because of thy father Kallikrates, and if thou dost fear or fail this I say to all of thy seed who come after thee, till at last a brave man be found among

---

* Nectanebes or Nectanebo II. The last native Pharaoh of Egypt fled from Ochus to Ethiopia, B.C. 339.—EDITOR.

them who shall bathe in the fire and sit in the place of the Pharaohs. I speak of those things, that though they be past belief, yet I have known, and I lie not."

"May the Lord forgive her for that," groaned Job, who had been listening to this marvellous composition with his mouth open.

As for myself, I said nothing; my first idea being that my poor friend, being demented, had composed the whole thing, though it scarcely seemed likely that such a story could have been invented by anybody. It was too original. To solve my doubts I took up the potsherd and commenced to read the close uncial Greek writing on it, and beautiful Greek it is to have been written by an Egyptian born. The English translation was, as I discovered on further investigation, both accurate and elegant.

Besides the uncial writing on the convex side of the sherd at the top, painted in dull red, on what had once been the lip of the amphora, was the cartouche[1] already mentioned as being on the *scarabæus*, which we had also found in the casket. The hieroglyphics or symbols, however, were reversed, just as though they had been pressed on wax. Whether this was the cartouche of the original Kallikrates, or of some Prince or Pharaoh from whom his wife Amenartas was descended, I am not sure, nor can I tell if it was drawn upon the sherd at the same time that the uncial Greek was inscribed, or copied on more recently from the Scarab by some other member of the family. Nor was this all. At the foot of the writing, painted in the same dull red, was the outline of a somewhat rude drawing of a Sphinx wearing two feathers, symbols of majesty, which, though common enough upon the effigies of sacred bulls and gods, I have never before met with on a Sphinx.

On the right-hand side of this surface of the sherd, painted obliquely in bright red on the space not covered by the uncial, and signed in blue paint, was the following quaint inscription:—

IN EARTH AND SKIE AND SEA
    STRANGE THYNGES THER BE.
HOC FECIT
    DOROTHEA VINCEY.[2]

---

[1] Ancient Egyptian oval seal containing the name of a god or pharaoh. As a priest, Kallikrates in fact would not have had his own cartouche.

[2] "Dorothea Vincey made (or wrote) this" (Latin).

Perfectly bewildered, I turned the relic over. It was covered from top to bottom with notes and signatures in Greek, Latin, and English. The first in uncial Greek was by Tisisthenes, the son to whom the writing was addressed. It was, "I cannot go. To thee, my son Kallikrates."

This Kallikrates (probably, in the Greek fashion, so named after his grandfather) evidently made some attempt to start on the quest, for his entry written in very faint and almost illegible uncial is, "I started to seek, but the gods were against me. To thee, my son."

Between these two ancient writings, the second of which was inscribed upside down—that, had it not been for the transcript of them executed by Vincey, I should not have been able to read, since, owing to their having been written on that portion of the tile which had, in the course of ages, undergone the most handling, they were nearly worn out—was the bold, modern-looking signature of one Lionel Vincey, "Ætate sua 17,"[1] which was written thereon, I think, by Leo's grandfather. To the right of this were the initials "J. B. V.," and below came a variety of Greek signatures, in uncial and cursive character, and what appeared to be some repetitions of the sentence "to thee my son," showing that the relic has been passed on from generation to generation.

The next legible thing after the Greek signatures was the word "ROMAE, A.U.C."[2] showing that the family had now migrated to Rome. Unfortunately, however, the date of their settlement there is for ever lost, for just where it had been placed a piece of the potsherd is broken away.

Then followed a dozen or more Latin signatures, jotted about here and there, wherever there was a space upon the tile suitable to their inscription. These signatures were, almost without exception, ended with the name "Vindex" or "the Avenger," which seems to have been adopted by the family after its migration to Rome as a kind of equivalent to the Grecian "Tisisthenes," which also means an avenger. Ultimately, of course, this Latin cognomen of Vindex was transformed first into De Vincey, and then into the plain, modern Vincey. It is very curious to observe how the idea of revenge, inspired by an Egyptian before the time of Christ, is thus, as it were, embalmed in an English family name.

A few of the Roman names inscribed upon the sherd I have actually since found mentioned in history and other records. They were, if I remember right,

---

[1]   "In his seventeenth year" (Latin).
[2]   *Ab urbe conditia*: "from the founding of the city" (Latin).

MVSSIVS.VINDEX
SEX.VARIVS. MARVLLVS.
C. FVFIDIVS. C. F.VINDEX.

and

LABERIA POMPEIANA. CONIVX. MACRINI.VINDICIS.

this last being, of course, the name of a Roman lady. After the Roman names there is evidently a gap of very many centuries. Nobody will ever know now what was the history of the relic during those dark ages, or how it came to have been preserved in the family. My poor friend Vincey had, it will be remembered, told me that his Roman ancestors finally settled in Lombardy, and when Charlemagne invaded it returned with him across the Alps, and made their home in Brittany, whence they crossed to England in the reign of Edward the Confessor. How he knew this I am not aware, for there is no reference to Lombardy or Charlemagne upon the tile, though, as will presently be seen, there is a reference to Brittany. To continue: the next entries on the sherd, if I may except a long splash either of blood or red colouring matter of some sort, consist of two crosses drawn in red pigments, and probably representing Crusaders' swords, and an almost obliterated monogram ("D.V.") in scarlet and blue, perhaps executed by that same Dorothea Vincey who wrote, or rather painted, the doggrel couplet.

Then came what was perhaps as curious an entry as anything upon this extraordinary relic of the past. It is executed in black letter, written over the crosses or Crusaders' swords, and dated fourteen hundred and forty-five. As the best plan will be to allow it to speak for itself, I here give the original Latin, of course without the contractions, from which it will be seen that the writer was a fair mediæval Latinist. Also we discovered what is still more curious, a modernised version of a black-letter translation of the Latin which we found inscribed on a second parchment that was in the coffer, apparently older in date than that on which was inscribed the Latin black letter translation of the uncial Greek:—

Expanded Version of the Black Letter Inscription on the Sherd of Amenartas.

"Ista reliquia est valde misticum et myrificum opus, quod majores mei ex Armorica, scilicet Britannia Minore, secum convehebant; et quidam sanctus clericus semper patri meo in manu ferebat quod penitus illud destrueret, affirmans quod esset ab ipso Sathana conflatum prestigiosa et dyabolica arte, quare pater meus confregit illud in duas partes, quas quidem ego Johannes de Vinceto salvas servavi et adaptavi sicut apparet die lune proximo post festum beate Marie Virginis anni gratie MCCCCXLV."

Modernised Version of the Black-Letter Translation.

"Thys rellike ys a ryghte mistycall worke and a marvaylous, the whyche myne aunceteres aforetyme dyd conveigh hider with them from Armoryke[1] which ys to seien Britaine the Lesse and a certayne holye clerke should allweyes beare my fadir on honde that he owghte uttirly for to frusshe[2] ye same, affyrmynge that yt was fourmed and conflatyd of Sathanas hym selfe by arte magike and dyvellysshe where-fore my fadir dyd take the same and to-brast yt yn tweyne,[3] but I, John de Vincey, dyd save whool the tweye partes therof and topeecyd them togydder agayne soe as yee se, on this daye mondaye next followynge after the feeste of Seynte Marye ye Blessed Vyrgyne yn the yeere of Salvacioun fowertene hundreth and fyve and fowerti."

The next and, save one, last entry was Elizabethan, and dated 1564, "A most strange historie, and one that did cost my father his life; for in seekynge for the place upon the east coast of Africa, his pinnace was sunk by a Portuguese galleon off Lorenzo Marquez,[4] and he himself perished.—JOHN VINCEY."

Then came the last entry, apparently, to judge by the style of writing, made by some representative of the family in the middle of the eighteenth century. It was the well-known quotation by Hamlet, "There are more things in Heaven and earth than are dreamt of in your philosophy, Horatio."*

"Well," I said, when I had read these paragraphs out, at least those of them

---

* Another thing that makes me fix the date of this entry at the middle of the eighteenth century is that I have an acting copy of "Hamlet," written about 1740, in which these two lines are misquoted almost exactly in the same way, and I have little doubt that the Vincey who wrote them on the potsherd may have heard them so misquoted at that date. Of course, the lines really run:—
  "There are more things in heaven and earth, Horatio,
  Than are dreamt of in your philosophy."—ED.

---

[1] Another name for Britanny, in northwestern France.
[2] Smash.
[3] Broke it in half.
[4] Portuguese settlement on Delagoa Bay in Mozambique.

that were still legible, "that is the conclusion of the whole matter, Leo, and now you can form your own opinion on it. I have already formed mine."

"And what is it?" he asked, in his quick way.

"It is this. I believe that potsherd to be perfectly genuine, and that, wonderful as it may seem, it has come down in your family from since the fourth century before Christ. The entries absolutely prove it, and therefore, however improbable it may seem, it must be accepted. But there I stop. That your remote ancestress, the Egyptian princess, or some scribe under her direction, wrote that which we see on the tile I have no doubt, nor have I the slightest doubt but that her sufferings and the loss of her husband had turned her head, and that she was not right in her mind when she did write it."

"How do you account for what my father saw and heard there?" asked Leo.

"Coincidence. No doubt there are bluffs on the coast of Africa that look something like a man's head, and plenty of people who speak bastard Arabic. Also, I believe that there are lots of swamps. Another thing is, Leo, and I am sorry to say it, but I do not believe that your poor father was quite right when he wrote that letter. He had met with a great trouble, and also he had allowed this story to prey on his imagination, and he was a very imaginative man. Anyway, I believe that the whole thing is the most unmitigated rubbish. I know that there are curious things and forces in nature which we rarely meet with, and, when we do meet them, cannot understand. But until I see it with my own eyes, which I am not likely to, I never will believe that there is any means of avoiding death, even for a time, or that there is or was a white sorceress living in the heart of an African swamp. It is bosh, my boy, all bosh!—What do you say, Job?"

"I say, sir, that it is a lie, and, if it is true, I hope Mr. Leo won't meddle with no such things, for no good can't come of it."

"Perhaps you are both right," said Leo, very quietly. "I express no opinion. But I say this. I am going to set the matter at rest once and for all, and if you won't come with me I will go by myself."

I looked at the young man, and saw that he meant what he said. When Leo means what he says he always puts on a curious little look about the mouth. It has been a trick of his from a child. Now, of course, I had no intention of letting Leo go anywhere by himself, for my own sake, if not for his. I was far too much attached to him for that. I am not a man of many ties or affections. Circumstances have been against me in this respect, and men and women shrink from me, or, at least, I fancy they do, which comes to the same thing, thinking, perhaps, that my forbidding exterior is a key to my character. Rather than endure this, I have, to a great extent, secluded myself from the world, and cut myself off from those opportunities which with most men result in the formation of relations more or less intimate. Therefore Leo was all the world to me—brother, child, and friend—and until he wearied of me, where he went there I should go too. But, of course, it would not do to let him see how great a hold he had over me; so I cast about for some means whereby I might let myself down easy.

"Yes, I shall go, Uncle; and if I don't find the 'rolling Pillar of Life,' at any rate I shall get some first-class shooting."

Here was my opportunity, and I took it.

"Shooting?" I said. "Ah! yes; I never thought of that. It must be a very wild stretch of country, and full of big game. I have always wanted to kill a buffalo before I die. Do you know, my boy, I don't believe in the quest, but I do believe in big game, and really, on the whole, if after thinking it over, you make up your mind to go, I will take a holiday, and come with you."

"Ah," said Leo, "I thought that you would not lose such a chance. But how about money? We shall want a good lot."

"You need not trouble about that," I answered. "There is all your income that has been accumulating for years, and besides that I have saved two-thirds of what your father left to me as I consider in trust for you. There is plenty of cash."

"Very well, then, we may as well store these things away and go up to town to see about our guns. By the way, Job, are you coming too? It's time you began to see the world."

"Well, sir," answered Job, stolidly, "I don't hold much with foreign parts, but if both you gentlemen are going you will want somebody to look after you, and I am not the man to stop behind after serving you for twenty years."

"That's right, Job," said I. "You won't find out anything wonderful, but you'll get some good shooting. And now look here, both of you. I won't have a word said to a living soul about this nonsense," and I pointed to the potsherd. "If it got out, and anything happened to me, my next of kin would dispute my will on the ground of insanity, and I should become the laughing-stock of Cambridge."

That day three months we were on the ocean, bound for Zanzibar.[1]

(*To be continued*)

---

[1]   Island off the east coast of Africa, held as a British protectorate in the 1880s. The east African coastline was also generally called the Zanzibar Coast.

"The top of the peak, which was about eighty feet high by one hundred and fifty thick at its base, was shaped like a negro's head and face."

IV

THE SQUALL

How different is the scene that I have now to tell from that which has just been told! Gone are the quiet college rooms, gone the wind-swayed English elms and cawing rooks, and the familiar volumes on the shelves, and in their place there rises a vision of the great calm ocean gleaming in shaded silver lights beneath the beams of the full African moon. A gentle breeze fills the huge sail of our dhow, and draws us through the water that ripples musically against our sides. Most of the men are sleeping forward, for it is near midnight, but a stout swarthy Arab, Mahomed by name, stands at the tiller, lazily steering by the stars. Three miles or more to our starboard is a low dim line. It is the Eastern shore of Central Africa. We are running to the southward, before the North-East monsoon, between the mainland and the reef that for hundreds of miles fringes that perilous coast. The night is quiet—so quiet that a whisper can be heard fore and aft the dhow; so quiet that a faint booming sound rolls across the water to us from the distant land.

The Arab at the tiller holds up his hand, and says one word:—"*Simba* (lion)!"

We all sit up and listen. Then it comes again, a slow, majestic sound, that thrills us to the marrow.

"To-morrow by ten o'clock," I say, "we ought, if the Captain is not out in his reckoning, which I think very probable, to make this mysterious rock with a man's head and begin our shooting."

"And begin our search for the ruined city and the Fire of Life," corrected Leo, taking his pipe from his mouth, and laughing a little.

"Nonsense!" I answered. "You were airing your Arabic with that man at the tiller this afternoon. What did he tell you? He has been trading (slave-trading probably) up and down these latitudes for half of his iniquitous life, and once landed on this very 'man' rock. Did he ever hear anything of the ruined city or the caves?"

"No," answered Leo. "He says that the country is all swamp behind, and full of snakes, especially pythons, and game, and that no man lives there. But then there is a belt of swamp all along the East African coast, so that does not go for much."

"Yes," I said, "it does—it goes for malaria. You see what sort of an opinion these gentry have of the country. Not one of them will go with us. They think that we are mad, and upon my word I believe that they are right. If ever we see old England again I shall be astonished. However, it does not greatly matter to me, at my age, but I am anxious for you, Leo and Job. It's a Tom Fool's business, my boy."

"All right, Uncle Horace. So far as I am concerned, I am willing to take my chance. Look! What is that cloud?" and he pointed to a dark blotch upon the starry sky, some miles astern of us.

"Go and ask the man at the tiller," I said.

He rose and stretched his long arms, and went. Presently he returned.

"He says it is a squall, but it will pass far on one side of us."

Just then Job came up, looking very stout and English in his shooting-suit of brown flannel, and with a sort of perplexed appearance upon his honest round face that had been very common with him since he got into these strange waters.

"Please, sir," he said, touching his sun hat, which was stuck on to the back of his head in a somewhat ludicrous fashion, "as we have got all those guns and things in the whale-boat astern, to say nothing of the provisions in the lockers, I think it would be best if I got down and slept in her. I don't like the looks" (here he dropped his voice to a portentous whisper) "of these black gentry; they have such a wonderful thievish way about them. Supposing now that some of them were to slip into the boat at night and cut the cable, and make off with her? That would be a pretty go, that would."

The whale-boat, I may explain, was one that we had had built at Dundee, in the North of England, and brought with us, as we knew that this coast was a network of creeks, and that we might require something to navigate them with. She was a beautiful boat, thirty-feet in length, with a centre-board for sailing, copper-bottomed to keep the worm out of her, and full of water-tight compartments. The captain of the dhow had told us that when we reached the rock, which he knew well, and which appeared to be identical with the one described upon the sherd and by Leo's father, he would not probably be able to run up to it on account of the shallows and breakers, so we had employed three hours that very morning, whilst we were totally becalmed, the wind having dropped at sunrise, in transferring most of our goods and chattels to the whaleboat, placing the guns, ammunition, and preserved provisions in the watertight lockers specially prepared for them, so that when we did sight the fabled rock, we should have nothing to do but step into the boat, and run her ashore. Another reason that induced us to take this precautionary step was that Arab captains are apt to run past the point that they are making, either from carelessness or owing to a mistake in its identity. Now, as sailors will know, it is quite impossible for a dhow which is only rigged to run before the monsoon to beat back against it. Therefore we got our boat ready to row for the rock at any moment.

"Well, Job," I said, "perhaps it would be as well. There are lots of blankets there, only be careful to keep out of the moon, or it may turn your head or blind you."

"Lord, sir! I don't think it would much matter if it did; it is that turned already with the sight of these blackamoors and their filthy, thieving ways. They are only fit for muck, they are; and they smell bad enough for it already."

Job, it will be perceived, was not attached to the manners and customs of our dark-skinned brothers.

Accordingly we hauled up the boat by the tow-rope till it was right under the stern of the dhow, and Job bundled into her about as gracefully as a sack of potatoes. Then we returned and sat down on the deck again, and smoked and talked in little gusts and jerks. The night was so lovely, and our brains were so full of suppressed excitement of one sort and another, that we did not feel inclined to turn in. For nearly an hour we sat thus, and then, I think, we both dozed off. At least I have a faint recollection of Leo sleepily explaining that the head was not a bad place to hit a buffalo, if you could catch him exactly between the horns, or send your bullet down his throat, or some nonsense of the sort.

Then I remember no more; till suddenly—a frightful roar of wind, a shriek of terror from the awakening crew, and a whip-like sting of water in our faces. Some of the men ran to let go the haulyards[1] and lower the sail, but the parrel[2] jammed and the yard would not come down. I sprang to my feet and hung on to a rope. The sky aft was dark as pitch, but the moon still shone brightly ahead of us and lit up the blackness. Beneath its sheen a huge white-topped breaker, twenty feet high or more, was rushing on to us. It was on the break—the moon shone on its crest and tipped its foam with light. On it rushed beneath the inky sky, driven by the awful squall behind it. Suddenly, in the twinkling of an eye, I saw the black shape of the whaleboat cast high into the air on the breaking wave. Then—a shock of water, a wild rush of

---

[1] Variant of halyards, ropes controlling the sail.
[2] Loop used to raise or lower the yard, which supports the rigging on the mast.

boiling foam, and I was clinging for my life to the shroud, ay, swept straight out from it like a flag in a gale.

We were pooped.[1]

The wave passed. It seemed to me that I was under water for minutes—really it was seconds. I looked forward. The blast had torn out the great sail, and high in the air it was fluttering away to leeward like a huge wounded bird. Then for a moment there was comparative calm, and in it I heard Job's voice yelling wildly, "Come here to the boat."

Bewildered and half drowned as I was, I had the sense to rush aft. I felt the dhow sinking under me—she was full of water. Under her counter the whale boat was tossing furiously, and I saw the Arab Mahomed, who had been steering, leap into her. I gave one desperate pull at the tow-rope to bring the boat alongside. Wildly I sprang also, and Job caught me with one arm and I rolled into the bottom of the boat. Down went the dhow bodily, and as she did so Mahomed drew his curved knife and severed the fibre-rope by which we were fast to her, and in another second we were driving before the storm over the place where the dhow had been.

"Great God!" I shrieked, "where is Leo? *Leo! Leo!*"

"He's gone, sir, God help him!" roared Job into my ear, and such was the fury of the squall that his voice sounded like a whisper.

I wrung my hands in agony. Leo was drowned, and I was left alive to mourn him.

"Look out!" yelled Job, "here comes another."

I turned; a second huge wave was overtaking us. I hoped it would drown me. With a curious fascination I watched its awful advent. The moon was nearly hidden now by the wreaths of the rushing storm, but a little light still caught the crest of the devouring breaker. There was something dark on it—a piece of wreckage. It was on us now, and the boat was nearly full of water. But she was built in airtight compartments—Heaven bless the man who invented them!—and lifted up through it like a swan. Through the foam and turmoil I saw the black thing on the wave hurrying right at me. I put out my right arm to ward it from me, and my hand closed on another arm, the wrist of which my fingers gripped like a vice. I am a very strong man, and had something to hold to, but my arm was nearly torn from its socket by the strain and weight of the floating body. Had the rush lasted another two seconds I must either have let go or gone with it. But it passed, leaving us up to our knees in water.

"Bail out! bail out!" shouted Job, suiting the action to the word.

---

[1]   Waves have swamped and submerged the deck astern.

But I could not bail just then, for as the moon went out and left us in total darkness, one faint, flying ray of light lit upon the face of the man I had gripped, who was now half lying half floating in the bottom of the boat.

It was Leo. Leo brought back by the wave—back, dead or alive, from the very jaws of Death.

"Bail out! bail out!" yelled Job, "or we shall founder."

I seized a large tin bowl with a handle to it, which was fixed under one of the seats, and the three of us bailed away for dear life. The furious tempest drove over and round us, flinging the boat this way and that, the wind and the storm wreaths and the sheets of stinging spray blinded and bewildered us, but through it all we worked like demons with the wild exhilaration of despair, for even despair can exhilarate. One minute! three minutes! six minutes! The boat began to lighten, and no fresh wave swamped us. Five minutes more, and she was fairly clear. Then, suddenly, above the awful shriekings of the hurricane came a duller, deeper roar. Great Heavens! It was the voice of breakers!

At that moment the moon began to shine out again—this time behind the path of the squall. Out far across the torn bosom of the ocean shot the ragged arrows of her light, and there, half-a-mile ahead of us, was a white line of foam, then a little space of open-mouthed blackness, and then another line of white. It was the breakers, and their roar grew clearer and yet more clear as we sped down upon them like a swallow. There they were, boiling up in snowy spouts of spray, smiting and gnashing together like the gleaming teeth of hell.

"Take the tiller, Mahomed!" I roared in Arabic, "we must try and shoot them." At the same moment I seized an oar, and got it out, motioning to Job to do likewise.

Mahomed clambered aft, and got hold of the tiller, and with some difficulty Job, who had sometimes pulled a tub[1] upon the homely Cam,[2] got out his oar. In another minute her head was straight on to the ever nearing line, towards which she plunged and tore with the speed of a racehorse. Just in front of us the first line seemed a little thinner than to the right or left—there was a gap of rather deeper water. I turned and pointed to it.

"Steer for your life, Mahomed!" I yelled. He was a skilful steersman, and well acquainted with the dangers of this most perilous coast, and I

---

[1] Rowed a boat.
[2] The river that runs through Cambridge in England.

saw him grip the tiller and bend his heavy frame forward, and stare at the foaming terror till his big round eyes looked as though they would start out of his head. The send of the sea was driving the boat's head round to starboard. If we struck the line of breakers fifty yards to starboard of the gap we must sink. It was a great field of twisting, spouting waves. Mahomed planted his foot against the seat before him, and, glancing at him, I saw his brown toes spread out like a hand with the weight he put upon them as he took the strain of the tiller. She came round a bit, but not enough. I roared to Job to back water, whilst I dragged and laboured at my oar. She answered now, and none too soon. Heavens, we were in them! And then followed a couple of minutes of heart-breaking excitement such as I cannot hope to describe. All I remember is a shrieking sea of foam, out of which the billows rose here, there, and everywhere like avenging ghosts from their ocean grave. Once we were turned right round, but either by chance, or through Mahomed's skilful steering, the boat's head came straight again before a breaker filled us. One more—a monster. We were through it or over it—more through than over—and then, with a wild yell of exultation from the Arab, we shot out into the comparative smooth water of the mouth of sea between the teeth-like lines of gnashing waves.

But we were half full of water again, and not more than half-a-mile ahead was the second line of breakers. Again we set to and bailed furiously. Fortunately the storm had now quite gone by, and the moon shone brightly, revealing a rocky headland running half-a-mile or more out into the sea, of which the second line of breakers appeared to be a continuation. At any rate, they boiled around its foot. Probably the ridge that made it ran out into the ocean, only at a lower level, and formed the reef. This headland was terminated by a curious peak that seemed not to be more than a mile away from us. Just as we got the boat pretty clear, for the second time, Leo, to my immense relief, opened his eyes and remarked that the clothes had tumbled off the bed, and that he supposed it was time to get up for chapel. I told him to shut his eyes and keep quiet, which he did without in the slightest degree realizing the position. As for myself, his reference to chapel made me reflect, with a sort of sick longing, on my comfortable rooms at Cambridge. Why had I been such a fool as to leave them? This is a reflection that has several times recurred to me since, with ever-increasing force.

But now again we are drifting down on the breakers, though with lessened speed, for the wind had fallen, and only the current or the tide (it afterwards turned out to be the tide) was driving us.

Another minute, and with a sort of howl to Allah from the Arab, a pious ejaculation from myself, and something that was not pious from Job, we were in them. And then the whole scene, down to our final escape, repeated itself, only not quite so violently. Mahomed's skilful steering and the air-tight compartments saved our lives. In five minutes we were through, and drifting—for we were too exhausted to do anything to help ourselves except keep her head straight—with the most startling rapidity round the headland which I have described.

Round we went with the tide, until we got well under the lee of the point, and then suddenly the speed slackened, we ceased to make way, and finally appeared to be in dead water. The storm had entirely passed, leaving a clean-washed sky behind it; the headland intercepted the heavy sea that had been occasioned by the squall, and the tide, which had been running so fiercely up the river (for we were in the mouth of a small river), was sluggish before it turned, so we floated quietly, and before the moon went down managed to bail out the boat thoroughly and get her a little ship-shape. Leo was sleeping profoundly, and on the whole I thought it wise not to wake him. It was true he was in his wet clothes, but the night was now so warm that I thought (and so did Job) that they were not likely to injure a man of his unusually vigorous constitution. Besides, we had no dry ones at hand.

Presently the moon went down, and left us floating on the waters, now only heaving like some troubled woman's breast. This gave us leisure to reflect upon all that we had gone through and all that we had escaped. Job stationed himself at the bow, Mahomed kept his post at the tiller, and I sat on a seat in the middle of the boat close to where Leo was lying.

The moon went slowly down in chastened loveliness; she departed like some sweet bride into her chamber, and long veil-like shadows crept up the sky through which the stars peeped shyly out. Soon, however, they, too, began to pale before a splendour in the east, and then the quivering footsteps of the dawn came rushing across the new-born blue, and shook them from their places. Quieter and more quiet grew the sea, quiet as the soft mists that brooded on her bosom, and covered up her troubling, as the illusive wreaths of sleep brood upon and cover up a pain-racked mind, causing it to forget its sorrow. From the east to the west sped the angels of the dawn, from sea to sea, from mountain top to mountain top, scattering light with both their hands. On they sped out of the darkness, perfect, glorious, like spirits of the just breaking from the tomb; on, over the quiet sea, over the low coast line, and the swamps beyond, and the mountains beyond them; over those who slept in peace, and over those who woke in sorrow; over the evil and the good; over the living and the dead; over the wide world and all that breathes or has breathed thereon.

It was a wonderfully beautiful sight, and yet sad, perhaps from the very excess of its beauty. The arising sun! the setting sun! There we have the symbol and the type of humanity, and all things with which humanity has to do. The symbol and the type, yes, and the earthly beginning, and the end also. And on that morning this came home to me with a peculiar force. The sun that arose to-day for us had set last night for eighteen of our fellow voyagers!—had set for ever for eighteen whom we knew!

The dhow had gone down with them, they were tossing about now among the rocks and seaweed, so much human drift on the great ocean of death! And we four were saved! But one day a sunrise will come when we shall be among those who are lost, and then others will watch those glorious rays, and grow sad in the midst of beauty, and dream of Death in the full glow of arising Life!

For this is the lot of man.

V

THE HEAD OF THE ETHIOPIAN

At length the heralds and forerunners of the Royal sun had done their work, and, searching out the shadows, had caused them to flee away. Then up he came in glory from his ocean-bed, and flooded the earth with warmth and light. I sat there in the boat listening to the gentle lapping of the water and watched him rise, till presently the slight drift of the boat brought the odd-shaped rock, or peak, at the end of the promontory, which we had weathered with so much peril, between me and the majestic sight, and blotted it from my view. I still continued to stare at the rock, however, absently enough, till presently it became edged with the fire of the growing light behind it, and then I started, as well I might, for I perceived that the top of the peak, which was about eighty feet high by one hundred and fifty thick at its base, was shaped like a negro's head and face, on which was stamped a most fiendish and terrifying expression. There was no doubt about it; there were the thick lips, the fat cheeks, and the squat nose standing out with startling clearness against the flaming background. There, too, was the round skull, washed into shape perhaps by thousands of years of wind and weather, and, to complete the resemblance, there was a scrubby growth of weeds or lichen upon it, which against the sun looked for all the world like the wool on a colossal negro's head. It certainly was very odd; so odd that now I believe it is not a mere freak of nature but a gigantic monument fashioned, like the well-known Egyptian Sphinx, by a forgotten people out of a pile of rock that lent itself to their design, perhaps as an emblem of warning and defiance to any enemies who approached the harbour. Unfortunately we were never able to ascertain whether or not this was the case, inasmuch as the rock was difficult of access both from the land and the water-side, and we had other things to attend to. Myself, considering the matter by the light of what we afterwards saw, I believe that it was fashioned by man, but whether or not this is so, there it stands, and sullenly stares from age to age out across the changing sea—there it stood two thousand years and more ago, when Amenartas, the Egyptian princess, and the wife of Leo's remote ancestor Kallikrates, gazed upon its devilish face—and there I have no doubt it will still stand when as many centuries as are numbered between her day and our own are added to the year that bore us to oblivion.

"What do you think of that, Job," I asked of our retainer, who was sitting on the edge of the boat, trying to get as much sunshine as possible, and generally looking uncommonly wretched, and I pointed to the fiery demoniacal head.

"Oh Lord, sir," answered Job, who now perceived the object for the first time, "I think that the Old Gentleman[1] must have been sitting for his portrait on them rocks."

I laughed, and the laugh woke up Leo.

"Hullo," he said, "what's the matter with me? I am all stiff—where is the dhow?"

"You may be thankful that you are not stiffer, my boy," I answered. "The dhow is sunk, and everybody on board her is drowned, with the exception of us four, and your own life was only saved by a miracle;" and whilst Job, now that it was light enough, searched about in a locker for the brandy, for which Leo asked, I told him the history of our night's adventure.

"Great Heavens!" he said, faintly; "and to think that we should have been chosen to live through it!"

By this time the brandy was forthcoming, and we all had a good pull at it, and thankful enough we were for it. Also the sun was beginning

---

[1]   Satan.

to get strength, and warm our chilled bones, for we had been wet through for five hours or more.

"Why," said Leo, with a gasp as he put down the brandy bottle, "there is the head the writing talks of,'the rock shaped like the head of an Ethiopian.'"

"Yes," I said, "there it is."

"Well, then," he answered, "the whole thing is true."

"I don't at all see that that follows," I answered. "We knew this head was here, your father saw it.Very likely it is not the same head that the writing talks of; or if it is, it proves nothing."

Leo smiled at me in a superior way. "You are an unbelieving Jew, Uncle Horace," he said. "Those who live will see."

"Exactly so," I answered, "and now perhaps you observe that we are drifting across a sandbank into the mouth of the river. Get hold of your oar, Job, and we will row in and see if we can't find a place to land."

The river mouth which we were entering did not appear to be a very wide one, though as yet the long banks of steaming mist that clung about its shores had not lifted sufficiently to enable us to see its exact width. There was, as is the case with nearly every East African river, a considerable bar at the mouth, which, no doubt, when the wind was on shore and the tide running out, was absolutely impassable even for a boat drawing only a few inches. But as things were it was manageable enough, and we did not ship a cupful of water. In twenty minutes we were well across it, with but slight assistance from ourselves, and being carried by a strong though somewhat variable breeze well up the harbour. By this time the mist was being sucked up by the sun, which was getting uncomfortably hot, and we saw that the mouth of the little estuary was here about half a mile across, and that the banks were very marshy, and crowded with crocodiles lying about on the mud like logs. About a mile ahead of us, however, was what appeared to be a strip of firm land, and for this we steered. In another quarter of an hour we were there, and making the boat fast to a beautiful tree with broad shining leaves, and flowers of the magnolia species, only they were rose-coloured and not white,* which hung over the water, we disembarked. This done we undressed, washed ourselves, and spread our clothes and the contents of the boat in the sun to dry, which they very quickly did, and then taking shelter from the sun under some trees, we made a

---

* There is a known species of magnolia with pink flowers. It is indigenous in Sikkim, and known as *Magnolia Campbellii.*—EDITOR.

hearty breakfast off a "Paysandu"[1] potted tongue, of which we had brought a good quantity with us from the Army and Navy Stores,[2] congratulating ourselves enormously on our good fortune in having loaded and provisioned the boat on the previous day before the hurricane destroyed the dhow. By the time that we had finished our meal our clothes were dry, and we hastened to get into them, feeling not a little refreshed. Indeed, with the exception of weariness and a few bruises, none of us were the worse for our terrifying adventure, which had been fatal to all our companions. Leo, it is true, had been half-drowned, but that is no great matter to a vigorous young athlete of five-and-twenty.

After breakfast we started to look about us. We were on a strip of dry land about two hundred yards broad by five hundred long, bordered on one side by the river, and on the other three by endless desolate swamps, that stretched as far as the eye could reach. This strip of land was raised about twenty-five feet above the level of the surrounding swamps and the river level: indeed it had every appearance of having been made by the hand of man.

"This place has been a wharf," said Leo, dogmatically.

"Nonsense," I answered. "Who would be fool enough to build a wharf in the middle of these dreadful marshes in a country inhabited by savages, that is if it is inhabited at all?"

"Perhaps it was not always marsh, and perhaps the people were not always savage," he said drily, looking down the steep bank, for we were standing by the river. "Look there," he went on, pointing to a spot where the hurricane of the previous night had torn up one of the magnolia trees, which had grown on the extreme edge of the bank just where it sloped down to the water, by the roots, that had lifted a large cake of earth with them. "Is not that stone work? If not, it is very like it?"

"Nonsense," I said again, and we clambered down to the spot, and got between the upturned roots and the bank.

"Well?" he said.

But I did not answer this time. I only whistled. For there laid bare by the removal of the earth was an undoubted facing of solid stone laid in large blocks and bound together with brown cement, so hard that I could make no impression on it with the file in my shooting knife. Nor was this all; seeing something projecting through the soil at the bottom

---

[1]   A brand of canned meat.
[2]   An English department store.

of the bared patch of walling, I removed the loose earth in my hands, and revealed a huge stone ring, a foot or more in diameter, and about three inches thick. This fairly staggered me.

"Looks rather like a wharf where good-sized vessels have been moored, does it not, Uncle Horace?" said Master Leo, with an excited grin.

I tried to say "Nonsense" again, but the word stuck in my throat— the ring spoke for itself. In some past age vessels had been moored there, and this stone wall was undoubtedly the remains of a solidly-constructed wharf. Probably the city to which it had belonged lay buried beneath the swamp behind it.

"Begins to look as though there were something in the story after all, Uncle Horace," said the exultant Leo; and reflecting on the mysterious negro's head and the equally mysterious stonework I made no direct reply.

"A country like Africa," I said, "is sure to be full of the relics of long dead and forgotten civilisations. Nobody knows the age of the Egyptian civilisation, and very likely it had offshoots. Then there were the Babylonians and the Phœnicians, and the Persians, and all manner of people, all more or less civilised, to say nothing of the Jews whom everybody 'wants' nowadays. It is possible that they, or any one of them, may have had colonies or trading stations about here. Remember those buried Persian cities that the consul showed us at Kilwa."*

"Quite so," said Leo, "but that is not what you said before."

"Well, what is to be done now?" I asked, turning the conversation.

As no answer was forthcoming we proceeded to the edge of the swamp, and looked over it. It was apparently boundless, and vast flocks of every sort of waterfowl flew from its recesses till it was sometimes difficult to see the sky. Now that the sun was getting high it drew thin sickly-looking clouds of poisonous vapour from the surface of the marsh and from the scummy pools of stagnant water.

"Two things are clear to me," I said, addressing my three companions, who stared at this spectacle in dismay, "first, that we can't go across

---

* Near Kilwa, on the East Coast of Africa, about 400 miles south of Zanzibar, is a cliff which has been recently washed by the waves. On the top of this cliff are Persian tombs known to be at least seven centuries old by the dates still legible on them. Beneath these tombs is a layer of *débris* representing a city. Farther down the cliff is a second layer representing an older city, and farther down yet a third layer, the remains of a still more ancient city of vast and unknown antiquity. Beneath the bottom city were found some specimens of glazed earthenware, such as are occasionally to be met with on that coast to this day. I believe that they are now in the possession of Sir John Kirk.—EDITOR.

there" (I pointed to the swamp), "and, secondly, that if we stop here we shall certainly die of fever."

"That's as clear as a haystack," said Job.

"Very well, then; there are two alternatives before us. One is to 'bout ship, and try and run for some port in the whaleboat, which would be a sufficiently risky proceeding, and the other to sail or row on up the river, and see where we come to."

"I don't know what you are going to do," said Leo, setting his mouth, "but I am going up that river."

Job turned up the whites of his eyes and groaned, and the Arab murmured "Allah," and groaned also. As for me, I remarked sweetly that as we seemed to be between the devil and the deep sea, it did not much matter where we went. But in reality I was as anxious to proceed as Leo. The colossal negro's head and the stone wharf had excited my curiosity to an extent of which I was secretly ashamed, and I was prepared to gratify it at any cost. Accordingly, having carefully fitted the mast, re-stowed the boat, and got out our rifles, we embarked. Fortunately the wind was blowing on shore from the ocean, so we were able to hoist the sail. Indeed, we afterwards found out that as a general rule the wind set on shore from daybreak for some hours, and off shore again at sunset, and the explanation that I offer of this is that, when the earth is cooled by the dew and the night, the hot air rises, and the draught rushes in from the sea till the sun has once more heated it through. At least that appeared to be the rule here.

Taking advantage of this favouring wind, we sailed merrily up the river for three or four hours. Once we came across a school of hippopotami, which rose, and bellowed dreadfully at us within ten or a dozen fathoms of the boat, much to Job's alarm, and, I will confess, to my own. These were the first hippopotami that we had ever seen, and, to judge by their insatiable curiosity, I should judge that we were the first white men that they had ever seen. Upon my word, I once or twice thought that they were coming into the boat to gratify it. Leo wanted to fire at them, but I dissuaded him, fearing the consequences. Also we saw hundreds of crocodiles basking on the muddy banks, and thousands upon thousands of waterfowl. Some of these we shot, and among them was a wild goose, which, in addition to the sharp curved spurs on its wings, had a spur about three-quarters of an inch long growing from the skull just between the eyes. We never shot another like it, so I do not know if it was a freak or a distinct species. In the latter case this incident may interest naturalists. Job named it the Unicorn Goose.

About mid-day the sun grew intensely hot, and the stench drawn up by it from the marshes which the river drains was something too awful, and caused us instantly to swallow precautionary doses of quinine.[1] Shortly afterwards the breeze died away altogether, and as rowing our heavy boat against stream in the heat was out of the question, we were thankful enough to get under the shade of a group of trees—a species of willow—that grew by the edge of the river, and lie there and gasp till at length the approach of sunset put a period to our miseries. Seeing what appeared to be an open space of water straight ahead of us, we determined to row there before settling what to do for the night. Just as we were about to loosen the boat, however, a beautiful water-buck, with great horns curving forward, and a white stripe across the rump, came down to the river to drink without perceiving us hidden away within fifty yards under the willows. Leo was the first to catch sight of it, and being an ardent sportsman, thirsting for the blood of big game, about which he had been dreaming for months, he instantly stiffened all over, and pointed like a setter dog. Seeing what was the matter, I handed him his express rifle, at the same time taking my own.

"Now then," I whispered, "mind you don't miss."

"Miss!" he whispered back contemptuously; "I could not miss it if I tried."

He lifted the rifle, and the roan-coloured buck, having drunk his fill, raised his head and looked out across the river. He was standing right against the sunset sky on a little eminence, or ridge of ground, that ran across the swamp, evidently a favourite path for game, and there was something very beautiful about him. Indeed, I do not think that if I live to a hundred I shall ever forget that desolate and yet most fascinating scene: it is stamped upon my memory. To the right and left wide stretches of lonely, death-breeding swamp, unbroken and unrelieved so far as the eye could reach, except here and there by ponds of black and peaty water that, mirror-like, flashed up the red rays of the setting sun. Behind us and before the vista of the sluggish river, ending in glimpses of a reed-fringed lagoon, on whose surface the long lights of the evening played as the faint breeze stirred the shadows. To the west the huge red ball of the sinking sun, now vanishing down the vapoury horizon, and filling the great heaven, high across whose arch the cranes and wild fowl streamed in line, square, and triangle, with flashes of flying

---

[1] Medicine used to combat malaria, which in Haggard's day was still thought to be caused by breathing swamp vapour. In reality, the disease is spread through the bite of the mosquito.

gold and the lurid stain of blood. And then ourselves—three modern Englishmen in a modern English boat—seeming to jar upon and looking out of tone with that measureless desolation; and in front of us the noble buck limned out upon a background of ruddy sky.

Bang! Away he goes with a mighty bound. Leo has missed him. Bang! right under him again. Now for a shot. I must have one though he is going like an arrow, and a hundred yards away and more. By Jove! over and over and over! "Well, I think I've wiped your eye there, Master Leo," I say, struggling against the ungenerous exultation that in such a supreme moment of one's existence will rise in the best-tutored sportsman's breast.

"Confound you, yes," growled Leo; and then, with that quick smile that is one of his charms lighting up his handsome face like a ray of light, "I beg your pardon, old fellow. I congratulate you; it was a lovely shot, and mine were vile."

We got out of the boat and ran to the buck, which was shot through the spine and stone dead. It took us a quarter of an hour or more to clean it and cut off as much of the best meat as we could carry, and, having packed this away, we had barely light enough to row up into the lagoon-like space, into which, there being a hollow in the swamp, the river here expanded. Just as the light vanished we cast anchor about fifty yards from the edge of the lake. We did not dare to go ashore, not knowing if we should find dry ground to camp on, and greatly fearing the poisonous exhalations from the marsh, which we thought we should be freer from on the water. So we lighted a lantern, and made our evening meal off another potted tongue in the best fashion that we could, and then prepared to go to sleep, only, however, to find that sleep was impossible. For, whether they were attracted by the lantern, or by the unaccustomed smell of a white man, for which they had been waiting for the last thousand years or so, I know not; but certainly we were presently attacked by tens of thousands of the most bloodthirsty, pertinacious, and huge mosquitoes that I ever saw or read of. In clouds they came, and pinged and buzzed and bit till we were nearly mad. Tobacco smoke only seemed to stir them into a merrier and more active life, till at length we were driven to covering ourselves with blankets, head and all, and sitting to slowly stew and continually scratch and swear beneath them. And as we sat, suddenly rolling out like thunder through the silence came the deep roar of a lion, and then of a second lion, moving among the reeds within fifty yards of us.

"I say," said Leo, sticking his head out from under his blanket, "lucky we ain't on the bank, eh, Avuncular?" (Leo sometimes addressed me in this disrespectful way.) "Hang it! a mosquito has bitten me on the nose," and the head vanished again.

Shortly after this the moon came up, and notwithstanding every variety of roar that echoed over the water to us from the lions on the banks, we began, thinking ourselves perfectly secure, gradually to doze off.

I do not quite know what it was that made me poke my head out of the friendly shelter of the blanket, perhaps because I found that the mosquitoes were biting right through it. Anyhow, as I did so I heard Job whisper, in a frightened voice,

"Oh, my stars, look there!"

Instantly we all of us looked, and this was what we saw in the moonlight. Near the shore were two wide and ever-widening circles of concentric rings rippling away across the surface of the water, and in the heart and centre of the circles were two dark moving objects.

"What is it?" asked I.

"It is those blessed lions, sir," answered Job, in a tone which was an odd mixture of a sense of personal injury, habitual respect, and acknowledged fear, "and they are swimming here to heat us," he added, nervously picking up an "h" in his agitation.

I looked again: there was no doubt about it; I could catch the glare of their ferocious eyes. Attracted either by the smell of the newly killed water-buck meat or of ourselves, the hungry beasts were actually storming our position.

Leo already had his rifle in his hand. I called to him to wait till they were nearer, and meanwhile grabbed my own. Some fifteen feet from us the water shallowed on a bank to the depth of about fifteen inches, and presently the first of them—it was the lioness—got on to it, and shook herself and roared. At that moment Leo fired, and the bullet went right down her open mouth and out at the back of her neck, and down she dropped, with a splash, dead. The other lion—a full-grown male— was some two paces behind her. At this second he got his forepaws on to the bank, when a strange thing happened. There was a rush and disturbance of the water, such as one sees in a pond in England when a pike takes a little fish, only a thousand times fiercer and larger, and suddenly the lion gave a most terrific snarling roar and sprang forward on to the bank, dragging something black with him.

"Allah!" shouted Mahomed, "a crocodile has got him by the leg!" and sure enough he had. We could see the long snout with its gleaming lines of teeth, and the reptile body behind it.

And then followed a scene that absolutely baffles description. The lion managed to get well on to the bank, the crocodile half standing and half swimming, still nipping his hind leg. He roared till the air quivered with the sound, and then, with a savage, shrieking snarl, turned round and clawed hold of the crocodile's head. The crocodile shifted his grip, having, as we afterwards discovered, had one of his eyes torn out, and slightly turned over, and instantly the lion got him by the throat and held on, and then over and over they rolled upon the bank struggling hideously. It was impossible to follow their movements, but when next we got a clear view the tables had turned, for the crocodile, whose head seemed to be a mass of gore, had got the lion's body in his iron jaws just above the hips, and was squeezing him and shaking him to and fro. For his part the tortured brute, roaring in agony, was clawing and biting madly at his enemy's scaly head, and fixing his great hind claws in the crocodile's comparatively speaking, soft throat, ripping it open as one would rip a glove.

Then, all of a sudden, the end came. The lion's head fell forward on the crocodile's back, and with an awful groan he died, and the crocodile, after standing for a minute motionless, slowly rolled over on to his side, his jaws still fixed across the carcase of the lion, which we afterwards found he had bitten almost in half.

This duel to the death was a wonderful and a shocking sight, and one that I suppose few men have seen—and thus it ended.

When it was all over, leaving Mahomed to keep a look-out, we managed to spend the rest of the night as quietly as the mosquitoes would let us.

(*To be continued*)

"I drew my revolver, and fired it by a sort of instinct straight at the diabolical
woman who had been caressing Mahomed."

VI

AN EARLY CHRISTIAN CEREMONY

Next morning, at the earliest blush of dawn, we rose, and performed such ablutions as circumstances would allow, and generally made ready to start. I am bound to say that when there was sufficient light to enable us to see each other's faces I, for one, burst out in a roar of laughter. Job's fat and comfortable countenance was swollen out to nearly twice its natural size from mosquito bites, and Leo's condition was not much better. Indeed, of the three I had come off much the best, probably owing to the toughness of my dark skin, and to the fact that a good deal of it was covered by hair, for since we started from England I had allowed my naturally luxuriant beard to grow at its own sweet will. But the other two were, comparatively speaking, clean shaven, which of course gave the enemy a larger extent of open country to operate on, though as for Mahomed the mosquitoes, recognising the taste of a true believer, would not touch him at any price. How often, I wonder, during the next week or so did we wish that we were flavoured like an Arab!

By the time that we had done laughing as heartily as our swollen lips would allow it was daylight, and the morning breeze was coming up from the sea, cutting lanes through the dense marsh mists, and here and there rolling them before it in great balls of fleecy vapour. So we set our sail, and having first taken a look at the two dead lions and the dead alligator,[1] which we were of course unable to skin, being destitute of means of curing the pelts, we started, and, sailing through the lagoon, followed the course of the river on the further side. At midday, when the breeze dropped, we were fortunate enough to find a convenient piece of dry land on which to camp and light a fire, and here we cooked some wild duck and some of the waterbuck's flesh—not in a very appetising way, it is true, but still, sufficiently. The rest of the buck's flesh we cut into strips and hung in the sun to dry into "biltong," as I believe the South African Dutch call flesh thus prepared. On this welcome patch of dry land we stopped till the following dawn, and, as before, spent the night in warfare with the mosquitoes, but without other troubles. The next day or two

---

[1]   Haggard uses this word interchangeably with "crocodile."

passed in similar fashion, and without noticeable adventures, except that we shot a specimen of a peculiarly graceful, hornless buck, and saw many varieties of water-lilies in full bloom, some of them of exquisite beauty, though few of the flowers were perfect, owing to the prevalence of a white water-maggot with a green head that fed upon them.

It was on the fourth day of our journey, when we had travelled, so far as we could reckon, about one hundred and thirty-five to a hundred and forty miles westwards from the coast, that the first event of any real importance occurred. On that morning the usual wind failed us about eleven o'clock, and after pulling a little way we were forced to halt more or less exhausted at what appeared to be the junction of our stream with another of a uniform width of about fifty feet. Some trees grew near at hand—the only trees in all this country were along the banks of the river, and under these we rested, and then, the land being fairly dry just here, walked a little way along the edge of the river to prospect, and shoot a few waterfowl for food. Before we had gone fifty yards we perceived that all hopes of getting further up the stream in the whale-boat were at an end, for not two hundred yards above where we had stopped were a succession of shallows and mudbanks, with not six inches of water over them. It was a watery *cul-de-sac*.

Turning back, we walked some way along the banks of the other river, and soon came to the conclusion, from various indications, that it was not a river at all, but an ancient canal, such as is to be seen above Mombasa,[1] on the Zanzibar coast, connecting the Tana River with the Ozy, in such a way as to enable the shipping coming down the Tana to cross to the other river, and reach the sea by it, and thus avoid the very dangerous bar that blocks the mouth of the Tana. The canal before us had evidently been dug out by man at some remote period of the world's history, and the results of his digging still remained in the shape of the raised banks that had no doubt once formed towing-paths. Except here and there, where they had been hollowed out or fallen in, the banks of stiff, binding clay were at a uniform distance from each other, and the depth also appeared to be uniform. Current there was little or none, and, as a consequence, the surface of the water was choked with vegetable growth, intersected by little paths of clear water, made, I suppose, by the constant passage of waterfowl, iguanas, and other vermin. Now, as it was

---

[1]   Port city in what is now Kenya in east Africa, north of Zanzibar Island. The Tana flows through Kenya to the Indian Ocean. Haggard has invented the remains of a canal in this location.

evident that we could not proceed up the river, it became equally evident that we must either try the canal or else return to the sea. We could not stop where we were, to be baked by the sun and eaten up by the mosquitoes, till we died of fever in that dreary marsh.

"Well, I suppose that we must try it," I said; and the others assented in their various ways—Leo, as though it were the best joke in the world; Job, in respectful disgust; and Mahomed, with an invocation to the Prophet, and a comprehensive curse upon all unbelievers and their ways of thought and travel.

Accordingly, as soon as the sun got low, having little or nothing more to hope for from our friendly wind, we started. For the first hour or so we managed to row the boat, though with great labour; but after that the weeds got too thick to allow of it, and we were obliged to resort to the primitive and most exhausting resource of towing her. For two hours we laboured, Mahomed, Job, and myself, who was supposed to be strong enough to pull against the two of them, on the bank, while Leo sat in the bow of the boat, and brushed away the weeds which collected round the cutwater with Mahomed's sword. At dark we halted till midnight to rest and enjoy the mosquitoes, but when the moon got up we went on again, taking advantage of the comparative cool of the night. At dawn we halted for three hours, and then started once more, and laboured on till about ten o'clock, when a thunderstorm, accompanied by a deluge of rain, overtook us, and we spent the next six hours practically under water.

I do not know that there is any necessity for me to describe the next four days of our voyage in detail, further than to say that they were, on the whole, the most miserable that I ever spent in my life, forming one monotonous record of heavy labour, heat, misery, and mosquitoes. All the way we passed through a region of almost endless swamp, and I can only attribute our escape from fever and death to the constant doses of quinine and purgatives which we took, and the unceasing toil which we were forced to undergo. On the third day of our journey up the canal we had sighted a round hill that loomed dimly through the vapours of the marsh, and on the evening of the fourth night, when we camped, this hill seemed to be within five-and-twenty or thirty miles of us. We were by now utterly exhausted, and felt as though our blistered hands could not pull the boat a yard farther, and that the best thing that we could do would be to lie down and die in that dreadful wilderness of swamp. It was an awful position, and one in which I trust no other white man will ever be placed; and as I threw myself down in the boat to sleep the sleep of utter exhaustion, I bitterly cursed my folly in ever having been a party to such a mad undertaking, which could, I felt, only end in our death in this ghastly land. I thought, I remember, as I slowly sank into a doze, of what the appearance of the boat and her unhappy crew would be in two or three months' time from that night. There she would lie, with gaping seams and half filled with fœtid water, which, when the mist-laden wind stirred her, would wash backwards and forwards through our mouldering bones, and that would be the end of her, and of those in her who would follow after myths and seek out the secrets of Nature.

Already I seemed to hear the water rippling against the desiccated bones and rattling them together, rolling my skull against Mahomed's, and Mahomed's against mine, till at last Mahomed's stood straight up upon its vertebræ, and glared at me through its empty eyeholes, and cursed me with its grinning jaws, because I, a dog of a Christian, disturbed the last sleep of a true believer. I opened my eyes, and shuddered at the horrid dream, and then shuddered again at something that was not a dream, for two great eyes were gleaming down at me through the misty darkness. I struggled up, and in my terror and confusion shrieked, and shrieked again, so that the others sprang up too, reeling, and drunken with sleep and fright. And then all of a sudden there was a flash of cold steel, and a great spear was held against my throat, and behind it other spears gleamed cruelly.

"Peace," said a voice, speaking in Arabic, or rather in some dialect into which Arabic entered very largely; "who are ye who come hither swimming on the water? Speak, or ye die," and the steel pressed sharply against my throat, sending a cold chill through me.

"We are travellers, and have come hither by chance," I answered in my best Arabic, which appeared to be understood, for the man turned his head, and, addressing a tall form that towered up in the background, said, "Father, shall we slay?"

"What is the colour of the men?" said a deep voice in answer.

"White is their colour."

"Slay not," was the reply. "Four suns since was the word brought to me from '*She-who-must-be-obeyed*,' 'White men come; if white men come, slay them not.' Let them be brought to the land of '*She-who-must-be-obeyed*.' Bring forth the men, and let that which they have with them be brought also."

"Come," said the man, half leading and half dragging me from the boat, and, as he did so I perceived other men doing the same kind office to my companions.

On the bank were gathered a company of some fifty men. In that light all I could make out was that they were armed with huge spears, were very tall, and strongly built, comparatively light in colour, and nude, save for a leopard-skin tied round the middle.

Presently Leo and Job were bundled out and placed beside me.

"What on earth is up?" said Leo, rubbing his eyes.

"Oh, Lord! sir, here's a rum go,"[1] ejaculated Job; and just at that moment a disturbance ensued, and Mahomed came tumbling between us, followed by a shadowy form with an uplifted spear.

"Allah! Allah!" howled Mahomed, feeling that he had little to hope from man, "protect me! protect me!"

"Father, it is a black one," said a voice. "What said '*She-who-must-be-obeyed*' about the black one?"

"She said nought; but slay him not. Come hither, my son."

The man advanced, and the tall shadowy form bent forward.

"Yes, yes," said the other, and chuckled in a somewhat blood-curdling tone.

"Are the three white men there?" asked the form.

"Yes, they are there."

"Then bring up that which is made ready for them, and let the men take all that can be brought from the thing that floats."

Hardly had he spoken when men came running up, carrying on their shoulders neither more nor less than palanquins[2]—four bearers and two spare men to a palanquin—and in these it was promptly indicated we were expected to stow ourselves.

"Well!" said Leo, "it is a blessing to find anybody to carry us after having to carry ourselves so long."

Leo always takes a cheerful view of things.

There being no help for it, after seeing the others into theirs I tumbled into my own litter, and very comfortable I found it. It appeared to be manufactured of cloth woven from grass-fibre, which stretched and yielded to every motion after the body, and, being bound top and bottom to the bearing pole, gave a grateful support to the head and neck.

Scarcely had I settled myself when, accompanying their steps with a monotonous song, the bearers started at a swinging trot. For half-an-hour or so I lay there reflecting on the very remarkable experiences that we were going through, and wondering if any of my eminently respectable

---

[1]   A strange and difficult situation.
[2]   Enclosed couch supported on poles, carried on the shoulders of bearers.

fossil friends down at Cambridge would believe me if I were to be miraculously set at the familiar dinner-table for the purpose of relating them. I don't want to convey any disrespectful notion or slight when I call those good and learned men fossils, but my experience is that people are apt to fossilise even at a University if they follow the same paths too persistently. I was getting fossilised myself, but of late my stock of ideas has been very much enlarged. Well, I lay, and reflected, and wondered what on earth would be the end of it all, till at last I ceased to wonder, and went to sleep.

I suppose I must have slept for seven or eight hours, getting the first real rest that I had had since the night before the loss of the dhow, for when I woke the sun was high in the heavens. We were still journeying on at a pace of about four miles an hour. Peeping out through the mist-like curtains of the litter, which were ingeniously fixed to the bearing pole, I perceived to my infinite relief that we had passed out of the region of eternal swamp, and were now travelling over swelling grassy plains towards a cup-shaped hill. Whether or not it was the same hill that we had seen from the canal I do not know, and have never since been able to discover, for, as we afterwards found out, these people will give little information upon such points. Next I glanced at the men who were bearing me. They were of a magnificent build, none of them being under six feet in height, and yellowish in colour. Generally their appearance had a good deal in common with that of the East African Somali, but their hair was not frizzed up, but hung in thick black locks upon their shoulders. Their features were aquiline, and in many cases exceedingly handsome, the teeth being especially regular and beautiful. But notwithstanding their beauty, it struck me that, on the whole, I had never seen a more evil-looking set of faces. There was an aspect of cold and sullen cruelty stamped upon them that revolted me, and which in some cases was almost uncanny in its intensity.

Another thing that struck me about them was that they never seemed to smile. Sometimes they sang the monotonous song of which I have spoken, but when they were not singing, they remained almost perfectly silent, and the light of a laugh never came to brighten their sombre and evil faces. Of what race could these people be? Their language was a bastard Arabic, and yet they were not Arabs; I was quite sure of that. For one thing they were too dark, or rather, too yellow. I could not say why, but I knew that their appearance filled me with a sick fear of which I felt ashamed. While I was still wondering another litter came up alongside of mine. In it—for the curtains were drawn— sat an old man, clothed in a whitish robe, made apparently from coarse linen, that hung loosely about him, who, I at once jumped to the conclusion, was the shadowy figure that had stood on the bank, and been addressed as "Father." He was a wonderful-looking old man, with a snowy beard, so long that the ends of it hung over the sides of the litter, and he had a hooked nose, above which flashed out a pair of eyes as keen as a snake's, whilst his whole countenance was instinct with a look of wise and sardonic humour impossible to describe on paper.

"Art thou awake, stranger?" he said, in a deep and low voice.

"Surely, my father," I answered, courteously, feeling certain that I should do well to conciliate this ancient Mammon[1] of Unrighteousness.

He stroked his beautiful white beard, and smiled faintly.

"From whatever country thou camest," he said, "and by the way it must be from one where somewhat of our language is known, they teach their children courtesy there, my stranger son. And now wherefore comest thou unto this land, which scarce an alien foot has pressed from the time that man knoweth? Art thou and those with thee aweary of life?"

"We came to find new things," I answered boldly. "We are tired of the old things; we have come up out of the sea to know that which is unknown. We are of a brave race who fear not death, my very much respected father—that is, if we can get a little fresh information before we die."

"Humph!" said the old gentleman; "that may be true, it is rash to contradict, otherwise I should say that thou wast lying, my son. However, I daresay that '*She-who-must-be-obeyed*' will meet thy wishes in the matter."

"Who is '*She-who-must-be-obeyed*?'" I asked, curiously.

The old man glanced at the bearers, and then answered, with a little smile that somehow sent my blood to my heart,

"Surely, my stranger son, thou wilt learn soon enough if it be her pleasure to see thee at all in the flesh."

"In the flesh?" I answered. "What may my father wish to convey?"

But the old man only laughed a dreadful laugh, and made no reply.

"What is the name of my father's people?" I asked.

"The name of my people is Amahagger" (the People of the Rocks).[2]

"And if a son might ask, what is the name of my father?"

---

[1]   Greed personified, in the Christian tradition; see Luke 16:9.
[2]   "Hajar" is the Arabic word for rocks. In Swahili, an African language that includes words based in Arabic, the plural of "zulu" is "amazulu." Haggard may also intend to invoke the Koreish, Arabs thought to be descended from Abraham and Hagar the Egyptian, i.e., the "people of Hagar."

"My name is Billali."

"And whither go we, my father?"

"That shalt thou see," and at a sign from him the bearers started forward at a run till they reached the litter in which Job was reposing (with one leg hanging over the side). Apparently, however, he could not make much out of Job, for presently I saw his bearers trot forward to Leo's litter.

And after that, as nothing fresh occurred, I yielded to the pleasant swaying motion of the litter, and went to sleep again. I was dreadfully tired. When I woke I found that we were passing through a rocky defile of a lava formation with precipitous sides, in which grew many beautiful trees and flowering shrubs.

Presently this defile took a turn, and a lovely sight unfolded itself to my eyes. Before us was a vast cup of green from four to six miles in extent, shaped like a Roman amphitheatre. The sides of this great cup were rocky, and clothed with bush, but the centre was of the richest meadow land, studded with single trees of magnificent growth, and watered by meandering streams. On this rich plain grazed herds of goats and cattle, but I saw no sheep. At first I could not imagine what this strange spot could be, but presently it flashed upon me that it must represent the crater of some long-extinct volcano, which had afterwards been a lake, and was ultimately drained in some unexplained way. And here I may state that from my subsequent experience of this and a much larger, but otherwise similar spot, which I shall have occasion to describe by and by, I have every reason to believe that this conclusion was correct. What puzzled me, however, was that, although there were people moving about herding the goats and cattle, I saw no signs of any human habitation. Where did they all live, I wondered. My curiosity was soon destined to be gratified. Turning to the left the string of litters followed the cliffy sides of the crater for a distance of about half a mile, or perhaps a little less, and then halted. Seeing the old gentleman, my adopted 'father,' Billali, emerge from his litter I did the same, and so did Leo and Job. The first thing I saw was our wretched Arab companion, Mahomed, lying exhausted on the ground. It appeared that he had not been provided with a litter, but had been forced to run the entire distance, and, as he was already quite worn out when we started, his condition now was one of great prostration.

On looking round we discovered that the place where we had halted was a platform in front of the mouth of a great cave, and piled upon this platform were the entire contents of the whale-boat, even down to the oars and sail. Round the cave stood groups of the men who had escorted us, and other men of a similar stamp. They were all tall and all handsome, though they varied in their degree of darkness of skin, some being as dark as Mahomed, and some as yellow as a Chinese. They were naked, except for the leopard skin round the waist, and each of them carried a huge spear.

There were also some women among them, who, instead of the leopard skin, wore a tanned hide of a small red buck, something like that of the oribé,[1] only rather darker in colour. These women were, as a class, exceedingly good-looking, with large, dark eyes, well-cut features, and a thick bush of curling hair—not crisped like a negro's—and ranging from black to chestnut in hue, with all shades of intermediate colour. Some, but very few of them, wore a yellowish linen garment, such as I have described as worn by Billali, but this, as we afterwards discovered, was a mark of rank, rather than an attempt at clothing. For the rest, their appearance was not quite so terrifying as that of the men, and they sometimes, though rarely, smiled. As soon as we had alighted, they gathered round us and examined us with curiosity, but without excitement. Leo's tall, athletic form and clear-cut Grecian face, however, evidently excited their attention, and when he politely lifted his hat to them, and showed his curling yellow hair, there was a slight murmur of admiration. Nor did it stop there; for, after regarding him critically from head to foot, the handsomest of the young women—one wearing a robe, and with hair of a shade between brown and chestnut—deliberately advanced to him, and, in a way that would have been winning had it not been so determined, quietly put her arm round his neck, bent forward, and kissed him on the lips.

I gave a gasp, expecting to see Leo instantly speared; and Job ejaculated, "The hussy—well, I never!" As for Leo, he looked slightly astonished; and then remarking that we had got into a country where they clearly followed the customs of the early Christians,[2] deliberately returned the embrace.

Again I gasped, thinking that something would happen; but to my surprise, though some of the young women showed traces of vexation, the older ones and the men only smiled slightly. When we came to understand the customs of this extraordinary people the mystery was explained.

---

[1] Antelope native to South Africa.
[2] Leo refers to the kiss of charity exchanged by early Christians, as recommended by Peter and Paul in the New Testament (e.g., Romans 16:16).

It then appeared that, in direct opposition to the habits of almost every other savage race in the world, women among the Amahagger are not only upon terms of perfect equality with the men, but are not held to them by any binding ties. Descent is traced only through the line of the mother, and while individuals are as proud of a long and superior female ancestry as we are of our families in Europe, they never pay attention to, or even acknowledge, any man as their father, even when their male parentage is perfectly well known. There is but one titular male parent of each tribe, or, as they call it, "Household," and he is its immediate ruler, with the title of "Father." For instance, the man Billali was the father of this "household," which consisted of about seven thousand individuals all told, and no other man was ever called by that name. When a woman took a fancy to a man she signified her preference by advancing and kissing him publicly, in the same way that this handsome and exceedingly prompt young lady, who was called Ustane, had done to Leo. If he kissed her back it was a token that he accepted her, and the arrangement continued till one of them wearied of it. I am bound, however, to say that the change of husbands was not nearly so frequent as might have been expected. Nor did quarrels arise out of it, at least among the men, who, when their wives deserted them in favour of a rival, accepted the whole thing much as we accept the income-tax or our marriage laws, as something not to be disputed, and as tending to the good of the community, however disagreeable they may in particular instances prove to the individual.

It is very curious to observe how the customs of mankind on this matter vary in different countries, making what is right and proper in one place wrong and improper in another. It must, however, be understood that, as all civilised nations appear to accept it as an axiom that ceremony is the touchstone of morality, there was even according to our canons, nothing immoral about this custom, seeing that the interchange of the embrace answers to our ceremony of marriage, which, as we know, justifies all things.

VII

USTANE SINGS

When the kissing operation was finished—by the way none of the young ladies offered to pet me in this fashion, though I saw one hovering round Job, to that respectable individual's evident alarm—the old man Billali advanced, and graciously waved us into the cave, whither we went, followed by Miss Ustane, who did not seem inclined to take the hints I gave her that we liked privacy.

Before we had gone five paces it struck me that the cave that we were entering was none of Nature's handiwork, but, on the contrary, had been hollowed by the hand of man. So far as we could judge it appeared to be about one hundred feet in length by fifty wide, and very lofty, resembling a cathedral aisle more than anything else. From this main aisle opened passages at a distance of every twelve or fifteen feet, leading, I supposed, to smaller chambers. About fifty feet from the entrance of the cave, just where the light began to get dim, a fire was burning, and threw huge shadows upon the gloomy walls around. Here Billali halted, and asked us to be seated, saying that they would bring us food, and accordingly we squatted ourselves down upon rugs of skins which were spread for us, and waited. Presently the food, consisting of goat's flesh boiled, fresh milk in an earthenware pot, and boiled cobs of Indian corn, was brought by young girls. We were almost starving, and I do not think that I ever in my life before ate with such satisfaction. Indeed, before we had finished we literally ate up everything that was set before us.

When we had done our somewhat saturnine host, Billali, who had been watching us in perfect silence, rose, and addressed us. He said that it was a wonderful thing that had happened. No man had ever known or heard of white strangers arriving in the country of the People of the Rocks. Sometimes, very rarely, black men had come here, and from them they had heard of the existence of men much whiter than themselves, who sailed on the sea in ships, but for the arrival of such there was no precedent. We had, however, been seen dragging the boat up the canal, and he told us frankly that he had at once given orders for our destruction, seeing that it was unlawful for any stranger to enter here, when a message had come from "*She-who-must-be-obeyed*," saying that our lives were to be spared, and that we were to be brought hither.

"Pardon me, my father," I interrupted at this point; "but if, as I understand, '*She-who-must-be-obeyed*' lives yet farther off, how could she have known of our approach?"

Billali turned, and seeing that we were alone—for the young lady, Ustane, had withdrawn when he began to speak—said, with a curious little laugh,

"Are there none in your land who can see without eyes and hear without ears? Ask no questions; *She* knew."

I shrugged my shoulders at this, and he proceeded to say that no further instructions had been received on the subject of our disposal, and this being so he was about to start to interview "*She-who-must-be-obeyed*," generally spoken of, for the sake of brevity, as "Hiya"[1] or *She* simply, who he gave us to understand was the Queen of the Amahagger, and learn her wishes.

I asked him how long he proposed to be away, and he said that by travelling hard he might be back on the fifth day, but there were many miles of marsh to cross before he came to where *She* was. He then said that every arrangement would be made for our comfort during his absence, and that, as he personally had taken a fancy to us, he sincerely trusted that the answer he should bring from *She* would be one favourable to the continuation of our existence, but at the same time he did not wish to conceal from us that he thought this doubtful, as every stranger who had ever come into the country during his grandmother's life, his mother's life, and his own life, had been put to death without mercy, and in a way he would not harrow our feelings by describing; and this had been done by the order of *She* herself, at least he supposed it was by her order. At any rate, she never interfered to save them.

"Why," I said, "but how can that be? You are an old man, and the time you talk of must reach back three men's lives. How therefore could *She* have ordered the death of anybody at the beginning of the life of your grandmother, seeing that herself she would not have been born?"

Again he smiled—that same faint, peculiar smile, and with a deep bow departed, without making any answer; nor did we see him again for five days.

When we had gone we discussed the situation, which filled me with alarm. I did not at all like the accounts of this mysterious Queen, "*She-who-must-be-obeyed*," or more shortly *She*, who apparently ordered the execution of any unfortunate stranger in a fashion so unmerciful. Leo, too, was depressed about it, but proceeded to console himself by triumphantly pointing out that this *She* was undoubtedly the person referred to in the writing on the potsherd and in his father's letter, in proof of which he advanced Billali's allusions to her age and power. I was by this time so overwhelmed with the whole course of events that I had not even got the heart left to dispute a proposition so absurd, so I proposed that we should try to go out and get a bath, of which we stood sadly in need.

---

[1]   "She" (Arabic).

Accordingly, having indicated our wish to a middle-aged individual of an unusually saturnine cast of countenance, even among the saturnine people who appeared to be deputed to look after us now that the Father of the hamlet had departed, we started in a body—having first lit our pipes. Outside the cave we found quite a crowd of people evidently watching for our appearance, but when they saw us come out smoking they vanished this way and that, calling out that we were great magicians. Indeed, nothing about us created so great a sensation as our tobacco smoke—not even our fire-arms.★ After this we succeeded in reaching a stream and taking our bath in peace, though some of the women, not excepting Ustane, showed a decided inclination to follow us even there.

By the time that we had finished this most refreshing bath the sun was setting; indeed, when we got back to the big cave it had already set. The cave itself was full of people gathered round fires—for several more had now been lighted—and eating their evening meal by their lurid light, and by that of various lamps which were set about or hung up on the walls. These lamps were of a rude manufacture of baked earthenware, and of all shapes, some of them graceful enough. The larger ones were formed of big red earthenware pots, filled with clarified melted fat, and having a reed wick stuck through a wooden dish which filled the top of the pot, and this sort of lamp required the most constant attention to prevent its going out whenever the wick burnt down, as there were no means of turning it up. The smaller hand lamps, however, which were also made of baked clay, had a wick manufactured from the pith of a palm tree, or sometimes from the stem of a very handsome variety of fern. This wick came up through a round hole at the end of the lamp, to which a sharp piece of hard wood was attached to pierce and draw it up with whenever it showed signs of burning low.

For a while we sat down and watched this grim people eating their evening meal in silence as grim as themselves, till at length, getting tired of contemplating them and the huge moving shadows on the rocky walls, I suggested to our new keeper that we should like to go to bed.

Without a word he rose, and, taking me politely by the hand, advanced with a lamp to one of the small passages that I had noticed opening out of the central cave. This we followed for about five paces,

---

★ We found tobacco growing in this country as it does in every other part of Africa, and although they are so absolutely ignorant of its other blessed qualities, the Amahagger use it habitually in the form of snuff, also for medicinal purposes.—L.H.H.

when it suddenly widened out into a small chamber, about eight feet square, and hewn out of the living rock. On one side of this chamber was a stone slab, about three feet from the ground, and running its entire length like a bunk in a cabin, and on this he indicated that I was to sleep. There was no window or airhole to the chamber, and no furniture; and, on looking at it more closely, I came to the disturbing conclusion (in which, as I afterwards discovered, I was quite right) that it had originally served for a sepulchre for the dead rather than a sleeping-place for the living, the slab being designed to receive the corpse of the departed. The thought made me shudder in spite of myself; but, seeing that I must sleep somewhere, I got over the feeling as best I might, and returned to the cavern to get my blanket, which had been brought up from the boat with the other things. There I met Job, who, having been inducted to a similar apartment, had flatly declined to sleep in it, saying that the look of the place gave him the horrors, and that he might as well be dead and buried in his grandfather's brick grave at once, and expressed his determination of sleeping with me if I would allow him.

The night passed very comfortably on the whole. I say on the whole, for personally I went through a most horrible nightmare of being buried alive, induced, no doubt, by the sepulchral nature of my surroundings. At dawn we were aroused by a loud trumpeting sound, produced, by a young Amahagger blowing through a hole bored in its side into a hollowed elephant tusk.

Taking the hint, we got up and went down to the stream to wash, after which the morning meal was served. At breakfast one of the women, no longer quite young, advanced, and publicly kissed Job. I think it was in its way the most delightful thing (putting its impropriety aside for a moment) that I ever saw. Never shall I forget the respectable Job's abject terror and disgust. Job, like myself, is a bit of a misogynist—I fancy chiefly owing to the fact of his having been one of a family of seventeen—and the feelings expressed upon his countenance when he realised that he was not only being embraced publicly, and without authorisation on his own part, but also in the presence of his masters, were too mixed and painful to admit of accurate description. He sprang to his feet, and pushed the woman, a buxom party of about thirty, from him.

"Well, I never!" he gasped, whereupon she embraced him again.

"Be off with you! Get away, you minx!" he shouted, waving the wooden spoon, with which he was eating his breakfast, up and down before the lady's face. "Beg your pardon, gentlemen, I am sure I haven't encouraged her. Oh, Lord! she's coming for me again. Hold her, Mr. Holly! please, hold her! I can't stand it; I can't, indeed. This has never happened to me before, gentlemen, never! There's nothing against my character," and here he broke off, and ran as hard as he could go down the cave, and for once I saw the Amahagger laugh. As for the woman, however, she did not laugh. On the contrary, she seemed to bristle with fury, which the mockery of the other women about only served to intensify. She stood there literally snarling and shaking with indignation, and seeing her, I wished Job's scruples had been at Jericho,[1] forming a shrewd guess that his admirable behaviour had endangered our throats. Nor, as the sequel shows, was I wrong.

The lady having retreated, Job returned in a great state of nervousness, and keeping his weather eye[2] fixed upon every woman who came near him. I took an opportunity to explain to our hosts that Job was a married man, and had had very unhappy experiences in his domestic relations, which accounted for his presence here and his terror at the sight of women, but my remarks were received in grim silence, it being evident that our retainer's behaviour was considered as a slight to the "household" at large, although the women, after the manner of their more civilised sisters, made merry at the rebuff of their companion.

After breakfast we took a walk and inspected the Amahagger herds, and also their cultivated lands. They have two breeds of cattle, one large and angular, with no horns, but yielding beautiful milk; and the other, a red breed, very small and fat, excellent for meat, but of no value for milking purposes. This last breed closely resembles the Norfolk red-poll strain, only it has horns which generally curve forward over the head, sometimes to such an extent that they have to be cut to prevent them from growing into the bones of the skull. The goats are long-haired, and are used for eating only, at least I never saw them milked. As for the Amahagger cultivation, it is primitive in the extreme, being all done by means of a spade made of iron, for these people smelt and work iron. This spade is shaped more like a big spear-head than anything else, and has no shoulder to it on which the foot can be set. As a consequence, the labour of digging is very great. It is, however, all done by the men, the women, contrary to the habits of most savage races, being entirely exempt from all manual toil. But then, as I think I have said elsewhere, among the Amahagger the weaker sex has established its rights.

---

[1]   A euphemism meaning somewhere far away, equivalent to "at the devil."
[2]   A watchful eye, one sharp at detecting changes in the weather.

At first we were much puzzled as to the origin and constitution of this extraordinary race, points upon which they were singularly uncommunicative. As the time went on—for the next four days passed without any striking event—we learnt something from Leo's lady friend Ustane, who, by the way, stuck to that young gentleman like his own shadow. As to origin, they had none, at least so far as she was aware. There were, however, she informed us, mounds of masonry and many pillars near the place where *She* lived, which was called Kôr, and which the wise said had once been houses wherein men lived, and it was suggested that they were descended from these men. No one, however, dared go near these great ruins, because they were haunted: they only looked on them from a distance. Other similar ruins were to be seen, she had heard, in various parts of the country, that is, wherever one of the mountains rose above the level of the swamp. Also the caves in which they lived had been hollowed out of the rocks by men, perhaps the same who built the cities. They themselves had no written laws, only custom, which was, however, quite as binding as law. If any man offended against the custom, he was put to death by order of the Father of the "Household." I asked how he was put to death, and she only smiled, and said that I might see one day soon.

They had a Queen, however. *She* was their Queen, but she was very rarely seen, perhaps once in two or three years, when she came forth to pass sentence on some offenders, and when seen was muffled up in a big cloak, so that nobody could look upon her face. Those who waited upon her were deaf and dumb, and therefore could tell no tales, but it was reported that she was lovely as no other woman was lovely, or ever had been. It was rumoured also that she was immortal, and had power over all things, but she, Ustane, could say nothing of all that. What she believed was that the Queen chose a husband from time to time, and as soon as a female child was born this husband, who was never again seen, was put to death. Then the female child grew up and took the place of the Queen when its mother died, and had been buried in the great caves. But of these matters none could speak for certain. Only *She* was obeyed throughout the length and breadth of the land, and to question her command was certain death. She kept a guard, but had no regular army, and to disobey her was to die.

I asked what the land was, and how many people lived in it. She answered that there were ten "Households" like this that she knew of, including the big "Household," where the Queen was, that all the "Households" lived in caves, in places resembling this stretch of raised country, dotted about in a vast extent of swamp, which was only to be threaded by secret paths. Often the "Households" made war on each other until *She* sent word that it was to stop, and then they instantly ceased. That and the fever which they caught in crossing the swamps was what kept their numbers from increasing too much. They had no connection with any other race, indeed none lived near them, or were able to thread the vast swamps. Once an army from the direction of the great river (presumably the Zambesi) had attempted to attack them, but they got lost in the marshes, and at night, seeing the great balls of fire that move about there, tried to come to them, thinking that it was the enemy's camp, and half of them were drowned. As for the rest, they soon died of fever and starvation, not a blow being struck at them. The marshes, she told us, were absolutely impassable except to those who knew the paths, adding that we should never have reached this place where we then were had we not been brought there.

These and many other things we learnt from Ustane during the four days' pause before our real adventures began, and, as may be imagined, they gave us considerable cause for thought. The whole thing was exceedingly remarkable, almost incredibly so indeed, and the oddest part of it was that so far it did more or less correspond to the ancient writing on the sherd. And now it appeared that there was a mysterious Queen clothed by rumour with awful and wonderful attributes, and commonly known by the impersonal, but, to my mind, rather awesome title of *She*. Altogether, I could not make it out, nor could Leo, though of course he was exceedingly triumphant over me because I had persistently mocked at the whole thing. As for Job, he had long since abandoned any attempt to call his reason his own, and left it to drift upon the sea of circumstance. Mahomed, the Arab, who was, by the way, treated civilly indeed, but with chilling contempt, by the Amahagger, was, I discovered, in a great fright, though I could not quite make out what he was frightened about. He would sit crouched up in a corner of the cave all day long, calling upon Allah and the Prophet to protect him. When I pressed him about it he said that he was afraid because these people were not men and women at all, but devils, and that this was an enchanted land; and once or twice since then I have been inclined to agree with him. So the time went on, till the night of the fourth day after Billali had left, when something happened.

We three and Ustane were sitting round the fire in the cave just before bedtime, when suddenly the woman, who had been brooding in silence, rose, and laid her hand upon Leo's golden curls and addressed him. Even now, when I shut my eyes, I can see her proud, imperial form, clothed alternately in dense shadow and the red flickering of the fire, as she stood, the wild centre of as weird a scene as I ever witnessed, and delivered herself of the burden of her thoughts and forebodings in a kind of rhythmical speech that ran something as follows:—

"Thou art my chosen—I have waited for thee from the beginning!
Thou art very beautiful. Who hath hair like unto thee, or skin
    so white?
Who hath so strong an arm, who is so much a man?
Thine eyes are the sky, and the light in them is the stars.
Thou art perfect and of a happy face, and my heart turned itself
    toward thee.
Ay, when mine eyes fell on thee, I did desire thee,—
Then did I take thee to me—thou, my Beloved,
And hold thee fast, lest harm should come unto thee.
Ay, I did cover thine head with mine hair, lest the sun should
    strike it;
And altogether was I thine, and thou wast altogether mine.
And so it went for a little space, till Time was in labour with
    an evil Day;
And then what befell upon that day? Alas! my Beloved, I know
    not!
But I, I saw thee no more—I, I was lost in the blackness.
And she who is stronger did take thee; ay, she who is fairer
    than Ustane.
Yet did'st thou turn and call upon me, and let thine eyes wander
    in the darkness.
But, nevertheless, she prevailed by Beauty, and led thee down
    horrible places,
And then, ah! then, my Beloved——"

Here this extraordinary woman broke off her speech, or chant, which was so much musical gibberish to us, for all that we understood of what she was driving at, and seemed to fix her flashing eyes upon the deep shadow before her. All in a moment they acquired a vacant, terrified stare, as though they were trying to realise some half-seen horror. She lifted her hand from Leo's head, and pointed into the darkness. We all looked and could see nothing; but she saw something, or thought she did, and something evidently that affected even her iron nerves, for, without another sound, down she fell senseless between us.

Leo, who was growing really attached to this remarkable young person, was in a great state of alarm and distress, and I, to be perfectly candid, was in a condition not far removed from superstitious fear. The whole scene was an uncanny one.

Presently, however, she recovered, and sat up with an extraordinary convulsive shudder.

"What did'st thou mean, Ustane?" asked Leo, who, thanks to years of tuition, spoke Arabic very prettily.

"Nay, my chosen," she answered, with a little forced laugh. "I did but sing unto thee after the fashion of my people. Surely, I meant nothing. How could I speak of that which is not yet?"

"And what did'st thou see, Ustane?" I asked.

"Nay," she answered again; "I saw nought. Ask me not what I saw. Why should I fright ye?" and then turning to Leo with a look of the most utter tenderness that I ever saw upon the face of woman, civilised or savage, she took his head between her hands, and kissed him on the forehead as a mother might. "When I am gone from thee, my chosen; when at night thou stretchest out thine hand and canst not find me, then shouldst thou think at times of me, for of a truth I love thee well, though I be not fit to wash thy feet. And now let us love and take that which is given us, and be happy; for in the grave there is no love and no warmth, nor any touching of the lips. Nothing perchance, or perchance but bitter memories of what might have been. To-night the hours are our own: how know we to whom they shall belong to-morrow?"

NOTE.—Our illustration on page [84] will be described next week.

(*To be continued*)

"I took this cold fragment of mortality in my hand, and looked at it in the light
of the lamp with feelings which I cannot describe."

VIII

THE FEAST, AND AFTER!

On the day following this remarkable scene, a scene calculated to make a deep impression upon anybody who beheld it, more because of what it suggested and seemed to foreshadow than for what it revealed, it was announced to us that a feast would be held that evening in our honour. I did my best to get out of it, saying that we were modest people, and cared little for feasts, but my remarks being received with the silence of displeasure, I thought it wisest to hold my tongue.

Accordingly, just before sundown, I was informed that everything was ready, and, accompanied by Job, went into the cave, where I met Leo, who was, as usual, followed by Ustane. These two had been out walking somewhere, and knew nothing of the projected festivity till that moment. When Ustane heard of it I saw an expression of horror spring up upon her handsome features. Turning, she caught a man who was passing up the cave by the arm, and asked him something in an imperious tone. His answer seemed to reassure her a little, for she looked relieved, though far from satisfied. Next she appeared to attempt some remonstrance with the man, who was a person in authority, but he spoke angrily to her, and shook her off, and then changing his mind, led her by the arm, and sat her down between himself and another man in the circle round the fire, and I perceived that for some reason of her own she thought it best to submit.

The fire in the cave was an unusually big one that night, and in a large circle round it were gathered about thirty-five men and two women, Ustane and the woman to avoid whom Job had played the *rôle* of another Scriptural character.[1] The men were sitting in perfect silence, as was their custom, each with his great spear stuck upright behind him, in a socket cut in the rock for that purpose. Only one or two wore the yellowish linen garment of which I have spoken, the rest had nothing on except the leopard's skin about the middle.

"What's up now, sir?" said Job, doubtfully. "Bless us and save us,

---

[1]   Besides his Biblical namesake, Job has played the part of Joseph who rejected Potiphar's wife; Genesis 39:1–20.

there's that woman again. Now, surely, she can't be after me, seeing that I have given her no encouragement. They give me the creeps, the whole lot of them, and that's a fact. Why, look, they have asked Mahomed to dine, too. There, that lady of mine is talking to him in as nice and civil a way as possible. Well, I'm glad it isn't me, that's all."

We looked up, and sure enough the woman in question had risen, and was escorting the wretched Mahomed from the corner, where, overcome by some acute prescience of horror, he had been seated, shivering, and calling on Allah. He appeared unwilling enough to come, if for no other reason perhaps because it was an unaccustomed honour, for hitherto his food had been given to him apart. Anyway I could see that he was in a state of great terror, for his tottering legs would scarcely support his stout, bulky form, and I think it was rather owing to the resources of barbarism behind him, in the shape of a huge Amahagger with a proportionately huge spear, than to the seduction of the lady who led him by the hand, that he consented to come at all.

"Well," I said to the others, "I don't at all like the look of things, but I suppose that we must face it out. Have you fellows got your revolvers on? because, if so, you had better see that they are loaded."

"I have, sir," said Job, tapping his Colt, "but Mr. Leo has only got his hunting-knife, though that is big enough, surely."

Feeling that it would not do to wait while the missing weapon was fetched, we advanced boldly, and seated ourselves in a line, with our backs against the side of the cave.

As soon as we were seated, an earthenware jar was passed round containing a fermented fluid, of by no means unpleasant taste, though apt to turn upon the stomach, made of crushed grain,—not Indian corn, but a small brown grain that grows upon the stem in clusters, not unlike that which in the southern part of Africa is known by the name of Kafir corn. The vase in which this liquid was handed round was very curious, and as it more or less resembled many hundreds of others in use among the Amahagger I may as well describe it. These vases are of a very ancient manufacture, and of all sizes. None such can have been made in the country for hundreds, or rather thousands, of years. They are found in the rock tombs, of which I shall give a description in their proper place, and my own belief is that, after the fashion of the Egyptians, with whom the former inhabitants of this country may have had some connection, they were used to receive the viscera of the dead. Leo, however, is of opinion that, like the Etruscan amphoræ, they were placed there for the spiritual use of the deceased. They are mostly two-handled, and of all sizes, some being nearly three feet in height, and running from that down to as many inches. In shape they vary, but are all exceedingly beautiful and graceful, being made of a very fine black ware, not lustrous, but slightly rough. On this groundwork were inlaid figures much more graceful and lifelike than any others I have seen on antique vases. Some of these inlaid pictures represented love-scenes with a child-like simplicity and freedom of manner which would not commend itself to the taste of the present day. Others again were pictures of maidens dancing, and others again were hunting-scenes. For instance, the very vase from which we were now drinking had on one side a most spirited drawing of men, apparently white in colour, attacking a bull-elephant with spears, while on the reverse was a picture, not quite so well done, of a hunter shooting an arrow at a running ante-lope, I should say from the look of it either an eland or a koodoo.

This is a digression at a critical moment, but it is not too long for the occasion, for the occasion itself was very long. With the exception of the periodical passing of the vase, and the movement necessary to throw fuel on to the fire, nothing happened for the best part of a whole hour. Nobody spoke a word. There we all sat in perfect silence, staring at the glare and glow of the large fire, and at the shadows thrown by the flickering earthenware lamps (which, by the way, were not ancient). On the open space between us and the fire lay a large wooden tray, with four short handles to it, exactly like a butcher's tray, only not hollowed out. By the side of the tray was a great pair of long-handled iron pincers, and on the other side of the fire was a similar pair. Somehow I did not at all like the appearance of the tray and the accompanying pincers. There I sat and stared at them and at the silent circle of the fierce moody faces of the men, and reflected that it was all very awful, and that we were absolutely in the power of this alarming people, who, to me at any rate, were all the more formidable because their true character was still very much of a mystery to us. They might be better than I thought them, or they might be worse. I feared that they were worse, and I was not wrong. It was a curious sort of a feast, I reflected, in appearance, indeed, an entertainment of the Barmecide stamp,[1] for there was absolutely nothing to eat.

At last, just as I was beginning to feel as though I were being mesmerised, a move was made. Without the slightest warning, a man from the other side of the circle called out in a loud voice,

---

[1]   Alluding to a banquet in the *Arabian Nights* at which no food is actually served.

"Where is the flesh that we shall eat?"

Thereon everybody in the circle answered in a deep measured tone, and stretching out the right arm towards the fire as they spoke,

"*The flesh will come.*"

"Is it a goat?" said the same man.

"*It is a goat without horns, and more than a goat, and we shall slay it,*" they answered with one voice, and turning half round, they one and all grasped the handles of their spears with the right hand, and then simultaneously let them go.

"Is it an ox?" said the man, again.

"*It is an ox without horns, and more than an ox, and we shall slay it,*" was the answer, and again the spears were grasped, and again let go.

Then came a pause, and I noticed, with horror and a rising of the hair, that the woman next to Mahomed began to fondle him, patting his cheeks, and calling him by names of endearment, while her fierce eyes played up and down his trembling form. I don't know why the sight frightened me so, but it did frighten us all dreadfully, especially Leo. The caressing was so snake-like, and so evidently a part of some ghastly formula that had to be gone through.* I saw Mahomed turn white under his brown skin, sickly white with fear.

"Is the meat ready to be cooked?" asked the voice, more rapidly.

"*It is ready; it is ready.*"

"Is the pot hot to cook it?" it continued, in a sort of scream that echoed painfully down the great recesses of the cave.

"*It is hot; it is hot.*"

"Great heavens!" roared Leo, "remember the writing,'*The people who put pots upon the heads of strangers.*'"

As he said the words, before we could stir, or even take the matter in, two great ruffians jumped up, and seizing the long pincers, plunged them into the heart of the fire, and the woman who had been caressing Mahomed suddenly produced a fibre noose from under her girdle or moocha, and, slipping it over his shoulders, ran it tight, while the men next him seized him by the legs. The two men with the pincers gave a heave, and scattering the fire this way and that upon the rocky floor, lifted from it a large earthenware pot, heated to a white heat. In an instant, almost with a single movement, they had reached the spot where

---

* We afterwards learnt that its object was to pretend to the victim that he was the object of love and admiration, and so to soothe his injured feelings, and cause him to expire in a happy and contented frame of mind.—L.H.H.

Mahomed was struggling, and then—even now I can scarcely bear to write it—there was one awful, heartrending shriek, ending and smothered in a hissing sound, and the next thing that I saw was the poor wretch, broken loose from his captors, in the despairing effort of a hideous death, and rushing and rolling into the darkness beyond the lamps, *the red hot pot jammed upon his head*, completely covering it from view.

I sprang to my feet with a yell of horror, and drawing my revolver, fired it by a sort of instinct straight at the diabolical woman who had been caressing Mahomed, and was now gripping him in her arms. The bullet struck her in the back and killed her, and to this day I am glad that it did, for, as it afterwards transpired, she had availed herself of the anthropophagous customs of the Amahagger to organise the whole thing in revenge of the slight put upon her by Job.

For a moment there was a silence of astonishment. They had never heard the report of a firearm before, and its effects dismayed them. But the next a man close to us recovered himself, and seized his spear preparatory to making a lunge with it at Leo, who was the nearest to him.

"Run for it!" I halloaed, setting the example by going up the cave as hard as my legs would carry me. I would have bolted for the open air if it had been possible, but there were men in the way, and, besides, I had caught sight of the forms of a crowd of people standing out clear against the skyline beyond the entrance to the cave. Up the cave I went, and after me came the others, and after them thundered the whole crowd of cannibals, mad with fury at the death of the woman. With a bound I cleared the prostrate form of Mahomed. As I flew over him I felt the heat from the red hot pot, strike upon my legs, and by its glow saw his poor hands—for he was not quite dead—still feebly beating at the hissing torment on his head. At the top of the cave was a little platform of rock three feet or so high by about eight deep, on which two large lamps were placed at night. Whether this platform had been left as a seat, or as a raised point afterwards to be cut away when it had served its purpose as a standing-place from which to carry on the excavations, I do not know—at least, I did not then. At any rate, we all three reached it, and, jumping on it, prepared to sell our lives as dearly as we could. For a few minutes the crowd that was pressing on our heels hung back when they saw us face round upon them. Job was on one side of the rock to the left, Leo in the centre, and I to the right. Behind us were the lamps. Leo bent forward, and looked down the long lane of shadows, terminated in the fire and lighted lamps, through which the quiet forms of our would-be murderers flitted to and fro with the faint light glinting on their spears, for even their fury was silent as a bulldog's. The only other thing visible was the red hot pot still glowing angrily in the gloom. There was a curious light in Leo's eyes, and his handsome face was set like a stone. In his right hand was his heavy hunting-knife. He shifted its thong a little up his wrist and then put his arm round me and gave me a good hug.

"Good bye, old fellow," he said, "my dear friend—my more than father. We have no chance against those scoundrels; they will finish us in a few minutes, and eat us afterwards, I suppose. Good bye. I led you into this. I hope you will forgive me. Good bye, Job."

"God's will be done," I said, setting my teeth, as I prepared for the end. At that moment, with an exclamation, Job lifted his revolver and fired, and hit a man—not the man he had aimed at by the way: anything that Job shot *at* was perfectly safe.

On they came with a rush, and I fired too as fast as I could, and checked them—between us, Job and I killed or mortally wounded five men with our pistols before they were emptied, besides the woman. But we had no time to reload, and they still came on in a way that was almost splendid in its recklessness, seeing that they did not know but that we could go on firing for ever.

A great fellow bounded up upon the platform, and Leo struck him dead with one blow of his powerful arm, sending the knife right through him. I did the same by another, but Job missed his stroke, and I saw a brawny Amahagger grip him by the middle, and whirl him off the rock. The knife not being secured by a thong fell from his hand as he did so, and, by a most happy accident for Job, lit upon its handle on the rock, just as the body of the Amahagger being undermost hit upon its point and was transfixed upon it. What happened to Job after that I am sure I do not know, but my own impression is that he lay still upon the corpse of his deceased assailant, "playing 'possum" as the Americans say. As for myself, I was soon involved in a desperate encounter with two ruffians who, luckily for me, had left their spears behind them; and for the first time in my life the great physical power with which Nature has endowed me stood me in good stead. I had hacked at the head of one man with my hunting knife, which was almost as big and heavy as a short sword, with such vigour, that the sharp steel had split his skull down to the eyes, and was held so fast by it, that as he suddenly fell sideways the knife was twisted right out of my hand.

Then it was that the two others sprung upon me. I saw them coming, and got an arm round the waist of each, and down we all fell upon the floor of the cave together, rolling over and over. They were strong men, but I was mad with rage, and that awful lust for slaughter which will creep into the hearts of the most civilised of us when blows are flying, and life and death tremble on the turn. My arms were round the two swarthy demons, and I hugged them till I heard their ribs crack and crunch up beneath my gripe. They twisted and writhed like snakes, and clawed and battered at me with their fists, but I held on. Lying on my back there, so that their bodies should protect me from spear thrusts from above, I slowly crushed the life out of them, and as I did so, strange as it may seem, I thought of what the amiable Head of my College at Cambridge and my brother Fellows would say if by clairvoyance they could see me, of all men, playing such a bloody game. Soon my assailants grew faint, and almost ceased to struggle, their breath had left them, and they were dying, but still I dare not leave them, for they died very slowly. I knew that if I relaxed my grip they would revive. The other ruffians probably thought—for we were all three lying in the shadow of the ledge—that we were all dead together, at any rate they did not interfere with our little tragedy.

I turned my head, and as I lay gasping in the throes of that awful struggle I could see that Leo was off the rock now, for the lamplight fell full upon him. He was still on his feet, but in the centre of a surging mass of struggling men, who were striving to pull him down as wolves pull down a stag. Up above them towered his beautiful pale face crowned with its bright curls (for Leo was six feet two high), and I saw that he was fighting with a desperate abandonment and energy that was at once splendid and hideous to behold. He drove his knife through one man—they were so close to him and mixed up with him that they could not get at him to kill him with their big spears, and they had no knives or sticks. The man fell, and then somehow the knife was wrenched from his hand, leaving him defenceless, and I thought the end had come. But no, with a desperate effort he broke loose from them, seized the body of the man he had just slain, and lifting it high in the air hurled it right at the mob of his assailants, so that the shock and weight of it swept some five or six of them to the earth. But in a minute they were all up again, except one, whose skull was smashed, and had once more fastened upon him. And then slowly, and with infinite labour and struggling, the wolves bore the lion down. Once even then he recovered himself, and felled an Amahagger with his fist, but it was more than man could do to hold his own for long against so many, and at last he came crashing down upon the rock floor, falling as an oak falls, and bearing with him to the earth all those who clung about him. They gripped him by his arms and legs, and then cleared off his body.

"A spear," cried a voice, "a spear to cut his throat, and a vessel to catch his blood."

I shut my eyes, for I saw the man coming with a spear, and myself, I could not stir to Leo's help, for I was growing weak, and the two men on me were not yet dead, and a deadly sickness overcame me.

Then suddenly there was a disturbance, and involuntarily I opened my eyes again, and looked towards the scene of murder. The girl Ustane had suddenly thrown herself on the top of Leo's prostrate form, covering his body with her body, and fastening her arms about his neck. They tried to drag her from him, but she twisted her legs round his, and hung on like a bulldog, or rather like a creeper to a tree, and they could not. Then they tried to stab him in the side without hurting her, but somehow she shielded him, and he was only wounded.

At last they lost patience.

"Drive the spear through the man and the woman together," said a voice, the same voice that had asked the questions at that ghastly feast, "so of a verity shall they be wed."

Then I saw the man with the weapon straighten himself for the effort. I saw the cold steel gleam on high, and once more I shut my eyes.

As I did so, I heard a voice of a man thunder out in tones that rang and echoed down the rocky ways.

"*Cease!*"

Then I fainted, and as I did so it flashed through my darkening mind that I was passing down into the last oblivion of death.

IX

A LITTLE FOOT

When I opened my eyes again I found myself lying on a skin mat not far from the fire round which we had been gathered for the dreadful feast. Near me lay Leo, still apparently in a swoon, and over him was bending the tall form of the girl Ustane, who was washing a deep spear wound in his side with water preparatory to binding it up with linen. Leaning against the wall of the cave behind her was Job, apparently unhurt, but bruised and trembling. On the other side of the fire, tossed about this way and that, as though they had thrown themselves down to sleep in some moment of absolute exhaustion, were the bodies of those whom we had killed in our frightful struggle for life. I counted them: there were twelve beside the woman, who had died by my hand, as well as the corpse of poor Mahomed, which, the fire-stained pot at its side, was placed at the end of the irregular line. To the left a body of men were engaged in binding the arms of the survivors of the cannibals behind them, and then fastening them two and two. The villains were submitting with a look of sulky indifference upon their faces that accorded ill with the baffled fury that gleamed in their sombre eyes. In front of these men, directing the operations, stood no other than our friend Billali, looking rather tired, but particularly patriarchal with his flowing beard, and as cool and unconcerned as though he were superintending the cutting up of an ox.

Presently he turned, and perceiving that I was sitting up advanced to me, and with the utmost courtesy said that he trusted that I felt better. I answered that at present I scarcely knew how I felt, except that I ached all over.

Then he bent down and examined Leo's wound.

"It is a nasty cut," he said, "but the spear has not pierced the entrails. He will recover."

"Thanks to your arrival, my father," I answered. "In another minute we should all have been beyond the reach of recovery, for those devils of yours would have slain us as they would have slain our servant," and I pointed towards Mahomed.

The old man ground his teeth, and I saw an extraordinary expression of malignity light up his eyes.

"Fear not, my son," he answered. "Vengeance shall be taken on them such as would make the flesh twist upon the bones merely to hear of it. To *She* shall they go, and her vengeance shall be worthy of her greatness. That man," pointing to Mahomed, "I tell you that man has died a merciful death to the death these hyæna-men shall die. Tell me, I pray of thee, how it came about."

In a few words I sketched what had happened.

"Ah, so," he answered. "Thou seest, my son, here there is a custom that if a stranger comes into this country he may be slain by 'the pot,' and eaten."

"It is hospitality turned upside down," I answered feebly. "In our country we entertain a stranger, and give him food to eat. Here ye eat him, and are entertained."

"It is a custom," he answered, with a shrug. "For myself I think it an evil one; but then," he added by an afterthought, "I do not like the taste of strangers, especially after they have wandered through the swamps and lived on wildfowl. When *She-who-must-be-obeyed* sent orders that ye were to be saved she said nought of the black man, therefore, being hyænas, these men lusted after his flesh, and the woman it was whom thou didst rightly slay who put it into their evil hearts to hot-pot him. Well, they will have their reward. Better for them would it be if they had never seen the light than that they should stand before *She* in her terrible anger. Happy are those of them that died by your hands.

"Ah," he went on, "it was a gallant fight that ye fought. Knowest thou, that thou, long-armed old Baboon that thou art, hast crushed in the ribs of those two who are laid out there as though they were but as the shell on an egg? And the young one, the lion, it was a beautiful fight that he made—one against so many—three did he slay outright, and that one there"—and he pointed to a body that was still moving a little—"will die anon, for his head is cracked across, and others of those who are bound are hurt. It was a gallant fight, and ye and he have made a friend of me by it, for I love to see a well-fought fray. But tell me, my son, the Baboon—and now I think of it thy face, too, is hairy, and alto- gether like a baboon's—how was it that ye slew those with a hole in them?—Ye made a noise, they say, and slew them— they fell down on their faces at the noise!"

I explained to him as well as I could, but very shortly—I was terri- bly wearied, and only persuaded to talk at all through fear of offending one so powerful if I refused to do so—what were the properties of gunpowder, and he instantly suggested that I should illustrate what I said by operating on the person of one of the prisoners. One, he said, never would be missed, and it would not only be very interesting to him, but would give me an opportunity of an instalment of revenge. He was greatly astounded when I told him that it was not our custom to avenge ourselves in cold blood, and that we left vengeance to the law and a higher Power, of which he knew nothing. I added, however, that when I recovered I would take him out shooting with us, and he should kill an animal for himself, and at this he was as pleased as a child at the promise of a new toy.

Just then, Leo opened his eyes beneath the stimulus of some brandy (of which we still had a little) that Job had poured down his throat, and our conversation came to an end.

After this we managed to get Leo, who was in a very poor way indeed, and only half conscious, safely off to bed, supported by Job and that brave girl Ustane, to whom, had I not been afraid she might resent it, I would certainly have given a kiss for her splendid behaviour in saving my dear boy's life at the risk of her own. But Ustane was not the sort of young person with whom one would care to take liberties unless one were perfectly certain that they would not be misunderstood, so I repressed my inclinations. Then, bruised and battered, but with a sense of safety in my breast to which I had for some days been a stranger, I crept off to my own little sepulchre, not forgetting before I lay down in it to thank God from the bottom of my heart that it was not a sepulchre indeed, as were it not for a merciful combination of events, that I can only attribute to Him, it would certainly have been for me that night. Few men have been nearer their end and yet escaped it than we were on that dreadful day.

My dreams that night when at last I got to sleep were not of the pleasantest. The awful vision of poor Mahomed struggling to escape the red-hot pot would haunt them, and then in the background, as it were, a veiled form was always hovering, which, from time to time, seemed to draw the coverings from its body, revealing now the perfect shape of a lovely blooming woman, and now again the white bones of a grinning skeleton, and which, as it veiled and unveiled, uttered the mysterious and apparently meaningless sentence:

"*That which is alive hath known death, and that which is dead yet can never die, for in the Circle of the Spirit life is nought and death is nought. Yea, all things live for ever, though at times they sleep and are forgotten.*"

The morning came at last, but when it came I found that I was too stiff and sore to rise. About seven Job arrived, limping terribly, and with his face the colour of a rotten apple, and told me that Leo had slept fairly, but was very weak. Two hours afterwards Billali (Job called him "Billy-goat," to which, indeed, his white beard gave him some resemblance, or more familiarly "Billy,") came too, bearing a lamp in his hand, his towering form reaching nearly to the roof of the little chamber. I pretended to be asleep, and through the cracks of my eyelids watched his sardonic, but handsome old face. He fixed his hawk-like eyes upon me, and stroked his glorious white beard, which, by the way, would have been worth a hundred a-year to any London barber as an advertisement.

"Ah!" I heard him mutter (Billali had a habit of muttering to himself), "he is ugly—ugly as the other is beautiful—a very Baboon, it was a good name. But I like the man. Strange now, at my age, that I should like a man. What says the proverb—'Mistrust all men, and slay him whom thou mistrustest overmuch; and as for women, flee from them, for they are evil, and in the end will destroy thee.' It is a good proverb, especially the last part: I think it must have come down from the ancients. Nevertheless I like this Baboon, and I wonder where they taught him his tricks, and I trust that *She* will not bewitch him. Poor Baboon! he must be wearied after that fight. I will go lest I should awake him."

I waited till he had turned and was nearly through the entrance, walking softly on tiptoe, and then I called after him.

"My father," I said, "is it thou?"

"Yes, my son, it is I; but let me not disturb thee. I did but come to see how thou did'st fare, and to tell thee that those who would have slain thee, my Baboon, are by now well on their road to *She*. *She* said that ye were to come also at once, but I fear ye cannot yet."

"Nay," I said, "not till we have recovered a little; but have me borne out into the daylight, my father. I like not this place."

"Ah, no," he answered, "it hath a sad air. I remember when I was a boy I found the body of a fair woman lying where you lie now, yes, on that very bench. She was so beautiful that I used to creep in here with a lamp and gaze upon her. Had it not been for her cold hands, almost could I think that she slept and would one day awake, so fair and peaceful was she in her robe of white. White was she, too, and her hair was yellow, and lay down her almost to the feet. There are many such still in the tombs at the place where *She* is, for those who set them there had a way I know nought of, of keeping their beloved out of the crumbling hand of Decay, even when Death had slain them. Ay, day by day I came hither, and gazed on her till at last—laugh not at me, stranger, for I was but a silly lad—I learnt to love that dead form, that shell that once had held a life that no more is. I would creep up to her and kiss her cold face, and wonder how many men had lived and died since she was, and who had loved her and embraced her in the days that long had passed away. And my Baboon, I think I learnt wisdom from that dead one, for of a truth it taught me of the littleness of life, and the length of Death, and how all things that are under the sun go down one path, and are for ever forgotten. And so I mused, and it seemed to me that wisdom flowed into me from that dead one, till one day my mother, a watchful woman, but hasty-minded, seeing I was changed, followed me, and saw the beautiful white one, and feared I was bewitched, as, indeed, I was. So half in fear, and half in anger, she took the lamp, and standing the dead one up against the wall there, set fire to her hair, and she burnt fiercely, even down to the feet, for those who are thus kept burn excellently well. See, my son, there on the roof is yet the smoke of her burning."

I looked up doubtfully, and there, sure enough, on the roof of the sepulchre was a peculiarly unctuous and sooty mark, three feet or more across. Doubtless it had in the course of years been rubbed off the sides of the little cave, but on the roof it remained, and there was no mistaking its appearance.

"She burnt," he went on in a meditative way, "even to the feet, but the feet I came back and saved, cutting the burnt bone from them, and hid them under the stone bench there, wrapped up in a piece of linen. Surely, I remember it as though it were but yesterday. Perchance they are there if none have found them, even to this hour. Of a truth I have not entered this chamber from that time to this very day. Stay, I will look," and, kneeling down, he groped about with his long arm in the recess under the stone bench. Presently his face brightened, and with an exclamation he pulled something forth that was caked in dust; which he shook on to the floor. It was covered with the remains of a rotting rag, which he undid, and revealed to my astonished gaze a beautifully shaped and almost white woman's foot, looking as fresh and as firm as though it had been placed there yesterday.

"Thou seest, my son, the Baboon," he said, in a sad voice, "I spake the truth to thee, for here is yet one foot remaining. Take it, my son, and gaze upon it."

I took this cold fragment of mortality in my hand and looked at it in the light of the lamp with feelings which I cannot describe, so mixed up were they between astonishment, fear, and fascination. It was light, much lighter I should say than it had been in the living state, and the flesh to all appearance was still flesh, though about it there clung a faintly aromatic odour. For the rest it was not shrunk or shrivelled, or even black and unsightly, like the flesh of Egyptian mummies, but plump and fair, and, except where it had been slightly burnt, perfect as on the day of death—a very triumph of embalming.

Poor little foot! I set it down upon the stone bench where it had lain for so many thousand years, and wondered whose was the beauty that it had upborne through the pomp and pageantry of a forgotten civilisation—first as a merry child's, then as a blushing maid's, and lastly as a perfect woman's. Through what halls of life had its soft step echoed, and in the end, with what courage had it trodden down the dusty ways of death! To whose side had it stolen in the hush of night when the black slave slept upon the marble floor, and who had listened for its stealing? Shapely little foot! Well might it have been set upon the proud neck of a conqueror bent at last to woman's beauty, and well might the lips of nobles and of kings have been pressed upon its jewelled whiteness.

I wrapped up this relic of the past in the remnants of the old linen rag which had evidently formed a portion of its owner's grave-clothes, for it was partially burnt, and put it away in my Gladstone bag,[1] which I had bought at the Army and Navy Stores, a strange combination I thought. Then with Billali's help I staggered off to see Leo. I found him dreadfully bruised, worse even than myself, perhaps owing to the excessive whiteness of his skin, and faint and weak with the loss of blood from the flesh wound in his side, but for all that cheerful as a cricket, and asking for some breakfast. Job and Ustane got him on to the bottom, or rather the sacking of a litter, which was removed from its pole for that purpose, and carried him out into the shade at the mouth of the cave, from which, by the way, every trace of the slaughter of the previous night had now been removed, and there we all breakfasted, and indeed spent that day, and most of the two following ones.

On the third morning Job and myself were practically recovered. Leo also was so much better that I yielded to Billali's often expressed entreaty, and agreed to start at once upon our journey to Kôr, which we were told was the name of the place where the mysterious *She* lived, though I still feared for its effects upon Leo, and especially lest the motion should cause his wound, which was scarcely skinned over, to break open again. Indeed, had it not been for Billali's evident anxiety to get off, which led us to suspect that some difficulty or danger might threaten us if we did not comply with it, I would not have consented to go.

(*To be continued*)

---

[1] A large piece of luggage named after William Gladstone (1809–98), the British politician and Prime Minister, after he said in 1882 that the Turks should be thrown "bag and baggage" out of Bulgaria.

"'Behold the House of *She-who-must-be-obeyed*,' said Billali. 'Had ever a queen such a throne before?' 'It is wonderful, my father,' I answered."

X

SPECULATIONS

Within an hour of our finally deciding to start five litters were brought up to the door of the cave, each accompanied by four regular bearers and two spare hands, also a band of about fifty armed Amahagger, who were to form the escort and carry the baggage. Three of these litters, of course, were for us, and one for Billali, who, I was immensely relieved to hear, was to be our companion, while the fifth I presumed was for the use of Ustane.

"Does the lady go with us, my father?" I asked of Billali, as he stood superintending things generally.

He shrugged his shoulders as he answered,

"If she wills. In this country the women do what they please. We worship them, and give them their way, because without them the world could not go on; they are the source of life."

"Ah," I said, the matter never having struck me in that light before.

"We worship them," he went on, "up to a certain point, till at last they get unbearable, which," he added, "they do about every second generation."

"And then what do you do?" I asked, with curiosity.

"Then," he answered, with a faint smile, "we rise, and kill the old ones as an example to the young ones, and to show them that we are the strongest. My poor wife was killed in that way three years ago. It was very sad, but to tell thee the truth, my son, life has been happier since, for my age protects me from the young ones."

"In short," I replied, quoting the saying of a great man[1] whose wisdom has not yet lightened the darkness of the Amahagger, "thou hast found thy position one of greater freedom and less responsibility."

This phrase puzzled him a little at first from its vagueness, though I think my translation hit off its sense very well, but at last he saw it, and appreciated it.

---

[1] British politician William Gladstone. In 1880, Gladstone backed off from pugnacious statements made about Austria before he became Prime Minister, saying that he had made them when he was in "a position of greater freedom and less responsibility." Haggard disliked Gladstone and his policies.

"Yes, yes, my Baboon," he said, "I see it now, but all the 'responsibilities' are killed, at least most of them are, and that is why there are so few old women about just now. Well, they brought it on themselves. As for this girl," he went on, in a graver tone, "I know not what to say. She is a brave girl, and she loves the Lion (Leo): thou sawest how she clung to him, and saved his life. Also, she is, according to our custom, wed to him, and has a right to go where he goes, unless," he added significantly, "*She* should say her no, for her word overrides all rights."

"And if *She* bade her leave him, and the girl refused? What then?"

"If," he said, with a shrug, "the hurricane bids the tree to bend, and it will not; what happens?"

And then, without waiting for an answer, he turned and walked to his litter, and in ten minutes from that time we were all well under weigh.

It took us an hour and more to cross the cup of the volcanic plain, and another half-hour or so to climb the edge on the further side. Once there, however, the view was a very fine one. Before us was a long steep slope of grassy plain, broken here and there by clumps of trees mostly of the thorn tribe. At the bottom of the gentle slope, some nine or ten miles away, we could make out a dim sea of marsh, on which the foul vapours hung like smoke about a city. It was easy going for the bearers down the slopes, and by mid-day we had reached the borders of the dismal swamp. Here we halted to eat our mid-day meal, and then, following a winding and devious path, plunged into the morass. Presently the path, at any rate to our unaccustomed eye, seemed to grow so faint as to be almost indistinguishable from those made by the aquatic beasts and birds, and it is to this day a mystery to me how our bearers found their way across the marshes. Ahead of the cavalcade marched two men with long poles, which they now and again plunged into the ground before them, the reason being that the nature of the soil frequently changed from causes with which I am not acquainted, so that places that would be safe enough to cross one month would certainly swallow the wayfarer the next. Never did I see a more dreary and depressing scene. Miles on miles of quagmire, varied only by bright green strips of comparatively solid ground, and by deep and sunken pools fringed with tall rushes, in which the bitterns boomed and the frogs croaked incessantly: miles on miles of it without a break, unless the fever fog can be called a break. The only life in this great morass was that of the aquatic birds, and the animals that fed on them, of both of which there were vast numbers. Geese, cranes, ducks, teal, coot, snipe, and plover swarmed all round us, many being of varieties that were quite new to me, and all so tame that one could almost have knocked them over with a stick. Among those birds I especially noticed a very beautiful variety of painted snipe, almost the size of woodcock, and with a flight more resembling that bird's than an English snipe's. In the pools, too, was a species of small alligator or enormous iguana, I do not know which, that fed, Billali told me, upon the waterfowl, also large quantities of a hideous black water snake, of which the bite is very dangerous, though not, I gathered, so deadly as a cobra's or a puff adder's. The bull-frogs were also very large, and with voices proportionate to their size; and as for the mosquitoes, they were, if possible, even worse than they had been on the river, and tormented us greatly. Undoubtedly, however, the worst feature of the swamp was the awful smell of rotting vegetation that hung about it, that was at times positively overpowering, and the malarious exhalations that accompanied it, which we were, of course, obliged to breathe.

On we went through it all, till at last the sun sank in sullen splendour just as we reached a spot of rising ground about two acres in extent—a little oasis of dry in the midst of the miry wilderness—where Billali announced that we were to camp. The camping, however, turned out to be a very simple process, and consisted, in fact, in sitting down on the ground round a scanty fire made of dry reeds and some wood that had been brought with us. However, we made the best we could of it, and smoked and ate with such appetite as the smell of damp, stifling heat would allow, for it was very hot on this low land, and yet, oddly enough, chilly at times. But, however hot it was, we were glad enough to keep near the fire, because we found that the mosquitoes did not like the smoke. Presently we rolled ourselves up in our blankets and tried to go to sleep, but so far as I was concerned the bull-frogs, and the extraordinary roaring and alarming sound produced by hundreds of snipe hovering high in the air, made sleep an impossibility, to say nothing of our other discomforts. I turned and looked at Leo, who was next me; he was dozing, but his face had a flushed appearance that I did not like, and by the flickering firelight I saw Ustane, who was lying on the other side of him, raise herself from time to time upon her elbow, and look at him anxiously enough.

However, I could do nothing for him, for we had all already taken a good dose of quinine, which was the only preventive we had; so I lay and watched the stars come out by thousands, till all the immense arch of Heaven was sewn with glittering points, and every point a world! Here was a glorious sight by which man might well measure his own insignificance! Soon I gave up thinking about it, for the mind wearies easily when it strives to grapple with the Infinite, and to trace the footsteps of the Almighty as He strides from sphere to sphere, or deduce His purpose from His works. Such things are not for us to know. Knowledge is to the strong, and we are weak. Too much wisdom would blind our imperfected sight, and too much strength would make us drunk, and overweight our feeble reason till it fell, and we were drowned in the depths of our own vanity. What is the first result of man's increased knowledge interpreted from Nature's book by the persistent effort of his purblind observation? Is it not nearly always to make him question the existence of his Maker, or indeed of any intelligent purpose beyond his own? The truth is veiled, because we could no more look upon her glory than we can upon the sun. It would destroy us. Full knowledge is not for man as man is here, for his capacities, which he is apt to think so great, are indeed but small. The vessel is soon filled, and, were one-thousandth part of the unutterable and silent wisdom that directs the rolling of the shining spheres and the force which makes them roll, pressed into it, it would be shattered into fragments. Perhaps in some other place and time it may be otherwise, who can tell? Here the lot of man born of the flesh is but to live midst toil and tribulation, to catch at the bubbles blown by Fate, which he calls pleasures, thankful if before they burst they rest a moment in his hand, and when the tragedy is played out and his hour comes to perish, to pass humbly whither he knows not.

Above me, as I lay, shone the eternal stars, and there at my feet the impish marsh-born balls of fire rolled this way and that, vapour-tossed and earth-desiring, and methought that in the two I saw a type and image of what man is, and what perchance man may one day be, if the living Force that ordained him and them should so ordain this also. Oh, that it might be ours to rest year by year upon that high level of the heart to which at times we momentarily attain! Oh, that we could shake loose the prisoned pinions of the soul and soar to that superior point, whence, like to some traveller looking out through space from Darien's[1] giddiest peak, we might gaze with the spirit eyes of noble thoughts deep into Infinity!

What would it be to cast off this earthy robe, to have done for ever with these earthy thoughts and miserable desires; no longer, like those

---

[1] Another name for Panama, from a peak in which Balboa first sighted the Pacific Ocean; alluding to Keats' sonnet, "On First Looking into Chapman's Homer."

corpse candles,[1] to be tossed this way and that, by forces beyond our control; or, if we can theoretically control them, are yet driven by the exigencies of our nature to obey! Yes, to cast them off, to have done with the foul and thorny places of the world; and like to those glittering points above me, to sit on high wrapped for ever in the brightness of our better selves, that even now shines in us as fire faintly shines within those lurid balls, and lay down our littleness in that wide glory of our dreams, that invisible but surrounding Good, from which all Truth and Beauty comes!

These and many such thoughts passed through my mind that night. They come to torment us all at times. I say to torment, for alas! thinking can only serve to measure out the helplessness of thought. What is the use of our feeble crying in the awful silences of space? Can our dim intelligence read the secrets of that star-strewn sky? Does any answer come out of it? Never any at all, nothing but echoes and fantastic visions. And yet we believe that there is an answer, and that upon a time a new Dawn will come blushing down the ways of our enduring night. We believe it, for its reflected beauty even now shines up continually in our hearts from beneath the horizon of the grave, and we call it Hope. Without Hope we should suffer moral death, and by the help of Hope we yet may climb to Heaven, or at the worst, if she also prove but a kindly mockery given to hold us from despair, be gently lowered into the abysses of eternal sleep.

Then I fell to reflecting upon the undertaking on which we were bent, and what a wild one it was, and yet how strangely the story seemed to fit in with what had been written centuries ago upon the sherd. Who was this extraordinary woman, Queen over a people apparently as extraordinary as herself, and reigning amidst the vestiges of a lost civilisation? And what could be the meaning of this story of the Fire that gave unending life? Could it be possible that any fluid or essence could exist that could so fortify these fleshly walls that they should from age to age resist the mines and batterings of decay? It was possible, though not probable. The indefinite continuation of life would not after all be half so marvellous a thing as the production of life and its temporary endurance. And if it were true, what then? The person who found it could no doubt rule the world. He could accumulate all the wealth in the world, and all the power, and all the wisdom that is

---

[1] Flickering lights seen in cemeteries at night, like the "marsh-born balls of fire" referred to here.

power. He might give a lifetime to the study of each art or science. Well, if that were so, and this *She* were practically immortal, which I did not for one moment believe, how was it that, with all these things at her feet, she preferred to remain in a cave amongst a society of cannibals? That surely settled the question. The whole story was monstrous, and only worthy of the superstitious days in which it was written. At any rate I was very sure that *I* would not attempt to attain unending life. I had had far too many worries and disappointments and secret bitternesses during my forty odd years of existence to wish that this state of affairs should be continued indefinitely. And yet I suppose that my life has been, comparatively speaking, a happy one.

And then, reflecting that at the present moment there was far more likelihood of our earthly careers being cut exceedingly short than of their being unduly prolonged, I at last managed to get to sleep, a fact for which anybody who reads this narrative, if anybody ever does, may very probably be thankful.

When I woke again it was just dawning, and the guard and bearers were moving about like ghosts through the dense morning mists, getting ready for our start. The fire had died quite down, and I rose and stretched myself, shivering in every limb from the damp cold of the dawn. Then I looked at Leo. He was sitting up, holding his hands to his head, and I saw that his face was flushed and his eye bright, and yet yellow round the pupil.

"Well, Leo," I said, "how do you feel?"

"I feel as though I were going to die," he answered hoarsely. "My head is splitting, my body is trembling, and I am as sick as a cat."

I whistled, or if I did not whistle, I felt inclined to—Leo had got a sharp attack of fever. I went to Job, and asked him for the quinine, of which fortunately we had still a good supply, only to find that Job himself was not much better. He complained of pains across the back, and dizziness, and was almost incapable of helping himself. Then I did the only thing it was possible to do under the circumstances—gave them both about ten grains of quinine, and took a slightly smaller dose myself as a matter of precaution. After that I found Billali, and explained to him how matters stood, asking at the same time what he thought had best be done. He came with me, and looked at Leo and Job (whom, by the way, he had named the Pig on account of his fatness, round face, and small eyes).

"Ah," he said, when we were out of earshot, "the fever! I thought so. The Lion has it badly, but he is young, and he may live. As for the

Pig, his attack is not so bad; it is the 'little fever' that he has; that always begins with pains across the back, it will spend itself upon his fat."

"Can they go on, my father?" I asked.

"Nay, my son, they must go on. If they stop here they will certainly die, and, besides, they will be better in the litters than on the ground. By to-night, if all goes well, we shall be across the marsh and in good air. Come, let us lift them into the litters and start, for it is very bad to stand still in this morning fog. We can eat our morning meal as we go."

This we accordingly did, and with a heavy heart I once more set out upon our strange journey. For the first three hours all went as well as could be expected, and then an accident happened that nearly lost us the pleasure of the company of our venerable friend, Billali, whose litter was leading the cavalcade. We were going through a particularly danger-ous piece of quagmire, in which the bearers sometimes sank up to their knees. Indeed, it was a mystery to me how they contrived to carry the heavy litters at all over such ground as that which we were traversing, though the two spare hands, as well as the four regular ones, had of course to put their shoulders to the pole.

Presently, as we blundered and floundered along, there was a sharp cry, then a storm of exclamations, and, last of all, a most tremendous splash, and the whole caravan halted.

I jumped out of my litter, and ran forward. About twenty yards ahead was the edge of one of those sullen peaty pools of which I have spoken, the path we were following running along the top of its bank, which, as it happened, was a steep one. Looking towards this pool, to my horror I saw that Billali's litter was floating on it, and as for Billali himself, he was nowhere to be seen. To make matters clear I may as well explain at once what had happened. One of Billali's bearers had unfortunately trodden on a basking snake, which had bitten him in the leg, whereon he had, not unnaturally, let go of the pole, and then finding he was tumbling down the bank, grasped at the litter to save himself. The result of this was what might have been expected. The litter was pulled over the edge of the bank, the bearers let go, and the whole thing, including Billali and the man who had been bitten, rolled into the slimy pool. When I got to the edge of the water neither of them were to be seen, and, indeed, the unfortunate bearer never was seen again. Either he struck his head against something, or got wedged in the mud, or possibly the snake-bite paralysed him. At any rate, he vanished. But though Billali was not to be seen, his whereabouts was clear enough, from the agitation of the float-ing litter, in the bearing cloth and curtains of which he was entangled.

"He is there! Our father is there!" said one of the men, but he did not stir a finger to help him, nor did any of the others. They simply stood and stared at the water.

"Out of the way, you brutes," I shouted in English, and throwing off my hat, I took a run and sprang well out into the horrid slimy-looking pool. A couple of strokes took me to where Billali was struggling beneath the cloth.

Somehow, I don't quite know how, I managed to push this free of him, and his venerable head all covered in green slime, like that of a yellowish Bacchus[1] with ivy leaves, emerged upon the surface of the water. The rest was easy, for Billali was an eminently practical individual, and had the common sense not to grasp hold of me as drowning people often do, so I got him by the arm, and towed him to the bank, through the mud of which we were with difficulty dragged. Such a filthy spectacle as we presented I have never seen before or since, and it will perhaps give some idea of the almost superhuman dignity of Billali's appearance when I say that, coughing, half-drowned, and covered with mud and green slime as he was, with his beautiful beard coming to a dripping point, like a Chinaman's freshly-oiled pig-tail, he still looked venerable and imposing.

"Ye dogs," he said, addressing the bearers, as soon as he had sufficiently recovered to speak, "ye left me, your father, to drown. Had it not been for this stranger, my son the Baboon, assuredly I should have drowned. Well, I will remember it," and he fixed them with his gleaming, though slightly watery eye, in a way I saw they did not like, though they tried to appear sulkily indifferent.

"As for thee, my son," the old man went on turning towards me, and grasping my hand, "rest assured that I am thy friend through good and evil. Thou hast saved my life, perchance a day may come when I shall save thine."

After that we cleaned ourselves as best we could, fished out the litter, and went on, *minus* the man who had been drowned. I don't know if it was owing to his being an unpopular character, or from native indifference and selfishness of temperament, but I am bound to say that nobody seemed to grieve much over his sudden and final disappearance, unless, perhaps, it was the men who had to do his share of the work.

---

[1] Greek god of wine, often depicted as crowned with leaves.

XI

THE PLAIN OF KÔR

About an hour before sundown we at last, to my unbounded gratitude, emerged from the great belt of marsh on to land that swelled upwards in a succession of rolling waves. Just on the hither side of the crest of the first wave we halted for the night. My first act was to examine Leo's condition. It was, if anything, worse than in the morning, and a new and very distressing feature, vomiting, set in, and continued till dawn. Not one wink of sleep did I get that night, for I passed it in assisting Ustane, who was one of the most gentle and indefatigable nurses I ever saw, to wait upon Leo and Job. However, the air here was warm and genial without being too hot, and there were no mosquitoes to speak of. Also we were above the level of the marsh mist, which lay stretched beneath us like the dim smoke-pall over a city, lit up here and there by the wandering globes of fen fire. Thus it will be seen that we were, speaking comparatively, in clover.

By dawn on the following morning Leo was quite light-headed, and fancied that he was divided into halves. I was dreadfully distressed, and began to wonder with a sort of sick fear what the termination of the attack would be. Alas! I had heard but too much of how these attacks generally terminate. As I was doing so Billali came up and said that we must be getting on, more especially as, in his opinion, if Leo did not reach some spot where he could be quiet, and have proper nursing, within the next twelve hours, his life would only be a matter of a day or two. I could not but agree with him, so we got him into the litter, and started on, Ustane walking by his side to keep the flies off him, and see that he did not throw himself out on to the ground.

Within half-an-hour of sunrise we had reached the top of the rise of which I have spoken, and a most beautiful view broke upon our gaze. Beneath us was a rich stretch of country, verdant with grass and lovely with foliage and flowers. In the background, at a distance, so far as I could judge, of some eighteen miles from where we then stood, a huge and extraordinary mountain rose abruptly from the plain. The base of this great mountain appeared to consist of a grassy slope, but rising from this, I should say, from subsequent observation, at a height of about five hundred feet above the level of the plain, was a most tremendous and absolutely precipitous wall of bare rock, quite twelve or fifteen hundred feet in height. The shape of the mountain, which was undoubtedly of volcanic origin, was round, and, of course, as only a segment of its circle was visible, it was difficult to estimate its exact size, which was enormous. I afterwards discovered that it could not cover less than fifty square miles of ground. Anything more grand and imposing than the sight presented by this great natural castle, starting in solitary grandeur from the level of the plain, I never saw, and I suppose never shall. Its very solitude added to its majesty, and its towering cliffs seemed to kiss the sky. Indeed, generally speaking, they were clothed in clouds that lay in fleecy masses upon their broad and level battlements.

I sat up in my hammock and gazed out across the plain at this thrilling and majestic sight, and I suppose that Billali noticed it, for he brought his litter alongside.

"Behold the house of '*She-who-must-be-obeyed!*'" he said. "Had ever a queen such a throne before?"

"It is wonderful, my father," I answered. "But how does one enter? Those cliffs look hard to climb."

"Thou shalt see, my Baboon. Look now at the plain below us. What thinkest thou that it is? Thou art a wise man. Come, tell me."

I looked, and saw what appeared to be the line of roadway running straight towards the base of the mountain, though it was covered with turf. There were high banks on each side of it, broken here and there, but fairly continuous on the whole, the meaning of which I did not understand. It seemed so very odd that anybody should embank a roadway.

"Well, my father," I answered, "I suppose that it is a road, otherwise I should have been inclined to say that it was the bed of a river, or rather," I added, observing the extraordinary directness of the cutting, "of a canal."

Billali—who, by the way, was none the worse for his immersion of the day before—nodded his head sagely as he replied,

"Thou art right, my son. It is a channel cut out by those who were before us in this place to carry away water. Of this I am sure: within the rocky circle of the great mountain whither we journey was once a great lake. But those who were before us, by wonderful arts of which I know nought, hewed a path for the water through the solid rock of the mountain, piercing even to the bed of the lake. But first they cut the channel that thou seest across the plain. Then when at last the water burst out, it rushed down the channel that had been made to receive it, and crossed this plain till it reached the low land behind the rise, and there, perchance, it made the swamp through which we have come. Then when the lake was drained dry, the people whereof I speak built a mighty city, whereof nought but ruins and the name of Kôr yet remaineth, on its bed, and from age to age hewed the caves and passages that thou wilt see."

"It may be," I answered; "but if so, how is it that the lake does not fill up again with the rains?"

"Nay, my son, the people were a wise people, and they left a drain to keep it clear. Seest thou the river to the right?" and he pointed to a fair-sized stream that wound away across the plain, some four miles from us. "That is the drain, and it comes out through the mountains where this cutting goes in. At first, perhaps, the water ran down this canal, but afterwards the people turned it, and used the cutting for a road."

"And is there then no other place where one may enter into the great mountain," I asked, "except through the drain?"

"There is a place," he answered, "where cattle and men on foot may cross with much labour, but it is secret. A year mightest thou search and should'st never find it. It is only used once a year, when the herds of cattle that have been fatting on the slopes of the mountain, and on this plain, are driven into the space within."

"And does *She* live there always?" I asked, "or does she come at times without the mountain?"

"Nay, my son, where she is, there she is."

By now we were well on to the great plain, and I was examining with delight the varied beauty of its semi-tropical flowers and trees, the latter of which grew singly, or at most in clumps of three or four, much of the timber being of large size, and belonging apparently to a variety of evergreen oak. There were also many palms, some of them more than one hundred feet high, and the largest and most beautiful tree ferns that I ever saw, about which hung clouds of jewelled honeysuckers and great-winged butterflies. Wandering about among the trees or crouching in the long and feathered grass were all varieties of game, from rhinoceroses down. I saw a rhinoceros, buffalo (a large herd), eland,[1] quagga,[2] and sable antelope, the most beautiful of all the bucks, not to mention many smaller varieties of game, and three ostriches which scudded away at our approach like white drift before a gale. So plentiful was the game that at last I could stand it no longer. I had a single barrel sporting Martini[3] with me in the litter, the "Express" being too

---

[1] African antelope with spiral horns.

[2] A wild horse native to southern Africa, related to the Zebra, that has since become extinct.

[3] The Martini-Henry, a brand of breech-action rifle popular in the wars of the British Empire; Holly here uses a civilian "sporting" version.

cumbersome, and espying a beautiful fat eland rubbing himself under one of the oak-like trees, I jumped out of the litter, and proceeded to creep as near to him as I could. He let me come within eighty yards, and then turned his head, and stared at me, preparatory to running away. I lifted the rifle, and taking him about midway down the shoulder, for he was side on to me, fired. I never made a cleaner shot or a better kill in all my small experience, for the great buck sprang right up into the air and fell dead. The bearers, who had all halted to see the performance, gave a murmur of surprise, an unwonted compliment from these sullen people, who never appear to be surprised at anything, and a party of the guard at once ran off to cut the animal up. As for myself, though I was longing to have a look at him, I sauntered back to my litter as though I had been in the habit of killing eland all my life, feeling that I had gone up several degrees in the estimation of the Amahagger, who looked on the whole thing as a very high-class manifestation of witch-craft. As a matter of fact, however, I had never seen an eland in a wild state before. Billali received me with enthusiasm.

"It is wonderful, my son the Baboon," he cried; "wonderful! Thou art a very great man, though so ugly. Had I not seen, surely I would never have believed. And thou sayest that thou wilt teach me to slay in this fashion?"

"Certainly, my father," I said, airily; "it is nothing."

But all the same I firmly made up my mind that when "my father" Billali began to fire I would without fail lie down or take refuge behind a tree.

After this little incident nothing happened of any note till about an hour and a half before sundown, when we arrived beneath the shadow of the towering volcanic mass that I have already described. It is quite impossible for me to describe its grim grandeur as it appeared to me while my patient bearers toiled along the bed of the ancient watercourse towards the spot where the rich brown-clad cliff shot up from precipice to precipice till its crown lost itself in cloud. All I can say is that it almost awed me by the intensity of its lonesome and most solemn greatness. On we went up the bright and sunny slope, till at last the creeping shadows from above swallowed up its brightness, and presently we began to pass through a cutting hewn in the living rock. Deeper and deeper grew this marvellous work, which must, I should say, have employed thousands of men for many years. Indeed how it was ever executed at all without the aid of blasting-powder or dynamite I cannot to this day imagine. It is and must remain one of the mysteries of this wild land. I can only suppose that these cuttings and the vast caves that had been hollowed out of the rocks it pierced were the State undertakings of the people of Kôr, who lived here in the dim lost ages of the world, and, as in the case of the Egyptian monuments, were executed by the forced labour of tens of thousands of captives, carried on through an indefinite number of centuries. But who were the people?

At last we reached the face of the precipice itself, and found ourselves looking into the mouth of a dark tunnel that forcibly reminded me of those undertaken by our nineteenth-century engineers in the construction of railway lines. Out of this tunnel flowed a considerable stream of water. Indeed, though I do not think that I have mentioned it, we had followed this stream, which ultimately developed into the river I have already described as winding away to the right from the spot where the cutting in the solid rock commenced. Half of this cutting formed a channel for the stream, and half, which was placed on a slightly higher level—eight feet, perhaps—was devoted to the purposes of a roadway. At the termination of the cutting, however, the stream turned off across the plain and followed a channel of its own. At the mouth of the cave the cavalcade was halted, and while the men employed themselves in lighting some earthenware lamps they had brought with them, Billali, descending from his litter, informed me politely but firmly that the orders of *She* were that we were now to be blindfolded, so that we should not learn the secret of the paths through the bowels of the mountains. To this I of course assented cheerfully enough, but Job, who was now very much better, notwithstanding the journey, did not like it at all, fancying, I believe, that it was but a preliminary step to being hot-potted. He was, however, a little consoled when I pointed out to him that there were no hot pots handy, and, so far as I knew, no fire to heat them in. As for poor Leo, after turning restlessly for hours, he had, to my deep thankfulness, at last dropped off into a sleep or stupor, I don't know which, so there was no need to blindfold him. The blindfolding was performed by binding tightly round the eyes a piece of the yellowish linen whereof those of the Amahagger who condescended to wear anything in particular made their dresses. This linen I afterwards discovered was taken from the tombs, and was not, as I had at first supposed, of native manufacture. The bandage was then knotted at the back of the head, and finally brought down again and the ends bound under the chin to prevent its slipping. Ustane, by the way, was also blindfolded. I do not know why, unless it was from fear that she should impart the secrets of the route to us. This operation performed we started on once more, and soon, by the echoing sound of the footsteps of the bearers and the increased noise of the water caused by reverberation in a confined space, I knew that we were entering into the bowels of the great mountain. It was an eerie sensation, being borne along into the heart of a mountain we knew not whither, but I was getting used to eerie sensations by this time, and by now was pretty well prepared for anything. So I lay still, and listened to the tramp, tramp of the bearers and the rushing of the water, and tried to believe that I was enjoying myself. Presently the men set up the melancholy little chant that I had heard on the first night when we were captured in the whale-boat, and the effect produced by their voices was very curious, and quite inde-scribable on paper. After a while the air began to get exceedingly thick and heavy, so much so, indeed, that I felt as though I were going to choke, till at length I felt the litter take a sharp turn, then another and another, and the sound of the running water ceased. After this the air got fresher again, but the turns were continuous, and to me, blindfolded as I was, most bewildering. I tried to keep a map of them in my mind in case it might ever be necessary for us to try and escape by this route, but, needless to say, failed utterly. Another half-hour or so passed, and then suddenly I became aware that we were once more in the open air. I could see the light through my bandage and feel the freshness of it on my face. A few more minutes and the caravan halted, and I heard Billali order Ustane to remove her bandage and undo ours. Without waiting for her attentions I got the knot of mine loose, and looked out.

As I anticipated, we had passed right through the precipice, and were now on its further side, and immediately beneath its beetling face. The first thing I noticed was that it was not nearly so high here, not so high I should say by five hundred feet, which proved that the bed of the lake, or rather of the vast ancient crater in which we stood, was much higher than the surrounding plain. For the rest, we found ourselves in a huge rock-surrounded cup, not unlike that of the first place where we had sojourned, only ten times the size. Indeed, one could only just make out the frowning line of the opposite cliffs. A great portion of the plain thus enclosed by nature was cultivated, and fenced in with walls of stone placed there to keep the cattle and goats, of which there were large herds about, from breaking into the gardens. Here and there rose great grass mounds, and some miles away towards the centre I thought that I could see the outline of colossal ruins. I had no time to observe anything more at the moment, for we were instantly surrounded by crowds of Amahagger, similar in every particular to those with whom we were already familiar, who, though they spoke little, pressed round us so closely as to obscure the view to a person lying in a hammock. Then all of a sudden a number of armed men arranged in companies, and marshalled by officers who held an ivory wand in their hands, came running swiftly towards us, having, so far as I could make out, emerged from the face of the precipice like ants from their burrows. These men as well as their officers were all robed in addition to the usual leopard skin, and, as I gathered, formed the body guard of *She* herself.

Their leader advanced to Billali, saluted him by placing his ivory wand transversely across his forehead, and then asked some question which I could not catch, and Billali having answered him the whole regiment turned and marched along the side of the cliff, our cavalcade of litters following in their track. After going thus for about half a mile we halted once more in front of the mouth of a tremendous cave, measuring about fifty feet in height by eighty wide, and here Billali descended finally, and requested Job and myself to do the same. Leo of course was far too ill to do anything of the sort. I did so, and we entered the great cave, into which the light of the setting sun penetrated for some distance, while beyond the reach of the light it was faintly illuminated with lamps which seemed to me to stretch away for an almost immeasurable distance, like the gas lights of an empty London street. Another thing I noticed was that the walls were covered with sculptures in bas-relief, of a sort, pictorially speaking, similar to those that I have described upon the vases, love-scenes principally, then hunting pictures, and pictures of executions, and the torture of criminals by the placing of a hot, presumably red-hot, pot upon the *head*, showing whence our hosts had derived this pleasant practice. There were very few battle-pieces, though many of duels, and men running and wrestling, and from this fact I am led to believe that this people were not much subject to attack by exterior foes, either on account of the isolation of their position, or because of their great strength. Between the pictures were columns of stone characters of a formation absolutely new to me; at any rate they were neither Greek nor Egyptian, nor Hebrew, nor Assyrian—that I can swear to. They looked more like Chinese than anything else. Near to the entrance of the cave both pictures and writings were worn away, but further in they were in many cases absolutely fresh and perfect as the day on which the sculptor had ceased work on them.

The regiment of guards did not come further than the entrance to the cave, where they formed up to let us pass through. On entering the place itself we were, however, met by a man robed in white, who bowed humbly, but said nothing, which, as it afterwards appeared that he was a deaf mute, was not very wonderful.

Running at right angles to the main cave at a distance of some twenty feet from the entrance was a smaller cave or wide gallery, that was pierced into the rock both to the right and to the left of the main cave. At the mouth of this gallery to our left stood two guards, and from this circumstance I argued that it was the entrance to the apartments of *She* herself. The entrance to the right gallery was unguarded, and down this the mute indicated we were to proceed. A few yards down this gallery, which was lighted with lamps, we came to the entrance to a chamber with a curtain made of some grass material, not unlike a Zanzibar mat[1] in appearance, hung over the doorway. This the mute drew back with another profound obeisance, and led the way into a good-sized apartment, hewn, of course, out of the solid rock, but to my great delight lighted by means of a shaft pierced in the face of the precipice. In this room was a stone bedstead, pots full of water for washing, and beautifully tanned leopard skins to serve as blankets.

Here we left Leo, who was still sleeping heavily, and with him stayed Ustane. I noticed that the mute gave her a very sharp look, as much as to say "Who are you, and by whose orders do you come here?" Then he conducted us to another similar room which Job took, and then to two more that were respectively occupied by Billali and myself.

(*To be continued*)

---

[1]   A rug or mat made of closely woven natural fibers.

"The hand grasped the curtain, and drew it aside."

XII

"SHE"

The first care of Job and myself, after seeing to Leo, was to wash ourselves and put on clean clothing, for what we were wearing had not been changed since the loss of the dhow. Fortunately, as I think that I have said, by far the greater part of our personal baggage had already been packed into the whale-boat, and was therefore saved—and brought hither by the bearers—although all the stores laid in by us for barter and presents to the natives were lost. Nearly all our clothing was made of a well shrunk and very strong grey flannel, and excellent I found it for travelling in these places, because though a Norfolk jacket, shirt, and pair of trousers of it only weighed about four pounds, a great consideration in a tropical country, where every extra ounce tells on the wearer, it was warm, and offered a good resistance to the rays of the sun, and best of all to chills, which are so apt to result from sudden changes of temperature.

Never shall I forget the comfort of the "wash and brush-up," and of those clean flannels. The only thing that was wanting to complete my joy was a cake of soap, of which we had none.

Afterwards I discovered that the Amahagger, who do not reckon dirt among their many disagreeable qualities, use a kind of burnt earth for washing purposes, which, though unpleasant to the touch till one gets accustomed to it, forms a very fair substitute for soap.

By the time that I was dressed, and had combed and trimmed my black beard, the previous condition of which was certainly sufficiently unkempt to give weight to Billali's appellation for me, the Baboon, I began to feel most uncommonly hungry. Therefore I was by no means sorry when, without the slightest preparatory sound or warning, the curtain over the entrance to my cave was flung aside, and another mute, a young girl this time, announced to me by signs that I could not misunderstand—that is, by opening her mouth and pointing down it—that there was something ready to eat. Accordingly I followed her into the next chamber, which we had not yet entered, where I found Job, who had also, to his great embarrassment, been conducted thither by a fair mute. Job had never got over the advances the former lady had made to him, and suspected every girl who came near to him of similar designs.

"These young parties have a way of looking at one, sir," he would say apologetically, "which I don't call respectable."

This fresh room was twice the size of the sleeping caves, and I saw at once that it had originally served as a refectory, and also probably as an embalming room for the Priests of the Dead; for I may as well say at once that these hollowed-out caves were nothing more nor less than vast catacombs, in which for tens of ages the mortal remains of the great extinct race whose monuments surrounded us had been first preserved, with an art and a completeness that has never since been equalled, and then hidden away for all time. On each side of this rock-chamber was a long solid stone table, about three feet wide by three feet six in height, hewn out of the living rock, of which it had formed part, and was still attached to, at the base. These tables were slightly hollowed out or curved inward, to give room for the knees of any one sitting on the stone ledge that had been cut for a bench along the side of the cave at a distance of about two feet from them. Each of them was so arranged that it ended right under a shaft pierced in the rock for the admission of light and air. On examining them carefully, however, I saw that there was a difference between them that had at first escaped my attention, viz., that one of the tables, that to the left as we entered the cave, had evidently been used, not to eat upon, but for the purpose of embalming bodies. That this was beyond all question the case was clear from five shallow depressions in the stone of the table, all shaped like a human form, with a separate place for the head to lie in, and a little bridge to support the neck, each depression being of a different size, so as to fit bodies varying in stature from a full-grown man's to a small child's, and with little holes bored at intervals to carry off fluid. And, indeed, if any further confirmation was required, one had but to look at the wall of the cave above to find it. For there, sculptured all round the apartment, and looking nearly as fresh as the day it was done, was the pictorial representation of the death, embalming, and burial of an old man with a long beard, probably an ancient king or grandee of this country.

The first picture represented his death. He was lying upon a couch which had four short curved posts at the corners coming to a knob at the end, in appearance something like a written note of music, and was evidently in the very act of expiring. Gathered round the couch were women and children weeping, the former with their hair hanging down their back. The next scene represented the embalming of the body, which lay nude upon a table with depressions in it, similar to the one before us; probably, indeed, it was a picture of the same table. Three men were employed at the work—one superintending, one holding a funnel shaped exactly like a port wine strainer, of which the narrow end was fixed in an incision in the breast, no doubt in the great pectoral artery, while the third, who was represented as standing straddle-legged over the corpse, held a kind of large jug high in his hand, and poured from it some steaming fluid, which fell accurately into the funnel. The most curious part of this sculpture is that both the man with the funnel and the man who poured the fluid are represented as holding their noses, either I suppose because of the stench arising from the body, or more probably to keep out the aromatic fumes of the hot fluid which was being forced into the dead man's veins. Another curious thing which I am unable to explain was that all three men had a band of linen tied round the face, with holes in it for the eyes.

The third sculpture represented the burial of the deceased. There he was, stiff and cold, clothed in a linen robe and laid out on a stone slab such as I had slept upon at our first sojourning-place. At his head and feet burnt a lamp, and by his side were placed several of the beautiful painted vases that I have described, which were probably supposed to be full of provisions. The little chamber was crowded with mourners, and with musicians playing on a sort of lyre, while near the foot of the corpse stood a man with a sheet, with which he was preparing to cover it from view.

These sculptures, looked at merely as works of art, were so remarkable that I make no apology for describing them rather fully. They struck me also as being of surpassing interest as representing, probably with studious accuracy, the last rites of the dead as practised among an utterly lost people, and even then I thought how envious some antiquarian friends of my own at Cambridge would be if ever I got an opportunity of describing these wonderful remains to them. Probably they would say that I was exaggerating, notwithstanding that every page of this history must bear so much internal evidence of its truth that it would obviously have been quite impossible for me to have invented it.

To return. As soon as I had hastily examined these sculptures, which I think I omitted to mention were executed in relief, we sat down to a very excellent meal of boiled goat's-flesh, fresh milk, and cakes made of meal, the whole being served upon clean wooden platters.

When we had eaten we returned to see how Leo was getting on, Billali saying that he must now wait upon *She* and hear her commands.

On reaching Leo's room we found the poor boy in a very bad way. He had woke up from his torpor, and was altogether off his head, babbling about some boat-race on the Cam, and was inclined to be violent. Indeed, when we entered the room Ustane was holding him down. I spoke to him, and my voice seemed to soothe him; at any rate he grew much quieter, and was persuaded to swallow a dose of quinine.

I had been sitting with him for an hour, perhaps—at any rate I know that it was just getting so dark that I could only just make out his head lying like a gleam of gold upon the pillow we had extemporised of a bag covered with a blanket—when suddenly Billali arrived with an air of great importance, and informed me that *She* herself had deigned to express a wish to see me—an honour, he added, accorded to but very few. I think that he was a little horrified at my cool way of taking the honour, but the fact was that I did not feel overwhelmed with gratitude at the prospect of seeing some savage dusky queen, however absolute and mysterious she might be, more especially as my mind was full of dear Leo, for whose life I began to have great fears. However, I rose to follow him, and as I did so I caught sight of something bright lying on the floor, which I picked up. Perhaps the reader will remember that with the potsherd in the casket was a composition scarabæus marked with a round O, a large bird, and another curious hieroglyphic, the meaning of which signs is "Suten se Rā," or "Royal Son of the Sun." This scarab, which is a very small one, Leo had insisted upon having set in a massive gold ring, such as is generally used for signets, and it was this very ring that I now picked up. He had pulled it off in the paroxysm of his fever, at least I suppose so, and flung it down upon the rock-floor. Thinking that if I left it about it might get lost, I slipped it on to my own little finger, and then followed Billali, leaving Job and Ustane with Leo.

We passed down the passage, crossed the great aisle-like cave, and came to the corresponding passage on the other side, at the mouth of which the guards stood like two statues. As we came they bowed their heads in salutation, and then lifting their long spears placed them transversely across their foreheads, as the leaders of the troop that had met us had done with their ivory wands. We stepped between them, and found ourselves in an exactly similar passage to that which led to our own apartments, only this passage was comparatively speaking, brilliantly lighted. A few paces down it we were met by four mutes—two men and two women—who bowed low and then arranged themselves, the women in front of and the men behind us, and in this order we continued our procession past several doorways hung with curtains similar to those leading to our own quarters, and which I afterwards found opened out into chambers occupied by the mutes who attended on *She*. A few paces more and we came to another doorway facing us, and not to our left like the others, which seemed to mark the termination of the passage. Here two more white, or rather yellow-robed guards were standing, and they, too, bowed, saluted, and let us pass through heavy curtains into a great antechamber, quite forty feet long by as many wide, in which some eight or ten women, most of them young and handsome, with yellowish hair, sat on cushions working with ivory needles at what had the appearance of being embroidery frames. These women were also deaf and dumb. At the further end of this great lamp-lit apartment was another doorway closed in with heavy Oriental-looking curtains, quite unlike those that hung before the doors of our own apartments, and here stood two particularly handsome girl mutes, their heads bowed upon their bosoms and their hands crossed in an attitude of the humblest submission. As they came they each stretched out an arm and drew back the curtains. Thereupon Billali did a curious thing. Down he went, that venerable-looking old gentleman—for Billali is a gentleman at the bottom—down on to his hands and knees, and in this undignified position, with his long white beard trailing on the ground, he began to creep into the apartment beyond. I followed him, standing on my feet in the usual fashion. Looking over his shoulder he perceived it.

"Down, my son; down, my Baboon; down on to thy hands and knees. We enter the presence of *She*, and, if thou art not humble, of a surety she will blast thee where thou standest."

I halted, and felt scared. Indeed, my knees began to give way of their own mere motion; but reflection came to my aid. I was an Englishman, and why, I asked myself, should I creep into the presence of some savage woman as though I were a monkey in fact as well as in name? I would not and could not do it, that is, unless I was absolutely sure that my life depended upon it. If once I began to creep upon my knees I should always have to do so, and it would be a patent acknowledgment of inferiority. So, fortified by an insular prejudice against "kootooing,"[1] which has, like most of our so-called prejudices, a good deal of common sense to recommend it, I marched in boldly after Billali. I found myself in another apartment, considerably smaller than the anteroom, of which the walls were entirely hung with rich-looking curtains of the same

---

[1]   Variant of kowtowing, meaning showing extreme deference and respect.

make as those over the door, the work, as I subsequently discovered, of the mutes who sat in the antechamber and wove them in strips, which were afterwards sewn together. Also, here and there about the room, were settees of a beautiful black wood of the ebony tribe, inlaid with ivory, and all about the floor were other tapestries, or rather rugs. At the top end of this apartment was what appeared to be a recess, also draped with curtains, through which shone rays of light. There was nobody in the place except ourselves.

Painfully and slowly old Billali crept up the length of the cave, and with the most dignified stride that I could command I followed after him. But I felt that it was more or less of a failure. To begin with, it is not possible to look dignified when you are following in the wake of an old man writhing along on his stomach like a snake, and then, in order to go sufficiently slowly, either I had to keep my leg some seconds in the air at every step, or else to advance with a full stop between each stride, like Mary, Queen of Scots,[1] going to execution in a play. Billali was not good at crawling—I suppose his years stood in the way—and our progress up that apartment was a very long affair. I was immediately behind him, and several times I was sorely tempted to help him on with a good kick. It is so absurd to advance into the presence of savage royalty after the fashion of an Irishman driving a pig to market, for that is what we looked like, and the idea nearly made me burst out laughing then and there. I had to work my dangerous tendency to unseemly merriment off by blowing my nose, a proceeding which filled old Billali with horror, for he looked over his shoulder and made a ghastly face at me, and I heard him murmur, "Oh, my poor Baboon!"

At last we reached the curtains, and here Billali collapsed flat on to his stomach, with his hands stretched out before him as though he were dead, and I, not knowing what to do, began to stare about the place. But presently I distinctly felt that somebody was looking at me from behind the curtains. I could not see the person, but I could distinctly feel his or her gaze, and, what is more, it produced a very odd effect upon my nerves. I felt frightened, I don't know why. The place was a strange one, it is true, and looked lonely, notwithstanding its rich hangings and the soft glow of the lamps,—indeed these accessories added to, rather than detracted from, its loneliness, just as a lighted street at night has always a more solitary appearance than a dark one. It was so silent in the place,

---

[1] Mary Stuart, daughter of James V of Scotland, beheaded on the orders of Elizabeth I in 1487.

and there lay Billali like one dead before the heavy curtains, through which the odour of perfume seemed to float up towards the gloom of the arched roof above. Minute grew into minute, and still there was no sign of life, nor did the curtain move; but I felt the gaze of the unknown being sinking through and through me, and filling me with a nameless terror, till the perspiration stood in beads upon my brow.

At last the curtain began to move. Who could be behind it?—some naked savage queen, a languishing Oriental beauty, or a nineteenth-century young lady, drinking afternoon tea? I had not the slightest idea, and should not have been astonished at seeing any of the three. I was getting beyond astonishment. The curtain agitated itself a little, then suddenly between its folds there appeared a most beautiful white hand (white as snow), and with long tapering fingers, ending in the pinkest nails. The hand grasped the curtain, and drew it aside, and as it did so I heard a voice, I think the softest and yet most silvery voice I ever heard. It reminded me of the murmur of a brook.

"Stranger," said the voice in Arabic, but much purer and more classical Arabic than the Amahagger talk; "stranger, wherefore art thou so much afraid?"

Now I flattered myself that in spite of my inward terrors I had kept a very fair command of my countenance, and was, therefore, a little astonished at this question. Before I had made up my mind how to answer it, however, the curtain was drawn, and a tall figure stood before us. I say a figure, for not only her body, but also her face, was wrapped up in soft white, gauzy material in such a way as at first sight to remind me most forcibly of a corpse in its grave clothes. And yet I do not know why it should have given me that idea, seeing that the wrappings were so thin that one could distinctly see the gleam of the pink flesh beneath them. I suppose it was the way in which they were arranged, either accidentally, or more probably by design. Anyhow, I felt more frightened than ever at this ghost-like apparition, and my hair began to rise upon my head as the feeling crept over me that I was in the presence of something that was not canny. The swathed mummy-like form before me was that of a tall and lovely woman, instinct with beauty in every part, and also with a certain snakelike grace that I have never seen anything like before. When she moved a hand or foot her entire frame seemed to undulate, and the neck did not bend, it curved.

"Why art thou so frightened, stranger?" asked the sweet voice again—a voice that seemed to draw the heart out of me, like the strains of softest music. "Is there that about me that should affright a man? Then surely are men changed from what they used to be." And with a little coquettish movement, she turned herself and held up one arm, so as to show all her loveliness and the rich hair of raven blackness that streamed in soft ripples down her snowy robes, almost to her sandalled feet.

"It is thy beauty that makes me fear, oh queen," I answered, humbly, scarcely knowing what to say, and I thought that as I did so I heard old Billali, who was still lying prostrate on the floor, mutter, "Good, my Baboon, good."

"I see that men still know how to beguile us women with false words. Ah, stranger," she answered, with a laugh that sounded like distant silver bells, "thou wast afraid because mine eyes were searching out thine heart, therefore wast thou afraid. But being but a woman, I forgive thee for the lie, for it was courteously said. And now tell me how came ye hither to this land of the dwellers among caves—a land of swamps and evil things and dead old shadows of the dead? What came ye for to see? How is it that ye hold your lives so cheap as to place them in the hollow of the hand of *Hiya*, into the hand of '*She-who-must-be-obeyed*?' Tell me also how come ye to know the tongue that I talk. It is an ancient tongue. Liveth it yet in the world? Thou seest I dwell among the caves and the dead, and nought know I of the affairs of men, nor have I cared to know. I have lived, oh stranger, with my memories, and my memories are in a grave that mine own hands hollowed, for truly hath it been said that the child of man maketh his own path evil," and her beautiful voice quivered, and broke in a note as soft as any wood-bird's. Suddenly her eye fell upon the sprawling frame of Billali, and she seemed to recollect herself.

"Ah! thou art there, old man. Tell me how it is that things have gone wrong in thine household. Forsooth, it seems that these my guests were set upon. Ay, and one was actually slain by the hot pot to be eaten of those brutes, thy children, and had not the others fought gallantly they, too, had been slain, and not even I could have called back the life that had been loosed from the body. What means it, old man? What hast thou to say that I should not give thee over to those who execute my vengeance?"

Her voice had risen in her anger, and it rang clear and cold against the rocky walls. Also I thought I could see her eyes flash through the gauze that hid them. I saw poor Billali, whom I had believed to be a very fearless person, positively quiver with terror at her words.

"Oh 'Hiya!' oh *She*!" he said, without lifting his white head from the floor. "Oh *She*, as thou art great be merciful, for I am now as ever thy servant to obey. It was no plan or fault of mine, oh *She*, it was those wicked ones who are called my children. Led on by a woman whom thy guest the Pig had scorned, they would have followed the ancient custom of the land, and eaten the fat black stranger who came hither with these thy guests the Baboon and the Lion who is sick, thinking that no word had come from thee about the Black one. But when the Baboon and the Lion saw what they would do, they slew the woman. Then those evil ones, ay, those children of the Wicked One who lives in the Pit, they went mad with the lust of blood, and flew at the throats of the Lion and the Baboon and the Pig. But gallantly they fought. Oh *Hiya*! they fought like very men, and slew many, and held their own, and then I came and saved them, and the evildoers have I sent on hither to be judged of thy greatness, oh *She*! and here they are."

"Ay, old man, I know it, and to-morrow will I sit in the great hall and do justice upon them, fear not. And for thee, I forgive thee, though hardly. See that thou dost keep thine household better. Go."

Billali rose upon his knees with astonishing alacrity, bowed his head thrice, and, his white beard sweeping the ground, crawled down the apartment as he had crawled up it, till he finally vanished through the curtains, leaving me, not a little to my alarm, alone with this terrible but most fascinating person.

XIII

AYESHA UNVEILS

"There," she said, "he has gone, the white-bearded old fool. Ah, how little knowledge does a man acquire in his life. He gathers it up like water, but like water it runneth through his fingers, and yet if his hands be but wet as though with dew, behold a generation of fools call out, 'See, he is a wise man.' Is it not so? But how call they thee? 'Baboon,' he says," and she laughed; "but that is the fashion of these savages who lack imagination, and fly to the beasts they resemble for a name. How do they call thee in thine own country, stranger?"

"They call me Holly, oh Queen," I answered.

"'Holly,'" *She* answered, speaking the word with difficulty, and yet with a most charming accent, "and what is 'Holly?'"

"'Holly' is a prickly tree," I said.

"So. Well, thou hast a prickly and yet a tree-like look. Strong art thou, and ugly, but, if my wisdom be not at fault, honest at the core, and a staff to lean on. Also one who thinks. But stay, Holly, stand not there, enter with me and be seated by me. I would not see thee crawl before me like those slaves. I am aweary of their worship and their terror; sometimes when they vex me I could blast them for very sport, and to see the rest turn white, even to the heart," and *She* held the curtain aside with her ivory hand to let me pass in.

I entered, shuddering. This woman was very terrible. Within the curtains was a recess, about twelve feet by ten, and in the recess was a couch and a table whereon stood fruit and sparkling water. By it at its end was a vessel like a font cut in carved stone, also full of pure water. The place was softly lit with lamps formed out of the beautiful vessels of which I have spoken, and the air and curtains were full of a subtle perfume. Perfume too seemed to emanate from the glorious hair and white clinging vestments of *She* herself. I entered the little room, and there stood uncertain.

"Sit," said *She*, pointing to the couch. "At present thou hast no cause to fear me. If thou hast cause, thou shalt not fear for long, for I shall slay thee. Therefore let thy heart be light."

I sat down on the end of the couch near to the font-like basin of water, and *She* sank down softly on to the other end.

"Now, Holly," she said, "how comest thou to speak Arabic? It is mine own dear tongue, for Arabian am I by my birth. Yet dost thou not speak it as we used to speak. Some of the words seemed changed, even as among these men. The Amahagger have debased and defiled its purity, so that I have to talk to them in what is to me another tongue."

"I have learnt it," I answered, "for many years. The language is spoken in Egypt and elsewhere."

"So it is still spoken, and there is yet an Egypt? And what Pharaoh sits upon the throne? Still one of the spawn of the Persian Ochus,[1] or are the Archæmenians gone?"

"The Persians have been gone from Egypt for nigh two thousand years, and since then the Ptolemies, the Romans, and many others have flourished and held sway upon the Nile, and fallen when their time was ripe," I said, aghast. "What canst thou know of the Persian Artaxerxes?"

She laughed, and made no answer, and again a cold chill went through me. "And Greece," she said; "is there still a Greece? Ah, I loved the Greeks. Beautiful were they as the day, and clever, but fierce at heart and fickle, notwithstanding."

---

[1] Persian king Ataxerxes III, representing the Achaemenian dynasty, who conquered and ruled Egypt as a pharaoh from 343–338 BCE (the Thirty-First Dynasty).

"Yes," I said, "there is a Greece; and, just now, it is once more a people.[1] Yet the Greeks of to-day are not what the Greeks of the old time were, and Greece herself is but a mockery of the Greece that was."

"So. The Hebrews, are they yet at Jerusalem? And does the Temple that the wise king built stand, and if so, what God do they worship therein? Is their Messiah come of whom they talked so much, and does He rule the earth?"

"The Jews are broken and gone, and the fragments of their people strew the world, and Jerusalem is no more. As for the temple that Herod built——"

"Herod?" she said. "I know not Herod. But go on."

"The Romans burnt it, and the Roman eagles flew across its ruins."[2]

"So, so! They were a great people, those Romans, and went straight to their end—ay, they sped to it like Fate, or like their own eagles on their prey!—and left peace behind them."

"Solitudinem faciunt, pacem appellant," I suggested.[3]

"Ah, thou canst speak the Latin tongue, too!" she said, in surprise. "It hath a strange ring in my ears after all these days, and it seems to me that thy accent does not fall as the Romans put it. Who was it wrote that? I know not the saying, but it is a true one of that great people. It seems that I have met a learned man—one whose hands have held the water of the world's knowledge. Knowest thou Greek also?"

"Yes, oh Queen, and something of Hebrew, but not to speak them. They are all dead languages now."

She clapped her hands in childish glee. "Of a truth, ugly tree that thou art, thou growest the fruits of wisdom. Oh, Holly," she said, "but of those Jews whom I hated, for they called me 'heathen' when I would have taught them my philosophy. Did their Messiah come, and doth He rule the world?"

"Their Messiah came," I answered with reverence; "but He came poor and lowly, and they would have none of Him. They scourged Him, and crucified Him upon a tree, but yet His words and His works live on, for He was the Son of God, and now of a truth He rules half the world, but not with an Empire of the World."

---

[1] In 1829, Greece had declared its independence from the Ottoman Empire.

[2] Ayesha is remembering the Temple of King Solomon (1 Kings 6), but Holly refers to Herod's later re-creation of it, which was destroyed by the Romans in 70 CE.

[3] The Latin phrase (from Tacitus' *Agricola*, written in 98 CE) means, "They make a solitude and call it peace."

"Ah, the fierce-hearted wolves," she said, "the followers of Sense and of many gods—greedy of gain and faction-torn. I can see their dark faces yet. So they crucified their Messiah? Well can I believe it. That He was a Son of the Living Spirit would be naught to them, if indeed He was so, and of that we will talk afterwards. They would care nought for any God if He came not with pomp and power. They, a chosen people, a vessel of Him they call Jehovah, ay, and a vessel of Baal, and a vessel of Astoreth,[1] and a vessel of the gods of the Egyptians—a high-stomached people greedy of aught that brought them wealth and power. So they crucified their Messiah because He came in lowly guise—and now are they scattered about the earth. Why, if I remember, so said one of their prophets that it should be. Well, let them go—they broke my heart, those Jews, and made me look with evil eyes across the world, ay, and drove me to this wilderness of a people that was before them. When I would have taught them wisdom in Jerusalem they stoned me, ay, at the Gate of the Temple those white-bearded hypocrites and rabbis hounded the people on to stone me! See, here is the mark of it to this day!" and with a sudden move she pulled up the gauzy wrapping on her rounded arm, and pointed to a little scar that showed red against its milky beauty.

I shrank back horrified.

"Pardon me, oh Queen!" I said, "but I am bewildered. Nearly two thousand years have rolled across the earth since the Jewish Messiah hung upon His cross at Golgotha. How then canst thou have taught thy philosophy to the Jews before He was? Thou art a woman, and no spirit. How can a woman live two thousand years? Why dost thou befool me, oh Queen?"

She leaned back upon the couch, and once more I felt the hidden eyes playing upon me and searching out my heart.

"Oh man!" she said at last, speaking very slowly and deliberately, "it seems that there are still things upon the earth of which thou knowest naught. Dost thou still believe that all things die, even as those very Jews believed? I tell thee that naught really dies. There is no such thing as Death, though there be a thing called Change. See," and she pointed to some sculptures on the rocky wall. "Three times two thousand years have passed since the last of the great race that hewed those pictures fell before the breath of the pestilence that destroyed them, yet are they not

---

[1] Phoenician god and goddess of life and fertility, whom the Jews would have regarded as false idols.

dead. E'en now they live; perchance their very spirits are drawn toward us now." She glanced round. "Of a surety it sometimes seems to me that my eyes can see them."

"Yes, but to the world they are dead."

"Ay, for a time; but even to the world are they born again and again. I, even I, Ayesha*—for that is my name, stranger—I say to thee that I wait now for one I loved to be born again, and here I tarry till he finds me, knowing of a surety that hither he will come, and that here, and here only, shall he greet me. Why, dost thou suppose that I, who am all powerful, I, whose loveliness is greater than the loveliness of the Grecian Helen,[1] of whom they used to sing, and whose wisdom is greater, ay, ten times more great than the wisdom of Solomon the Wise[2]—I, who know the secrets of the earth and its riches, and can turn all things to my uses,—I, who have even for a while overcome Change, that ye call Death,—why, I say, oh stranger, dost thou think that I herd here with barbarians lower than the beasts?"

"I know not," I said humbly.

"Because I wait for him I love. My life has perchance been evil, I know not—for who can say what is evil and what good?—so I fear to die even if I could die, which I cannot, to go and seek him where he is; for between us there might be a wall I could not climb, at least, I fear so. Surely easy would it be to lose the way in those great spaces wherein the suns wander on for ever. But the day will come, maybe when ten thousand more years have passed, and are lost and melted into the vault of Time, even as the little clouds melt into the gloom of night, when he shall be born again, and then, following a law that is stronger than any human plan, he will find me *here*, and of a surety his heart will soften towards me though I sinned against him; ay, even though he knows me not again, yet will he love me, if only for my beauty's sake."

For a moment I was dumbfounded, and could not answer. The matter was too overpowering for my intellect to grasp.

"But even so, oh Queen," I said at last, "even if we men be born again and again, that is not so with thee, if thou speakest truly." Here she looked up sharply, and once more I caught the flash of those hidden eyes; "Thou," I went on hurriedly, "who hast never died?"

---

* Pronounced Assha.—L.H.H.

---

[1] Helen, beautiful wife of the Greek king Menelaus, was taken by Paris of Troy, thus causing the Trojan War.
[2] King Solomon of Biblical history, renowned for his wisdom.

"'Tis so," she said; "and it is so because I have, half by chance and half by learning, solved one of the great secrets of the world. Tell me, stranger: life is—why therefore should not life be lengthened for a while? What are ten or twenty or fifty thousand years in the history of life? Why in ten thousand years scarce will the rain and storms lessen a mountain top by a span in thickness? In two thousand years these caves have not changed, nought has changed, but the beasts and man, who is as the beasts. There is nought that is wonderful about the matter, couldst thou but understand. Life is wonderful, ay, but that it should be a little lengthened is not wonderful. Nature hath her animating spirit as well as man, who is Nature's child, and he who can find that spirit, and let it breathe upon him, shall live with her life. He shall not live eternally, for Nature is not eternal, and she herself must die, even as the nature of the moon hath died. She herself must die, I say, or rather change and sleep till it be time for her to live again. But when shall she die? Not yet, I ween, and while she lives, so shall he who hath all her secret live with her. All I have it not, yet have I some, more perchance than any who were before me. Now, to thee I doubt not this thing is a great mystery, therefore I will not overcome thee with it now. Another time I will tell thee more if the mood be on me, though perchance I shall never speak of it again. Dost thou wonder how I knew that ye were coming, and so saved your heads from the hot pot?"

"Ay, oh Queen," I answered, feebly.

"Then gaze in the water," and she pointed to the font-like vessel, and then, bending forward, held her hand over it.

I rose and gazed, and instantly the water darkened. Then it cleared, and I saw as distinctly as I ever saw anything in my life—I saw, I say, our boat upon that horrible canal. There was Leo lying at the bottom asleep in it, with a coat thrown over him to keep off the mosquitoes, in such a fashion as to hide his face, and myself, Job, and Mahomed towing on the bank.

I started back aghast, and cried out that it was magic, for I recognised the whole scene—it was one that had actually occurred.

"No, no; oh, Holly," she answered, "it is no magic; that is a fiction of ignorance. There is no such thing as magic, though there is such a thing as a knowledge of the secrets of Nature. That is my glass; in it I see what passes if I care to summon up the pictures which is not often. In the water I can show thee what thou wilt of the past, if it be anything to do with this country and with what I have known, or anything that thou, the gazer, hast known. Think of a face if thou wilt, and it shall be reflected from thy mind upon the water. I know not all the secret yet—

I can read nothing in the future. But it is an old secret; I did not discover it. In Arabia and in Egypt the sorcerers knew it centuries ago. So one day I chanced to bethink me of that old canal—some twenty centuries since I sailed up it, and I was minded to look upon it again. And so I looked, and there I saw the boat and three men walking, and one, whose face I could not see, but a youth of a noble form, sleeping in the boat, and so I sent and saved ye. And now farewell. But stay, tell me of this youth—the Lion, as the old man calls him. I would look upon him, but he is sick, thou sayest—sick with the fever, and also wounded in the fray."

"He is very sick," I answered sadly; "canst thou do nothing for him, oh Queen! who knowest so much?"

"Of a surety I can. I can cure him; but why speakest thou so sadly? Dost thou love the youth? Is he perchance thy son?"

"He is my adopted son, oh Queen! Shall he be brought in before thee?"

"Nay. How long hath the fever taken him?"

"This is the third day."

"Good; then let him lie another day. Then will he perchance throw it off by his own strength, and that is better than that I should cure him, for my medicine is of a sort to shake the life in its very citadel. If, however, by to-morrow night, at that hour when the fever first took him, he doth not begin to mend, then will I come to him and cure him. Stay, who nurses him?"

"Our white servant, him whom Billali names the Pig; also," and here I spoke with some little hesitation, "a woman named Ustane, a very handsome woman of this country, who came and kissed him when first she saw him, and hath stayed by him ever since, as I understand is the fashion of thy people, oh Queen."

"My people! speak not to me of my people," she answered, hastily; "these slaves are no people of mine, they are but dogs to do my bidding till the day of my redemption comes; and, as for their customs, nought have I to do with them. Also, call me not Queen—I am sick of flattery and titles—call me Ayesha, the name hath a sweet sound in mine ears, it is an echo from the past. As for this Ustane, I know not. I wonder if it be she against whom I was warned, and whom I in turn did warn? Hath she? Stay, I will see;" and, bending forward, she passed her hand over the font of water and gazed intently into it. "See," she said, quietly, "is that the woman?"

I looked into the water, and there, mirrored upon its placid surface, was the silhouette of Ustane's stately face. She was bending forward, with a look of infinite tenderness upon her features, watching something beneath her, and with her chestnut locks falling on to her right shoulder.

"It is her," I said, in a low voice, for once more I felt much disturbed at this most uncommon sight. "She watches Leo asleep."

"Leo!" said Ayesha, in an absent voice; "why, that is 'lion' in the Latin tongue. The old man hath named happily for once. It is very strange," she went on, "very. So like—but it is not possible!" With an impatient gesture she passed her hand over the water once more. It darkened, and the image vanished silently and mysteriously as it had risen, and once more the lamplight, and the lamplight only, shone on the placid surface of that limpid, living mirror.

"Hast thou aught to ask me before thou goest, oh Holly?" she said, after a few moments' reflection. "It is but a rude life that thou must live here, for these people are savages, and know not the ways of cultivated man. Not that I am troubled thereby, for behold my food," and she pointed to the fruit upon the little table. "Nought but fruit doth ever pass my lips—fruit and a little water. I have bidden my girls to wait upon thee. They are mutes thou knowest, deaf are they and dumb, and therefore the safest of servants, save to those who can read their faces and their signs. I bred them so—it hath taken many centuries and much trouble; but at last I have succeeded. Once I succeeded before, but the race was too ugly, so I did away with it; but now, as thou seest, they are otherwise. Once, too, I bred a race of giants, but after a while Nature would no more of it, and it died away. Hast thou aught to ask of me?"

"Ay, one thing, oh Ayesha," I said boldly; but feeling by no means as bold as I trust I looked. "I would gaze upon thy face."

She laughed out in her bell-like notes. "Bethink thee, Holly," she answered; "bethink thee. It seems that thou knowest the old myths of the gods of Greece. Was there not one Actæon[1] who perished miserably because he looked on too much beauty? If I show thee my face, perchance thou wouldst perish miserably also; perchance thou wouldst eat out thy heart in impotent desire; for know I am not for thee—I am for no man, save one, who hath been, but is not yet."

"As thou wilt, Ayesha," I said. "I fear not thy beauty. I have put my heart away from such vanities as woman's loveliness that passes like a flower."

"Nay, thou errest," she said; "that does *not* pass. My beauty endures

---

[1]   In Greek myth, a young huntsman who, in punishment for watching the goddess Artemis as she bathed, was transformed into a stag and torn apart by his own dogs. Artemis was a virginal deity of archery and the hunt.

even as I endure; still if thou wilt, oh rash man, have thy will; but blame not me if passion mount thy reason, as the Egyptian breakers used to mount a horse, and guide it whither thou wilt not. Never may the man to whom my beauty has been unveiled put it from his mind, and therefore even with these savages do I go veiled, lest they vex me, and I should slay them. Say, wilt thou see?"

"I will," I answered, my curiosity overpowering me.

She lifted her white and rounded arms—never had I seen such arms before—and slowly, very slowly, withdrew some fastening beneath her hair. Then all of a sudden the long, corpse-like wrappings fell from her, and my eyes travelled up her form now only robed in a garb of clinging white that did but serve to show its perfect and imperial shape, instinct with a life that was more than life, and with a certain serpent-like grace that was more than human. On her little feet were sandals, fastened with studs of gold. Then came ankles more perfect than ever sculptor dreamed of. About the waist her white kirtle was fastened by a double-headed snake of solid gold, above which her gracious form swelled up in lines as pure as they were lovely, till the kirtle ended on the snowy argent of her breast, whereon her arms were folded. I gazed above them at her face, and—I do not exaggerate—shrank back blinded and amazed. I have heard of the beauty of celestial beings, now I saw it; only this beauty, with all its awful loveliness and purity, was *evil*—at least, at the time, it struck me as evil. How am I to describe it? I cannot—simply, I cannot! The man does not live whose pen could convey a sense of what I saw. I might talk of the great changing eyes of deepest, softest black, of the tinted face, of the broad and noble brow, on which the hair grew low, and delicate, straight features. But, beautiful, surpassingly beautiful as they all were, her loveliness did not lie in them. It lay rather, if it can be said to have any fixed abiding place, in a visible majesty, in an imperial grace, in a godlike stamp of softened power, that shone upon that radiant countenance like a living halo. Never before had I guessed what beauty made sublime could be—and yet, the sublimity was a dark one—the glory was not all of heaven—though none the less was it glorious. Though the face before me was that of a young woman in perfect health, and the first flush of ripened beauty, yet it had stamped upon it a look of unutterable experience, and of deep acquaintance with grief and passion. Not even the lovely smile that crept about the dimples of her mouth could hide this shadow of sin and sorrow. It shone even in the light of the glorious eyes, it was present in the air of majesty, and it seemed to say: "Behold me, lovely as no woman was or is, undying and half-divine; memory haunts me from age to age, and passion leads me by the hand—evil have I done, and with sorrow have I made acquaintance from age to age, and from age to age evil I shall do, and sorrow shall I know till my redemption comes."

Drawn by some magnetic force which I could not resist, I let my eyes rest upon her shining orbs, and felt a current pass from them to me that bewildered and half-blinded me.

She laughed—ah, how musically! and nodded her little head at me with an air of sublimated coquetry that would have done credit to a Venus Victrix.[1]

"Rash man!" she said; "like Actæon, thou hast had thy will; be careful lest, like Actæon, thou, too, dost perish miserably, torn to pieces by the ban-hounds[2] of thine own passions. I, too, oh Holly, am a virgin goddess, not to be moved of any man, save one, and it is not thou. Say, hast thou seen enough!"

"I have looked on beauty, and I am blinded," I said hoarsely, lifting my hand to cover up my eyes.

"So! what did I tell thee? Beauty is like the lightning; it is lovely, but it destroys—especially trees, oh Holly!"

Suddenly, she paused, and through my fingers I saw an awful change come over her countenance. Her great eyes suddenly fixed themselves into an expression in which horror seemed to struggle with some tremendous hope arising through the depths of her dark soul. The lovely face grew rigid, and the gracious, willowy form seemed to erect itself.

"Man," she half whispered, half hissed, throwing back her head like a snake about to strike, "man, where didst thou get that scarab on thy hand? Speak, or by the Spirit of Life I will blast thee where thou standest!" and she took one light step towards me, and from her eyes there shone such an awful light—to me it seemed almost like a flame—that I fell, then and there, on the ground before her, babbling confusedly in my terror.

"There," she said, with a sudden change of manner, and speaking in her former soft voice, "I did affright thee! Forgive me! But at times oh, Holly, the almost infinite mind grows impatient of the slowness of the very finite, and I am tempted to use my power out of sheer vexation— very nearly wast thou dead, but I remembered——. But the scarab— about the scarabæus!"

---

[1] "Venus Triumphant" (Latin), the Roman goddess of love as depicted in her conquering aspect.

[2] Supernatural hunting hounds summoned as part of a curse.

"When the lamps were held up I saw that it was nothing
but one vast charnel-house."

"I picked it up," I gurgled feebly, as I got on to my feet again, and it is a solemn fact that my mind was so disturbed that at the moment I could remember nothing else about the ring except that I picked it up in Leo's cave.

"It is very strange," she said, with a sudden access of woman-like trembling and agitation that seemed out of place in this awful woman—"but once I knew a scarab like that. It—hung round the neck—of one I loved," and she gave a little sob, and I saw that after all she was only a woman, although she might be a very old one.

"There," she went on, "it must be one like it. Also in old Egypt many there were who bore the name of the Royal son of Rā. The scarab that I knew was not set thus in the bezil of a ring. Go now, Holly, go, and, if thou canst, try to forget that thou hast looked upon Ayesha's beauty," and, turning from me, she flung herself on her couch, and buried her face in the cushions.

As for me, I stumbled from her presence, and I do not remember how I reached my own cave.

(*To be continued*)

PART 8 (20 NOVEMBER 1886)

XIV

A SOUL IN HELL

It was nearly ten o'clock at night when I cast myself down upon my bed, and began to gather my scattered wits, and reflect upon what I had seen and heard. But the more I reflected the less I could make of it. Was I mad, or drunk, or dreaming, or was I merely the victim of a gigantic and most elaborate hoax? How was it possible that I, a rational man, not unacquainted with the leading scientific facts of our history, and hitherto an absolute and utter disbeliever in all the hocus-pocus that in Europe goes by the name of the supernatural, could believe that I had within the last few minutes been engaged in conversation with a woman two thousand

and odd years old? The thing was contrary to the experience of human nature, and absolutely and utterly impossible. It must be a hoax, and yet, if it were a hoax, what was I to make of it? What, too, was to be said of the figures on the water, of the woman's extraordinary acquaintance with the remote past, and her ignorance, or apparent ignorance, of any subsequent history? What, too, of her wonderful and awful loveliness? That, at any rate, was a patent fact, and beyond the experience of the world. No merely mortal woman could shine with such a supernatural radiance. About that she had, at any rate, been in the right—it was not safe for any man to look upon such beauty. I was a hardened vessel in such matters, having, with the exception of one painful experience of my green and tender youth, put the softer sex (I sometimes think that this is a misnomer) almost entirely out of my thoughts. But now, to my intense horror, I *knew* that I could never put away the vision of those glorious eyes; and alas, the very *diablerie*[1] of the woman, whilst it horrified and repelled, attracted even in a greater degree. A person with the experience of two thousand years at her back, with the command of such tremendous powers and the knowledge of a mystery that could hold off death, was certainly worth falling in love with, if ever woman was. But, alas, it was not a question of whether or no she was worth it, for so far as I could judge, not being versed in such matters, I, a fellow of my college, noted for what my friends are pleased to call my misogyny, and a respectable man now well on in middle life, had fallen absolutely and hopelessly in love with this white sorceress. Nonsense; it must be nonsense! She had warned me fairly, and I had refused to take the warning. Curses on the fatal curiosity that is ever prompting man to draw the veil from woman, and curses on the natural impulse that begets it! It is the cause of half, ay, and more than half of our misfortunes. Why cannot man be content to live alone and be happy, and let the women live alone and be happy too? But perhaps they would not be happy, and I am not sure that we should either. Here was a nice state of affairs. I, at my age, to fall a victim to this modern Circe![2] But then she was not modern, at least she said not. She was almost as ancient as the original Circe.

I tore my hair, and jumped up off my couch, feeling that if I did not do something I should also go off my head. What did she mean about the scarabæus too? It was Leo's scarabæus, and had come out of the old

---

[1]   Devilishness, diabolism (French).
[2]   In Homer's *Odyssey*, a beautiful sorceress who seduces Odysseus and turns his crew into swine.

coffer that Vincey had left in my rooms nearly one-and-twenty years before. Could it be after all that the whole story was true, and the writing on the sherd was *not* a forgery, or the invention of some crack-brained, long-forgotten individual? And if so, could it be that *Leo* was the man that *She* was waiting for—the dead man who was to be born again! Impossible again! The whole thing was gibberish; who ever heard of a man being born again?

But if it were possible that a woman could exist for two thousand years, this might be possible also—anything might be possible. I myself might, for aught I knew, be a reincarnation of some other forgotten self, or perhaps the last of a long line of ancestral selves. Well, *vive la guerre,*[1] why not? Only, unfortunately, I had no recollection of these previous conditions. The idea was so absurd to me that I burst out laughing, and, addressing the sculptured picture of a grim-looking warrior on the cave wall, called out to him aloud, "Who knows, old fellow?—perhaps I was your contemporary. By Jove! perhaps I was you and you are I," and then I laughed again at my own folly, and the sound of it rang dismally along the vaulted roof, as though the ghost of the warrior had uttered the ghost of a laugh.

Next I bethought me that I had not been to see how Leo was, so, taking up one of the lamps that burnt away at my bedside, I slipped off my shoes and crept down the passage to the entrance of his cave. The draught of night air was lifting his curtain to and fro gently, as though spirit hands were drawing and re-drawing it. I slid into the vault-like apartment, and looked. There was a light by it, and Leo was lying on the couch, tossing restlessly in his fever, but asleep. By his side, half lying on the floor, half leaning against the stone couch, was Ustane. She held his hand in one of hers, but she, too, was dozing, and the two made a pretty or rather a pathetic picture. Poor Leo! his cheek was burning red, there were dark shadows beneath his eyes, and his breath came heavily. He was very, very ill; and again the horrible fear seized me that he might die, and I be left alone in the world. And yet if he lived he would perhaps be my rival with Ayesha; even if he were not the man, what chance should I, middle-aged and hideous, have against his bright youth and beauty? Well, thank heaven! my sense of right was not dead. *She* had not killed that yet; and, as I stood there, I prayed to the Almighty in my heart that my boy, my more than son, might live, ay, even if he proved to be the man.

---

[1] "Long live war" (French), here used to mean something like "what the hell."

Then I went back as softly as I had come, but still I could not sleep, the sight and thought of dear Leo lying there so ill had but added fuel to the fire of my unrest. My wearied body and overstrained mind had awakened all my imagination into preternatural activity. Ideas, visions, almost inspirations, floated before it with startling vividness. Most of them were grotesque enough, some were ghastly, some recalled thoughts and sensations that had for years been buried in the *débris* of my past life. But, behind and above them all, hovered the shape of that awful woman, and through them gleamed the memory of her entrancing loveliness. Up and down the cave I strode—up and down.

Suddenly I observed what I had not noticed before, that there was a narrow aperture in the rocky wall. I took up the lamp and examined it; the aperture led to a passage. Now, I was still sufficiently sensible to remember that it is not pleasant, in such a situation as ours was, to have passages running into one's bed-chamber from no one knows where. If there are passages, people can come up them; they can come up when one is asleep. Partly to see where it went to, and partly from a restless desire to be doing something, I followed the passage. It led to a stone stair, which I descended; the stair ended in another passage, or rather tunnel, also hewn out of the bed-rock, and running, so far as I could judge, exactly beneath the passage that led to the entrance of our rooms, and across the great central cave. I went on down it; it was as silent as the grave, but still, drawn by some sensation or attraction that I cannot describe, I followed on, my stockinged feet falling without noise on the smooth and rocky floor. When I had traversed some fifty yards of space, I came to another passage running at right angles, and here an awful thing happened to me: the sharp draught caught my lamp and extinguished it, leaving me in utter darkness in the bowels of that mysterious place. I took a couple of strides forward so as to clear the bisecting tunnel, being terribly afraid lest I should turn up it in the dark if once I got confused as to the direction, and then paused to think. What was I to do? I had no match; it seemed awful to attempt that long journey back through the utter gloom, and yet I could not stand there all night, and, if I did, probably it would not help me much, for in the bowels of the rock it would be as dark at midday as at midnight. I looked back over my shoulder—not a sight or a sound. I peered forward down the darkness: surely, far away I saw something like the faint glow of fire. Perhaps it was a cave where I could get a light—at any rate, it was worth investigating. Slowly and painfully, I crept along the tunnel, keeping my hand against its wall, and feeling at every step with my foot before I put it down, fearing lest I should fall into some pit. Thirty paces—there was a light, a flickering light shining through curtains! Fifty paces—it was close at hand! Sixty—oh, great heaven!

I was at the curtains, and they did not hang close, so I could see clearly into the little cavern beyond them. It had all the appearance of being a tomb, and was lit up by a fire that burnt in its centre with a whitish flame and without smoke. Indeed, there to the left, was a stone shelf with a little ledge to it three inches or so high, and on the shelf lay what I took to be a corpse; at any rate, it looked like one, with something white thrown over it. To the right was a similar shelf, on which lay some broidered coverings. Over the fire bent the figure of a woman; she was sideways to me and facing the corpse, wrapped in a dark mantle that hid her like a nun's cloak. She seemed to be staring at the flickering flame. Suddenly, as I was trying to make up my mind what to do, with a convulsive movement that somehow gave an impression of despairing energy, the woman rose to her feet and cast the dark cloak from her.

It was *She* herself!

She was clothed, as I had seen her when she unveiled, in the kirtle of clinging white, cut low upon her bosom, and bound in at the waist with the barbaric double-headed snake, and, as before, her rippling black hair fell in heavy masses down her back. But her face was what caught my eye, and held me as in a vice, not this time by the force of her beauty, but by the power of fascinated terror. The beauty was still there, indeed, but the agony, the blind passion, and the awful vindictiveness displayed upon those quivering features, and in the tortured look of the upturned eyes, were such as surpasses my powers of description.

For a moment she stood still, her hands raised high above her head, and as she did so the white robe slipped from her down to her golden girdle, baring the blinding loveliness of her form. She stood there, her fingers clenched, and the awful look of malevolence gathered and deepened on her face.

Suddenly, I thought of what would happen if she discovered me, and the reflection made me turn sick and faint. But, even if I had known that I must die if I stopped, I do not believe that I could have moved, for I was absolutely fascinated. But still I knew my danger. Supposing she should hear me, or see me through the curtain, supposing I even sneezed, or that her magic told her that she was being watched—swift indeed would be my doom. I should certainly be blasted.

Down came the clenched hands to her sides, then up again above her head, and, as I am a living and honourable man, the flame of the fire leapt up after them, almost to the roof, throwing a fierce and vivid glare upon *She* herself, upon the white figure beneath the covering, and every scroll and detail on the rockwork.

Down came the ivory arms again, and as they did so she spoke, or rather hissed, in Arabic, in a note that curdled my blood, and for a second stopped my heart.

"Curse her, may she be everlastingly accursed."

The arms fell and the flames sank. Up they went again, and the broad tongue of fire shot up after them; then again they fell.

"Curse her memory—accursed be the memory of the Egyptian."

Up again, and again down.

"Curse her, the fair daughter of the Nile, because of her beauty."
"Curse her, because her magic has prevailed against me."
"Curse her, because she kept my beloved from me."

And again the flame dwindled and shrank.
She put her hands before her eyes, and, stopping the hissing tone, cried aloud:—

"What is the use of cursing?—she prevailed, and she is gone."

Then she commenced again with an even more frightful energy.

"Curse her where she is. Let my curses reach her where she is and disturb her rest."
"Curse her through the starry spaces. Let her shadow be accursed."
"Let my power find her even there."
"Let her hear me even there. Let her hide herself in the blackness."
"Let her go down into the pit of despair, because I shall one day find her."

Again the flame fell, and again she covered her eyes with her hands.
"It is no use—no use," she wailed; "who can reach those who sleep? Not even I can reach them."
Then once more she began her unholy rites.

"Curse her when she shall be born again. Let her be born accursed."

"Let her be utterly accursed from the hour of her birth until sleep finds her."

"Yes, then, let her be accursed; for then shall I overtake her with my vengeance, and utterly destroy her."

And so on. The flame rose and fell, reflecting itself in her agonised eyes, the hissing sound of her terrible maledictions, and no words of mine, especially on paper, can convey how terrible they were, ran round the walls and died away in little echoes, and the fierce light and deep gloom alternated themselves on the white and dreadful form stretched upon that bier of stone.

But at length she seemed to wear herself out, and ceased. She sat herself down upon the rocky floor, and shook the dense cloud of her beautiful hair over her face and breast, and commenced to sob terribly in the torture of a heartrending despair.

"Two thousand years," she moaned; "two thousand years have I waited and endured; but though century doth still creep on to century, the sting of memory hath not lessened, the light of hope doth not shine more bright. Oh! to have lived two thousand years, with all my passion eating at my heart, and with my sin ever before me. Oh, that for me life cannot bring forgetfulness! Oh, for the weary years that have been and are yet to come, and still to come, endless and without end!

"My love! my love! my love! Why did that stranger bring thee back to me after this sort? For five hundred years I have not suffered thus. Oh, if I sinned against thee have I not wiped away the sin! When wilt thou come back to me who have all, and yet without thee have naught! What is there that I can do? What? What? What? And perchance she— perchance that Egyptian doth abide with thee where thou art, and doth mock my memory. Oh, why could I not die with thee, I who slew thee? Alas, that I cannot die! Alas! Alas!" and she flung herself prone upon the ground, and sobbed and wept till I thought her heart must burst.

Suddenly she ceased, raised herself to her feet, and tossing back her long locks impatiently, swept across to where the figure lay upon the stone.

"Oh Kallikrates," she cried, and I trembled at the name, "I must look upon thy face again, though it be agony. It is a generation since I looked upon thee whom I slew—slew with mine own hand," and with trembling fingers she seized the corner of the wrapping that lay over the form upon the stone bier, and then paused. When she spoke again, it was in a kind of awed whisper, as though her idea were terrible even to herself.

"Shall I raise thee," she said, apparently addressing the corpse, "so that thou standest there before me, as of old? I *can* do it," and she held out her hands over the sheeted dead, while her whole frame became rigid and terrible to see, and her eyes grew fixed and dull. I shrank in horror behind the curtain, my hair stood up upon my head, and, whether it was my imagination or a fact I am unable to say, but I thought that the quiet form beneath the covering began to quiver, and the winding sheet to lift as though it lay on the breast of one who slept. Suddenly she withdrew her hands.

"What is the use?" she said gloomily. "Of what use is it to recall the semblance of life when I cannot recall the spirit? Even if thou stoodest before me thou would'st not know me, and could'st but do what I bid thee. The life in thee would be *my* life, and not *thy* life, Kallikrates."

For a moment she stood there, and then cast herself down on her knees beside the form, and began to press her lips against the sheet, and weep. There was something so horrible about the sight of this fearsome woman letting loose her passion on the dead—so much more horrible even than anything that had gone before, that I could no longer bear to look at it, and, turning, commenced to creep, shaking as I was in every limb, slowly along the pitch-dark passage, feeling in my heart that I had a vision of a Soul in Hell.

On I stumbled, I scarcely know how. Twice I fell, once I turned up the bisecting passage, but fortunately found out my mistake in time. Twenty minutes or more I crept along, till at last it occurred to me that I must have passed the little stair by which I had descended. So utterly exhausted, and nearly frightened to death, I sank down at length there on the stone flooring, and sank into oblivion.

When I came to I noticed a faint ray of light in the passage just behind me. I crept to it, and found it was the little stair down which the weak dawn was stealing. Passing up it I gained my chamber in safety, and flinging myself on the couch, was soon lost in slumber, or rather stupor.

XV

AYESHA GIVES JUDGMENT

The next thing that I remember was opening my eyes and perceiving the form of Job, who had now practically recovered from his attack of fever. He was standing in the ray of light that pierced into the cave from the outer air, shaking out my clothes as a makeshift for brushing them, which he could not do because there was no brush, and then folding them up neatly and laying them on the foot of the stone couch. This done, he got my travelling dressing-case out of the Gladstone bag, and opened it ready for my use. First, he stood it on the foot of the couch also, then, being afraid, I suppose, that I should kick it off, he placed it on a leopard skin on the floor, and stood back a step or two to observe the effect. It was not satisfactory, so he shut up the bag, turned it on end, and, having rested it against the foot of the couch, placed the dressing-case on it. Next he looked at the pots full of water, which constituted our washing apparatus. "Ah!" I heard him murmur, "no hot water in this beastly place. I suppose these poor creatures only use it to boil each other in," and he sighed deeply.

"What is the matter, Job?" I said.

"Beg pardon, sir," he said, touching his hair. "I thought you were asleep, sir; and I am sure you look as though you want it. One might think from the look of you that you had been having a night of it."

I only groaned by way of answer. I had, indeed, been having a night of it, such as I hope never to have again.

"How is Mr. Leo, Job?"

"Much the same, sir. If he don't soon mend, he'll end, sir; and that's all about it; though I must say that that there savage, Ustane, do do her best for him almost like a baptised Christian. She is always hanging round and looking after him, and if I ventures to interfere, it's awful to see her; her hair seems to stand on end, and she curses and swears away in her heathen talk—at least I fancy she must be cursing, from the look of her."

"And what do you do then?"

"I make her a polite bow, and I say, 'Young woman, your position is one that I don't quite understand, and can't recognise. Let me tell you that I has a duty to perform to my master as is incapacitated by illness, and that I am going to perform it until I am incapacitated too,' but she don't take no heed, not she—only curses and swears away worse than ever. Last night she put her hand under that sort of nightshirt she wears and whips out a knife with a kind of a curl in the blade, so I whips out my revolver, and we walks round and round each other till at last she bursts out laughing. It isn't nice treatment for a Christian man to have to put up with from a savage, however handsome she may be, but it is what people must expect as is *fools* enough" (Job laid great emphasis on the "fools") "to come to such a place to look for things no man is meant to find. It's a judgment on us, sir—that's my opinion; and I, for one, is of opinion that the judgment isn't half done yet, and when it is done, we shall be done too, and just stop in these beastly caves with the ghosts and the corpses for once and all. And now, sir, I must be seeing about Mr. Leo's broth, if that wild cat will let me; and, perhaps, you would like to get up, sir, because it's past nine o'clock."

Job's remarks were not of a cheering order to a man who had passed such a night as I had; and, what is more, they had the weight of truth. Taking one thing with another, it appeared to me to be an utter impossibility that we should escape from the place we were. Supposing that Leo recovered, and supposing that *She* would let us go, which was exceedingly doubtful, and that she did not "blast" us in some moment of vexation, and that we were not hot-potted by the Amahagger, it would be quite impossible for us to find our way across the network of marshes which, stretching for scores and scores of miles, formed a stronger and more impassable fortification round the various Amahagger households than any that could be built or designed by man. No, there was but one thing to do—face it out; and, speaking for my own part, I was so intensely interested in the whole weird story that, so far as I was concerned, notwithstanding the shattered state of my nerves, I asked nothing better, even if my life paid forfeit to my curiosity. What man for whom physiology has charms could forbear to study such a character as that of this Ayesha when the opportunity of doing so presented itself? The very terror of the pursuit added to its fascination, and besides, as I was forced to own to myself even now in the sober light of day, she herself had attractions that I could not forget. Not even the dreadful sight which I had witnessed during the night could drive that folly from my mind; and alas! that I should have to admit it, it has not been driven thence to this hour.

After I had dressed myself I passed into the eating, or rather embalming chamber, and had some food, which was as before brought to me by the girl mutes. When I had finished I went and saw poor Leo, who was quite off his head, and did not even know me. I asked Ustane how she thought he was; but she only shook her head and began to cry a little. Evidently her hopes were small; and I then and there made up my mind that, if it were in any way possible, I would get *She* to come and see him. Surely she could cure him if she chose—at any rate she said she could. While I was in the room Billali entered, and also shook his head.

"He will die at night," he said.

"God forbid, my father," I answered, and turned away with a heavy heart.

"*She-who-must-be-obeyed* commands thy presence, my Baboon," said the old man as soon as we got to the curtain; "but, oh my dear son, be more careful. Yesterday I made sure in my heart that *She* would blast thee when thou didst not crawl upon thy stomach before her. *She* is sitting in the great hall to do justice upon those who would have smitten thee and the Lion. Come on, my son; come swiftly."

I turned, and followed him down the passage, and when we reached the great central cave, saw that many Amahagger, some robed, and some merely clad in the sweet simplicity of a leopard skin, were hurrying up it. We mingled with the throng, and walked up the enormous, and, indeed, almost interminable, cave. All the way up it the walls were elaborately sculptured, and every twenty paces or so passages opened out of it at right angles, leading, Billali told me, to tombs, hollowed in the rock by "the people who were before." Nobody visited those tombs now, he said; and I must say that my heart rejoiced when I thought of the opportunities of antiquarian research which opened out before me.

At last we came to the head of the cave, where there was a rock daïs almost exactly similar to the one on which we had been so furiously attacked, a fact that proved to me that these daïs must have been used as altars, probably for the celebration of religious ceremonies, and more especially of rites connected with the interment of the dead. On either side of this daïs were passages leading, Billali informed me, to other caves full of dead bodies. "Indeed," he added, "the whole mountain is full of dead, and nearly all of them are perfect."

In front of the daïs were gathered a great number of people of both sexes, who stood staring about in their peculiar gloomy fashion, which would have reduced Mark Tapley[1] himself to misery in about five minutes. On the daïs was a rude chair of black wood inlaid with ivory, having a seat made of grass fibre, and a footstool formed of a wooden slab attached to the chair.

Suddenly there was a cry of "Hiya! Hiya!" ("*She! She!*") and thereupon the entire crowd instantly precipitated itself upon the ground, and lay there as though it were individually and collectively stricken dead, leaving me standing up like some solitary survivor of a massacre. As they did so a long string of guards began to defile from a passage to the left, and ranged themselves on either side of the daïs. Then followed about a score of male mutes, then as many women mutes bearing lamps, and then a tall white figure, swathed from head to foot, in whom I recognised *She* herself. She mounted the daïs and sat down upon the chair, and spoke to

---

[1]   A character in Charles Dickens' novel *Martin Chuzzlewit* (1844) who is always extremely cheerful.

me in *Greek*, I suppose because she did not wish those present to understand what she said.

"Come hither, Holly," she said, "and sit at my feet, and see me do justice on those who would have slain thee. Forgive me if my Greek doth halt like a lame man; it is so long since I have heard the sound of it that my tongue is stiff, and will not bend to the words."

I bowed, and, mounting the daïs, sat down at her feet.

"How didst thou sleep, my Holly?" she asked.

"I slept not well, oh Ayesha!" I answered with perfect truth, and with an inward fear that perhaps she knew how I had passed the heart of the night.

"So," she said, with a little laugh, "I, too, have not slept well. Last night I had dreams, and methinks that thou did'st call them to me, oh Holly."

"Of what didst thou dream, Ayesha?" I asked, indifferently.

"I dreamed," she answered, quickly, "of one I hate and one I love," and then, as though to turn the conversation, she addressed the captain of her guard in Arabic. "Let the men be brought before me."

The captain bowed low, for the guard and her attendants did not prostrate themselves, but had remained standing, and departed with his underlings down a passage to the right.

Then came a silence. *She* leant her swathed head upon her hand and appeared to be lost in thought, while the multitude before her continued to grovel upon their stomachs, only screwing their heads round a little so as to get a view of us with one eye. It seemed that their Queen so rarely appeared in public that they were willing to undergo this inconvenience, and even graver risks, to have the opportunity of looking on her, or rather, on her garments, for no living man there except myself had ever seen her face. At last we caught sight of the waving of lights, and heard the tramp of men coming along the passage, and in filed the guard, and with them the survivors of our would-be murderers to the number of a score or more, on whose countenances the natural expression of sullenness struggled with the terror that evidently filled their savage hearts. They were ranged in front of the daïs, and would have cast themselves down on the floor of the cave like the spectators, but *She* stopped them.

"Nay," she said in her softest voice, "stand; I pray ye stand. Perchance the time will soon be when ye shall grow weary of being stretched out," and she laughed melodiously.

I saw a cringe of terror run along the rank of the doomed wretches, and, wicked villains as they were, I felt sorry for them. Some minutes, perhaps two or three, passed before anything fresh occurred, during which

She appeared from the movement of her head—for, of course, we could not see her eyes—to be slowly and carefully examining each delinquent. At last she spoke, addressing herself to me in a quiet and deliberate tone.

"Dost thou, oh my guest, who art known in thy country by the name of the Prickly Tree, recognise these men?"

"Ay, oh Queen, nearly all of them," I said, and I saw them glower at me as I said it.

"Then tell me, and this company, the tale whereof I have heard."

Thus abjured, I, in as few words as I could, related the history of the cannibal feast, and of the torture of our poor servant.

The narrative was received in perfect silence, both by the accused and by the audience, and also by *She* herself. When I had done, Ayesha called upon Billali by name, and, lifting his head from the ground, but without rising, the old man confirmed my story. No further evidence was taken.

"Ye have heard," said *She* at length, in a cold, clear voice, very different from her usual tones—indeed, it was one of the most remarkable things about this extraordinary creature, that her voice had the power of suiting itself in a wonderful manner to the mood of the moment. "What have ye to say, ye rebellious children, why vengeance should not be done upon ye?"

For some time there was no answer, but, at last, one of the men, a fine, broad-chested fellow, well on in middle-life, with deep-graven features and an eye like a hawk's, spoke, and said that the orders that they had received were not to harm the white men; nothing was said of their black servant, so, egged on thereto by a woman who was now dead, they proceeded to hot-pot him after the ancient and honourable custom of their country, with a view of eating him in due course. As for their attack upon ourselves, it was made in an access of sudden fury, and they deeply regretted it. He ended by humbly praying that mercy might be extended to them; or, at least, that they might be banished into the swamps, to live or die as it might chance; but I saw on his face that he had but little hope of mercy.

Then came a pause, and the most intense silence reigned over the whole scene, which, illuminated as it was by the flickering lamps that struck out broad patterns of light and shadow upon the rocky walls, was as strange a one as I ever saw, even in that weird land. Upon the ground before the daïs were stretched scores of forms of the spectators, till at last the long lines of them were lost in the gloomy background. Before the outstretched audience were the knots of evildoers, trying to cover up their natural terrors with a brave appearance of unconcern. On the right and left were the guards, robed in white and armed with great spears and daggers, and the men and women mutes watching with hard, curious eyes. Then, seated in her barbaric chair above them all, with myself at her feet, was the veiled white woman, whose loveliness and awesome power seemed to shine about her like a halo, or rather like the glow from some unseen light. Never have I seen her veiled shape look more terrible than it did in that space, while she gathered herself up as it were for vengeance.

At last it came.

"Dogs and serpents," *She* began in a low voice that gradually gathered power as she went on, till the place rang with it. "Eaters of human flesh, two things have ye done. First ye have attacked these strangers, being white men, and have slain their servant, and for that alone death is your reward. But that is not all. Ye have dared to disobey me. Did I not send my word unto ye by Billali, my servant, and the father of your household? Did I not bid ye to hospitably entertain these strangers, whom now ye have striven to slay, and whom, had not they been brave and strong beyond the strength of men, ye would cruelly have murdered? Hath it not been taught to ye from childhood that the law of *She* is an ever fixed law, and that he who breaketh it by so much as one jot or tittle[1] shall perish? And is not my lightest word a law? Have not your fathers taught ye this, I say, whilst as yet ye were but children? Do ye not know that as well might ye bid these great caves to fall upon ye, or the sun to cease his journeying, as to hope to turn me from my courses, or make my word light or heavy, according to your minds. Well do ye know it, ye Wicked Ones. But ye are all evil—evil to the core—the wickedness bubbles up in ye like a fountain in the spring time. Were it not for me, generations since had ye ceased to be, for of your own evil way had ye destroyed each other. And now because ye have done this thing, because ye have striven to put these men, my guests, to death, and yet more because ye have dared to disobey my word, this is the doom that I doom ye to. That ye be taken to the cave of torture,* and given over

---

* "The cave of torture." I afterwards saw this dreadful place, also a legacy from the prehistoric people who lived in Kôr. The only objects in the cave itself were slabs of rock arranged in various positions to facilitate the operations of the torturers. Many of these slabs, which were of a porous stone, were stained quite dark with the blood of ancient victims that had soaked into them. Also in the centre of the room was a place for a furnace, with a cavity to heat the historic pot in. But the most dreadful thing about the cave was that over each slab was a sculptured illustration of the appropriate torture being applied. These sculptures were so awful that I will not harrow the reader by attempting a description of them.—L.H.H.

[1] Little bit. The phrase recalls Jesus' words in Matthew 5:18.

to the torturers to wreak their will upon ye, and that on the going down of to-morrow's sun, those of ye who yet remain alive be slain by the hot pot, as ye have slain the servant of this my guest."

She ceased, and a faint murmur of horror ran round the cave. As for the victims, as soon as they realised the full hideousness of their doom, their stoicism forsook them, and they flung themselves down upon the ground, and wept and implored for mercy in a way that was dreadful to behold. I, too, turned to Ayesha, and begged her to spare them, or at least to mete out their fate in some less awful way. But she was hard as adamant about it.

"My Holly," she said, again speaking in Greek, which, to tell the truth, although I have always been considered as good a scholar of the language as most, I found it rather difficult to follow, chiefly because of the change in the fall of the accent. Ayesha, of course, talked with the accent of her contemporaries, whereas we have only tradition and the modern accent to guide us as to the exact pronunciation: "My Holly, it cannot be. Were I to show mercy to those wolves, your lives would not be safe among this people for a day. Thou knowest them not. They are tigers to lap blood, and even now they hunger after your lives. How thinkest thou that I rule this people? I have but a regiment of guards to do my bidding, therefore it is not by force. It is by terror. My empire is a moral one. Once in a generation mayhap I do as I am doing now, and slay a score by torture. Believe not that I would be cruel, or take vengeance on anything so low. What can it profit me to be avenged on such as these? Those who live long, my Holly, have no passions, save where they have interests. Though I may seem to slay in wrath, or because my mood is crossed, it is not so. Thou hast seen how in the heavens the little clouds blow this way and that without a cause, yet behind them is the great wind sweeping on its path whither it listeth. So it is with me, oh Holly. My moods and changes are the little clouds, and fitfully these seem to turn; but behind them ever blows the great wind of my wise purpose. Nay, the men must die; and die as I have said." Then, suddenly turning to the captain of the guard:

"My word is spoken—let my doom be done."

XVI

THE TOMBS OF KÔR

After the prisoners had been removed, Ayesha waved her hand, and the spectators turned round, and began to crawl off down the cave like a scattered flock of sheep. When they got a fair distance from the daïs, however, they rose and walked away, leaving the Queen and myself alone, with the exception of the mutes and a few guards, most of latter having departed with the doomed men. Thinking this a good opportunity, I asked *She* to come and see Leo, telling her of his serious condition, but she would not, saying that he certainly would not die before the night, as people never died of that sort of fever except at nightfall or dawn. Also she said that it would be better to let the fever spend its course as much as possible before she cured it. Accordingly, I was rising to leave, when she bade me follow her, as she would talk with me, and show me the wonders of the caves.

I was too much involved in the web of her fatal fascinations to say her no, even if I had wished to, which I did not. She rose from her chair, and, making some signs to the mutes, descended from the daïs. Thereon four of the girls took lamps, and ranged themselves two in front and two behind us, but the others went away.

"Now," she said, "wouldst thou see some of the wonders of this place, oh Holly? Look upon this great cave. Saw ye ever the like? Yet was it, and many more like it, hollowed by the hands of the dead race that once lived here in the city on the plain. A great and wonderful people must they have been, these men of Kôr, but, like the Egyptians, they thought more of the dead than the living. How many men, think ye, working for how many years, did it require to hollow out this cave and all the galleries thereof?"

"Tens of thousands," I answered.

"So, oh Holly. This people was an old people before the Egyptians were. A little can I read of their inscriptions, having found the key thereto—and, see here, this was one of the last of the caves that they dug," and turning to the rock behind her, she motioned the mutes to hold up the lamps. Carven over the daïs was the figure of an old man seated in a chair, with an ivory rod in his hand. It struck me at once that his features were exceedingly like those of the man who was represented as being embalmed in the chamber where we took our meals. Beneath the chair, which, by the way, was shaped exactly like the one in which Ayesha had sat to give judgment, was a short inscription in the extraordinary characters of which I have already spoken, but which I do not remember sufficient of to illustrate. It looked more like Chinese writing than any other that I am acquainted with. This inscription Ayesha proceeded, with some difficulty and hesitation, to read aloud and translate. It ran as follows:—

In the year four thousand two hundred and fifty-nine from the founding of the City of Imperial Kôr was this cave (or burial place) completed by Tisno, King of Kôr, the people thereof and their slaves having laboured thereat for three generations, to be a tomb for their citizens of rank who shall come after. May the blessing of the heaven above the heaven rest upon their work, and make the sleep of Tisno, the mighty monarch, the likeness of whose features is graven above, a sound and happy sleep till the day of awakening,* and also the sleep of his servants, and of those of his race who, rising up after him, shall yet lay their heads as low.

"Thou seest, oh Holly," she said, "this people founded the city, of which the ruins yet cumber the plain yonder, four thousand years before this cave was finished. Yet, when first I saw it, two thousand years ago, was it even as it is now. Judge, therefore, how old must the place have been! And now, follow thou me, and I will show thee after what fashion this great city fell when the time was come for it to fall," and she led the way down to the centre of the cave, and stopped at a spot where a round rock had been let into a sort of large manhole in the flooring, accurately filling it just as the iron plates fill the spaces in the London pavements down which the coals are thrown. "Thou seest," she said. "Tell me, what is it?"

"Nay, I know not," I answered; whereon she crossed to the left-hand side of the cave (looking towards the entrance) and bid the mutes hold up the lamps. On the wall, something was painted with a red pigment in similar characters to those hewn beneath the sculpture of Tisno, King of Kôr. This she proceeded to translate to me, the pigment still being quite fresh enough to show the form of the letters.

"I, Junis, a priest of the Great Temple of Kôr, write this upon the rock in the year four thousand eight hundred and three from the founding of Kôr. Kôr is fallen. No more shall the mighty feast in her halls, no more shall she rule the world, and her navies go out to commerce with the

---

* This phrase is remarkable, as seeming to indicate a belief in a future state.—EDITOR.

world. Kôr is fallen, and her mighty works and all the cities of Kôr, and all the harbours that she built and the canals that she made, are for the wolf and the owl and the wild swan, and the barbarian who comes after. Twenty and five moons ago did a cloud settle upon Kôr, and the hundred cities of Kôr, and out of the cloud came a pestilence that slew her people, old and young, one with another, and spared not. One with another they turned black and died—the young and the old, the rich and the poor, the man and the woman, the prince and the slave. The pestilence slew and slew, and ceased not by day or by night, and those who escaped from the pestilence were slain of the famine. No longer could the bodies of the children of Kôr be preserved according to the ancient rites, because of the number of the dead, therefore were they hurled into the great pit beneath the cave through the hole in the cave. Then, at last, a remnant of this the great people, the light of the whole world, went down to the coast and took ship and sailed northwards; and now am I, the Priest Junis, who write this, the last man left alive of this great city of men, but whether there be any yet left in the other cities I know not. This do I write in misery of heart before I die, because Kôr the Imperial is no more, and because there are none to worship in her temple, and all her palaces are empty, and her princes and her traders and her fair women have passed off the face of the earth."

I gave a sigh of astonishment,—the utter desolation depicted in this rude scrawl was so overpowering. It was terrible to think of this solitary survivor of a mighty people recording its fate before he, too, went down into darkness. What must the old man have felt as, in ghastly terrifying solitude, by the light of one lamp feebly illuminating a little space of gloom, he in a few brief lines daubed the history of his nation's death upon the cavern wall? What a subject for the moralist, or the painter, or indeed for any one who can think!

"Doth it not occur to thee, oh Holly," said Ayesha, laying her hand upon my shoulder, "that those men who sailed North may have been the fathers of the first Egyptians?"

"Nay, I know not," I said; "it seems that the world is very old."

"Old?—Yes, it is old indeed. Time after time have nations, ay, and rich and strong nations, learned in all the arts, been and passed away and been forgotten, so that no memory of them remains. This is but one of many; for Time eats up the works of man, unless, indeed, he digs in caves like the people of Kôr, and then mayhap the sea swallows them, or the earthquake shakes them in. Who knows what hath been on the earth, or what shall be? There is no new thing under the sun, as the wise Hebrew wrote long ago.[1] Yet were not these people utterly destroyed, as I think. Some few remained in the other cities, for their cities were many. But the barbarians, or perchance my people, the Arabs, came down upon them, and took their women to wife, and the race of the Amahagger that now is is a bastard brood of the mighty sons of Kôr, and behold it dwelleth in the tombs with its fathers' bones. But I know not: who can know? My arts cannot pierce so far into the blackness of Time's night. A great people were they. They conquered till none were left to conquer, and then they dwelt at ease within their rocky mountain walls, with their man servants and their maid servants, their minstrels, their sculptors, and their concubines, and traded and quarrelled, and ate and hunted and slept and made merry, till their time came. But come, I will show thee the great hall beneath the cave whereof the writing speaks. Never shall thine eyes witness such another sight."

Accordingly I followed her on to a side passage opening out of the main cave, then down a great number of steps, and along an underground shaft that cannot have been less than sixty feet beneath the surface of the rock, and was ventilated by curious borings that ran upward, I do not know where. Suddenly the passage ended, and she halted, and bid the mutes hold up the lamps, and I saw such a scene as she had prophesied I was not likely to see again. We were standing in an enormous pit, or rather on the edge of it, for it went down deeper— I don't know how much—than where we were, and was edged in with a low wall of rock. So far as I could judge, the pit was about the size of the space beneath the dome of St. Paul's, and when the lamps were held up I saw that it was nothing but one vast charnel-house, being literally full of thousands of human skeletons, which lay piled up in an enormous gleaming pyramid, formed by the slipping down of the bodies from the apex as fresh ones were dropped in from above. Anything more appalling than this jumbled mass of the remains of a departed race I cannot imagine, and what made it even more dreadful was that in this dry air a good number of the bodies had simply become desiccated with the skin on them, and now, fixed in every conceivable position, stared at one out of the heaps of white bones, grotesquely horrible caricatures of humanity. In my astonishment I made an ejaculation, and the echoes of my voice ringing in the vaulted place disturbed a skull that had been accurately balanced for many thousands of years near the apex of the pile. Down it came with a run, bounding along merrily towards

---

[1] King Solomon; see Ecclesiastes 1:9.

"Next second her tall and willowy form was staggering back across the room."

us, and of course bringing an avalanche of other bones after it, till at last the whole place rattled with their movement, as though the skeletons were getting up to greet us.

(*To be continued*)

PART 9 (27 NOVEMBER 1886)

CHAPTER XVI (*CONTINUED*)

"Come," I said, "I have seen enough. These are the bodies of those who died of the great sickness, I suppose?" I added, as we turned away.

"Yes. The people of Kôr always embalmed their dead, like the Egyptians, but their art is greater than the art of the Egyptians, because whereas the Egyptians disembowelled and drew the brain, the people of Kôr injected fluid into the veins, and thus reached every part. But stay, thou shalt see," and she halted at haphazard at one of the little doorways opening out of the passage along which we were walking, and motioned to the mutes to light us in. We entered into a little chamber similar to the one in which I had slept at our first stopping-place, only there were two stone benches or beds in it. On the benches lay figures covered with yellow linen,* on which a fine and impalpable dust had gathered in the course of ages, but nothing like to the extent that one would have anticipated, for in these deep-hewn caves there was no material to turn to dust. About the bodies on the stone shelves and floor of the tomb were many painted vases, but I saw very few ornaments in any of the vaults.

"Lift the cloth up, oh Holly," she said, but though I put out my hand to do so I drew it back again. It seemed like sacrilege, and to speak the truth I was awed by the dread solemnity of the place, and of the presences before us. Then with a little laugh at my fears she drew it herself, only to

---

* All the linen that the Amahagger wore was taken from the tombs, which accounted for its yellow hue. If it was well washed, however, and properly bleached, it acquired its former snowy whiteness, and was the softest and best linen I ever saw.—L.H.H.

discover another and yet finer cloth lying over the forms upon the stone bench. This also she withdrew, and then for the first for thousands upon thousands of years did living eyes look upon the faces of those chilly dead. It was a woman; she might have been thirty-five years of age, or perhaps a little less, and had certainly been beautiful. Even now her calm clear-cut features, marked out with delicate black eyebrows and long eyelashes that threw little lines of shadow from the lamp upon the ivory face, were wonderfully beautiful. There robed in white, down which her blue-black hair was streaming, she slept her last long sleep, and on her arm, its face pressed against her breast, there lay a little babe. So sweet was the sight, although so awful, that—I confess it without shame—I could scarcely withhold my tears. It took one back across the dim gulf of the ages to some happy home in dead Imperial Kôr, where this winsome lady girt about with beauty had lived and died, and dying taken her last-born with her to the tomb. There they were, mother and babe, the white memories of a forgotten human history speaking more eloquently to the heart than could any written record of their lives. Reverently I replaced the grave cloths, and with a sigh that flowers so fair, should, in the purpose of the Everlasting, have only bloomed to be gathered to the grave, I turned to the body on the opposite shelf, and gently unveiled it. It was that of a man in advanced life, with a long grizzled beard, and also robed in white, prob-ably the husband of the lady who, after surviving her many years, came at the last to sleep once more for good and all beside her.

We left the place and entered others. It would be too long to describe the many things I saw in them. Each one had its occupants, for the five hundred and odd years that had elapsed between the completion of the cave and the destruction of the race had evidently sufficed to fill these catacombs, numberless as they were, and each appeared to have been undisturbed since the day that they were laid there. I could fill a book with the description of them, but to do so would only be to repeat what I have said, with variations.

Nearly all the bodies, so masterly was the art with which they had been treated, were as perfect as on the day of death thousands of years before. Nothing came to injure them in the deep silence of the living rock: they were beyond the reach of heat and cold and damp, and the aromatic drugs with which they had been saturated were evidently practically everlasting in their effect. Here and there, however, we saw an exception, and in these cases, although the flesh looked sound enough externally, if one touched it it fell in, and revealed the fact that the figure was but a pile of dust.

This arose, Ayesha told me, from these particular bodies having, either owing to haste in the burial or other causes, been soaked in the preservative,* instead of its being injected into the substance of the flesh. About the last tomb we visited I must, however, say one word, for its contents spoke even more eloquently to one's human sympathies than those of the first. It had but two occupants, and they lay together on a single shelf. I withdrew the grave cloths, and, there clasped heart to heart, were a young man and a blooming girl. Her head rested on his arm, and his lips were pressed against her brow. I opened the man's linen robe, and there over his heart was a dagger-wound, and beneath the girl's fair breast was a like cruel stab, through which her life had ebbed away. On the rock above was an inscription in three words. Ayesha translated it. It was *Wedded in Death*.

What was the life-history of these two, who, of a truth, were beautiful in their lives, and in their death were not divided?[1]

I closed my eyelids, and imagination taking up the thread of thought shot its swift shuttle[2] back across the ages, weaving a picture on their blackness so real and vivid in its details that I could almost for a moment think that I had triumphed o'er the Past, and that my spirit's eyes had pierced Time's mystery.

I seemed to see this fair girl's form—the yellow hair streaming down her, glittering against her garments snowy white, and the bosom that was whiter than the robes, even dimming with its lustre her ornaments of burnished gold. I seemed to see the great cave filled with warriors, bearded and clad in mail, and, on the lighted daïs where Ayesha had given judgment, a man standing, robed, and surrounded by the symbols of his priestly office. And up the cave there came one clad in purple,

---

* Ayesha afterwards showed me the tree from the leaves of which this ancient preservative was manufactured. It is a low bush-like tree, that to this day grows in wonderful plenty upon the sides of the mountains, or rather upon the slopes leading up to the rocky walls. The leaves are long and narrow, a vivid green in colour, but turning a bright red in the autumn, and not unlike those of a laurel in general appearance. They have no smell when green, but if boiled the aromatic odour from them is so strong that one can hardly bear it. The best mixture, however, was made from the roots, and among the people of Kôr there was a law, which Ayesha showed me alluded to on some of the inscriptions, to the effect that under heavy penalties no one under a certain rank was to be embalmed with the drugs prepared from the roots. The object and effect of this was, of course, to preserve the trees from extermination. The sale of the leaves and roots was a Government monopoly, and from it the Kings of Kôr derived a large proportion of their private revenue.—L.H.H

[1]   A reference to Saul and Jonathan in the Old Testament. See 2 Samuel 1:23.
[2]   The device that passes thread through the warp as it moves across a weaving-loom.

and before him and behind him came minstrels and fair maidens, chanting a wedding song. White stood the maid against the altar, fairer than the fairest there—purer than a lily, and more cold than the dew that glistens in its heart. But as the man drew near she shuddered. Then out of the press and throng there sprang a dark-haired youth, and put his arm about her—this long-forgotten maid—and kissed her pale face, in which the blood shot up like lights of the red dawn across the quiet sky. And next there was turmoil and uproar, and a flashing of swords, and they tore the youth from her arms, and stabbed him, but with a cry she snatched the dagger from his belt, and drove it into her snowy breast, home to the heart, and down she fell, and then, with cries and wailing, and every sound of lamentation, the pageant rolled away from the arena of my vision, and once more the past shut up its book.

Let him who reads this forgive the intrusion of a dream into a history of fact. But it came so home to me—I saw it all so clear in a moment, as it were; and, besides, who shall say what proportion of fact, past, present, or to come, may lie in imagination? What is imagination? Perhaps it is the shadow of the intangible truth, perhaps it is the soul's thought.

In a moment the whole thing had passed through my brain, and *She* was addressing me.

"Behold the lot of man," said the veiled Ayesha, as she drew the winding sheets back over the dead lovers, speaking in a solemn, thrilling voice, that accorded well with the dream that I had dreamed, "to the tomb, and to the forgetfulness that hides the tomb, must we all come at last! Ay, even I who live so long. Even for me, oh Holly, thousands upon thousands of years hence; thousands of years after thou hast gone through the gate and been lost in the mists, a day will dawn whereon I shall die, and be even as thou art and these are. And then what will it matter that I have lived a little longer, holding off death by the knowledge I have wrung from Nature, since at last I, too, must die? What is a span of ten thousand years, or ten times ten thousand years, in the history of time? It is as nought—it is as the mists that roll up in the sunlight; it fleeth away like an hour of sleep or a breath of the Eternal Spirit. Behold the lot of man! Certainly it shall overtake us, and we shall sleep. Certainly, too, we shall awake, and live again, and again shall sleep, and so on and on, through periods, spaces, and times, from æon unto æon, till the world is dead, and the worlds beyond the worlds are dead, and nought liveth save the Spirit that is Life. But for us twain and for these dead ones shall the end of ends be Life, or shall it be Death? As yet Death is but Life's Night, but out of the night is the Morrow born again, and doth again beget the

Night. Only when Day and Night, and Life and Death, are ended and swallowed up in that from which they came, what shall be our fate, oh Holly? Who can see so far? Not even I!"

And then, with a sudden change of tone and manner,

"Hast thou seen enough, my stranger guest, or shall I show thee more of the wonders of these tombs that are my palace halls? If thou wilt, I can lead thee to where Tisno, the mightiest and most valorous King of Kôr, in whose day these caves were ended, lies in a pomp that seems to mock at nothingness, and bid the empty shadows of the past do homage to his sculptured vanity!"

"I have seen enough, oh Queen," I answered. "My feeble breast is overwhelmed by the strength of the present Death. Mortality is weak, and easily broken down by a sense of the companionship that waits upon its end. Take me hence, oh Ayesha!"

XVII

THE BALANCE TURNS

In a few minutes, following the lamps of the mutes, that, held out from the body as a bearer holds water in a vessel, had the appearance of float-ing down the darkness by themselves, we came to a stair which led us to *She*'s ante-room, the same that Billali had crept up upon on all fours on the previous day. Here I would have bade the Queen adieu, but she would not.

"Nay," she said, "enter with me, oh Holly, for of a truth thy conver-sation pleaseth me. Think, oh Holly: for two thousand years have I had none to converse with save slaves and my own thoughts, and though of all this thinking hath much wisdom come, and many secrets been made plain, yet am I weary of my thoughts, and have come to loathe mine own society, for surely the food that memory gives to eat is bitter to the taste, and it is only with the teeth of hope that we can bear to bite it. Now though thy thoughts are green and tender, as becometh one so young, yet are they those of a thinking brain, and in truth thou dost bring back to my mind certain of those old philosophers with whom in days bygone I have disputed at Athens and in Arabia, for thou hast the same crabbed air and dusty look as though thou hadst passed thy days in reading ill-writ Greek, and been stained dark with the grime of manuscripts. So draw the curtain, and sit here by my side, and we will eat fruit, and talk of pleasant things. See, I will again unveil to thee. Thou hast brought it on thyself, oh Holly; fairly have I warned thee, and thou shalt call me beautiful as even those old philosophers were wont to do. Fie upon them, forgetting their philosophy!"

And without more ado she stood up and shook the white wrappings from her, and came forth shining and splendid like some glittering snake when she has cast her slough; ay, and fixed her wonderful eyes upon me—more deadly than any basilisk's[1]—and pierced me through and through with their beauty, and sent her light laugh ringing through the air like chimes of silver bells.

A new mood was on her, and the very colour of her mind seemed to change beneath it. It was no longer torture-torn and hateful, as I had seen it when she was cursing her dead rival by the leaping flames, no longer icily terrible as in the judgment-hall, no longer rich, and sombre, and splendid, like a Tyrian[2] cloth, as in the dwellings of the dead. No, her mood now was that of Aphrodité triumphing. Life—radiant, ecstatic, wonderful—seemed to flow from her and around her. Softly she laughed and sighed, and swift her glances flew. She shook her heavy tresses, and their perfume filled the place; she struck her little sandalled foot upon the floor, and hummed a snatch of some old Greek epithalamium. All the majesty was gone, or did but lurk and faintly flicker through her laughing eyes, like lightning seen through sunlight. She had cast off the terror of the leaping flame, the cold power of judgment that was even now being done, and the wise sadness of the tombs—cast them off and put them behind her, like the white shroud she wore, and now stood out the incarnation of lovely tempting womanhood, made more perfect—and in a way more spiritual—than ever woman was before.

"There, my Holly, sit there where thou canst see me. It is by thine own wish, remember—again I say, blame me not if thou dost spend the rest of thy little span with such a sick pain at the heart that thou wouldst fain have died before ever thy curious eyes were set upon me. There, sit so, and tell me, for in truth I am inclined for praises—tell me, am I not beautiful? Nay, speak not so hastily; consider well the point; take me feature by feature, forgetting not my form, and my hands and feet, and my hair, and the whiteness of my skin, and then tell me truly hast thou ever known a woman who in aught, ay, in one little portion of her beauty, in the curve of an eyelash even, or the modelling of a shell-like

---

[1] A mythological creature whose gaze kills its victims.
[2] A rich purple dye from the ancient Phoenician city of Tyre.

ear, is justified to hold a light before my loveliness? Now, my waist! Perchance thou thinkest it too large, but of a truth it is not so; it is this golden snake that is too large, and doth not bind it as it should. It is a wise snake, and knoweth that it is ill to tie in the waist. But see, give me thy hands—so—now press them round me, there, with but a little force, thy fingers touch, oh Holly."

I could stand it no longer. I am but a man, and she was more than a woman. Heaven knows what she was—I don't! But then and there I fell upon my knees before her, and told her in a sad mixture of languages—for such moments confuse the thoughts—that I worshipped her as never woman was worshipped, and that I would give my immortal soul to marry her, which at that time I certainly would have done, and so, indeed, would any other man, or all the race of men rolled into one. For a moment she looked a little surprised, and then she began to laugh, and clap her hands in glee.

"Oh, so soon, oh Holly!" she said. "I wondered how many minutes it would take to bring thee to thy knees. I have not seen a man kneel before me for so many days, and, believe me, to a woman's heart the sight is sweet, ay, wisdom and length of days take not from that dear pleasure which is our sex's only right.

"What wouldst thou?—what wouldst thou? Thou dost not know what thou doest. Have I not told thee that I am not for thee? I love but one, and it is not thee. Ah Holly, for all thy wisdom—and in a way thou art wise—thou art but a fool running after folly. Thou wouldst look into mine eyes—thou wouldst kiss me. Well, if it pleaseth thee, *look*," and she bent herself towards me, and fixed her dark and thrilling orbs upon my own; "ay, and *kiss*, too, if thou wilt, for, thanks be given to the scheme of things, kisses leave no marks, except upon the heart. But if thou dost kiss, I tell thee of a surety thou wilt eat out thy heart with love of me, and die!" and she bent yet further towards me till her soft hair brushed my brow, and her fragrant breath played upon my face, and made me faint and weak. Then of a sudden, even as I stretched out my hands to clasp, she straightened herself, and a quick change passed over her. Reaching out her hand, she held it over my head, and it seemed to me that something flowed from it that chilled me back to common sense, and a knowledge of propriety and the domestic virtues.

"Enough of this wanton play," she said with a touch of sternness. "Listen, Holly. Thou art a good and honest man, and I fain would spare thee; but, oh! it is so hard for a woman to be merciful. I have said I am not for thee, therefore let thy thoughts pass by me like an idle wind, and the dust of thy imagination sink again into the depths—well, of despair, if thou wilt. Thou dost not know me, Holly. Hadst thou seen me but ten hours ago when my passion seized me, thou hadst shrunk from me in fear and trembling. I am a woman of many moods, and, like the water in that vessel, I reflect many things; but they pass, my Holly; they pass, and are forgotten. Only the water is the water still, and I still am I, and that which maketh the water maketh it, and that which maketh me maketh me, nor can my quality be altered. Therefore, pay no heed to what I seem, seeing that thou canst not know what I am. If thou troublest me again I will veil myself, and thou shalt behold my face no more."

I rose, and sank on the cushioned couch beside her, yet quivering with emotion, though for a moment my mad passion had left me, as the leaves of a tree quiver still, although the gust be gone that stirred them. I did not dare to tell her that I *had* seen her in that deep and hellish mood, muttering incantations to the fire in the tomb.

"So," she went on, "now eat some fruit; believe me, it is the only true food for man. Oh, tell me of the philosophy of the Hebrew Messiah, who came after me, and whom thou sayest doth now rule Rome and Greece and Egypt and the barbarians beyond. It must have been a strange philosophy that He taught, for in my day the people would have naught of our philosophies. Revel and lust and drink, blood and cold steel, and the shock of men gathered in the battle—these were the canons of their creeds."

I had recovered myself a little by now, and, feeling bitterly ashamed of the weakness into which I had been betrayed, I did my best to expound to her the doctrines of Christianity, to which, however, with the single exception of our conception of Heaven and Hell, I found that she paid but faint attention, her interest being all directed towards the Man who taught them.

"Ah!" she said; "I see—a new religion! I have known so many, and doubtless there have been many more since I knew aught beyond these caves of Kôr. Mankind asks ever of the skies to vision out what lies behind them. It is terror for the end, and but a subtler form of selfishness—this it is that breeds religions. Mark, my Holly, each religion claims the future for its followers; or, at the least, the good thereof. The evil is for those benighted ones who will have none of it, seeing the light the true believers worship, as the fishes see the stars, but dimly. The religions come and the religions pass, and the civilisations come and pass, and nought endures but the world and human nature. Ah! if man would but see that hope is from within and not from without—that he himself must work out his own salvation! He is there, and within him is the breath of life and a knowledge of good and evil as good and evil is to him. Thereon let him build and stand erect, and not cast himself before the image of some unknown God, modelled like himself, but with a bigger brain to think evil; and a longer arm to do it."

I thought to myself, which shows how old such reasoning is, being, indeed, one of the recurring quantities of theological discussion, that her argument sounded very like some I have heard in the nineteenth century, and in other places than the caves of Kôr, and with which, by the way, I personally disagree, but I did not care to try and discuss the question with her. To begin with, my mind was too weary with all the emotions through which I had passed, and, in the second place, I knew that I should get the worst of it. It is hard enough to argue with an ordinary materialist, who hurls statistics and whole strata of geological facts at your head, whilst you can only buffet him with deductions and instincts and the snowflakes of faith, that are, alas! so apt to melt in the hot embers of our troubles. How little chance, then, should I have against one whose brain was supernaturally sharpened, and who had two thousand years of experience, besides all manner of knowledge of the secrets of Nature at her command? Feeling that she would be more likely to convert me than I should to convert her, I thought it best to leave the matter alone, and so sat silent. Many a time since then have I bitterly regretted that I did so, for thereby I lost the only opportunity I can remember having had of ascertaining what Ayesha really believed.

"Well, my Holly, art thou tired of me already, that thou dost sit so silent?" she said presently, with a little yawn. "Faithless man! And but half an hour since thou wast upon thy knees—the posture does not suit thee, Holly,—swearing that thou didst love me. What shall we do?—Nay, I have it. I will come and see this youth, the Lion, as the old man Billali calls him, who came with thee, and who is now so sick. The fever must have run its course by now, and if he is about to die I will recover him. Fear not, my Holly, I shall use no magic. Have I not told thee that there is no such thing as magic, though there is such a thing as understanding and applying the forces which are in Nature? Go now, and presently when I have made the drug ready I will follow thee."*

---

* Ayesha was a great chemist, indeed chemistry appears to have been her only amusement and occupation. She had one of the caves fitted up as a laboratory, and although her appliances were necessarily rude, the results that she attained were, as will become clear in the course of this narrative, sufficiently surprising.—L.H.H.

Accordingly I went only to find Job and Ustane in a great state of grief, and declaring that Leo was in the throes of death, and that they had been searching for me everywhere. I rushed to the couch, and glanced at him: clearly he was dying. He was senseless, and breathing heavily, but his lips were quivering, and every now and again a little shudder ran down his frame. I knew enough of doctoring to see that in another hour he would be beyond the reach of earthly help,—perhaps in another five minutes. How I cursed my selfishness and the folly that had kept me lingering by Ayesha's side while my dear boy lay dying! Alas! and alas! how easily the best of us are lighted down to evil by the gleam of woman's eyes! What a wicked wretch was I! Actually, for the last half-hour I had scarcely thought of Leo, and this, be it remembered, of the man who for twenty years had been my dearest companion, and the one interest of my existence. And now, perhaps, it was too late!

I wrung my hands, and glanced round. Ustane was sitting by the couch, and in her eyes burnt the dull light of despair. Job was blubbering—I am sorry I cannot name his distress by any more delicate word—audibly in the corner. Seeing my eye fixed upon him he went outside to give way to his grief in the passage. Obviously the only hope lay in Ayesha. She, and she alone—unless, indeed, she was an imposter, which I could not believe—could save him. I would go, and implore her to come. As I started to do so, however, Job came flying into the room, his hair literally standing on end with terror.

"Oh, God help us, sir!" he ejaculated in a frightened whisper, "here's a corpse coming sliding down the passage!"

For a moment I was puzzled, but presently, of course, it struck me that he must have seen Ayesha, wrapped in her grave-like garment, and been deceived by the extraordinary undulating smoothness of her walk into a belief that she was a white ghost gliding towards him. Indeed, at that very moment the question was settled, for Ayesha herself was in the apartment, or rather cave. Job turned, and saw her sheeted form, and then, with a convulsive howl of "Here it comes!" sprang into a corner, and jammed his face against the wall, and Ustane, guessing whose the dread presence must be, prostrated herself upon her face.

"Thou comest in a good time, Ayesha," I said, "for my boy lies at the point of death."

"So," she said softly; "provided he be not dead, it is no matter, for I can bring him back to life, my Holly. Is that man there thy servant, and is that the method wherewith thy servants greet strangers in thy country?"

"He is frightened of thy garb—it hath a death-like air," I answered.

She laughed.

"And the girl? Ah, I see now. It is her of whom thou didst speak to me. Well, bid them both to leave us, and we will see to this sick Lion of thine. I love not that underlings should perceive my wisdom."

Thereon I told Ustane in Arabic and Job in English both to leave the room; an order which the latter obeyed readily enough, and was glad to obey, for he could not in any way subdue his fear. But it was otherwise with Ustane.

"What does *She* want?" she whispered, divided between her fear of the terrible Queen and her anxiety to remain near Leo. "It is surely the right of a wife to be near her husband when he dieth. Nay, I will not go, my lord the Baboon."

"Why doth not that woman leave us, my Holly?" asked Ayesha, from the other end of the cave, where she was engaged in carelessly examining some sculptures on the wall.

"She doth not like to leave Leo," I answered, not knowing what to say. Ayesha wheeled round, and pointing to the girl Ustane, said one word, and one only, but it was quite enough, for the tone in which it was said meant volumes.

"Go!"

And sullenly Ustane crept past her on her hands and knees, and went.

"Thou seest, my Holly," said Ayesha, with a little laugh, "it was time that I gave these people a lesson in obedience. The girl went nigh to disobeying me, but then she did not learn this morning how I treat the disobedient. Well, she has gone; and now let me see the youth," and she glided towards the couch on which Leo lay, with his face in the shadow and turned towards the wall.

"He hath a noble shape," she said, as she bent over him to look upon his face.

Next second her tall and willowy form was staggering back across the room, as though she had been shot or stabbed, staggering back till at last she struck the cavern-wall, and then there burst from her lips the most awful and unearthly scream that I ever heard in all my life.

"What is it, Ayesha?" I cried. "Is he dead?"

She turned, and sprang towards me like a tigress.

"Thou dog!" she said, in her terrible whisper, which sounded like the hiss of a snake, "why didst thou hide this from me?" and she stretched out her arm, and I thought she was going to slay me.

"What?" I ejaculated, in the most lively terror; "what?"

"Ah!" she said, "perchance thou didst not know. Learn, my Holly, learn; there lies—there lies my lost Kallikrates. Kallikrates, who has come back to me at last, as I knew he would, as I knew he would," and she began to sob and to laugh, and generally to go on like any other lady who is a little upset, murmuring "Kallikrates, Kallikrates."

"Nonsense," thought I to myself, but I did not like to say it; and, indeed, at that moment I was thinking of Leo's life, having forgotten everything else in that terrible anxiety. What I feared now was that he should die whilst she was "carrying on."

"Unless thou canst help him, Ayesha," I put in, by way of a reminder, "thy Kallikrates will soon be far beyond thy calling. Surely he dieth even now."

"True," she said, with a start. "Oh, why did I not come before! I am unnerved—my hand trembles, even mine—and yet it is very easy. Here, thou Holly, take this phial," and she produced a tiny jar of pottery from the folds of her garment, "and pour the liquid in it down his throat. It will cure him if he be not dead. Swift, now! swift! the man dies!"

I glanced towards him; it was true enough, Leo was in his death-struggle. I saw his poor face turning ashen, and the breath began to rattle in his throat. The phial was stoppered with a little piece of wood. I drew it with my teeth, and a drop of the fluid within flew upon my tongue. It had a sweet flavour, and for a second made my head swim and a mist gather before my eyes, but happily the effect passed away as swiftly as it had arisen.

When I reached Leo's side he was plainly expiring —his golden head was slowly turning from side to side, and his mouth was slightly open. I called to Ayesha to hold his head, and this she managed to do, though the woman was quivering from head to foot, like an aspen-leaf or a startled horse. Then, forcing the jaw a little more open, I poured the contents of the phial into his mouth. Instantly a little vapour arose from it, as happens when one disturbs nitric acid, and this sight did not increase my hopes, already faint enough, of the efficacy of the treatment.

One thing, however, was certain, the death throes ceased—at first I thought because he had got beyond them, and crossed the awful river. His face turned a livid pallor, and his heart-beats, which had been feeble enough before, seemed to die away altogether—only the eyelid still twitched a little. In my doubt I looked up at Ayesha, whose head-wrapping had slipped back in her excitement when she went reeling across the room. She was still holding Leo's head, and with a face as pale as his watching his countenance with such an expression of agonised anxiety as I have never seen before. Clearly she did not know if he would live or die. Five minutes passed, and I saw that she was abandoning hope; her lovely oval face seemed to fall in and grow visibly thinner beneath the pressure of a mental agony, whose pencil drew black lines about the hollows of her eyes. The coral faded even from her lips, till they were as white as Leo's face, and quivered pitifully. It was shocking to see her; even in my own grief I felt for hers.

"Is it too late?" I gasped.

She hid her face in her hands, and made no answer, and I, too, turned away. But as I did so I heard a deep-drawn breath, and looking down perceived a line of colour creeping up Leo's face, then another and another, and then, wonder of wonders, the man we had thought dead turned over on his side.

"Thou seest," I said, in a whisper.

"I see," she answered, hoarsely. "He is saved. I thought we were too late—another moment—one little moment more—and he had been gone!" and she burst into an awful flood of tears, sobbing as though her heart would break, and yet managing to look lovelier than ever as she did it. At last she ceased.

"Forgive me, my Holly—forgive me for my weakness," she said. "Thou seest after all I am a very woman. Think—now think of it. This morning didst thou speak of the place of torment appointed by this new religion of thine. Hell or Hades thou didst call it—a place where the vital essence lives and retains an individual memory, and where all the errors and faults of judgment and unsatisfied passions and the unsubstantial terrors of the mind wherewith it hath at any time had to do come to mock and haunt and gibe and wring the heart for ever and for ever with the vision of its own hopelessness. Thus, even thus, have I lived for two thousand years—for some sixty generations, as ye reckon time—in a Hell, as thou callest it—tormented by the memory of a crime, tortured day and night with an unfulfilled desire—without companionship, without comfort, without death, and led on only down my dreary road by the marsh lights of Hope, which though they flickered here and there, and now glowed strong, and now were not, yet, as my skill told me, would one day lead unto my deliverer.

"And then—think of it still, oh Holly, for never shalt thou hear such another tale, or see such another scene, nay, not even if I give thee ten thousand years of life—and thou shalt have it in payment if thou wilt—think: at last my deliverer came—he whom I had watched and waited for through the generations—at the appointed time he came to seek me, as I knew he must come, for my wisdom could not err, though I knew not

"'Even now, mayhap, *She* heareth us.'"

when or how. Yet see how ignorant I was! See how small my knowledge, and how faint my strength! For hours he lay here sick unto death, and I felt it not—I who had waited for him for two thousand years—I knew it not. And then at last I see him, and behold, my chance is gone but by a hair's breadth even before I had it, for he is in the very jaws of death; whence no power of mine can draw him. And if he die, surely must the Hell be lived through once more—once more must I face the weary centuries, and wait, and wait till the time in its fulness shall bring my beloved back to me. And then thou gavest him the medicine, and that five minutes dragged along before I knew if he would live or die, and I tell thee that all the sixty generations that are gone were not so long as that five minutes. But they passed at last, and still he showed no sign, and I knew that if the drug works not then it, so far as I have had knowledge, works not at all. Then thought I that he was once more dead, and all the tortures of all the years gathered themselves into a single venomed spear, and pierced me through and through, because once again I had lost Kallikrates! And then, when all was done, behold! he sighed, behold! he lived, and I knew that he would live, for none die on whom the drug takes hold. Think of it now, my Holly—think of the wonder of it! He will sleep for twelve hours, and then the fever will have left him!"

And she stopped, and laid her hand upon the golden head, and then bent down and kissed the brow with a chastened abandonment of tenderness that would have been beautiful to behold had not the sight cut me to the heart—for I was jealous!

(*To be continued*)

PART 10 (4 DECEMBER 1886)

XVIII

"GO, WOMAN!"

Then followed a silence of a minute or so, during which *She* appeared, if one might judge from the almost angelic rapture of her face—for she looked angelic sometimes—to be plunged in a happy ecstasy. Suddenly, however, a new thought struck her, and her expression became the very reverse of angelic.

"Almost had I forgotten," she said, "that woman, Ustane. What is she to Kallikrates—his servant, or——" and she paused, and her voice trembled.

I shrugged my shoulders. "I understand that she is wed to him according to the custom of the Amahagger," I answered; "but I know not."

Her face grew dark as a thunder-cloud. Old as she was, Ayesha had not outlived jealousy.

"Then there is an end," she said; "she must die, even now!"

"For what crime?" I asked, horrified; "she is guilty of nought that thou art not guilty of thyself, oh Ayesha. She loves the man, and he has been pleased to accept her love; where, then, is her sin?"

"Truly, oh Holly, thou art foolish," she answered, almost petulantly. "Where is her sin? Her sin is that she stands between me and my desire. Well, I know that I can take him from her—for dwells there a man upon this earth, oh Holly, who could resist me if I put out my strength? Men are faithful for so long only as temptations pass them by. If the temptation be but strong enough, then will the man yield, for every man, like every rope, hath his breaking strain, and passion is to them what gold and power are to women—the weight upon their weakness. Believe me, ill will it fare with mortal woman in that heaven of which thou speakest, if only the spirits be more fair, for their lords will never turn to look upon them, and their heaven will become their hell. For man can be bought with woman's beauty, if it be but beautiful enough; and woman's beauty can be ever bought with gold, if only there be gold enough. So was it in my day, and so it will be to the end of time. The world is a great mart, my Holly, where all things are for sale to him who bids the highest in the currency of our desires."

These remarks, which were as cynical as might have been expected from a woman of Ayesha's age and experience, jarred upon me, and I answered, testily, that in our heaven there was no marriage or giving in marriage.[1]

"Else would it not be heaven, dost thou mean?" she put in. "Fie upon thee, Holly, to think so ill of us poor women! Is it, then, marriage that marks the line between thy heaven and thy hell? But enough of this. This is no time for disputing and the challenge of our wits. Why dost thou always dispute? Art thou also a philosopher of these latter

---

[1] Mark 12:25.

days? As for this woman, she must die; for though I can take her husband from her, yet, while she lived, might he think tenderly of her, and that I cannot away with. No woman shall dwell in his thoughts; my empire shall be all my own. She hath had her day, let her be content; for better is an hour with love than a century of loneliness—now night shall swallow her."

"Nay, nay," I cried, "it would be a wicked crime; and from a crime naught comes but what is evil. For thy own sake do not this deed."

"Is it, then, a crime, oh foolish man, to put away that which stands between us and our ends? Then is our life one long crime, my Holly; for day by day we destroy that we may live, since in this world none, save the strongest, can endure. Those who are weak must perish; the earth is to the strong, and the fruits thereof. For every tree that grows a score shall wither, that the strong ones may take their share. We run to place and power over the dead bodies of those who fail and fall; ay, we win the food we eat from out the mouths of starving babes. It is the scheme of things. Thou sayest, too, that a crime breeds evil, but therein thou dost lack experience; for out of crimes come many good things, and out of good grows much evil. The cruel rage of the tyrant may prove a blessing to the thousands who come after him, and the sweet-heartedness of a holy man may make a nation slaves. Man doeth this and doeth that from the good or evil of his heart; but he knoweth not to what end his moral sense doth prompt him; for when he striketh he is blind to where the blow shall fall, nor can he count the airy threads that weave the web of circumstance. Good and evil, love and hate, night and day, sweet and bitter, man and woman, heaven above and the earth beneath—all these things are necessary, one to the other, and who knows the end of each? I tell thee that there is a hand of Fate that twines them up to bear the burden of its purpose, and all things are gathered in that great rope to which all things are needful. Therefore doth it not become us to say this thing is evil and this good, or the dark is hateful and the light lovely; for to other eyes than ours the evil may be the good and the darkness more beautiful than the day, or all alike be fair. Hearest thou, my Holly?"

I felt it was hopeless to argue against casuistry of this nature, which, if it were carried to its logical conclusion, would absolutely destroy all morality, as we understand it. But her talk gave me a fresh thrill of fear; for what may not be possible to a being who, unconstrained by human law, is also absolutely unshackled by a moral sense of right and wrong, which, however partial and conventional it may be, is yet based, as our conscience tells us, upon the great wall of individual responsibility that marks off mankind from the beasts.

But I was deeply anxious to save Ustane, whom I liked and respected, from the dire fate that overshadowed her at the hands of her mighty rival. So I made one more appeal.

"Ayesha," I said, "thou art too subtle for me; but thou thyself hast told me that each man should be a law unto himself, and follow the teaching of his heart. Hath thy heart no mercy towards her whose place thou wouldst take? Bethink thee, as thou sayest—though to me the thing is incredible—him whom thou desirest has returned to thee after many years, and but now thou hast, as thou sayest also, wrung him from the jaws of death. Wilt thou celebrate his coming by the murder of one who loved him, and whom perchance he loved, one, at any rate, who saved his life for thee when the spears of thy slaves would have made an end thereof? Thou sayest also that in past days thou didst grievously wrong this man, that with thine own hand thou didst slay him because of the Egyptian Amenartas whom he loved."

"How knowest thou that, oh stranger? How knowest thou that name? I spoke it not to thee," she broke in with a cry, catching at my arm.

"Perchance I dreamed it," I answered; "strange dreams do hover about these caves of Kôr. It seems that the dream was, indeed, a shadow of the truth. What came to thee of thy mad crime?—two thousand years of waiting, was it not? And now wouldst thou repeat the history? Say what thou wilt, I tell thee that evil will come of it; for to him who doeth, at the least, good breeds good and evil evil, even though in after days out of evil cometh good. Offences must needs come; but woe to him by whom the offence cometh.[1] So said that Messiah of whom I spoke to thee, and it was truly said. If thou slayest this innocent woman, I say unto thee that thou shalt be accursed, and pluck no fruit from thine ancient tree of love. Also, what thinkest thou? How will this man take thee red-handed from the slaughter of her who loved and tended him?"

"As to that," she answered, "I have already answered thee. Had I slain thee as well as her, yet should he love me, Holly, because he could not help himself any more than thou couldst help dying, if by chance I slew thee, oh Holly. And yet maybe there is truth in what thou dost say; for in some way it presseth on my mind. If it may be, I will spare this woman; for have I not told thee that I am not cruel for the sake of cruelty? I love not to see suffering, or to cause it. Let her come before

---

[1]   Matthew 18:7.

me—quick now, before my mood changes," and she hastily covered her face with its gauzy wrapping.

Well pleased to have succeeded even to this extent, I passed out into the passage and called to Ustane, whose white garment I caught sight of some yards away, huddled up against one of the earthenware lamps that were placed at intervals along the tunnel. She rose, and ran towards me.

"Is my lord dead? Oh, say not he is dead," she cried, lifting her noble-looking face, all stained as it was with tears, up to me with an air of infinite beseeching that went straight to my heart.

"Nay, he lives," I answered. "*She* hath saved him. Enter."

She sighed deeply, and entered, and fell upon her hands and knees, after the custom of the Amahagger people, in the presence of the dread *She*.

"Stand," said Ayesha in her coldest voice, "and come hither."

Ustane obeyed, standing before her with bowed head.

Then came a pause, which she broke.

"Who is this man?" she said, pointing to the sleeping form of Leo.

"The man is my husband," she answered in a low voice.

"Who gave him to thee for a husband?"

"I took him according to the custom of our country, oh *She*."

"Thou hast done evil, woman, in taking this man, who is a stranger. He is not a man of thine own race, and the custom fails. Listen: perchance thou didst this thing through ignorance, therefore, woman, do I spare thee, otherwise hadst thou died. Listen again. Go from hence back to thine own place, and never dare to speak to, or set thine eyes upon, this man again. He is not for thee. Listen a third time. If thou breakest this my law, that moment thou diest. Go."

But Ustane did not move.

"Go, woman!"

Then she looked up, and I saw that her face was torn with passion.

"Nay, oh *She*, I will not go," she answered in a choked voice; "the man is my husband, and I love him—I love him, and I will not leave him. What right hast thou to make me leave my husband?"

I saw a little quiver pass down Ayesha's frame, and shuddered myself, fearing the worst.

"Be pitiful," I said in Greek; "it is but Nature working."

"I am pitiful," she answered coldly; "had I not been pitiful she had been dead even now." Then addressing Ustane: "Woman, I say to thee, go, before I destroy thee where thou art!"

"I will not go! He is mine—mine!" she cried in anguish. "I took him, and I saved his life! Destroy me, then, if thou hast the power! I will not give thee my husband—never—never!"

Ayesha made a movement so swift that I could scarcely follow it, but it seemed to me that she lightly struck the poor girl upon the hair with her hand. I looked at Ustane's head, and then staggered back in horror, for there upon her hair, right across her bronze-like tresses, were three finger-marks as *white as snow*. As for the girl herself, she had put her hands to her head, and was looking dazed.

"Great heavens!" I said, perfectly aghast at this dreadful manifestation of unhuman power; but *She* did but laugh a little.

"Thou thinkest, poor ignorant fool," she said to the bewildered woman, "that I have not the power to slay. Stay, there lies a mirror," and she pointed to Leo's round shaving-glass that had been arranged by Job with other things upon his portmanteau; "give it to this woman, my Holly, and let her see that which lies across her hair, and whether or no I have power to slay."

I picked up the glass, and held it before Ustane's eyes. She gazed, then felt at her hair, then gazed again, and then sank upon the ground with a sort of sob.

"Now, wilt thou go, or must I strike a second time?" asked Ayesha, in mockery. "See, I have set my seal upon thee so that I may know thee till thy hair is all as white as it. If I see thy face here again be sure, too, that thy bones shall soon be whiter than my mark upon thy hair."

Utterly awed and broken down, the poor creature rose, and, marked with that awful mark, crept from the room, sobbing bitterly.

"Look not so frighted, my Holly," said Ayesha, when she had gone. "I tell thee I deal not in magic—there is no such thing. 'Tis only a force that thou dost not understand. I marked her to strike terror to her heart, else must I have slain her. And now I will bid my servants bear my Lord Kallikrates to a chamber near mine own, that I may watch over him, and be ready to greet him when he wakes; and thither, too, shalt thou come, my Holly, and the white man, thy servant. But one thing remember at thy peril. Nought must thou say to Kallikrates as to how this woman went, and as little as may be of me. Now, I have warned thee!" and she slid away to give her orders, leaving me more absolutely confounded than ever. Indeed, so bewildered was I, and racked and torn with such a succession of various emotions, that I began to think that I must be going mad. However, perhaps fortunately, I had but little time to reflect, for presently the mutes arrived to carry the sleeping Leo and our possessions across the central cave, so for a while all was bustle. Our new rooms were situated immediately behind what we used to call Ayesha's boudoir—the curtained space where I had first seen her. Where she herself slept I did not then know, but it was somewhere quite close.

That night I passed in Leo's room, but he slept through it like the dead, never once stirring. I also slept fairly well, as, indeed, I needed to do, but my sleep was full of dreams of all the horrors and wonders I had undergone. Chiefly, however, I was haunted by that frightful piece of diablerie by which Ayesha left her finger marks upon her rival's hair. There was something so terrible about the swift, snake-like movement, and the instantaneous blanching of that three-fold line, that, if the results to Ustane had been much more tremendous, I doubt if they would have impressed me so deeply. To this day, I often dream of that dread scene, and see the weeping woman, bereaved, and marked like Cain, cast a last look at her lover, and creep from the presence of her dread Queen.

Another dream that troubled me was about the huge pyramid of bones. I dreamed that they all stood up and marched past me in thousands and tens of thousands—in squadrons, companies, and armies— with the sunlight shining through their hollow ribs. On they rushed across the plain to Kôr, their imperial home; I saw the drawbridges fall before them, and heard their bones clank through the brazen gates. On they went, up the splendid streets, on past fountains, palaces, and temples such as the eye of man never saw. But there was no man to greet them in the market-place, and no woman's head appeared at the windows-only a bodiless voice went before them, calling: "*Fallen is Imperial Kôr!—fallen!—fallen!— fallen!*"[1] On, right through the city, marched those gleaming phalanxes, and the rattle of their bony tread went echoing through the silent air as they pressed grimly on. They passed through the city and clomb the wall, and marched along the great roadway that was made upon it, till at length they once more reached the drawbridge. Then, as the sun was sinking, they returned again towards their sepulchre, and luridly his light shone through them, throwing gigantic shadows of their bones, that stretched away, and moved like huge spider's legs as they wound across the plain. Back they came to the cave, and once more flung themselves in unending files through the hole into the huge pyramid of bones, and I awoke, shuddering, to see *She*, who had evidently been standing between my couch and Leo's, glide like a shadow from the room.

After this I slept again, soundly this time, till morning, when I awoke much refreshed, and got up. At last the hour drew near at which,

---

[1]   Compare Revelation 18:2.

according to Ayesha, Leo was to awake, and with it came *She* herself, as usual, veiled.

"Thou shalt see, Holly," she said; "presently shall he awake in his right mind, the fever having left him."

Hardly were the words out of her mouth, when Leo turned round and stretched out his arms, yawned, opened his eyes, and, perceiving a female form bending over him, threw his arms round her and kissed her, mistaking her, perhaps, for Ustane; because, next minute, he said, in Arabic, "Hullo, Ustane, why have you tied your head up like that? Have you got the toothache?" and then, in English, "I say, I'm awfully hungry. Why, Job, you old son of a gun, where the deuce have we got to now—eh?"

"I am sure I wish I knew, Mr. Leo," said Job, edging suspiciously past Ayesha, whom he still regarded with the utmost disgust and horror, being by no means sure that she was not an animated corpse; "but you mustn't talk, Mr. Leo, you've been very ill, and given us a great deal of hanxiety, and, if this lady," looking at Ayesha, "would be so kind as to move, I'll bring you your soup."

This turned Leo's attention to the "lady," who was standing by in perfect silence. "Hullo!" he said; "that is not Ustane—where is Ustane?"

Then, for the first time, Ayesha spoke to him, and her first words were a lie. "She has gone from hence upon a visit," she said; "and, behold, I am here as thine handmaiden."

Ayesha's silver notes seemed to puzzle his half-awakened intellect, as also did her corpse-like wrappings. However, he said nothing at the time, but drank off his soup greedily enough, and then turned over and slept again till the evening. When he woke for the second time he saw me, and began to question me as to what had happened, but I had to put him off as best I could till the morrow, when he awoke almost miraculously better. Then I told him something of his illness and of my doings, but as Ayesha was present I could not tell him much except that she was the Queen of the country, and well-disposed towards us, and that it was her pleasure to go veiled; for, though of course I spoke in English, I was afraid that she might understand what we were saying from the expression of our faces, and besides, I remembered her warning.

On the following day Leo got up almost entirely recovered. The flesh wound in his side was healed, and his constitution, naturally a vigorous one, had shaken off the exhaustion consequent on his terrible fever with a rapidity that I can only attribute to the effects of the wonderful drug which Ayesha had given to him, and also to the fact that his illness had been too short to reduce him very much. With his returning health came back full recollection of all his adventures up to the time when he had lost consciousness in the marsh, and of course of Ustane also, to whom I discovered he had grown considerably attached. Indeed, he overwhelmed me with questions about the poor girl, which I did not dare to answer, for after Leo's first awakening *She* had sent for me, and again warned me solemnly that I was to reveal nothing of the story to him, delicately hinting that if I did it would be the worse for me. She also, for the second time, cautioned me not to tell Leo anything more than I was obliged about herself, saying that she would tell him in her own time.

Indeed, her whole manner changed. After all that I had seen I had expected that she would take the earliest opportunity of claiming the man she believed to be her old-world lover, but this, for some reason of her own, which was at the time quite inscrutable to me, she did not do. All that she did was to attend to his wants quietly, and with a humility that was in striking contrast with her former imperious bearing, addressing him always in a tone of something very like respect, and keeping him with her as much as possible. Of course his curiosity was as much excited about this mysterious woman as my own had been, and he was particularly anxious to see her face, which I had, without entering into particulars, told him was as lovely as her form and voice. This in itself was enough to raise the expectations of any young man to a dangerous pitch, and had it not been that he had not as yet completely shaken off the effects of illness, and was much troubled in his mind about Ustane, of whose affection and brave devotion he spoke in touching terms, I have no doubt that he would have entered into her plans, and fallen in love with her by anticipation. As it was, however, he was simply wildly curious, and also, like myself, considerably awed, for though no hint had been given to him by her of her extraordinary age, he not unnaturally came to identify her with the woman spoken of on the potsherd. At last, quite driven into a corner by his continual questions, which he showered on me while he was dressing on this third morning, I referred him to Ayesha, saying, with perfect truth, that I did not know where Ustane was. Accordingly, after he had eaten a hearty breakfast, we adjourned into *She*'s presence, for her mutes had orders to admit us at all hours.

She was, as usual, seated in what, for want of a better term, we called her boudoir, and, on the curtains being drawn, she rose from her couch and, stretching out both hands, came forward to greet us, or rather Leo; for I, as may be imagined, was now quite left in the cold. It was a pretty sight to see her veiled form gliding towards the sturdy young

Englishman, dressed in his grey flannel suit; for, though he is half a Greek in blood, Leo is, with the exception of his hair, one of the most English-looking men I ever saw. He has nothing of the supple form or slippery manner of the modern Greek about him, though I presume that he got his remarkable personal beauty from his foreign mother, whose portrait he resembles not a little. He is very tall and big-chested, and yet not awkward, as so many big men are, and his head is set upon him in such a fashion as to give him a proud and vigorous air, which was well translated in his Amahagger name of the Lion.

"Greeting to thee, my young stranger lord," she said in her softest voice. "Right glad am I to see thee upon thy feet. Believe me, had I not saved thee at the last, never wouldst thou have stood upon those feet again. But the danger is done, and it shall be my care"—and she flung a world of meaning into the words—"that it doth never return again."

Leo bowed to her, and then, in his best Arabic, thanked her for all her kindness and courtesy in caring for one unknown to her.

"Nay," she answered softly, "ill could the world spare such a man. Beauty is too rare upon it. Give me no thanks, who am made happy by thy coming."

"Humph! old fellow," said Master Leo aside to me in English, "the lady is uncommonly civil. We seem to have tumbled into clover. I hope you have made the most of your opportunities. By Jove! what a pair of arms she has got!"

I nudged him in the ribs to make him keep quiet, for I caught sight of a gleam from Ayesha's hidden eye regarding me curiously.

"I trust," went on Ayesha, "that my servants have attended well upon thee; if there can be comfort in this poor place, be sure it waits on thee. Is there aught that I can do for thee more?"

"Yes, oh *She*," answered Leo hastily. "I would fain know where the young lady who was looking after me has gone to."

"Ah," said Ayesha; "the girl—yes, I saw her. Nay, I know not; she said that she would go. I know not whither. Perchance she will return, perchance not. It is wearisome waiting on the sick, and these savage women are fickle."

Leo looked both sulky and distressed at this intelligence.

"It's infernally odd," he said to me in English; and then, addressing *She*, "I cannot understand," he said; "the young lady and I—well, you know exactly—in short, we had a regard for each other."

Ayesha laughed a little very musically, and then turned the subject.

XIX

"GIVE ME A BLACK GOAT!"

The conversation after this was of such a desultory order that I do not quite recollect it. For some reason, perhaps from a desire to keep her identity and character in reserve, Ayesha did not talk freely, as she usually did. Presently, however, she informed Leo that she had arranged a dance that night for our amusement. I was astonished to hear this, as I fancied that the Amahagger were much too gloomy a folk to indulge in any such frivolity; but, as will presently more clearly appear, it turned out that an Amahagger dance had little in common with such fantastic festivities in other countries, savage or civilised. Then, as we were about to withdraw, she suggested that Leo might like to see some of the wonders of the caves, and as he gladly assented thither we departed, accompanied by Job and Billali. To describe our visit would only be to repeat a great deal of what I have already said. The tombs we entered were indeed different, for the whole rock was a honeycomb of sepulchres,* but the contents were nearly always the same. Afterwards we visited the pyramid of bones that had haunted my dreams on the previous night, and from thence went down a long passage to one of the great vaults occupied by the bodies of the poor citizens of Imperial Kôr. These bodies were not nearly so well preserved, and many of them had no linen covering on them, also they were buried from five hundred to one thousand in a single large vault, the corpses in many instances being thickly piled one upon another, like a heap of slain.

Leo was of course intensely interested in this stupendous and unequalled sight, which was, indeed, enough to awake all the imagination a man had in him into the most active life. But to poor Job it did not prove attractive. His nerves—already seriously shaken by what he had undergone since we had arrived in this terrible country—were, as may be imagined, still further disturbed by the spectacle of all this mass of departed humanity, whose forms still remained perfect before his eyes, though their voices were for ever lost in the eternal silence of the tomb. Nor was he comforted when old Billali, by way of soothing his

---

* For a long while it puzzled me to know what could have been done with the enormous quantities of rock that must have been dug out of these vast caves; but I afterwards discovered that it was for the most part built into the walls and palaces of Kôr, and also used to line the reservoirs and sewers.—L.H.H.

evident agitation, informed him that he should not be frightened of these dead things, as he would soon be like them himself.

"There's a nice thing to say of a man, sir," he ejaculated, when I translated this little remark; "but there, what can one expect of an old man-eating savage? Not but what I daresay he's right," and Job sighed.

When we had finished inspecting the caves, we returned and had our meal, for it was now past four in the afternoon, and we needed some food and rest—especially Leo. At six o'clock we all, including Job, waited on Ayesha, who set to work to terrify our poor servant still further by showing him pictures on the pool of water in the font-like vessel. She learnt from me that he was one of seventeen children, and then bid him think of all his brothers and sisters, or as many of them as he could, gathered together in his father's cottage. Then she told him to look in the water, and there, reflected from its stilly surface, was that dead scene of many years gone by, as it was recalled to our poor servant's brain. Some of the faces were clear enough, but some were mere blurs and splotches, or with one feature grossly exaggerated; the fact being that, in these instances, Job had been unable to recall the exact appearances of the individuals, or remembered them only by a peculiarity of his tribe, and the water could only reflect what he saw with his mind's eye. For it must be remembered that *She's* power in this matter was strictly limited; she could apparently, except in very rare instances, only photograph upon the water what was actually in the mind of some one present, and then only by his will. But if she was personally acquainted with a locality, she could, as in the case of ourselves and the whaleboat, throw its reflection upon the water, and also the reflection of anything extraneous that was passing there at the time. This power, however, did not extend to the minds of others. For instance, she could show me the interior of my college chapel, as I remembered it, but not as it was at the moment of reflection; for, where other people were concerned, her art was strictly limited to the facts or memories present to *their* consciousness at the moment. So much was this so, that when we tried, for her amusement, to show her pictures of noted buildings, such as St. Paul's or the Houses of Parliament, the result was most imperfect; for, of course, though we had a good general idea of their appearance, we could not recall all the architectural details, and therefore the minutiæ necessary to a perfect reflection were wanting. But Job could not be got to understand this, and, so far from accepting a natural explanation of the matter, which was after all, though strange enough in all conscience, nothing more than an instance of glorified and perfected telepathy, he set the whole thing down as a manifestation of the blackest magic. I shall never forget the howl of terror which he uttered when he saw the more or less perfect portraits of his long-scattered brethren staring at him from the quiet water, or the merry peal of laughter with which Ayesha greeted his consternation. As for Leo, he did not half like it either, but ran his fingers through his yellow curls, and remarked that it gave him the creeps.

After about an hour of this amusement, in the latter part of which Job did *not* participate, the mutes by signs indicated that Billali was waiting for an audience. Accordingly he was told to "crawl up," which he did as awkwardly as usual, and announced that the dance was ready to begin if *She* and the white strangers would be pleased to attend. Shortly afterwards we all rose, and Ayesha having thrown a dark cloak (the same, by the way, that she had worn when I saw her cursing by the fire) over her white wrappings, we started. The dance was to be held in the open air, on the smooth rocky plateau in front of the great cave, and thither we made our way. About fifteen paces from the mouth of the cave we found three chairs placed, and here we sat and waited, for as yet no dancers were to be seen. The night was almost, but not quite, dark, the moon being not risen as yet, which made us wonder how we should be able to see the dancing.

"Thou wilt presently understand," said Ayesha, with a little laugh, when Leo asked her, and we certainly did. Scarcely were the words out of her mouth when from every point we saw dark forms rushing up, each bearing with them what we at first took to be enormous flaming torches. Whatever they were they were burning furiously, for the flames stood out a yard or more behind each bearer. On they came, fifty or more of them, looking like devils from hell, with their flaming burdens. Leo was the first to discover what these burdens were.

"Great heaven!" he said, "they are corpses on fire!"

I stared and stared again—he was perfectly right—the torches that were to light our entertainment were human mummies from the caves!

On rushed the bearers of the flaming corpses, and meeting at a spot about twenty paces in front of us built their ghastly burdens crossways into a huge bonfire. Heavens! how they roared and flared. No tar barrel could have burnt as those mummies did. Nor was this all. Suddenly I saw one great fellow seize a flaming human arm that had fallen from its parent frame, and rush off into the darkness. Presently he stopped, and a tall streak of fire shot up into the air, illumining the gloom, and also the lamp from which it sprang. The lamp was the mummy of a woman tied to a stout stake let into the rock, and he had fired her hair. On he went a few paces and touched a second, then a third, and a fourth, till at last we were surrounded on all three sides by a great ring of bodies flaring furiously, the material with which they were preserved having rendered them so inflammable that the flames would literally spout out of the ears and mouth in tongues of fire a foot or more long.

Nero[1] illuminated his gardens with live Christians soaked in tar, and we were now treated to a similar spectacle, probably for the first time since his day, only happily our lamps were not living ones.

But although this element of horror was fortunately wanting, to describe the awful and hideous grandeur of the spectacle thus presented to us is, I feel, so absolutely beyond my poor powers, that I scarcely dare attempt it. To begin with, it appealed to the moral as well as the physical susceptibilities. There was something very terrible, and yet very fascinating, about the employment of the remote dead to illumine the orgies of the living; in itself the thing was a satire, both on the living and the dead. Cæsar's dust—or is it Alexander's?—may stop a bunghole, but the functions of these dead Cæsars of the past was to light up a savage orgie.[2] To such base uses do we come, of so little account are we in the minds of the eager multitudes we have bred, most of whom, so far from revering our memory, will live to curse us for begetting them into such a world of woe.

Then there was the physical side of the spectacle, and a weird and splendid one it was. Those old citizens of Kôr burnt, as to judge from their inscriptions they had lived, very fast, and with the utmost liberality. What is more, there were plenty of them. As soon as ever a mummy had burnt down to the ancles, which it did in about twenty minutes, the feet were kicked away, and another one put in its place. The bonfire was kept going on the same generous scale, and its flames shot up, with a hiss and a crackle, twenty or thirty feet into the air, throwing great flashes of light far out into the gloom, through which the dark forms of the Amahagger flitted to and fro like devils replenishing the infernal fires. We all stood and stared aghast—shocked, and yet fascinated—at so strange a spectacle, and half-expecting to see the spirits those flaming forms had once enclosed come creeping from the shadows to work vengeance on their desecrators.

---

[1] Roman emperor (58–64 CE) legendary for his cruelty who, according to Tacitus, burned crucified Christians to illuminate one of his parties.

[2] In this sentence and the next, Holly is alluding to *Hamlet* V.i. 197–208.

"I promised thee a strange sight, my Holly," laughed Ayesha, whose nerves alone did not seem to be affected; "and, behold, I have not failed thee. Also, it hath its lesson. Trust not to the future, for who knows what the future may bring! Therefore, live for the day and endeavour not to escape the dust which seems to be man's end. What thinkest thou those long-forgotten nobles and ladies would have felt had they known that they should one day flare to light the dance or boil the pot of savages? But see, here come the dancers; a merry crew—are they not? The stage is lit—now for the play."

As she spoke, we perceived two lines of figures, one male and the other female, to the number of about a hundred, each advancing round the human bonfire, arrayed only in the usual leopard and buck skins. They formed up, in perfect silence, in two lines, facing each other between us and the fire, and then the dance—a sort of infernal and fiendish cancan—began. To describe it is quite impossible, but, though there was a good deal of tossing of legs and double-shuffling, it seemed to our untutored minds to be more of a play than a dance, and, as usual with this dreadful people, whose minds seem to have taken their colour from the caves in which they live, and whose jokes and amusements are drawn from the inexhaustible stores of preserved mortality with which they share their homes, the subject appeared to be a most ghastly one. I know that it represented an attempted murder first of all, and then the burial alive of the victim and his struggling from the grave, each act of the abominable drama, which was carried on in perfect silence, being rounded off and finished with a furious and most revolting dance round the supposed victim, who writhed upon the ground in the red light of the fire.

Presently, however, this pleasing piece was interrupted. Suddenly there was a slight commotion, and a great, powerful woman, whom I had noted as one of the most vigorous of the dancers, came, made mad and drunken with unholy excitement, bounding and staggering towards us, shrieking out as she came:—

"I want a black goat, I must have a black goat, bring me a black goat!" and down she fell upon the rocky floor foaming and writhing, and shrieking for a black goat, about as hideous a spectacle as can well be conceived.

Instantly most of the dancers came up, and got round her, though some still continued their capers in the background.

"She has got a Devil," sung out one of them. "Run and get a black goat. There, Devil, keep quiet! keep quiet! You shall have the goat presently. They have gone to fetch it, Devil."

"I want a black goat, I must have a black goat!" shrieked the foaming rolling creature again.

"All right, Devil, the goat will be here presently, keep quiet, there's a good Devil!"

And so on till the goat taken from a neighbouring kraal,[1] did at last arrive, being dragged bleating on to the scene by its horns.

"Is it a black one, is it a black one?" shrieked the possessed.

"Yes, yes, Devil, as black as night," then aside, "keep it behind thee, don't let the Devil see that it has got a white spot on its rump and another on its belly. In one minute, Devil. There, cut its throat quick. Where is the saucer?"

"The goat! the goat! the goat! Give me the blood of my black goat! I must have it, don't you see I must have it? Oh! oh! oh! give me the blood of the goat."

At this moment a terrified *bah!* announced that the poor goat had been sacrificed, and the next minute a woman ran up with a saucer full of the blood. This the possessed creature, who was then raving and foaming her wildest, seized and *drank*, and instantly recovered, and without a trace of hysteria, or fits, or being possessed, or whatever dreadful thing it was she was suffering from. She stretched her arms, smiled faintly, and walked quietly back to the dancers, who presently withdrew in a double line as they had come, leaving the space between us and the bonfire deserted.

I thought the entertainment (*sic*) was now over, and feeling rather queer, was about to ask *She* if we could rise, when suddenly what at first I took to be a baboon came hopping round the fire, and was instantly met upon the other side by a lion, or rather a human being dressed in a lion's skin. Then came a goat, then a man wrapped in an ox's hide, with the horns wobbling about in a ludicrous way. After him followed a blesbok, then an impala, then a koodoo,[2] then more goats, and many other animals, including a girl sewn up in the shining scaly hide of a boa-constrictor, several yards of which trailed along the ground behind her. When all the beasts had collected they began to dance about in a lumbering, unnatural fashion, and to imitate the sounds produced by the respective animals they represented, till the whole air was alive with roars and bleating and the hissing of snakes. This went on for a long time, till, getting tired of the pantomime, I asked Ayesha if there would be any objection to Leo and myself walking round to inspect the human

---

[1]   Corral for holding livestock (Afrikaans).

[2]   Blesboks, impalas, and koodoos are all types of African antelope.

torches, and, as she had nothing to say against it, we started, striking round to the left. After looking at one or two of the flaming bodies we were about to return, thoroughly disgusted with the grotesque weirdness of the spectacle, when our attention was attracted by one of the dancers, a particularly active leopard, that had separated itself from its fellow beasts, and was whisking about in our immediate neighbourhood, but gradually drawing into a spot where the shadow was darkest, equidistant between two of the flaming mummies. Drawn by curiosity, we followed it, when suddenly it darted past us into the shadows beyond, and as it did so erected itself and whispered, "Come," in a voice that we both recognised as that of Ustane. Without waiting to consult me Leo turned and followed her into the outer darkness, and I, feeling sick enough at heart, went after them. The leopard crawled on for about fifty paces—a sufficient distance to be quite beyond the light of the fire and torches—and then Leo came up with it, or, rather, with Ustane.

"Oh, my lord," I heard her whisper, "so I have found thee! Listen. I am in peril of my life from '*She-who-must-be-obeyed.*' Surely the Baboon has told thee how she drove me from thee? I love thee, my lord, and thou art mine according to the custom of the country. I saved thy life! My Lion, wilt thou cast me off now?"

"Of course not," ejaculated Leo; "I have been wondering whither thou hadst gone. Let us go and explain matters to the Queen."

"Nay, nay, she would slay us. Thou knowest not her power—the Baboon there, he knoweth, for he saw. Nay, there is but one way: if thou wilt cleave to me, thou must flee with me across the marshes even now, and then perchance we may escape."

"For Heaven's sake, Leo," I began, but she broke in.

"Nay, listen not to him. Swift—be swift—death is in the air we breathe. Even now, mayhap, *She* heareth us," and without more ado, she proceeded to back her arguments by throwing herself into his arms. As she did so the leopard's head slipped from her hair. I saw the three white finger-marks upon it, gleaming faintly in the starlight. Once more realising the desperate nature of the situation, I was about to interpose, for I knew that Leo was not too strong-minded where women were concerned, when—oh! horror!—I heard a little silvery laugh behind me. I turned round, and there was *She* herself, and with her Billali and two male mutes. I gasped and nearly sank to the ground, for I knew that such a situation must result in some dreadful tragedy, of which it seemed exceedingly probable to me that I should be the first victim. As for Ustane, she untwined her arms and covered her eyes with her hands,

"As we were returning Billali met us."

while Leo, not knowing the full terror of the position, merely coloured up, and looked as silly as a man caught in such a trap would naturally do.

(To be continued)

PART II (II DECEMBER 1886)

XX

TRIUMPH

Then followed a moment of the most painful silence that I ever endured. It was broken by Ayesha, who addressed herself to Leo.

"Nay, now my lord and guest," she said, in her softest tones, which yet had the ring of steel about them, "look not so bashful. Surely the sight was a pretty one—the leopard and the lion!"

"Oh, hang it all," said Leo, in English.

"And thou Ustane," she went on, "surely I should have passed thee by had not the light fallen on the white across thy hair. Well! well! the dance is done—see, the tapers have burnt down, and all things end in darkness and in ashes. So thou thoughtest it a fit time for love, Ustane, my servant—and I, dreaming not that I could be disobeyed, thought thee already far away."

"Play not with me," moaned the wretched woman; "slay me, and let there be an end."

"Nay, why? It is not well to go so swift from the hot lips of love down to the cold mouth of the grave," and she made a motion to the mutes, who instantly stepped up and caught the girl by either arm. With an oath Leo sprung upon the nearest, and hurled him to the ground, and then stood over him with his face set, and his fist ready.

Again Ayesha laughed. "It was well thrown, my guest: thou hast a strong arm for one who so late was sick. But now out of thy courtesy I pray thee let that man live and do my bidding. He shall not harm the girl; the night air grows chill, and I would welcome her in mine own place. Surely she whom thou dost favour shall be favoured of me also."

I took Leo by the arm, and pulled him from the prostrate mute, and he, half bewildered, obeyed the pressure. Then we all set out for the cave across the plateau, where a great pile of white human ashes was all that remained of the fire that had lit the dancing, for the dancers had vanished.

In due course we gained Ayesha's boudoir—all too soon it seemed to me, having a sad presage of what was to come lying heavy on my heart.

Ayesha seated herself upon her cushions, and having dismissed Job and Billali, by signs bade the mutes tend the lamps and retire, all save one girl, who was her favourite personal attendant. We three remained standing, the unfortunate Ustane a little to the left of the rest of us.

"Now, oh Holly," Ayesha began, "how came it that thou who didst hear my words bidding this evil-doer"—and she pointed to Ustane—"to go from hence—thou at whose prayer I did weakly spare her life—how came it, I say, that thou wast a sharer in what I saw to-night? Answer, and for thine own sake, I say, speak the truth, for I am not minded to hear lies upon this matter!"

"It was by accident, oh Queen," I answered. "I knew nought of it."

"I do believe thee, oh Holly," she answered coldly, "and well it is for thee that I do—then does all the guilt rest upon her."

"I don't see any particular guilt about it," broke in Leo. "She is not anybody else's wife, and it appears that she has married me according to the custom of this awful place, so who is the worse? Any way, madam," he went on, "whatever she has done I have done too, so if she is to be punished let me be punished also; and I tell thee," he went on, working himself up into a fury, "that if thou biddest one of those deaf and dumb villains to touch her again I will tear him to pieces!" And he looked as though he meant it.

Ayesha listened in icy silence, and made no remark. When he had finished, however, she addressed Ustane.

"Hast thou aught to say, woman? Thou silly straw, thou feather, who didst think to float towards thy passion's petty ends, even against the great wind of my will! Tell me, for I fain would understand. Why didst thou this thing?"

And then I think I saw the most tremendous exhibition of moral courage and intrepidity that it is possible to conceive. For the poor doomed girl, knowing what she had to expect at the hands of her terrible Queen, knowing, too, from bitter experience how great was her power, yet gathered herself together, and out of the very depths of her despair found materials to defy her.

"I did it, oh Queen," she answered, drawing herself up to the full of her stately height, and throwing back the panther skin off her head, "because my love is stronger than the grave. I did it because my life without this man whom my heart chose would be but a living death. Therefore did I risk my life, and now that I know that it is forfeit to thine anger, yet am I glad that I did risk it, and pay it away in the risking, ay, because he embraced me once, and told me that he yet loved me."

Here Ayesha half rose from her couch, and then sank down again.

"I have no magic," went on Ustane, her rich voice ringing strong and full, "and I am not a Queen, nor do I live for ever, but a woman's heart is heavy to sink through waters, however deep, oh Queen! And a woman's eyes are quick to see, even through thy veil, oh Queen!

"Listen: I know it, thou dost love this man thyself, and therefore wouldst thou destroy me who stand across thy path. Ay, I die—I die, and go into the darkness, nor know I whither I go. But this I know. There is a light shining in my breast, and by that light, as by a lamp, I see the truth and the future that I shall not share unroll itself before me like a scroll. When first I knew my lord," and she pointed to Leo, "I knew also that death would be the bridal gift he gave me—it rushed upon me of a sudden, but I turned not back, being ready to pay the price, and, behold, death is here! And now, even as I knew that, so do I, standing on the steps of doom, know that thou shalt not reap the profits of thy crime. Mine he is, and, though thy beauty shine like a sun among the stars, mine shall he remain for thee. Never here upon this earth shall he look thee in the eyes and call thee wife. Thou, too, art doomed, I see"—and her voice rang like the cry of an inspired prophetess; "ah, I see"——

Then came an answering cry of mingled rage and terror. I turned my head. Ayesha had risen, and was standing with her outstretched hand pointing at Ustane, who had suddenly stopped speaking. I gazed at the poor woman, and as I gazed there grew upon her face that same, woful, fixed expression of terror that I had seen once before when she had broken out into her wild chant. Her eyes grew large, her nostrils dilated, and her lips blanched.

Ayesha said nothing, she made no sound, she only drew herself up, stretched out her arm, and, her tall veiled frame quivering like an aspen leaf, appeared to look fixedly at her victim. Even as she did so Ustane put her hands to her head, uttered one piercing scream, turned round twice, and then fell backwards with a thud prone upon the floor. Both Leo and myself rushed to her—she was stone dead—blasted into death by some mysterious electric agency or overwhelming will-force whereof the dread *She* had command.

For a moment Leo did not quite realise what had happened. But when he did, his face was awful to see. With a savage oath he rose from beside the corpse, and, turning, literally sprang at Ayesha. But she had been watching, and seeing him coming, stretched out her hand again, and he came staggering back towards me, and would have fallen, had I not caught him. Afterwards he told me that he felt as though he had suddenly received a violent blow in the chest, and, what is more, cowed as though all the manhood had been taken out of him.

Then Ayesha spoke. "Forgive me, my guest," she said softly, addressing him, "if I have shocked thee with my justice."

"Forgive thee, thou fiend!" roared poor Leo, wringing his hands, in his rage and grief. "forgive thee, thou murderess! By Heaven I will kill thee if I can!"

"Nay, nay," she answered in the same soft voice, "thou dost not understand—the time has come for thee to learn. Thou art my love, my Kallikrates, my Beautiful, my Strong! For two thousand years, Kallikrates, have I waited for thee, and now at length thou hast come back to me; and as for this woman," pointing to the corpse, "she stood between me and thee, and therefore I have removed her, Kallikrates."

"It is an accursed lie!" said Leo. "My name is not Kallikrates! I am Leo Vincey, my ancestor was Kallikrates—at least, I believe he was."

"Ah, thou sayest it—thine ancestor was Kallikrates, and thou, even thou, art Kallikrates come back—and mine own dear lord!"

"I am not Kallikrates, and as for being thy lord, or having anything to do with thee, I had rather be the lord of a fiend from hell, for she would be better than thou."

"Sayest thou so—sayest thou so, Kallikrates? Nay, but thou hast not seen me for so many years that no memory remains. Yet am I very fair, Kallikrates!"

"I hate thee, murderess, and I do not wish to see thee. What is it to me how fair thou art? I hate thee, I say."

"Yet within a very little space shalt thou creep to my knee, and swear that thou dost love me," answered Ayesha, with a sweet, mocking laugh. "Come, there is no time like the present time: here, before this dead girl, who loved thee, let us put it to the proof.

"Look now on me, Kallikrates!" and with a sudden motion she shook her gauzy covering from her, and stood forth in her low kirtle and her snaky zone, in her glorious, radiant beauty and her imperial grace, rising from her wrappings, as it were, like Venus from the wave, or Galatea from her marble,[1] or a beatified spirit from the tomb. She stood forth, and fixed her deep and glowing eyes upon his own, and I saw his clenched fists unclasp, and his set and quivering features relax beneath her gaze. I saw his wonder and astonishment grow into admiration, and then into fascination, and the more he struggled the more I saw the power of her dread beauty fasten on him and take possession of his senses, drugging them, and drawing the heart out of him. Did I not know the process? Had not I, who was twice his age, gone through it myself? Was I not going through it afresh even then, though her sweet and passionate gaze was not for me? Yes, alas, I was! Alas, that I should have to confess that at that very moment I was rent by mad and furious jealousy. I could have flown at his throat, shame upon me! The woman had confounded and almost destroyed my moral sense, as she was bound to confound all who looked upon her superhuman loveliness. But somehow, I do not know how, I got the better of myself, and once more turned to see the climax of the tragedy.

"Oh, heavens!" gasped Leo, "art thou a woman?"

"A woman in truth—in very truth—and thine own spouse, Kallikrates!" she answered, stretching out her rounded ivory arms towards him, and smiling, ah, so sweetly!

He looked and looked, and slowly I perceived that he was drawing nearer to her. Suddenly his eye fell upon the corpse of poor Ustane, and he shuddered and stopped.

"How can I?" he said hoarsely. "Thou art a murderess; she loved me."

Observe, he was already forgetting that he had loved her.

"It is nought," she murmured, and her voice sounded sweet as the night-wind passing through the trees. "It is nought at all. If I have sinned, let my beauty answer for my sin. If I have sinned it is for love of thee; let my sin, therefore, be put away and forgotten;" and once more she stretched out her arms and whispered "Come," and then in another few seconds it was over. I saw him struggle—I saw him even turn to fly; but her eyes drew him stronger than iron bonds, and the magic of her beauty and concentrated will and passion entered into him and overpowered him, ay, even there, in the presence of the body of the woman who had loved him well enough to die for him. It sounds

---

[1] In Greek myth, Pygmalion sculpted Galatea from stone and, after falling in love with his creation, prayed that she turn into a living woman. His prayer was answered by Aphrodite. Venus from the wave] the Roman goddess of love was supposed to have been born from the ocean, fully formed.

horrible and wicked enough, but he cannot be blamed too much, and be sure his sin will find him out. The temptress who drew him into evil was more than human, and her beauty was greater than the loveliness of the daughters of men.

I looked up again, and now her perfect form lay in his arms, and her lips were pressed against his own; and thus, with the corpse of his dead love for an altar, did Leo Vincey plight his troth to her red-handed murderess—plight it for ever and a day. For those who sell themselves into a like dominion, paying down the price of their own honour, and throwing their soul into the balance to sink the scale to the level of their lusts, can hope for no deliverance here or hereafter. As they have sown, so shall they reap, and reap even when the poppy flowers of passion have withered in their hands, and their harvest is but bitter tares, garnered in satiety.

Suddenly, with a snake-like motion, she seemed to slip from his embrace, and then again broke out into her low laugh of mockery.

"Did I not tell thee that within a little space thou wouldst creep to my knee, oh Kallikrates! And surely the space has not been a great one!"

Leo groaned in shame and misery; for though he was overcome and stricken down, he was not so lost as to be unaware of the depth of the degradation to which he had sunk. On the contrary, his better nature rose up in arms against his fallen self, as I saw clearly enough later on.

Ayesha laughed again, and then quickly veiled herself, and made a sign to the girl mute who had been watching the whole scene with curious startled eyes. The girl left, and presently returned, followed by two male mutes, to whom the Queen made another sign. Thereon they all three seized the body of poor Ustane by the arms, and dragged it heavily down the cavern and away through the curtains at the end. Leo watched it for a little while, and then covered his eyes with his hand, and it, too, to our excited fancy, seemed to watch us as it went.

"There passes the dead past," said Ayesha, solemnly, as the curtains shook and fell back into their places, when the ghastly procession had vanished behind them, and then, with one of those extraordinary transitions of which I have already spoken, she again threw off her veil, and broke out into a kind of pæan of triumph or epithalamium, which, wild and beautiful as it was, is exceedingly difficult to render into English. It was divided into two parts—one descriptive or definatory, and the other personal; and, as nearly as I can remember, ran as follows:—

Love is like a flower in the desert.
It is like the aloe of Arabia that blooms but once and dies; it blooms in

the salt emptiness of Life, and the brightness of its beauty is set upon the waste as a star is set upon a storm.

It hath the sun above that is the spirit, and above it blows the air of its own divinity.

At the echoing of a step, Love blooms, I say; I say Love blooms, and bends her beauty down to him who passeth by.

He plucketh it, yea, he plucketh the red cup that is full of honey, and beareth it away, away across the desert, away till the flower be withered, away till the desert be done.

There is only one perfect flower in the wilderness of Life.

That flower is Love!

There is only one fixed star in the mist of our wandering.

That star is Love!

There is only one hope in our despairing night.

That hope is Love!

All else is false. All else is shadow moving upon water. All else is wind and vanity.

Who shall say what is the weight or the measure of Love?

It is born of the flesh, it dwelleth in the spirit. From each does it draw its comfort.

For beauty it is as a star.

Many are its shapes, but all are beautiful, and none know where the star rose, or the horizon where it shall set.

Then turning to Leo, and laying her hand upon his shoulder, she went on in a fuller and more triumphant tone, and in balanced sentences that gradually swelled from idealised prose into pure and majestic verse:

Long have I loved thee, oh, my love; yet has my love not lessened.

Long have I waited for thee, and behold my reward is at hand—is here!

Far away I saw thee once, and thou wast taken from me.

Then in a grave sowed I the seed of patience, and shone upon it with the sun of hope, and watered it with tears of repentance, and breathed on it with the breath of my knowledge. And now, lo! it hath sprung up, and borne fruit. Lo! out of the grave hath it sprung. Yea, from among the dry bones and ashes of the dead.

I have waited, and my reward is with me.

I have overcome Death, and Death brought back to me him that was dead.

Therefore do I rejoice, for fair is the future.

Green are the paths that we shall tread across the everlasting meadows.
The hour is at hand. Night hath fled away into the valleys.
The dawn kisseth the mountain tops.
Soft shall we lie, my love, and easy shall we go,
Crowned shall we be with the diadem of Kings.
Worshipping and wonder-struck, all peoples of the world,
Blinded, shall fall before our beauty and our might.
From time unto times shall our greatness thunder on,
Rolling like a chariot through the dust of endless days.
Laughing shall we speed in our victory and pomp,
Laughing like the Daylight as he leaps along the hills.
Onward, still triumphant to a triumph ever new!
Onward, in our power to a power unattained!
Onward, never weary, clad with splendour for a robe!
Till accomplished be our fate, and the night is rushing down.

She paused in her strange and most thrilling allegorical chant, of which I am, unfortunately, only able to give the burden, and that feebly enough, and then said—

"Perchance thou dost not believe my word, Kallikrates—perchance thou thinkest that I do delude thee, and that I have not lived these many years, and that thou hast not been born again to me. Now will I show thee, and thee also, my Holly, who dost stand staring there as though of a truth thou hadst taken root in this unkindly soil. Bear each one of you a lamp, and follow after me whither I shall lead ye."

Without pausing to think—indeed, speaking for myself, I had almost abandoned the function in circumstances under which to think seemed to be absolutely useless, since thought fell hourly helpless against a black wall of wonder—we took the lamps and followed her. Going to the end of her "boudoir," she raised a curtain and revealed a little stair of the sort that was so common in these dim caves of Kôr. As we hurried down the stair I observed that the steps were worn in the centre to such an extent that some of them had been reduced from seven and a half inches, at which I guessed their original height, to about three and a half. Now, as all the other steps that I had seen in the caves had been practically unworn, as was to be expected, seeing that the only traffic that ever passed upon them was that of those who bore a fresh burden to the tomb, this fact struck my notice with that curious pertinacity with which little things do strike us when our minds are absolutely overwhelmed with a rush of powerful sensations, beaten flat as it were like a sea beneath a hurricane, so that every little object on the surface stands up like a mountain. At the bottom of the staircase, I stood and stared at the worn steps, and *She*, turning, saw me.

"Wonderest thou whose are the feet that have worn away the rock, my Holly?" she asked. "Behold! they are mine—even mine own light feet! I can remember when the stairs were fresh and level, but for two thousand years have I gone down hither day by day, and see, my sandals have worn out the solid rock!"

I made no answer, but I do not think that anything that I had heard or seen brought home to my limited understanding so clear a sense of this being's overwhelming antiquity as that hard rock hollowed out by her soft, white feet. How many millions of times must she have passed up and down that stair to bring about such a result?

The stair led to a tunnel, and a few paces down the tunnel was one of the usual curtain-hung doorways, a glance at which told me that it was the same where I had been a witness of that terrible scene by the leaping flame. I recognised the pattern of the curtain, and the sight of it brought the whole event vividly before my eyes, and made me tremble even at its memory. Ayesha entered the tomb (for it was a tomb), and we followed her,—I, for one, rejoicing that the mystery of the place was about to be cleared up, and yet afraid to face its solution.

XXI

THE DEAD AND LIVING MEET

"Behold the place where I have slept for these two thousand years," said Ayesha, taking the lamp from Leo's hand and holding it above her head. Its rays fell upon a little hollow in the floor, where I had seen the leaping flame, but the fire was out now. They fell upon the white form stretched there beneath its wrappings upon its bed of stone, upon the fretted carving of the tomb, and upon another shelf of stone opposite the one on which the body lay, and separated from it by the breadth of the cave.

"Here," went on Ayesha, laying her hand upon the rock, "here have I slept night by night for all these generations, with but a cloak to cover me. It did not become me that I should lie soft when my spouse yonder," and she pointed to the rigid form, "lay stiff in death. Here night by night have I slept in his cold company—till, thou seest, this thick slab, like the stairs down which we passed, has worn thin with the tossing of my form—so faithful have I been to thee even in thy space of sleep, Kallikrates. And now, my love, thou shalt see a wonderful thing—living, thou shalt behold thyself dead—for well have I tended thee during all these years, Kallikrates. Art thou prepared?"

We made no answer, but gazed at each other with frightened eyes, the whole scene was so dreadful and so solemn. Ayesha advanced, and laid her hand upon the corner of the shroud, and once more spoke.

"Be not affrighted," she said; "though the thing seem wonderful to thee—all we who live have thus lived before; nor is the very shape that holds us a stranger to the sun! Only we know it not, because memory writes no record, and earth hath gathered in the earth she lent us, for none have saved our glory from the grave. But I, by my arts and by the arts of those dead men of Kôr which I have learned, have held thee back, oh Kallikrates, from the dust, that the waxy stamp of beauty on thy face should ever rest before mine eye. 'Twas a mask that memory might fill, serving to fashion out thy presence from the past, and give it strength to wander in the habitations of my thought, clad in a mummery of life that stayed my appetite with visions of dead days.

"Behold now, let the dead and living meet! Across the gulf of Time they still are one. Time hath no power against Identity, though sleep in mercy hath blotted out the tablets of our mind, and with oblivion sealed the sorrows up that else would hound us on from life to life, stuffing the brain with gathered misery till it burst in the madness of uttermost despair. Still are they one, for the wrappings of our sleep shall roll away as thunder clouds before the wind; the frozen voices of the past shall melt in music like mountain snows beneath the sun; and the weeping and the laughter of the lost hours shall be heard once more sweetly echoing up the cliffs of immeasurable Time.

"Ay, the sleep shall roll away, and the voices shall be heard, when down the completed chain, whereof our each existence is a link, the lightning of the Spirit hath passed to work out the purpose of our being; quickening and fusing those separated days of life, and shaping them to a staff whereon we may safely lean as we wend to our appointed fate.

"Therefore, have no fear, Kallikrates, when thou—living, and but lately born—shalt look upon thine own departed self, who breathed and died so long ago. I do but turn one page in thy Book of Being, and show thee what is writ thereon.

"*Behold!*"

With a sudden motion she drew the shroud from the cold form, and let the lamplight play upon it. I looked, and then shrank back horrified; since, say what she might in explanation, the sight was an uncanny one—for her explanations were beyond the grasp of our finite minds, and when they were separated from the mists of vague esoteric philosophy, and brought into conflict with the cold and horrifying fact, did not do much to break its force. For there, stretched upon the stone bier before us, robed in white and perfectly preserved, was what appeared to be the body of Leo Vincey. I stared from Leo, standing there alive, to Leo lying there dead, and could see no difference; except, perhaps, that the body on the bier looked older. Feature for feature they were the same, even down to the crop of little golden curls, which was Leo's most uncommon beauty. It even seemed to me, as I looked, that the expression on the dead man's face resembled that which I had sometimes seen upon Leo's when he was plunged into profound sleep. I can only sum up the closeness of the resemblance by saying that I never saw twins so exactly similar as that dead and living pair.

I turned to see what effect was produced upon Leo by this sight of his dead self, and found it to be one of partial stupefaction. He stood for two or three minutes staring and said nothing, and when at last he spoke it was only to ejaculate,

"Cover it up and take me away."

"Nay, wait," said Ayesha, who, standing with the lamp raised above her head, flooding with its light her own rich beauty and the cold wonder of the death-clothed form upon the bier, looked more like an inspired Sibyl[1] than a woman as she rolled out her majestic sentences with a grandeur and a freedom of utterance which I am, alas, quite unable to do justice.

"Wait; I would show thee something, that no tittle of my crime may be hidden from thee. Do thou, oh Holly, open the garment on the breast of the dead Kallikrates, for perchance my lord may fear to touch himself."

I obeyed with trembling hands. It seemed a desecration and an unhallowed thing to touch that sleeping image of the live man by my side. Presently his broad chest was bare, and there upon it, right over the heart, was a wound, evidently inflicted with a spear.

"Thou seest, Kallikrates," she said. "Behold, it was I who slew thee: in the Place of Life I gave thee death. I slew thee because of the Egyptian Amenartas, whom thou didst love, for by her arts she held thy heart, and her I could not slay as but now I slew the woman, for she was too strong for me. In my haste and bitter anger I slew thee, and now for all these days have I lamented thee, and waited for thy coming. And thou hast

---

[1] A female prophet of ancient Greece or Rome.

come, and none can stand between thee and me, and of a truth now for death I will give thee life—not life eternal, for that none can give, but life and youth that shall endure for thousands upon thousands of years, and with it pomp, and power, and wealth, and all things that are good and beautiful, such as have been to no man before thee, nor shall be to any man who comes after. And now one thing more, and thou shalt rest and make ready for the day of thy new birth. Thou seest this body, which was thine own. For all these centuries it hath been my comfort and my companion, but now I need it no more, for I have thy living presence, and it can but serve to stir up memories of that which I had fain forget. Let it therefore go back to the dust from which I kept it.

"Behold! I have prepared against this happy hour!" and going to the other shelf, or stone ledge, which, she said, had served her for a bed, she took from it a large vitrified double-handed vase, the mouth of which was tied up with a bladder. This she loosed, and then, having bent down and gently kissed the white forehead of the dead man, she undid the vase, and sprinkled its contents carefully over the form, taking, I observed, the greatest precautions against any drop of them touching us or herself, and then poured out what remained of the liquid upon the chest and head. Instantly a dense vapour arose, and the cave was filled with choking fumes that prevented us from seeing anything while the deadly acid (for I presume it was some tremendous preparation of that sort) did its work. From the spot where the body lay came a fierce fizzing and cracking sound, which ceased, however, before the fumes had cleared away. At last they were all gone, except a little cloud which still hung over the corpse. In a couple of minutes more this, too, had vanished, and, wonderful as it may seem, it is a fact that on the stone bench that had supported the mortal remains of the ancient Kallikrates for so many centuries there was now nothing to be seen but a few handsfull of smoking white powder. The acid had utterly destroyed the body, and even in places eaten into the stone. Ayesha stooped down, and, taking a handful of this powder in her grasp, threw it into the air, saying at the same time, in a voice of calm solemnity,

"Dust to dust!—the past to the past!—the dead to the dead!—Kallikrates is dead, and is born again!"

The ashes floated noiselessly to the rocky floor, and we stood in awed silence and watched them fall, too overcome for words.

"Now leave me," she said, "and sleep if ye may. I must watch and think, for to-morrow night we go hence, and the time is long since I trod the path that we must follow."

Accordingly we bowed, and left her.

As we passed to our own apartment I peeped into Job's sleeping place, to see how he fared, for he had gone away just before our interview with the murdered Ustane, quite prostrated by the terrors of the Amahagger festivity. He was sleeping soundly, good honest fellow that he was, and I rejoiced to think that his nerves, which, like those of most uneducated people, were far from strong, had been spared the closing scenes of that dreadful day. Then we entered our own chamber, and here at last poor Leo, who, ever since he had looked upon that frozen image of his living self, had been in a state not far removed from stupefaction, burst out into a torrent of grief. Now that he was no longer in the presence of the dread *She*, his sense of the awfulness of all that had happened, and more especially of the wicked murder of Ustane, who was bound to him by ties so close, broke upon him like a storm, and lashed him into an agony of remorse and terror which was painful to witness. He cursed himself—he cursed the hour when we had first seen the writing on the sherd, which was being so mysteriously verified, and bitterly he cursed his own weakness. Ayesha he dared not curse—who dared speak evil of such a woman, whose consciousness for aught we knew was watching us at this very moment?

"What am I to do, old fellow?" he groaned, resting his head against my shoulder in the extremity of his grief. "I let her be killed—not that I could help that, but within five minutes I was kissing her murderess over her body. I am a degraded brute, but I cannot resist that" (and here his voice sank) "that awful sorceress. I know I shall do it again to-morrow; I know that I am in her power for always; if I never saw her again I should never think of anybody else for all my life; I must follow her as a needle follows a magnet; I would not go away now if I could; I could not leave her, my legs would not carry me, but my mind is still clear enough, and in my mind I hate her—at least, I think so. It is all so horrible; and that— that body! What can I make of it? It was *me*! I am sold into bondage, old fellow, and she will take my soul as the price of herself!"

Then, for the first time, I told him that I was in a but very little better position, and I am bound to say that, notwithstanding his own infatuation, he had the decency to sympathise with me. Perhaps he did not think it worth while being jealous, realising that he had no cause so far as the lady was concerned. I went on to suggest that we should try to run away, but we soon rejected the project as futile, and, to be perfectly honest, I do not believe that either of us would really have left Ayesha even if some superior power had suddenly offered to convey us from these gloomy caves and set us down in Cambridge. We could no more have left her than a moth can leave the light that destroys it. We were like confirmed opium-eaters: in our moments of reason, we well knew the deadly nature of our pursuit, but we certainly were not prepared to abandon its terrible delights.

No man who once had seen *She* unveiled, and heard the music of her voice, and drunk in the bitter wisdom of her words, would willingly give up the sight for a whole sea of placid joys. How much more then was this likely to be so when, as in Leo's case, to put myself out of the question, this extraordinary creature declared her utter and absolute devotion, and gave what appeared to be proofs of its having lasted for some two thousand years?

No doubt she was a wicked person, and no doubt she had murdered Ustane when she stood in her path, but then she was very faithful, and by a law of nature man is apt to think but lightly of a woman's crimes, especially if that woman be beautiful, and the crime be committed for the love of him.

And then for the rest, when had such a chance ever come to a man before as that which now lay in Leo's hand? True, in uniting himself to this dread woman, he would place his life in the hand of a mysterious creature of evil tendencies,* but then that would be likely enough to

---

* After some months of consideration of this statement I am bound to confess that I am not quite satisfied of its truth. It is perfectly true that Ayesha committed a murder, but I shrewdly suspect that were we endowed with the same absolute power, and if we had the same tremendous interest at stake, we should be very apt to do likewise under parallel circumstances. Also, it must be remembered that she looked on it as an execution for disobedience under a system which made the slightest disobedience punishable by death. Putting aside this question of the murder, her evil-doing resolves itself into the expression of views and the acknowledgment of motives which are contrary to our preaching if not to our practice. Now at first sight this might be fairly taken as a proof of an evil nature, but when we come to consider the great antiquity of the individual it becomes doubtful if it was anything more than the natural cynicism which arises from age and bitter experience, and the possession of extraordinary powers of observation. It is a well-known fact that very often, putting the period of boyhood out of the question, the older we grow the more cynical and hardened we get, indeed many of us are only saved by timely death from utter moral petrifaction if not moral corruption. No one will deny that a young man is on the average better than an old one, for he is without that experience of the order of things that in certain thoughtful dispositions can hardly fail to produce cynicism, and that disregard of acknowledged methods and established custom which we call evil. Now the oldest man upon the earth was but a babe compared to Ayesha, and the wisest man upon the earth was not one-third as wise. And the fruit of her wisdom was this, that there was but one thing worth living for, and that was Love in its highest sense, and to gain that good thing she was not prepared to stop at trifles. This is really the sum of her evil doings, and it must be remembered on the other hand that whatever may be thought of them she had some virtues developed to a degree very uncommon in either sex—constancy, for instance.—L.H.H.

happen to him in any ordinary marriage. On the other hand, however, no ordinary marriage could bring him such awful beauty—for awful is the only word that can describe it—such divine devotion, such wisdom, and command over the secrets of nature, and the place and power that they must win, or lastly the royal crown of unending youth, if indeed she could give that. No, on the whole, it is not wonderful, that though Leo was plunged in bitter shame and grief, such as any gentleman would have felt under the circumstances, he was not ready to entertain the idea of running away from his extraordinary fortune.

My own opinion is that he would have been mad if he had done so. But then I confess that my statement on the matter must be accepted with qualifications. I am in love with the lady myself to this day, and I would rather have been the object of her affection for one short week than that of any other woman in the world for a whole life-time. And let me add that if anybody who doubts this statement, and thinks me foolish for making it, could have seen Ayesha draw her veil and flash out in beauty on his gaze, his view would exactly coincide with my own. Of course, I am speaking of any *man*. We never had the advantage of a lady's opinion of Ayesha, but I think it quite possible that she would have regarded the Queen with dislike, would have expressed her disapproval in some more or less pointed manner, and ultimately have got herself blasted.

For two hours or more Leo and I sat with shaken nerves and frightened eyes, and talked over the almost miraculous events through which we were passing. It seemed like a dream or a fairy tale, instead of the solemn, sober fact. Who would have believed that the writing on the potsherd was not only true, but that we should live to verify its truth, and that we two seekers should find her who was sought, patiently awaiting our coming in the tombs of Kôr? Who would have thought that in the person of Leo this mysterious woman should, as she believed, discover the being whom she awaited from century to century, and whose former earthly habitation she had till this very night preserved? But so it was. In the face of all we had seen it was difficult for us as ordinary reasoning men any longer to doubt its truth, and therefore at last, with humble hearts and a deep sense of the impotence of human knowledge, and the insolence of its assumption that denies that which it has no experience of to be possible, we laid ourselves down to sleep, leaving our fates in the hands of that watching Providence which had thus chosen to allow us to draw the veil of human ignorance, and reveal to us for good or evil some glimpse of the possibilities of life.

XXII

JOB HAS A PRESENTIMENT

It was nine o'clock on the following morning when Job, who still looked scared and frightened, came in to call me, and at the same time breathe his gratitude at finding us alive in our beds, which it appeared was more than he had expected. When I told him of the awful end of poor Ustane he was even more grateful at our survival, and much shocked, though Ustane had been no favourite of his, or he of hers, for the matter of that. She called him "pig" in bastard Arabic, and he called her "hussy" in good English, but these amenities were forgotten in the face of the catastrophe that had overwhelmed her at the hands of her Queen.

"I don't want to say anything as mayn't be agreeable, sir," said Job, when he had finished exclaiming at my tale, "but it's my opinion that that there *She* is the old gentleman himself, or perhaps his wife, if he has got one, which I suppose he has, for he couldn't be so wicked all by himself. The Witch of Endor[1] was a fool to her, sir; bless you, she would make no more of raising every gentleman in the Bible out of these here beastly tombs than I should of growing cress on an old flannel. It's a country of devils, this is, sir, and she's the master one of the lot; and if ever we get out of it it will be more than I expect to do. I don't see no way out of it. That witch isn't likely to let a fine young man like Mr. Leo go."

"Come," I said, "at any rate she saved his life."

"Yes, and she'll take his soul to pay for it. She'll make him a witch, like herself. I say it's wicked to have anything to do with those sort of people. Last night, sir, I lay awake and read in my little Bible that my poor old mother gave me about what is going to happen to sorceresses and them sort till my hair stood on end.[2] Lord, how the old lady would stare if she saw where her Job had got to!"

"Yes, it's a queer country, and a queer people too, Job," I answered, with a sigh, for, though I am not superstitious like Job, I admit to a natural shrinking (which will not bear investigation) from the things that are above Nature.

"You are right, sir," he answered, "and if you won't think me very foolish, I should like to say something to you now that Mr. Leo is out of the way"—(Leo had got up early and gone for a stroll)—"and that

---

[1]   In the Bible, a woman who raised the spirit of the prophet Samuel; see 1 Samuel 28.
[2]   Revelation 21:8.

is that I know it is the last country as ever I shall see in this world. I had a dream last night, and I dreamed that I saw my old father with a kind of night-shirt on him, something like these folks wear when they want to be in particular full-dress, and a bit of that feathery grass in his hand, which he may have gathered on the way, for I saw lots of it yesterday about three hundred yards from the mouth of this beastly cave.

"'Job,' he said to me, solemn like, and yet with a kind of satisfaction shining through him, more like a Methody parson when he has sold a neighbour a marked horse for a sound one and cleared twenty pounds by the job than anything I can think on, 'Job, time's up, Job; but I never did expect to have to come and hunt you out in this 'ere place, Job. Such ado as I have had to nose you up; it wasn't friendly to give your poor old father such a run, let alone that a wonderful lot of bad characters hail from this place Kôr.'"

"Regular cautions," I suggested.

"Yes, sir—of course, sir, that's just what he said they was—'cautions, downright scorchers,'[1] sir—and I'm sure I don't doubt it, seeing what I know of them and their hot-potting ways," went on Job, sadly. "Anyway, he was sure that time was up, and went away saying that we should see more than we cared for of each other soon, and I suppose he was alluding to the fact that father and I never could hit it off together for longer nor three days, and I daresay that things will be similar when we meet again."

"Surely," I said, "you don't think that you are going to die because you dreamed you saw your old father; if one dies because one dreams of one's father, what happens to a man who dreams of his mother-in-law?"

"Ah, sir, you're laughing at me," said Job; "but, you see, you didn't know my old father. If it had been anybody else—my Aunt Mary, for instance, who never made much of a job—I should not have thought so much of it; but my father was that idle, which he shouldn't have been with seventeen children, that he would never have put himself out to come here just to see the place. No, sir; I know that he meant business. Well, sir, I can't help it; I suppose every man must go some time or other, though it is a hard thing to die in a place like this, where Christian burial isn't to be had for its weight in gold. I've tried to be a good man, sir, and do my duty honest, and if it wasn't for the supercilus kind of way in which father carried on last night—a sort of sniffing at me as it were, as though he hadn't no opinion of my references and

---

[1]   Astonishing, alarming things or people (slang).

testimonials—I should feel easy enough in my mind. Any way, sir, I've been a good servant to you and Mr. Leo, bless him! Why it seems but the other day that I used to lead him about the streets with a penny whip; and if ever you get out of this place—which, as father didn't allude to you, perhaps you may—I hope you will think kindly of my whitened bones, and never have anything more to do with Greek writing on flower-pots, sir, if I may make so bold as to say so."

"Come, come, Job," I said, seriously, "this is all nonsense, you know. You mustn't be silly enough to go getting such ideas into your head. We've lived through some queer things, and I hope that we may go on doing so."

"No, sir," answered Job, in a tone of conviction that jarred on me unpleasantly, "it isn't nonsense. I'm a doomed man, and I feel it, and a most uncomfortable feeling it is, sir, for one can't help wondering how it's going to come about. If you are eating your dinner you think of poison and it goes against your stomach, and if you are walking along these dark rabbit-burrows you think of knives, and Lord, don't you just shiver about the back! I ain't particular, sir, provided it's sharp, like that poor girl, who, now that she's gone, I am sorry to have spoke hard on, though I don't approve of her morals in getting married, which I consider too quick to be decent. Still, sir," and poor Job turned a shade paler as he said it, "I do hope it won't be that hot-pot game."

"Nonsense," I broke in angrily, "nonsense!"

"Very well, sir," said Job, "it isn't my place to differ from you, sir, but if you happen to be going anywhere, sir, I should be obliged if you could manage to take me with you, seeing that I shall be glad to have a friendly face to look at when the time comes, just to help one through, as it were. And now, sir, I'll be getting the breakfast," and he went, leaving me in a very uncomfortable state of mind. I was deeply attached to old Job, who was one of the best and honestest men I have ever had to do with in any class of life, and really more of a friend than a servant, and the mere idea of anything happening to him brought a lump into my throat. Beneath all his ludicrous talk I could see that he himself was quite convinced that something was going to happen, and though in most cases these convictions turn out to be utter moonshine—and this particular one especially was to be amply accounted for by the gloomy and unaccustomed surroundings in which its victim was placed—still it did more or less carry a chill to my heart, as any thing that is obviously a genuine object of belief is apt to do, however absurd the belief may be. Presently the breakfast arrived, and with it Leo, who

" 'It is safe,' she called."

had been taking a walk outside the cave—to clear his mind, he said—and very glad I was to see both, for they gave me a respite from my gloomy thoughts. After breakfast we went for another walk, and watched some of the Amahagger sowing a plot of ground with the grain from which they make their beer. This they did in scriptural fashion—a man with a bag made of goat's-hide fastened round his waist walking up and down the plot and scattering the seed as he went. It was a positive relief to see one of these dreadful people do anything so homely and pleasant as sow a field, perhaps because it seemed to link them, as it were, with the rest of humanity.

As we were returning Billali met us, and informed us that it was *She's* pleasure that we should wait upon her, and accordingly we entered her presence, not without trepidation, for Ayesha was certainly an exception to the rule. Familiarity with her might and did breed passion and wonder and horror, but it certainly did *not* breed contempt.

(*To be continued*)

PART 12 (18 DECEMBER 1886)

CHAPTER XXII (*CONTINUED*)

We were as usual shown in by the mutes, and after these had retired Ayesha unveiled, and once more bade Leo embrace her, which, notwithstanding his heart-searchings of the previous night, he did with more alacrity and fervour than in strictness courtesy required.

She laid her white hand on his head, and looked him fondly in the eyes. "Dost thou wonder, my Kallikrates," she said, "when thou shalt call me all thine own, and when we shall of a truth be for one another and to one another? I will tell thee. First, must thou be even as I am, not immortal indeed, for that am I not, but so cased and hardened against the attacks of Time, that his arrows shall glance from the armour of thy vigorous life as the sunbeams glance from water. As yet I may not mate with thee, for thou and I are different, and the very brightness of my being would burn thee up, and perchance destroy thee. Thou couldst not even bear to look upon me for too long a time lest thine eyes should ache, and thy senses swim, and therefore" (with a little coquettish nod) "shall I presently veil myself again." (This by the way she did not do.) "No: listen, thou shalt not be tried beyond endurance, for this very evening, an hour before the sun goes down, shall we start hence, and by to-morrow's dark, if all goes well, and the road is not lost to me, which I pray it may not be, shall we stand in the place of Life, and thou shalt bathe in the fire, and come forth glorified, as no man ever was before thee, and then, Kallikrates, shalt thou call me wife, and I will call thee husband."

Leo muttered something in answer to this astonishing statement, I don't know what, and she laughed a little at his confusion, and went on,

"And thou, too, oh Holly; on thee also will I confer this boon, and then of a truth shalt thou be an evergreen tree, and this will I do—well, because thou hast pleased me, Holly, for thou art not altogether a fool, like most of the sons of men, and because, though thou hast a school of philosophy as full of nonsense as those of the old days, yet hast thou not forgotten how to turn a pretty phrase about a lady's eyes."

"Hulloa, old fellow!" whispered Leo, with a return of his old cheerfulness, "have you been paying compliments? I should never have thought it of you!"

"I thank thee, oh Ayesha," I replied, with as much dignity as I could command, "but if there be such a place as thou dost describe, and if in this strange place there can be found a fiery virtue that can hold off Death when he comes to pluck us by the hand, yet would I none of it. For me, oh Ayesha, the world has not proved so soft a nest that I would lie in it for ever. A stony-hearted mother is our earth, and stones are the bread she gives her children for their daily food.[1] Stones to eat and bitter water for their thirst, and stripes for tender nurture. Who would endure this for many lives? Who would so laden up his back with memories of lost hours and loves and of his neighbour's sorrows that he cannot lessen, and wisdom that brings not consolation? Hard is it to die, because our delicate flesh doth shrink back from the worm it will not feel, and from that unknown which the winding-sheet doth curtain from our view. But harder still, to my fancy, would it be to live on, green in the leaf and fair, but dead and rotten at the core, and feel that other secret worm of recollection gnawing ever at the heart."

"Bethink thee, Holly," she said; "yet doth long life and strength and beauty beyond measure mean power and all things that are dear to man."

---

[1] Matthew 7:9.

"And what, oh Queen," I answered, "are those things that are dear to man? Are they not bubbles? Is not ambition but an endless ladder by which no height is ever climbed till the last unreachable rung is mounted? For height leads on to height, and there is no resting-place upon them, and rung doth grow upon rung, and there is no limit to the number. Doth not wealth satiate and become nauseous, and no longer serve to satisfy or pleasure, or to buy an hour's ease of mind? And is there any end to wisdom that we may hope to reach it? Rather, the more we learn shall we not thereby be able only to better compass out our ignorance? Did we live ten thousand years could we hope to solve the secrets of the suns, and of the space beyond the suns, and of the Hand that hung them in the heavens? Would not our wisdom be but as a gnawing hunger calling our consciousness day by day to a knowledge of the empty craving of our souls? Would it not be but as a light in a great cavern, that though bright it burn, and brighter yet, doth but the more serve to show the depths of the gloom around it? And what good thing is there beyond that we may gain by length of days?"

"Nay, my Holly, there is love—love which makes all things beautiful, and doth breathe divinity into the very dust we tread. With love shall life roll gloriously on from year to year like the voice of some great music that hath power to hold the hearer's heart poised on eagle's wings above the sordid shame and folly of the earth."

"It may be so," I answered; "but if the loved one prove a broken reed to pierce us, or if the love be loved in vain—what then? Shall a man grave his sorrows upon a stone when he hath but need to write them on the water? Nay, oh *She*, I will live my day and grow old with my generation, and die my appointed death, and be forgotten. For I do hope for an immortality to which the little span that perchance thou canst confer will be but as a finger's length laid against the measure of the great world; and, mark this, the immortality to which I look, and which my faith doth promise me, shall be free from the bonds that here must tie my spirit down. For, while the flesh endures, sorrow and evil and the scorpion whips of sin[1] must endure also; but when the flesh hath fallen from us, then shall the spirit shine forth clad in the brightness of eternal good, and for its common air shall breathe so rare an ether of most noble thoughts, that the highest aspiration of our manhood, or the purest incense of a maiden's prayer, would prove too earthly gross to float therein."

---

[1]   1 Kings 12:11.

"Thou lookest high," answered Ayesha, with a little laugh, "and speakest clearly as a trumpet and with no uncertain sound. And yet methinks that but now didst thou talk of 'that unknown' from which the winding-sheet doth curtain us. But, perchance, thou seest with the eye of faith, gazing on that brightness that is to be, through the painted glass of thy imagination. Strange are the pictures of the future that mankind can thus draw with this brush of faith and this many-coloured pigment of imagination! Strange, too, that no one of them doth agree with another! I could tell thee—but there, what is the use? why rob a fool of his bauble? Let it pass, and I pray, oh Holly, that when thou dost feel old age creeping slowly toward thyself, and the confusion of senility making havoc in thy brain, thou mayest not bitterly regret that thou didst cast away the imperial boon I would have given to thee. But so it hath ever been, man can never be content with that which his hand can pluck. If a lamp be in his reach to light him through the darkness, he must needs cast it down because it is no star. Happiness danceth ever a pace before him, like the marsh-fires in the swamps, and he must catch the fire, and he must hold the star. Beauty is nought to him, because there are lips more honey-sweet; and wealth is nought, because others can weigh him down with heavier shekels; and fame is nought, because there have been greater men than he. Thyself thou saidst it, and I turn thy words against thee. Well, thou dreamest that thou shalt pluck the star. I believe it not, and I think thee a fool, my Holly, to throw away the lamp."

I made no answer, for I could not—especially before Leo—tell her that since I had seen her face I knew that it would always be before my eyes, and that I had no wish to prolong an existence which must always be haunted and tortured by her memory, and by the last bitterness of unsatisfied love. But so it was, and so, alas, is it to this hour!

"And now," went on *She*, changing her tone and the subject together, "tell me, my Kallikrates, for as yet I know it not, how came ye to seek me here? Yesternight thou didst say that Kallikrates—him whom thou sawest—was thine ancestor. How was it? Tell me—thou dost not speak overmuch!"

Thus adjured, Leo told her the wonderful story of the casket and of the potsherd that, written on by his ancestress, the Egyptian Amenartas, had been the means of guiding us to her. Ayesha listened intently, and, when he had finished, spoke to me.

"Did I not tell thee one day, when we did talk of good and evil, oh Holly—it was when my beloved lay so ill—that out of good came evil, and out of evil good,—that they who sowed knew not what the crop should be, nor he who struck where the blow should fall? See, now: this Egyptian Amenartas, this child of the Nile who hated me, and whom even now I hate, for in a way she did prevail against me—see, now, she herself hath been the very means to bring her lover to mine arms. For her sake I slew him, and now, behold, through her he hath come back to me! She would have done me evil, and sowed her seeds that I might reap tares, and behold she hath given me more than all the world can give, and there is a strange square for thee to fit into thy circle of good and evil, oh Holly!

"And so," she went on after a pause "and so she bade her son destroy me if he might, because I slew his father. And thou, my Kallikrates, art the father, and in a sense thou art likewise the son; and wouldst thou avenge thy wrong, and the wrong of that far-off mother of thine upon me, oh Kallikrates? See," and she slid to her knees, and drew the white corsage still farther down her ivory bosom,—"see, here beats my heart, and there by thy side is a knife, heavy, and long, and sharp, the very knife to slay an erring woman with. Take it now, and be avenged. Strike, and strike home, so shalt thou be satisfied, Kallikrates, and go through life a happy man, because thou hast paid back the wrong, and obeyed the mandate of the past."

He looked at her, and then stretched out his hand and lifted her to her feet.

"Rise, Ayesha," he said sadly; "well thou knowest that I cannot strike thee, no, not even for the sake of her whom thou slewest but last night. I am in thy power, and a very slave to thee. How can I kill thee?— sooner should I slay myself."

"Almost dost thou begin to love me, Kallikrates," she answered smiling. "And now tell me of thy country—'tis a great people, is it not? with an empire like that of Rome! Surely thou wouldst return thither, and it is well, for I mean not that thou shouldst dwell in these caves of Kôr. Nay, when once thou art even as I am, we will go hence—fear not I shall find a means—and then shall we cross to this England of thine, and live as it becometh us to live. Two thousand years have I waited for the day when I should see the last of these hateful caves and this gloomy-visaged folk, and now it is at hand, and my heart bounds up to meet it like a child's towards its holiday. For thou shalt rule this England."

"But we have got a queen already,"[1] broke in Leo, hastily.

"It is nought, it is nought," said Ayesha; "she can be overthrown."

---

[1] Queen Victoria ruled England from 1837 until 1901.

At this we both broke out into an exclamation of horror, and explained that we should as soon think of overthrowing ourselves.

"But here is a strange thing," said Ayesha, in astonishment; "a queen whom her people love! Surely the world must have changed since I dwelt in Kôr."

Again we explained that it was the character of monarchs that had changed, and that the one under whom we lived was venerated and beloved by all right-thinking people in her vast realms. Also, we told her that real power in our country rested in the hands of the people, and that we were in fact ruled by the votes of the lower and least educated classes of the community.[1]

"Ah," she said, "a democracy—then surely there is a tyrant, for I have long since seen that democracies, having no clear will of their own, in the end set up a tyrant, and worship him."

"Yes," I said, "we have our tyrants."

"Well," she answered, resignedly, "we can at any rate destroy these tyrants, and Kallikrates shall rule the land."

I instantly informed Ayesha that in England blasting was not an amusement that could be indulged in with impunity, and that any such attempt would meet with the consideration of the law, and probably end upon a scaffold.

"The law," she laughed with scorn, "the law! Canst thou not understand, oh Holly, that I am above the law, and so shall my Kallikrates be also? All human law will be to us as the north wind to a mountain. Does the wind bend the mountain, or the mountain the wind?

"And now leave me, I pray thee, and thou too, my own Kallikrates, for I would get me ready against our journey, and so must ye both, and your servant also. But bring no great quantity of things with thee, for I trust that we shall be but three days gone. Then shall we return hither, and I will make a plan whereby we can bid farewell for ever to these sepulchres of Kôr. Yes, surely thou mayst kiss my hand."

So we went, I, for one, meditating deeply on the awful nature of the problem that now opened out before us. The terrible *She* had evidently made up her mind to go to England, and it made me absolutely shudder to think what would be the result of her arrival there. What her powers were I knew, and I could not doubt but that she would exercise them to the full. It might be possible to control her for a while, but her proud,

---

[1]   Holly and Leo refer to the Third Reform Bill of 1884, which extended the vote to most working-class males.

ambitious spirit would be certain to break loose and avenge itself for the long centuries of its solitude. She would, if necessary, and if the power of her beauty did not unaided prove equal to the occasion, blast her way to any end she set before her, and as she could not die, and, for aught I knew, could not even be killed,* what was there to stop her? In the end she would, I had little doubt, assume absolute rule over the British dominions, and probably over the whole earth, and though I was sure that she would speedily make ours the most glorious and prosperous empire that the world has ever seen, it would be at the cost of a terrible sacrifice of life.

The whole thing sounded like a dream or some extraordinary invention of a speculative brain, and yet it was a fact—a dreadful fact—of which the whole world would soon be called on to take notice. What was the meaning of it all? After much thinking I could only conclude that this wonderful creature, whose passion had kept her for so many centuries chained as it were, and comparatively harmless, was now about to be used by Providence as a means to change the order of the world, and possibly, by the building up of a power that could no more be rebelled against or questioned than the decrees of Fate, to change it materially for the better.

XXIII

THE TEMPLE OF TRUTH

Our preparations did not take us very long. We put a change of clothing apiece and some spare boots into my Gladstone bag, also we took our revolvers and an express rifle each, together with a good supply of ammunition, a precaution to which, under Providence, we subsequently owed our lives over and over again. The rest of our gear, together with our heavy rifles, we left behind us.

A few minutes before the appointed time we once more attended in Ayesha's boudoir, and found her also ready, her dark cloak thrown over her winding-sheet like wrappings.

"Are ye prepared for the great venture?" she said.

---

* I regret to say that I was never able to ascertain if *She* was invulnerable against the accidents of life. Presumably this was so, else some misadventure would have been sure to put an end to her in the course of so many centuries. True, she offered to let Leo slay her, but very probably this was only an experiment to try his temper and mental attitude towards her. She never gave way to impulse without some valid object.—L.H.H.

"We are," I answered, "though for my part, Ayesha, I have no faith in it."

"Ah, my Holly," she said, "thou art of a truth like those old Jews—of whom the memory plagues me so sorely—unbelieving, and hard to accept that which they have not seen. But thou shalt see; for unless my mirror yonder lies," and she pointed to the font of crystal water, "the path is yet open as it was of old time. And now let us start upon the new life which shall end who knoweth where?"

"Ah," I echoed, "who knoweth where?" and we passed down into the great central cave, and out into the light of day. At the mouth of the cave we found a single litter with six bearers, all of them mutes, waiting, and with them I was relieved to see our old friend Billali, for whom I had conceived a sort of affection. It appeared that for reasons not necessary to explain at length Ayesha had thought it best that with the exception of herself we should proceed on foot, and this we were nothing loth to do, after our long confinement in caves, which, however suitable they might be for sarcophagi[1]—a singularly inappropriate word, by the way, for these particular tombs, which certainly did not consume the bodies given to their keeping—were depressing habitations for breathing mortals like ourselves. Either by accident or by the orders of *She*, the space in front of the cave where we had beheld that awful dance was perfectly clear of spectators. Not a soul was to be seen, and consequently I do not believe that our departure was known to anybody except perhaps the mutes who waited on *She*, and they were, of course, in the habit of holding their tongues as to what they saw.

In a few minutes we were stepping out sharply across the great cultivated plain or lake bed framed like a vast emerald in its setting of frowning cliff, and had another opportunity of wondering at the extraordinary nature of the site chosen by these old people of Kôr for their capital, and at the marvellous amount of labour, ingenuity, and engineering skill that must have been brought into requisition by the founders of the city to drain so huge a sheet of water, and to keep it clear of subsequent accumulations. It is, indeed, so far as my experience goes, an unequalled instance of what man can do in the face of nature, for in my opinion such achievements as the Suez Canal[2] or even the Mont Cenis Tunnel[3] do not approach this ancient undertaking in magnitude.

---

[1] Tombs. "Sarcophogus" means "flesh-eater" in Greek, and refers to limestone tombs which were originally believed to have the power to consume the dead.

[2] Completed in 1869, connecting the Mediterranean and the Red Sea.

[3] Completed in 1871, connecting France and Italy.

When we had been walking for about half-an-hour enjoying ourselves exceeding in the delightful cool which about this time of the day always appeared to descend upon the great plain of Kôr, and in some degree atoned for the want of any land or sea breeze, for all wind was kept off by the rocky mountain wall, we began to get a clear view of what Billali had informed us were the ruins of the great city. And even from that distance we could see how wonderful those ruins were, a fact that with every step we took became more evident. The city was not very large if compared to Babylon or Thebes, or other cities of remote antiquity; perhaps its outer wall contained some twelve square miles of ground, or a little more. Nor had the walls, so far as we could judge when we reached them, been very high, probably not more than forty feet, which was about their present height where they had not through the sinking of the ground or some such cause fallen into ruin. The reason of this, no doubt, was that the people of Kôr, being protected from any outside attack by far more tremendous ramparts than any that the hand of man could rear, only required them for show and to guard against civil discord. But on the other hand they were as broad as they were high, built entirely of dressed stone, hewn, no doubt, from the vast caves, and surrounded by a great moat about sixty feet in width, some portions of which were still filled with water. About ten minutes before the sun finally sank we reached this moat, and passed down and through it, clambering across what evidently were the piled-up fragments of a great bridge, in order to do so, and then with some little difficulty up the slope of the wall to its summit. I wish that it lay within the power of my pen to give some idea of the grandeur of the sight that then met our view. There, all bathed in the red glow of the sinking sun, were miles upon miles of ruins—columns, temples, shrines, and the palaces of kings, varied with patches of green bush. Of course, the roofs of these buildings had long since fallen into decay and vanished, but owing to the extreme massiveness of the style of building, and to the hardness and durability of the rock employed, most of the party walls and great columns still remained standing.*

---

* In connection with the extraordinary state of preservation of these ruins after so vast a lapse of time—at least six thousand years—it must be remembered that Kôr was not burnt or destroyed by an enemy or an earthquake, but deserted, owing to the action of a terrible plague. Consequently the houses were left unharmed; also the climate of the plain is remarkably fine and dry, and there is very little rain, the result of which is that these relics have only to contend against the unaided action of time, which works but slowly upon such massive blocks of masonry.—L.H.H.

There before us stretched away what had evidently been the main thoroughfare of the city, for it was very wide, wider than the Thames Embankment,[1] and regular. Being, as we afterwards discovered, paved, or rather built, throughout of blocks of dressed stone, such as were employed in the walls, it was but little overgrown even now with grass and shrubs, that could get no depth of soil to live in. What had been the parks and gardens on the contrary were now dense jungle. Indeed, it was easy even from a distance to trace the course of the various roads by the burnt-up appearance of the scanty grass that grew upon them. On either side of this great thoroughfare were vast blocks of ruins, each block, generally speaking, being separated from its neighbour by a space of what had once, I suppose, been garden-ground, but was now dense and tangled bush. They were all built of the same coloured stone, and most of them had pillars, which was as much as we could make out in the fading light as we passed swiftly up the main road, that I believe I am right in saying no living foot had pressed for thousands of years.[*]

Presently we came to an enormous pile, which we rightly took to be a temple, covering at least four acres of ground, apparently arranged in a series of courts, each one enclosing another of smaller size, on the principle of a Chinese nest of boxes, and separated one from the other by rows of huge columns. And, whilst I think of it, I may as well state a remarkable thing about the shape of these columns, which resembled none that I have ever seen or heard of, being made with a kind of waist in the centre, and swelling out above and below. At first we thought that this shape was meant to roughly symbolise or suggest the female form, as was a common habit amongst the ancient religious architects of all creeds. On the following day, however, as we went up the slopes of the mountain, we discovered a large quantity of the most stately looking palms, of which the trunks grew exactly in this shape, and I have now no doubt that the first designer of those columns drew his inspiration from

---

[*] Billali told me that the Amahagger believe that the site of the city was haunted, and could not be persuaded to enter it upon any consideration. Indeed, I could see that he himself did not at all like doing so, and was only consoled by the reflection that he was under the direct protection of *She*. It struck Leo and myself as very curious that a people which has no objection to living amongst the dead, with whom their familiarity has perhaps bred contempt, and even using them for purposes of fuel, should be terrified at approaching the habitations that these very departed had occupied when alive. After all, however, it is only a savage inconsistency.—L.H.H.

[1] Constructed between 1868 and 1874, a broad sloping path protecting London from floods of the river Thames.

the graceful bends of those very palms, or rather of their ancestors, which then, some eight or ten thousand years ago as now, beautified the slopes of the mountain, that had once formed the shores of the volcanic lake.

At the *façade* of this huge temple, which, I should imagine, is almost as large as that of El-Karnac, at Luxor,[1] some of the largest columns, which I measured, being between eighteen to twenty feet in diameter at the base, by some sixty feet in height, our little procession was halted, and Ayesha descended from her litter.

"There used to be a spot here, Kallikrates," she said to Leo, who had run up to lift her down, "where one might sleep. Two thousand years ago did thou and I and that Egyptian snake rest therein, but since then have I not set foot here, nor any man, and perchance it has fallen," and, followed by the rest of us, she passed up a vast flight of broken and ruined steps into the outer court, and looked round into the gloom. Presently she seemed to recollect, and, walking a few paces along the wall to the left, halted.

"It is here," she said, and at the same time beckoned to the two mutes, who were loaded with provisions and our little belongings, to advance. One of them came forward, and soon produced a lamp and lit it from his brazier, for the Amahagger when on a journey nearly always carried with them a little lighted brazier, from which to provide fire. The tinder of this brazier was made of broken fragments of mummy carefully damped, and if the admixture of moisture was properly managed, this unholy compound would smoulder away for hours. As soon as the lamp was lit we entered the place before which Ayesha had stopped. It turned out to be a chamber hollowed in the thickness of the wall, and, from the fact of there still being a massive stone table in it, I should think that it had probably served as a living-room, perhaps for one of the door keepers of the great temple.

Here we stopped, and after cleaning the place out and making it as comfortable as circumstances and the darkness would permit, we ate some cold meat, at least Leo, Job, and I did, for Ayesha, as I think I have said elsewhere, never touched anything except fruit and water. Whilst we were eating, the moon, which was at her full, rose above the mountain-wall, and began to flood the place with silver.

"Wot ye why I have brought ye here to-night, my Holly?" said Ayesha, leaning her head upon her hand and watching the great orb as

---

[1] The Temple of Karnac is in Thebes, across the Nile from Luxor. Haggard corrected the error in later editions.

she rose, like some heavenly queen, above the solemn pillars of the temple. "I brought ye—nay, it is strange, but knowest thou, Kallikrates, that thou liest at this moment upon the very spot where thy dead body lay when I bore thee back to those caves of Kôr so many years ago. It all returns to my mind now. I can see it, and horrible is it to my sight," and she shuddered.

Here Leo jumped up, and hastily changed his seat. However the reminiscence might affect Ayesha, it clearly had few charms for him.

"I brought ye," went on Ayesha presently, "that ye might look upon the most wonderful sight that ever the eye of man beheld—the full moon shining over ruined Kôr. When ye have done your eating—I would that I could teach thee to eat nought but fruit, Kallikrates, but that will come after thou hast laved in the fire. Once I, too, ate flesh like a brute beast. When ye have done we will go out, and I will show you this great temple and the God that men once worshipped therein."

Of course we got up at once, and started. And here again my pen fails me. To give a string of measurements and details of the various courts of the temple would only be wearisome, supposing that I had them, and yet I know not how I am to describe what we saw, magnif-icent as it was even in its ruin, almost beyond the power of realisation. Court upon dim court, row upon row of mighty pillars—some of them (especially at the gateways) sculptured from pedestal to capital—space upon space of empty chambers that spoke more eloquently to the imagination than any crowded streets. And over all, the dead silence of the dead, the sense of utter loneliness, and the brooding spirit of the Past! How beautiful it was, and yet how drear! We did not dare to speak aloud. Ayesha herself was awed in the presence of an antiquity compared to which even her length of days was but a little thing; we only whispered, and our whispers seemed to run from column to column, till they were lost in the quiet air. Bright fell the moonlight on pillar and court and shattered wall, hiding all their rents and imperfec-tions in its silver garment, and clothing their hoar majesty with the peculiar glory of the night. It was a wonderful sight to see the full moon looking down on the ruined fane of Kôr. It was a wonderful thing to think for how many thousands of years the dead orb above and the dead city below had gazed thus upon each other, and in the utter solitude of space poured forth each to each the tale of their lost life and long departed glory. The weird light fell, and minute by minute the quiet shadows crept across the grass-grown courts like the spirits of old priests haunting the habitations of their worship—the weird light fell, and the long shadows grew till the beauty and grandeur of the scene and the untamed majesty of its present Death seemed to sink into our very souls, and speak more loudly than the tongues of trumpets concerning the pomp and splendour that the grave had swallowed, and even memory had forgotten.

"Come," said Ayesha, after we had gazed and gazed, I know not for how long, "and I will show you the stony flower of Loveliness and Wonder's very crown, if yet it stands to mock time with its beauty and fill the heart of man with longing for that which is behind the veil," and, without waiting for an answer, she led us through two more pillared courts into the inner shrine of the old fane.

And there, in the centre of the inmost court that might have been some fifty yards square, or a little more, we stood face to face with what is perhaps the grandest allegorical work of Art that the genius of her children has ever given to the world. For in the exact centre of the court, placed upon a thick square slab of rock, was a huge round ball of dark stone, some forty feet in diameter, and standing on the ball was a colossal winged figure of a beauty so entrancing and divine that when I first gazed upon it, illumined and shadowed as it was by the soft light of the moon, my breath stood still, and for an instant my heart ceased its beating.

The statue was hewn from marble so pure and white that even now, after all those ages, it shone as the moonbeams danced upon it, and its height was, I should say, a trifle under twenty feet. It was the winged figure of a woman of such marvellous loveliness and delicacy of form that the size seemed rather to add to than to detract from its so human and yet more spiritual beauty. She was bending forward, and poising herself upon her half spread wings as though to preserve her balance as she leant. Her arms were outstretched like those of some woman about to embrace one she dearly loved, while her whole attitude gave an impression of the tenderest beseeching. Her perfect and most gracious form was nude—save, and here came the extraordinary thing—the face, which was thinly veiled, so that we could only trace the marking of her features. A gauzy veil was thrown round and about the head, and of its two ends one fell down across her left breast, which was outlined beneath it, and one, now broken, streamed away upon the air behind her.

"What is she?" I asked, as soon as I could take my eyes off the statue.

"Can'st thou not guess, oh Holly?" answered Ayesha. "Where then is thy imagination? It is Truth standing on the World, and calling to its children to unveil her face. See what is writ upon the pedestal. Without doubt it is taken from the book of the scriptures of these men of Kôr," and she led the way to the foot of the statue, where an inscription of the usual Chinese-looking hieroglyphics was so deeply graven as to be still quite legible, at least to Ayesha. According to her translation it ran thus—

"Is there no man that will draw my veil and look upon my face, for it is very fair? Unto him who draws my veil shall I be, and peace will I give him, and sweet children of knowledge and good works."

"And a voice said, Though all those who seek after thee desire thee, behold, Virgin art thou, and Virgin shalt thou go till Time be done. No man is there born of woman who may draw thy veil and live, nor shall be. In death only can thy veil be drawn, oh Truth."

"And Truth stretched out her arms and wept, because those who sought her might not find her, nor look upon her face to face."

"Thou seest," said Ayesha, when she had finished translating, "Truth was the Goddess of the people of old Kôr, and to her they built their shrines, and her they sought; knowing that they should never find, still sought they."

"And so," I added sadly, "do men seek to this very hour, but they find not; and, as this scripture says, nor shall they; for in Death only is Truth found."

Then with one more look at the veiled and spiritualised loveliness, which was so perfect and so pure, that one might almost fancy that the light of a living spirit shone through the marble prison to lead man on to high ethereal thoughts—this poet's dream of beauty frozen into stone, which I never shall forget while I live, though I find myself so helpless when I attempt to describe it; we turned and went back through the vast moonlit courts to the spot whence we had started. I never saw the statue again, which I the more regret, because on the great ball of stone representing the World whereon the figure stood lines were drawn, that probably had there been light enough we should have discovered to be a map of the Universe, as it was known to the people of Kôr. It is at any rate suggestive of some scientific knowledge that these worshippers of Truth had recognised the fact that the globe is round.

XXIV

WALKING THE PLANK

Next day the mutes woke us before the dawn; and by the time that we had got the sleep out of our eyes, and gone through a very perfunctory wash at a spring which still welled up into the remains of a marble basin in the centre of the north quadrangle of the vast outer court, we found *She* standing by the litter ready to start, while old Billali and the two bearer mutes were busy collecting the baggage. As usual, Ayesha was veiled like the marble Truth (by the way, I wonder if she originally got the idea of covering up her beauty from that statue?). I noticed however that she seemed very depressed, and had none of that proud and buoyant bearing which would have betrayed her among a thousand women of the same stature, even if they had been veiled like herself. She looked up as we came—for her head was bowed—and greeted us. Leo asked her how she had slept.

"Ill, my Kallikrates," she answered, "ill. This night have strange and hideous dreams come creeping through my brain, and I know not what they portend. Almost do I feel as though some evil overshadowed me; and yet how can evil touch me? I wonder," she went on, with a sudden outbreak of womanly tenderness, "I wonder if, should aught happen to me, so that I slept and left thee waking, wouldst thou think gently of me? I wonder, my Kallikrates, if thou wouldst tarry till I came again, as for so many centuries I have tarried for thy coming?" Then, without waiting for an answer, she went on: "Come, let us be setting forth, for we have far to go, and before another day is born in yonder blue should we stand in the place of Life."

In five minutes we were once more on our way through the vast ruined city, that loomed at us on either side in the grey dawning in a way that was at once grand and oppressive. Just as the first ray of the rising sun shot like a golden arrow athwart this storied desolation we gained the further gateway of the outer wall, and having given one more glance at the hoar and pillared majesty through which we had passed, and (with the exception of Job, for whom ruins had no charms) breathed a sigh of regret that we had not had more time to explore it, passed through the great moat, and on to the plain beyond.

As the sun rose so did Ayesha's spirits, till by breakfast-time they had regained their normal level, and she laughingly set down her previous depression to the associations of the spot where she had slept.

"These barbarians declare that Kôr is haunted," she said, "and of a truth I do believe their saying, for never did I know so ill a night save once. I remember it now. It was on that very spot when thou didst lie dead at my feet, Kallikrates. Never will I visit it again; it is a place of evil omen."

After a very brief halt for breakfast we pressed on with such good will that by two o'clock in the afternoon we were at the foot of the vast wall of rock that formed the lip of the volcano, and which at this point towered up precipitously above us for fifteen hundred or two thousand feet. Here we halted, certainly not to my astonishment, for I did not see how it was possible that we should go any farther.

"Now," said Ayesha, as she descended from her litter, "doth our labour but commence, for here do we part with these men, and henceforward must we bear ourselves;" and then, addressing Billali, "do thou and these slaves remain here, and abide our coming. By to-morrow at the midday shall we be with thee—if not, wait."

Billali bowed humbly, and said that her august bidding should be obeyed if they stopped there till they grew old.

"And this man, oh Holly," said She, pointing to Job; "best is it that he should tarry also, for if his heart be not high and his courage great, perchance some evil might overtake him. Also, the secrets of the place whither we go are not fit for common eyes."

I translated this to Job, who instantly and earnestly entreated me, almost with tears in his eyes, not to leave him behind. He said he was sure that he could see nothing worse than he had already seen, and that he was terrified to death at the idea of being left alone with those "dumb folk," who, he thought, would probably take the opportunity to hot-pot him.

I translated what he said to Ayesha, who shrugged her shoulders, and answered, "Well, let him come, it is naught to me; on his own head be it, and he will serve to bear the lamp and this," and she pointed to a narrow plank, some sixteen feet long, which had been bound above the long bearing-pole of her hammock, as I had thought to make curtains spread out better, but, as it now appeared, for some unknown purpose connected with our extraordinary undertaking.

Accordingly, the plank, which, though tough, was very light, was given to Job to carry, and also one of the lamps. I slung the other on to my back, together with a spare jar of oil, while Leo loaded himself with the provisions and some water in a kid's skin. When this was done She bade Billali and the six bearer mutes to retreat behind a grove of flowering magnolias about a hundred yards away, and remain there under pain of death till we had vanished. They bowed humbly, and went, and, as he departed, old Billali gave me a friendly shake of the hand, and whispered that he had rather that it was I than he who was going on this wonderful expedition with "She-who-must-be-obeyed," and upon my word I felt inclined to agree with him. In another minute they were gone, and then, having briefly asked us if we were ready, Ayesha turned, and gazed up the towering cliff.

"Goodness me, Leo," I said, "surely we are not going to climb that!"

Leo shrugged his shoulders, being in a condition of half fascinated, half expectant mystification, and as he did so, Ayesha with a sudden move began to climb the cliff, and of course we had to follow her. It was perfectly marvellous to see the ease and grace with which she sprung from rock to rock, and swung herself along the ledges. The ascent was not, however, so difficult as it looked, although there were one or two nasty places where it did not do to look behind you, the fact being that the rock still sloped here, and was not absolutely precipitous as it was higher up. In this way we, with no great labour, mounted to the height of some fifty feet above our last standing place, the only really troublesome thing to manage being Job's board, and in doing so drew some fifty or sixty paces to the left of our starting point, for we went up like a crab, sideways. Presently we reached a ledge, narrow enough at first, but which widened as we followed it, and what is more sloped inwards like the petal of a flower, so that as we followed it we gradually got into a kind of rut or fold of rock that grew deeper and deeper, till at last it resembled a Devonshire lane in stone, and hid us perfectly from the gaze of anybody on the slope below, if there had been anybody to gaze. This lane (which appeared to be a natural formation) continued for some fifty or sixty paces, and then suddenly ended in a cave, also natural, running at right angles to it. I am sure that it was a natural cave, and not hollowed by the hand of man, because of its irregular and contorted shape and course, which gave it the appearance of having been blown bodily in the mountain by some frightful eruption of gas following the line of the least resistance. All the caves hollowed by the ancients of Kôr, on the contrary, were cut out with the most perfect regularity and symmetry. At the mouth of this cave Ayesha halted, and bade us light the two lamps, which I did, giving one to her and keeping the other myself. Then, taking the lead, she advanced down the cavern, picking her way with great care, as, indeed, it was necessary to do, for the floor was most irregular—strewn with boulders like the bed of a stream, and in some places pitted with deep holes, in which it would have been easy to break one's leg.

This cavern we pursued for twenty minutes or more, it being, so far as I could form a judgment—owing to its numerous twists and turns, no easy task—about a quarter of a mile long.

At last, however, we halted at its farther end, and whilst I was still trying to pierce the gloom a great gust of air came tearing down it, and extinguished both the lamps.

Ayesha called to us, and we crept up to her, for she was a little in front, and were rewarded with a view that was positively appalling in its gloom and grandeur. Before us was a mighty chasm in the black rock, jagged and torn and splintered through it in a far past age by some awful convulsion of Nature, as though it had been cleft by stroke upon stroke of the lightning. This chasm, which was bounded by a precipice on the hither, and presumably, though we could not see it, on the further side also, may have measured any width across, but from its darkness I do not think it can have been very broad. It was impossible to make out much of its outline, or how far it ran, for the simple reason that the point where we were standing was so far from the upper surface of the cliff, at least fifteen hundred or two thousand feet, that only a very dim light struggled down to us from above. The mouth of the cavern gave on to a most curious and tremendous spur of rock, which jutted out in the gulf before us in mid air, for a distance of some fifty yards, coming to a sharp point at its termination, and resembling nothing that I can think of so much as the spur upon the leg of a cock in shape. This huge spur was attached only to the parent precipice at its base, which was, of course, enormous, just as the cock's spur is attached to its leg. Otherwise it was utterly unsupported.

"Here must we pass," said Ayesha. "Be careful lest giddiness overcome ye, or the wind sweep ye into the gulf beneath, for of a truth it hath no bottom;" and, without giving us any further time to get scared, she started walking along the spur, leaving us to follow her as best we might. I was next to her, then came Job, painfully dragging his plank, while Leo brought up the rear. It was a wonderful sight to see this intrepid woman gliding fearlessly along that dreadful place. For my part, when I had gone but a very few yards, what between the pressure of the air and the awful sense of the consequences that a slip would entail, I found it necessary to go down on my hands and knees and crawl, and so did the other two.

But *She* never condescended to this. On she went, leaning her body against the gusts of wind, and never seeming to lose her head or her balance.

In a few minutes we had crossed some twenty paces of this awful bridge, which got narrower at every step, and then all of a sudden a great gust came tearing along the gorge. I saw Ayesha lean herself against it, but the strong draught got under her dark cloak, and tore it from her, and away it went down the wind, flapping like a dying bird. It was dreadful to see it go, till it was lost in the blackness. I clung to the saddle of rock, and looked round, while the great spur vibrated with a humming sound beneath us, like a living thing. The sight was a truly awesome one. There we were poised in the gloom between earth and heaven. Beneath us were hundreds upon hundreds of feet of emptiness that gradually grew darker and darker, till at last it was absolutely black, and at what depth it ended is more than I can guess. Above was space upon space of giddy air, and far, far away a line of blue sky. And down this vast gulf upon which we were pinnacled the great draught dashed and roared, driving clouds and misty wreaths of vapour before it, till we were nearly blinded, and utterly confused.

The whole position was so tremendous and so absolutely unearthly, that I believe it actually lulled our sense of terror, but to this hour I often see it in my dreams, and wake up covered with cold perspiration at its mere phantasy.

"On! on!" cried the white form before us, for now the cloak had gone *She* was robed in white, and looked more like a spirit riding down the gale than a woman; "On, or ye will fall and be dashed to pieces. Keep your eyes fixed upon the ground, and closely hug the rock."

We obeyed her, and crept painfully along the quivering path, against which the wind shrieked and wailed as it shook it, causing it to murmur like a vast tuning-fork. On we went, I do not know for how long, only gazing round now and again, when it was absolutely necessary, until at last we saw that we were on the very tip of the spur, a slab of rock, little larger than an ordinary table, and that throbbed and jumped like any over-engined steamer. There we lay on our stomachs, clinging to the ground, and looked about, while Ayesha stood leaning out against the wind, down which her long hair streamed, and, absolutely heedless of the hideous depth that yawned beneath, pointed before her. Then we saw why the narrow plank, which Job and I had painfully dragged along between us, had been provided. Before us was an empty space, on the other side of which was something, as yet we could not see what, for here—either owing to the shadow of the opposite cliff, or from some other cause—the gloom was that of night.

"We must wait awhile," called Ayesha; "soon there will be light."

At the moment I could not imagine what she meant. How could more light than there was ever come to this dreadful spot? Whilst I was still debating in my mind, suddenly, like a great sword of flame, a beam from the setting sun pierced the Stygian[1] gloom, and smote upon the point of rock whereon we lay, illumining Ayesha's lovely form with an unearthly splendour. I only wish that I could describe the wild and marvellous beauty of that sword of fire, laid across the darkness and rushing mist-wreaths of the gulf. How it got there I do not to this moment know, but I presume that there was some cleft or hole in the

---

[1]   Of the neighborhood of the River Styx (i.e., in Hades).

opposing cliff, through which it pierced when the setting orb was in a direct line with it. All I can say is, that the effect was the most wonderful that I ever saw. Right through the heart of the darkness that flaming sword was stabbed, and where it lay there was the most surpassingly vivid light, so vivid that even at a distance one could see the grain of the rock, while, outside of it—yes, within a few inches of its keen edge—there was nought but clustering shadows.

And now, by this ray of light, for which *She* had been waiting, and timed our arrival to meet, knowing that at this season, for thousands of years, it had always struck thus at sunset, we saw what was before us. Within eleven or twelve feet of the very tip of the tongue-like rock whereon we lay there arose, presumably from the far bottom of the gulf, a sugarloaf-shaped cone, of which the summit was exactly opposite to us. But had there been a summit only it would not have helped us much, for the nearest point of its circumference was some forty feet from where we were. On the lip of this summit, however, which was circular and hollow, rested a tremendous flat stone, something like a glacier stone—indeed, perhaps it was one for all I know to the contrary—and the end of this stone approached to within twelve feet or so of us. This huge boulder was nothing more or less than a gigantic rocking-stone, accurately balanced upon the edge of the cone or miniature crater, like a half-crown on the rim of a wine-glass; for, in the fierce light that played upon it and us, we could see it oscillating in the gusts of wind.

"Quick!" said Ayesha; "the plank—we must cross while the light endures; presently it will be gone."

"Oh, Lord, sir!" groaned Job, "surely she don't mean us to walk across that there place on that there thing," as in obedience to my direction he pushed the long board towards me.

"That's it, Job," I halloaed in ghastly merriment, though the idea of the plank was no pleasanter to me than to him.

I pushed the plank on to Ayesha, who deftly ran it across the gulf so that one end of it rested on the rocking stone, the other remaining on the extremity of our trembling spur. Then placing her foot upon it to prevent it from being blown away, she turned to me.

"Since last I was here, oh Holly," she called, "the support of the moving stone hath lessened somewhat, so that I am not sure if it will bear our weight and fall or no. Therefore will I cross the first, because no harm will come unto me," and, without further ado, she trod lightly but firmly across the frail bridge, and in another second was standing safe upon the heaving stone.

"Ayesha turned towards it, and stretched her arms to greet it."

"It is safe," she called. "See, hold thou the plank! I will stand on the further side of the stone so that it may not overbalance with your greater weights. Now come, oh Holly, for presently the light will fail us."

(*To be continued*)

PART 13 (25 DECEMBER 1886)

CHAPTER XXIV (*CONTINUED*)

I struggled to my knees, and if ever I felt sick in my life I felt sick then, and I am not ashamed to say that I hesitated and hung back.

"Surely thou art not afraid," called this strange creature in a lull of the gale, from where she stood poised like a bird, on the highest point of the rocking stone. "Make then way for Kallikrates."

This settled me; it is better to fall down a precipice and die than be laughed at by such a woman; so I clenched my teeth, and in another instant I was on that horrible, narrow, bending plank, with bottomless space beneath and around me. I have always hated a great height, but never before did I realise the full horrors of which such a position is capable. Oh, the sickening sensation of that yielding board resting on the two moving supports! I grew dizzy, and thought that I must fall; my spine *crept*; it seemed to me that I was falling, and my delight at finding myself sprawling upon that stone, which rose and fell beneath me like a boat in a swell, cannot be expressed in words. All I know is that briefly, but earnestly enough, I thanked Providence for preserving me so far.

Then came Leo's turn, and, though he looked rather queer, he came across like a rope-dancer. Ayesha stretched out her hand to clasp his own, and I heard her murmur, "Bravely done, my love—bravely done! The old Greek spirit lives in thee yet!"

And now only poor Job remained on the further side of the gulf. He crept up to the plank, and yelled out, "I can't do it, sir. I shall fall into that beastly place."

"You must," I said, "you must, Job, it's as easy as catching flies." I suppose that I said this to satisfy my conscience, because the expression conveys a wonderful idea of facility. As a matter of fact I know no more difficult operation in the whole world than catching flies—that is, in warm weather, when they have all their faculties—unless, indeed, it is catching mosquitoes.

"I can't, sir—I can't, indeed."

"Let the man come, or let him stop and perish there. See, the light is dying! In a minute it will be gone!" said Ayesha.

I looked. She was right. The sun was passing below the level of the hole or cleft in the precipice through which the ray came.

"If you stop there, Job, you will die alone," I halloaed; "the light is going."

"Come, be a man, Job," roared Leo; "it's quite easy."

Thus adjured, the miserable Job, with, I think, the most awful yell that I ever heard, precipitated himself face downwards on the plank—he did not dare, small blame to him, to try to walk it, and commenced to draw himself across in little jerks, his poor legs hanging down on either side into the nothingness beneath.

His violent jerks at the frail board made the great stone, which was only balanced on a few inches of rock, oscillate in a most sickening manner, and, to make matters worse, just as he was half-way across the flying ray of lurid light suddenly went out just as though a lamp had been extinguished in a curtained room, leaving the whole howling wilderness of air in blackness.

"Come on, Job, for God's sake," I shouted in an agony of fear, while the stone, gathering motion with every swing, rocked so violently that it was difficult to hang on to it. It was a truly awful position.

"Lord have mercy on me!" halloaed poor Job from the darkness. "Oh, the plank's slipping!" and I heard a violent struggle, and thought that he was gone.

But at that moment his outstretched hand, clasping in agony at the air, met my own, and I hauled—ah, how I did haul, putting out all the strength that it has pleased Providence to give me in such abundance—and to my joy in another minute Job was gasping on the rock beside me. But the plank! I felt it slip, and heard it knock against a projecting knob of rock, and it was gone.

"Great Heavens!" I exclaimed. "How are we going to get back?"

"I don't know" answered Leo, out of the gloom. "'Sufficient to the day is the evil thereof.'[1] I am thankful enough to be here."

But Ayesha merely called to me to take her hand and creep after her.

---

[1]   Matthew 6:34.

XXV

THE SPIRIT OF LIFE

I did as I was bid, and in fear and trembling felt myself drawn over the edge of the stone. I sprawled my legs out, but could touch nothing.

"I am going to fall!" I gasped.

"Nay, let thyself go, and trust to me," answered Ayesha.

Now, if the position is considered, it will be easily understood that this was a greater demand upon my confidence than was justified by my knowledge of Ayesha's character. For all I knew she might be in the very act of consigning me to a horrible doom. But in life we sometimes have to lay our faith upon strange altars, and so it was now.

"Let thyself go!" she cried, and, having no choice, I did.

I felt myself slide a pace or two down the sloping surface of the rock, and then pass into the air, and the thought flashed through my brain that I was lost. But no. In another instant my feet struck against a rocky floor, and I felt that I was standing on something solid, and out of reach of the wind, which I could hear singing away overhead. As I stood there thanking my stars for these small mercies, there was a slip and a scuffle, and down came Leo alongside of me.

"Hulloa, old fellow!" he called out, "are you there? This is getting interesting, is it not?"

Just then, with a terrific yell, Job arrived right on the top of us, knocking us both down. By the time we had struggled to our feet again Ayesha was standing among us, and bidding us light the lamps, which fortunately remained uninjured, as did the spare jar of oil.

I got out my box of Bryant and May's wax matches, and they struck as merrily, there, in that awful place, as in a London drawing-room.

In a couple of minutes both the lamps were alight, and a curious scene they revealed. We were huddled up in a rocky chamber, some twelve feet square, and scared enough we looked; that is, except Ayesha, who was standing calmly with her arms folded, and waiting for the lamps to burn up. The chamber appeared to be partly natural, and partly hollowed out of the top of the cone. The roof of the natural part was formed of the swinging stone, and that of the back part of the chamber, which sloped downwards, was hewn from the live rock. For the rest, the place was warm and dry—a perfect haven of rest compared to the giddy pinnacle above, and the quivering spur that shot out to meet it in mid-air.

"There" said *She*, "safely have we come, though once I feared that the rocking stone would fall with ye, and precipitate ye into the bottomless deeps beneath, for I do believe that the cleft goeth down to the very womb of the world. The rock whereon the stone resteth hath crumbled beneath the swinging weight. And now that he," nodding towards Job, who was sitting on the floor, feebly wiping his forehead with a red cotton pocket-handkerchief, "whom they rightly call the 'Pig,' for as a pig is he stupid, hath let fall the plank, it will not be easy to return across the gulf, and to that end must I make a plan. But now rest a while, and look at this place. What think ye that it is?"

"We know not," I answered.

"Wouldst thou believe that once a man did choose this airy nest for a daily habitation, and did here endure for many years; leaving it only but one day in every ten to seek food and water and oil that the people brought, more than he could carry, and laid as an offering in the mouth of the tunnel through which we passed hither?"

We looked up wonderingly, and she continued—

"Yet so it was. There was a man—Noot, he named himself—who, though he lived in the latter days, had of the wisdom of the sons of Kôr. A hermit was he, and a philosopher, and skilled in the secrets of Nature, and he it was who discovered the Fire that I shall show ye, which is Nature's blood and life, and also that he who bathed therein, and breathed thereof, should live while Nature lives. But like unto thee, oh Holly, this man, Noot, would not turn his knowledge to account. 'Ill,' he said, 'was it for man to live, for man was born to die.' Therefore did he tell his secret to none, and therefore did he come and live here, where the seeker after Life must pass, and was revered of the Amahagger of the day as holy, and a hermit. And when first I came to this country—knowest thou how I came, Kallikrates? Another time I will tell thee, it is a strange tale—I heard of this philosopher, and waited for him when he came to fetch his food, and returned with him hither, though greatly did I fear to tread the gulf. Then did I beguile him with my beauty and my wit, and flatter him with my tongue, so that he led me down and showed me the Fire, and told me the secrets of the Fire, but he would not suffer me to step therein, and, fearing lest he should slay me, I refrained, knowing that the man was very old, and soon would die. And I returned, having learnt from him all that he knew of the wonderful Spirit of the World, and that was much, for the man was wise and very ancient, and by purity and abstinence, and the contemplations of his innocent mind, had worn thin the veil between that which we see and the great invisible truths, the whisper of whose wings at times we hear as they sweep through the gross air of the world. Then it was but a very few days after I met thee, my Kallikrates, who had wandered hither with the Egyptian Amenartas, and I learned to love for the first and last time, once and for ever, so that it entered into my mind to come hither with thee, and receive the gift of Life for thee and me. Therefore came we, with that Egyptian who would not be left behind, and, behold, we found the old man Noot lying but newly dead. There he lay, and his white beard lay on him like a garment," and she pointed to a spot near where I was sitting; "but surely he hath long since crumbled into dust, and the wind hath borne his ashes hence."

Here I put out my hand and felt in the dust, and presently my fingers touched something. It was a single human tooth, very yellow, but sound. I held it up and showed it to Ayesha, who laughed.

"Yes," she said, "it is his without a doubt. Behold what remaineth of Noot and the wisdom of Noot—one little tooth. And yet that man had all life at his command, and for his conscience sake would have none of it. Well, he lay there newly dead, and we descended whither I shall lead ye, and then, gathering up all my courage, and courting death that I might perchance win so glorious a crown of life, I stepped into the flames, and behold! life such as ye can never know until ye feel it also flowed into me, and I came forth undying, and lovely beyond imagining. Then did I stretch out mine arms to thee, Kallikrates, and bid thee take thine immortal bride, and behold, as I spoke, thou, blinded by my beauty, didst turn from me, and throw thine arms about the neck of Amenartas. And then a great fury filled me, and made me mad, and I seized the javelin that thou didst bear, and stabbed thee, so that there, at my very feet, in the place of Life, thou didst groan and go down into death. I knew not then that I had power to slay with mine eyes and will, therefore in my madness slew I with the javelin.*

"And when thou wast dead, ah! I wept, because I was undying and thou wast dead. I wept there in the place of Life so that had I been

---

* It will be observed that Ayesha's account of the death of Kallikrates differs materially from that written on the potsherd by Amenartas. The writing on the sherd says, "Then in her rage did she smite him *by her magic*, and he died." We never ascertained which was the correct version, but it will be remembered that the body of Kallikrates had a spear-wound in the breast, which seems conclusive, unless, indeed, it was inflicted after death. Another thing that we never ascertained was *how* the two women—*She* and the Egyptian Amenartas—managed to bear the corpse of the man they both loved across the dread gulf and along the shaking spur. What a spectacle the two distracted creatures must have presented in their grief and loveliness as they toiled along that awful place with the dead man between them! Probably however the passage was easier then.—L.H.H.

mortal any more my heart had surely broken. And she, the swart Egyptian—she cursed me by her gods. By Osiris did she curse me and by Isis, by Nephthys and by Hekt, by Sekhet, the lion-headed, and by Set,[1] calling down evil on me, evil and everlasting desolation. Ah! I can see her dark face now lowering o'er me like a storm, but she could not hurt me, and I—I know not if I could hurt her. I did not try; it was nought to me then; so between us we bore thee hence. And afterwards I sent her—the Egyptian—away through the swamps, and it seems that she lived to bear a son and to write the tale that should lead thee, her husband, back to me, her rival and thy murderess.

"Such is the tale, my love, and now is the hour at hand that shall set a crown upon it. Like all things on the earth, it is compounded of evil and of good—more of evil than of good, perchance; and writ in letters of blood. It is the truth; nought have I hidden from thee, Kallikrates. And now one thing before the final moment of thy trial. We go down into the presence of Death, for Life and Death are very near together, and—who knows? that might happen which should separate us for another space of waiting. I am but a woman, and no prophetess, and I cannot read the future. But this I know—for I learnt it from the lips of the wise man Noot—that my life is but prolonged and made more bright. It cannot live for aye. Therefore, before we go, tell me, oh Kallikrates, that of a truth thou dost forgive me, and dost love me from thy heart. See, Kallikrates: much evil have I done—perchance it was evil but two nights gone to strike that girl who loved thee cold in death—but she disobeyed me and angered me, prophesying misfortune to me, and I smote. Be careful when power comes to thee also, lest thou also shouldst smite in thine anger or thy jealousy, for unconquerable strength is a sore weapon in the hands of erring man. Yes, I have sinned—out of the bitterness born of a great love have I sinned—but yet do I know the good from the evil, nor is my heart altogether hardened. Thy love, oh Kallikrates, shall be the gate of my redemption, even as aforetime my passion was the path down which I ran to evil. For deep love unsatisfied is the hell of noble hearts and a portion of the accursed, but love that is mirrored back more perfect from the soul of our desired doth fashion wings to lift us above ourselves, and makes us what we might be. Therefore, Kallikrates, take me by the hand, and lift my veil with no more fear than though I were some peasant girl, and not the wisest and

---

[1] Osiris, Isis, Nephthys, Hekt, Sekhet, and Set are all ancient Egyptian deities, associated variously with the underworld, childbirth and fertility, darkness and war.

most beauteous woman in this world, and look me in the eyes, and tell me that thou dost forgive me with all thine heart, and that with all thine heart thou dost worship me."

She paused, and the strange tenderness in her voice seemed to hover round us like a memory. I know that the sound of it moved me more even than her words, it was so very human—so very womanly. Leo, too, was strangely touched. Hitherto he had been fascinated against his better judgment, something as a bird is fascinated by a snake, but now I think that all this passed away, and he realised that he really loved this strange and glorious creature, as, alas! I loved her also. At any rate, I saw his eyes fill with tears, and he stepped swiftly to her and undid the gauzy veil, and then took her by the hand, and, gazing into her deep eyes, said aloud,

"Ayesha, I love thee with all my heart, and so far as forgiveness is possible I forgive thee the death of Ustane. For the rest, it is between thee and thy Maker; I know nought of it. I only know that I love thee as I never loved before, and that I will cleave to thee to the end."

"Now," answered Ayesha, with proud humility, "now when my lord doth speak thus royally and give with so free a hand, it cannot become me to lag behind in words, and be beggared of my generosity. Behold!" and she took his hand and placed it upon her shapely head, and then bent herself slowly down till one knee for an instant touched the ground—"Behold! in token of submission do I bow me to my lord! Behold!" and she kissed him on the lips, "in token of my wifely love do I kiss my lord. Behold!" and she laid her hand upon his heart, "by the sin I sinned, by my lonely centuries of waiting wherewith it was wiped out, by the great love wherewith I love, and by the Spirit—the Eternal Thing that doth beget all life, from whom it ebbs, to whom it doth return again—I swear.

"I swear, even in this first most holy hour of completed Womanhood, I swear that I will abandon Evil and cherish Good. I swear that I will be ever guided by thy voice in the straightest path of Duty. I swear that I will eschew Ambition, and through all my length of endless days set Wisdom over me as a guiding star to lead me unto Truth and a knowledge of the Right. I swear also that I will honour and will cherish thee, Kallikrates, who hath been swept by the wave of time back into my arms, ay, till the very end, come it soon or late. I swear—nay, I will swear no more, for what are words? Yet shalt thou learn that Ayesha hath no false tongue. So I have sworn, and thou, my Holly, art witness to my oath. Here, too, are we wed, my husband—wed till the end of all things; here do we write our marriage vows upon the rushing winds which shall bear them up to heaven, and round and continually round the rolling world, with the gloom for bridal canopy.

"And for a bridal gift I give to thee my beauty's starry crown, and enduring life and wisdom without measure, and wealth that none can count. Behold! the great ones of the earth shall creep about thy feet, and their fair women shall cover up their eyes because of the shining glory of thy face, and their wise ones shall be abased before thee. Thou shalt read the hearts of men as an open writing, and hither and thither shalt thou lead them as thy pleasure listeth. Like that old Sphinx of Egypt shalt thou sit aloft from age to age, and ever shall they cry to thee to solve the riddle of thy greatness that doth not pass away, and ever shalt thou mock them with thy silence!

"Behold! once more I kiss thee, and by that kiss I give thee dominion over sea and earth, over the peasant in his hovel, over the monarch in his palace halls, and cities crowned with towers, and those who breathe therein. Where'er the sun shakes out his spears, where'er the lonesome waters mirror up the moon, where'er storms roll, and Heaven's painted bows arch in the sky—from the pure North shrouded in her snows, across the middle spaces of the world, to where the amorous South lying like a bride upon her azure seas breathes in sighs made sweet with myrtle bloom—there shall thy power pass, and thy dominion find a home. Nor sickness, nor icy fingered fear, nor sorrow, and pale waste of form and mind hovering ever o'er humanity shall so much as shadow thee with the shadow of their wings. As a God shalt thou be, holding good and evil in the hollow of thy hand, and I, even I, I humble myself before thee. Such is the power of Love, and such is the bridal gift I give unto thee, Kallikrates, royal son of Rā, my Lord and Lord of All.

"And now it is done, and come storm, come shine, come good, come evil, come life, come death, it never, never can be undone. For, of a truth, that which is, is, and being done, is done for aye, and cannot be altered. I have said.—Let us hence, that all things may be accomplished in their order;" and, taking one of the lamps, she advanced towards the end of the chamber that was roofed in by the swaying stone, where she halted.

We followed her, and perceived that in the wall of the cone there was a stair, or, to be more accurate, that some projecting knobs of rock had been so shaped as to form a good imitation of a stair. Down this Ayesha began to climb, springing from step to step, like a chamois, and, after her we followed with less grace. When we had descended some fifteen or sixteen steps we found that they ended in a tremendous rocky slope, running first outwards and then inwards—like the slope of an inverted cone, or tunnel. The slope was very steep, and often precipitous, but it was nowhere impassable, and by the light of the lamps we went down it with no great difficulty, though it was gloomy work enough travelling on thus, no one of us knew whither, in the dead heart of a volcano. As we went, however, I took the precaution of noting our route as well as I could; and this was not difficult, owing to the extraordinary and most fantastic shape of the rocks that were strewn about, many of which in that dim light looked more like the grim faces carven upon mediæval gargoyles than ordinary boulders.

For a long period we travelled on thus, half an hour I should say, till, after we had descended for many hundreds of feet, I perceived that we were reaching the point of the inverted cone. In another minute we were there, and found that at the very apex of the funnel was a passage, so low and narrow that we had to stoop as we crept along it in Indian file. After some fifty yards of this creeping, the passage suddenly widened into a cave, so huge that we could see neither the roof nor the sides. We only knew that it was a cave by the echo of our tread and the perfect quiet of the heavy air. On we went for many minutes in absolute awed silence, like lost souls in the depths of Tartarus,[1] Ayesha's white and ghost-like form flitting in front of us, till once more the cavern ended in a passage which opened into a second cavern much smaller than the first. Indeed, we could clearly make out the arch and stony banks of this second cave, and, from their rent and jagged appearance, discovered, that, like the first long passage through which we had passed in the cliff, before we came to the quivering spur, it had to all appearance been torn in the bowels of the rock by the terrific force of some explosive gas. At length this cave ended in a third passage, through which gleamed a faint glow of light.

I heard Ayesha give a sigh of relief as this light dawned upon us.

"It is well," she said; "prepare to enter the very womb of the Earth, wherein she doth conceive the Life that ye see brought forth in man and beast—ay, and in every tree and flower."

Swiftly she sped along, and after her we stumbled as best we might, our hearts filled like a cup with mingled dread and curiosity. What were we about to see? We passed down the tunnel; stronger and stronger the light beamed, reaching us in great flashes like the rays from a lighthouse, as one by one they are thrown wide upon the darkness of the waters. Nor was

---

[1] In Greek mythology, a realm of darkness and punishment located below Hades.

this all, for with the flashes came a soul-shaking sound like that of thunder and of crashing trees. Now we were through it, and—oh, heavens!

We stood in a third cavern, some fifty feet in length by, perhaps, as great a height, and thirty wide. It was carpeted with fine white sand, and its walls had been worn smooth by the action of I know not what. The cavern was not dark like the others, it was filled with a soft glow of rose-coloured light, more beautiful to look on than anything that can be conceived. But at first we saw no flashes, and heard no more of the thunderous sound. Presently, however, as we stood in amaze, gazing at the wonderful sight, and wondering whence the rosy radiance flowed, a dread and beautiful thing happened. Across the far end of the cavern with a grinding and crashing noise—a noise so dreadful and awe-inspiring that we all trembled, and Job actually sank to his knees—there flamed out an awful cloud or pillar of fire, like a rainbow, many-coloured, and, like the lightning, bright. For a space, perhaps forty seconds, it flamed and roared thus, turning slowly round and round, and then by degrees the terrible noise ceased, and with the fire it passed away—I know not whither—leaving behind it the same rosy glow that we had first seen.

"Draw near, draw near!" cried Ayesha, with a voice of thrilling exultation. "Behold the very Fountain and Heart of Life as it beats in the bosom of the great world. Behold the substance from which all things draw their energy, the bright Spirit of the Globe, without which it cannot live, but must grow cold and dead as the dead moon. Draw near, and wash ye in the living flames, and take their virtue into your poor frames in all its virgin strength—not as it now feebly glows within your bosoms, filtered thereto through all the fine strainers of a thousand intermediate lives, but as it is here in the very fount and seat of Being."

We followed her through the rosy glow up to the head of the cave, till at last we stood before the spot where the great pulse beat and the great flame passed. And as we went we became sensible of a wild and splendid exhilaration, of a glorious sense of such a fierce intensity of Life that the most buoyant moments of our strength seemed flat and tame and feeble beside it. It was the mere effluvium of the flame, the subtle ether that it cast off as it passed, working on us, and making us feel strong as giants and swift as eagles.

We reached the head of the cave, and gazed at each other in the glorious glow, and laughed aloud—even Job laughed, and he had not laughed for a week—in the lightness of our hearts and the divine intoxication of our brains. I know that I felt as though all the varied genius of which the human intellect is capable had descended upon me. I could have spoken in blank verse of Shakesperian beauty, all sorts of great ideas flashed through my mind, it was as though the bonds of my flesh had been loosened and left the spirit free to soar to the empyrean of its native power. The sensations that poured in upon me are indescribable. I seemed to live more keenly, to reach to a higher joy, and sip the goblet of a subtler thought than ever it had been my lot to do before. I was another and most glorified self, and all the avenues of the Possible were for a space laid open to the footsteps of the Real.

Then, suddenly, whilst I rejoiced in this splendid vigour of a new-found self, from far, far away there came a dreadful muttering noise, that grew and grew to a crash and a roar, which combined in itself all that is terrible and yet splendid in the possibilities of sound. Nearer it came, and nearer yet, till it was close upon us, rolling down like all the thunder-wheels of Heaven behind the horses of the lightning. On it came, and with it came the glorious blinding cloud of many-coloured light, and stood before us for a space, turning, as it seemed to us, slowly round and round, and then, accompanied by its attendant pomp of sound, passed away I know not whither.

So astonishing was the wondrous sight that one and all of us, save *She*, who stood up and stretched her hands towards the fire, sank down before it, and hid our faces in the sand.

When it was gone, Ayesha spoke.

"Now, Kallikrates," she said, "the mighty moment is at hand. When the great flame comes again thou must stand in it. First throw aside thy garments, for it will burn them, though thee it will not hurt. Thou must stand in the flame while thy senses will endure, and when it embraces thee suck the fire down into thy very heart, and let it leap and play around thy every part, so that thou lose no moiety of its virtue. Hearest thou me, Kallikrates?"

"I hear thee, Ayesha," answered Leo, "but, of a truth—I am no coward—but I doubt me of that raging flame. How know I that it will not utterly destroy me, so that I lose myself and lose thee also? Nevertheless will I do it," he added.

Ayesha thought for a minute, and then said,

"It is not wonderful that thou shouldst doubt. Tell me, Kallikrates: if thou seest me stand in the flame and come forth unharmed, wilt thou enter also?"

"Yes," he answered, "I will enter, even if it slay me. I have said that I will enter."

"And that will I also," I cried.

"What, my Holly!" she laughed, aloud; "methought that thou wouldst naught of length of days. Why, how is this?"

"Nay, I know not," I answered, "but there is that in my heart that calleth me to taste of the flame, and live."

"It is well," she said. "Thou art not altogether lost in folly. See now, I will for the second time bathe me in this living bath. Fain would I add to my beauty and my length of days if that be possible. If it be not possible, at the least it cannot harm me.

"Also," she continued, after a momentary pause, "is there another and a deeper cause why I would once again dip me in the flame. When first I tasted of its virtue full was my heart of passion and of hatred of that Egyptian Amenartas, and therefore, despite my strivings to be rid thereof, have passion and hatred been stamped upon my soul from that sad hour to this. But now it is otherwise. Now is my mood a happy mood, and filled am I with the purest part of thought, and so would I ever be. Therefore, Kallikrates, will I once more wash and make me clean, and yet more fit for thee. Therefore also, when thou dost in turn stand in the fire, empty all thy heart of evil, and let sweet contentment hold the balance of thy mind. Shake loose thy spirit's wings, and take thy stand upon the utter verge of holy contemplation; ay, dream upon thy mother's kiss, and turn thee towards the vision of the highest good that hath ever swept on silver wings across the silence of thy dreams. For from the germ of what thou art in that dread moment shall grow the fruit of what thou shalt be for all unreckoned time.

"Now prepare thee, prepare, even as though thy last hour were at hand, and thou wast about to cross to the land of shadows, and not through the gates of most glorious life. Prepare, I say!"

XXVI

WHAT WE SAW

Then came a few moments' pause, during which Ayesha seemed to be gathering up her strength for the fiery trial, while we clung to each other, and waited in utter silence.

At last from far far away, came the first murmur of sound, that grew and grew till it began to crash and bellow in the distance. As she heard it, Ayesha swiftly threw off her gauzy wrapping, loosened the golden snake from her kirtle, and then, shaking her lovely hair about her like a garment, beneath its cover slipped the kirtle off and replaced the snaky belt around her and outside the masses of her falling hair. There she stood before us as Eve might have stood before Adam, clad in nothing but her abundant locks, held round her by her golden band; and no words of mine can tell how sweet she looked—and yet how divine. Nearer and nearer came the thunder wheels of fire, and as they came she pushed one ivory arm through the dark masses of her hair and flung it round Leo's neck.

"Oh, my love, my love," she murmured, "wilt thou ever know how I have loved thee?" and she kissed him on the forehead, and then went and stood in the pathway of the flame of Life.

There was, I remember, to my mind something very touching about her words and that embrace upon the forehead. It was like a mother's kiss, and seemed to convey a benediction with it.

On came the crashing, rolling noise, and the sound thereof was as though a forest were being swept flat by a mighty wind, and then tossed up by it like so much grass, and thundered down a mountain side. Nearer and nearer it came; now flashes of light, forerunners of the revolving pillar of flame, were passing like arrows through the rosy air; and now the edge of the pillar itself appeared. Ayesha turned towards it, and stretched out her arms to greet it. On it came very slowly, and lapped her round with flame. I saw the fire run up her form. I saw her lift it with both hands as though it were water, and pour it over her head. I even saw her open her mouth and draw it down into her lungs, and a dread and wonderful sight it was.

Then she paused, and stretched out her arms, and stood there quite still, with a heavenly smile upon her face, as though she were the very Spirit of the Flame.

The mysterious fire played up and down her dark and rolling locks, twining and twisting itself through and around them like threads of golden lace; it gleamed upon her ivory breast and shoulder, from which the hair had slipped aside; it slid along her pillared throat and delicate features, and seemed to find a home in the glorious eyes that shone and shone more brightly even than the spiritual essence.

Oh, how beautiful she looked there in the flame! No angel out of heaven could have worn a greater loveliness. Even now my heart faints before the recollection of it, as she stood and smiled at our awed faces, and I would give half my remaining time upon this earth to see her once like that again.

But suddenly—more suddenly than I can describe—a kind of change came over her face, a change which I could not define or explain on paper, but none the less a change. The smile vanished, and in its place there came a dry, hard look; the rounded face seemed to grow pinched, as though some great anxiety were leaving its impress upon it. The glorious eyes, too, lost their light, and, as I thought, the form its perfect shape and erectness.

I rubbed my eyes, thinking that I was the victim of some hallucination, or that the refraction from the intense light produced an optical delusion; and, as I did so, the flaming pillar slowly twisted and thundered off whithersoever it passes to in the bowels of the great earth, leaving Ayesha standing where it had been.

As soon as it was gone, she stepped forward to Leo's side—it seemed to me that there was no spring in her step—and stretched out her hand to lay it on his shoulder. I gazed at her arm. Where was its wonderful roundness and beauty? It was getting thin and angular. And her face— by heaven!—*her face was growing old before my eyes!* I suppose that Leo saw it also; certainly he recoiled a step or two.

"What is it, my Kallikrates?" she said, and her voice—what was the matter with those deep and thrilling notes? They were quite high and cracked.

"Why, what is it—what is it?" she said confusedly. "I feel dazed. Surely the quality of the fire hath not altered. Can the principle of Life alter? Tell me, Kallikrates, is there aught wrong with my eyes? I see not clear," and she put her hand to her head and touched her hair —and oh, *horror of horrors!*—it all fell upon the floor, leaving her utterly bald.

"Oh, *look!—look! look!*" shrieked Job, in a shrill falsetto of terror, his eyes nearly dropping out of his head, and foam upon his lips. "*Look!—look!—look!* she's shrivelling up! she's turning into a monkey!" and down he fell upon the floor, foaming and gnashing in a fit.

True enough—I faint even as I write it in the living presence of that terrible recollection—she *was* shrivelling up; the golden snake that had encircled her gracious form slipped over her hips and fell upon the ground; smaller and smaller she grew; her skin changed colour, and in place of the perfect whiteness of its lustre it turned dirty brown and yellow, like an old piece of withered parchment. She felt at her bald head: the delicate hand was nothing but a claw now, a human talon like that of a badly-preserved Egyptian mummy, and then she seemed to realise what kind of change was passing over her, and she shrieked— ah, she shrieked!—she rolled upon the floor and shrieked!

Smaller she grew, and smaller yet, till she was no larger than a she baboon. Now the skin was puckered into a million wrinkles, and on

"Next instant I felt Leo seize me by the right wrist with both hands."

the shapeless face was the stamp of unutterable age. I never saw anything like it; nobody ever saw anything like the frightful age that was graven on that fearful countenance, no bigger now than that of a two-months' child, though the skull remained the same size, or nearly so, and let all men pray to God they never may, if they wish to keep their reason.

At last she lay still, or only feebly moving. She who, but two minutes before, had gazed upon us the loveliest, noblest, most splendid woman the world had ever seen, she lay still before us, near the masses of her own dark hair, no larger than a big monkey, and hideous—ah, too hideous for words. And yet, think of this—at that very moment I thought of it—it was the same woman!

She was dying: we saw it, and thanked God—for while she lived she could feel, and what must she have felt? She raised herself upon her bony hands, and blindly gazed around her, swaying her head slowly from side to side as a tortoise does. She could not see, for her whitish eyes were covered with a horny film. Oh, the horrible pathos of the sight! But she could still speak.

"Kallikrates," she said, in husky, trembling notes. "Forget me not, Kallikrates. Have pity on my shame; I shall come again, and shall once more be beautiful, I swear it—it is true! Oh—h—h—" and she fell upon her face, and was still.

On the very spot where more than twenty centuries before she had slain the old Kallikrates, she herself fell down and died.

Overcome with the extremity of horror, we, too, fell on the sandy floor of that dread place, and swooned away.

(*To be continued*)

PART 14 (1 JANUARY 1887)

CHAPTER XXVI (*CONTINUED*)

I know not how long we lay thus. Many hours, I suppose. When at last I opened my eyes, the other two were still outstretched upon the floor. The rosy light still beamed like a celestial dawn, and the thunder wheels of the Spirit of Life still rolled upon their accustomed track, for as I awoke the great pillar was passing away. There, too, lay the hideous little monkey frame, covered with crinkled yellow parchment, that once had been the glorious *She*. Alas! it was no hideous dream—it was an awful and unparalleled fact!

What had happened to bring this shocking change about? Had the nature of the life-giving Fire changed? Did it, perhaps, from time to time send forth an essence of Death instead of an essence of Life? Or was it that the frame once charged with its marvellous virtue could bear no more, so that were the process repeated—it mattered not at what lapse of time—the two impregnations neutralised each other, and left the body on which they acted as it was before it ever came into contact with the very essence of Life? This, and this alone, would account for the sudden and terrible ageing of Ayesha, as the whole length of her two thousand years took effect upon her. I have not the slightest doubt myself but that the frame now lying before me was just what the frame of a woman would be if by any extraordinary means life could be preserved in her till she at length died at the age of twenty-two centuries.

But who can tell what had happened? There was the fact. Often since that awful hour I have reflected that it required no great stretch of imagination to see the finger of Providence in the matter. Ayesha locked up in her living tomb waiting from age to age for the coming of her lover worked but a small change in the order of the World. But Ayesha strong and happy in her love, clothed in immortal youth and godlike beauty, and the wisdom of the centuries, would have revolutionised society, and even perchance have changed the destiny of Mankind. Thus she opposed herself against the eternal Law, and strong though she was, by it was swept back to nothingness, swept back with shame and hideous mockery.

For some minutes I lay faintly turning these terrors over in my mind, while my physical strength came back to me, which it soon did in that buoyant atmosphere. Then I bethought me of the others, and staggered to my feet, to see if I could arouse them. But first I took up Ayesha's kirtle and the gauzy scarf with which she had been wont to hide her dazzling loveliness from the eyes of men, and, averting my head so that I might not look upon it, covered up that dreadful relic of the glorious dead, that shocking epitome of human beauty and human life. I did this hurriedly, fearing lest Leo should recover, and see it again.

Then, stepping over the perfumed masses of dark hair that lay upon the sand, I stooped down by Job, who was lying upon his face, and turned him over. As I did so his arm fell back in a way that I did not like, and which sent a chill through me, and I glanced sharply at him. One look was enough. Our old and faithful servant was dead. His nerves, already shattered by all he had seen and undergone, had utterly broken down beneath this last dire sight, and he had died of terror, or in a fit brought on by terror. One had only to look at his face to see it.

It was another blow; but perhaps it may help people to understand how overwhelmingly awful was the experience through which we had passed—we did not feel it much at the time. It seemed quite natural that the poor old fellow should be dead. When Leo came to himself, which he did with a groan and trembling of the limbs about ten minutes afterwards, and I told him that Job was dead, he merely said, "Oh!" And, mind you, this was from no heartlessness, for he and Job were much attached to each other; and he often talks of him now with the deepest regret and affection. It was only that his nerves would bear no more. A harp can give out but a certain quantity of sound, however heavily it is smitten.

Well, I set myself to recovering Leo, who, to my infinite relief, I found was not dead, but only fainting, and in the end I succeeded, as I have said, and he sat up; and then I saw another dreadful thing. When we entered that awful place his curling hair had been of the ruddiest gold, now it was turning grey, and by the time we gained the outer air it was snow white. Besides, he looked twenty years older.

"What is to be done, old fellow?" he said in a hollow, dead sort of voice, when his mind had cleared a little, and a recollection of what had happened forced itself upon it.

"Try and get out, I suppose," I answered; "that is, unless you would like to go in there," and I pointed to the column of fire that was once more rolling by.

"I would go in if I were sure that it would kill me," he said with a little laugh. "It was my cursed hesitation that did this. If I had not been afraid she might never have tried to show me the road. But I am not sure. The fire might have the opposite effect upon me. It might make me immortal; and, old fellow, I have not the patience to wait a couple of thousand years for her to come back again as she did for me. I had rather die when my hour comes—and I should fancy that it isn't far off either—and go my ways to look for her. Do you go in if you like."

But I merely shook my head, my excitement was as dead as ditch-water, and my distaste for the prolongation of my mortal span had come back upon me more strongly than ever. Besides, we neither of us knew what the effects of the fire might be. The result upon *She* had not been of an encouraging nature, and of the exact causes that produced that result we were, of course, ignorant.

"Well, my boy," I said, "we can't stop here till we go the way of those two," and I pointed to the little heap under the white garment and to the stiffing corpse of poor Job. "If we are going we had better go. But, by the way, I expect that the lamps have burnt out," and I took one up and looked at it, and sure enough it had.

"There is some more oil in the vase," said Leo indifferently, "if it is not broken, at least."

I examined the vessel in question—it was intact. With a trembling hand I filled the lamps—luckily there was still some of the linen wick unburnt. Then I lit them with one of our wax matches. While I did so we heard the pillar of fire approaching once more as it went on its never-ending journey, if, indeed, it was the same pillar that passed and repassed in a circle.

"Let's see it come once more," said Leo; "we shall never look upon its like again in this world."

It seemed a bit of idle curiosity, but somehow I shared it, and so we waited till, turning slowly round upon its own axis, it had flamed and thundered by; and I remember wondering for how many thousands of years this same phenomenon had been taking place in the bowels of the earth, and for how many more thousands it would continue to take place. I wondered also if any mortal eyes would ever again mark its passage, or any mortal ears be thrilled and fascinated by the swelling volume of its majestic sound. I do not think that they will. I believe that we are the last human beings who will ever see that unearthly sight. Presently it had gone, and we, too, turned to go.

But before we did so we each took Job's cold hand in ours and shook it. It was a rather ghastly ceremony, but it was the only means in our power of showing our respect to the faithful dead and of celebrating his obsequies. The heap beneath the white garment we did not uncover. We had no wish to look upon that terrible sight again. But we went to the pile of rippling hair that had fallen from her in the agony of the hideous change which was worse than a thousand natural deaths, and each of us drew from it a shining lock, and these locks we still have, the sole memento that is left to us of Ayesha as we knew her in the fulness of her grace and glory. Leo pressed the perfumed hair to his lips.

"She called to me not to forget her," he said hoarsely; "and swore that we should meet again. By heaven! I never will forget her. Here I swear that, if we live to get out of this, I will not for all my days have anything to say to another living woman, and that wherever I go I will wait for her as faithfully as she waited for me."

"Yes," I thought to myself, "if she comes back as beautiful as we knew her. But supposing she came back like that!"*

Well, and then we went. We went, and left those two in the presence of the very well and spring of Life, but gathered to the cold company of Death. How lonely they looked as they lay there, and how ill-assorted! That little heap had been for two thousand years the wisest, loveliest, proudest creature—I can hardly call her woman—in the whole universe. She had been wicked, too, in her way; but, alas! such is the frailty of the human heart, her wickedness had not detracted from her charm. Indeed, I am by no means certain that it did not add to it. It was after all of a grand order, there was nothing mean or small about Ayesha.

And poor Job too! His presentiment had come true, and there was an end of him. Well, he had a strange burial-place—no Norfolk hind ever had a stranger, or ever will; and it is something to lie in the same sepulchre with the poor remains of the imperial *She*.

We looked our last upon them and the indescribable rosy glow in which they lay, and then with hearts far too heavy for words we left them, and crept thence broken-down men—so broken down, that we even renounced the chance of practically immortal life, because all that made life valuable had gone from us, and we knew even then that to prolong our days indefinitely would only be to prolong our sufferings. For we felt—yes, both of us—that having once looked Ayesha in the eyes, we could not forget her for ever and ever while memory and identity remained. We both loved her now and for always, she was stamped and carven on our hearts, and no other woman could ever raze that splendid die. And I—there lies the sting—I had and have no right to think thus of her. As she told me, I was nought to her, and never shall be through the unfathomed depths of Time, unless, indeed, conditions alter, and a day comes at last when two men may love one woman, and all three be happy in the fact. It is the only hope of my broken-heartedness, and a rather faint one. Beyond it I have nothing. I have paid down this heavy price, all that I am worth here and hereafter, and that

---

* What a terrifying reflection it is, by the way, that nearly all our deep love for women who are not our kindred depends—at any rate, in the first instance—upon their personal appearance. If we lost them, and found them again dreadful to look on, though otherwise they were the very same, should we still love them?—L.H.H.

is my sole reward. With Leo it is different, and often and often I bitterly envy him his happy lot, for if *She* was right, and her wisdom and knowledge did not fail her at the last, which arguing from the precedent of her own case I think unlikely, he has some future to look forward to. But I have none, and yet—mark the folly and the weakness of the human heart, and let him who is wise learn wisdom from it—yet I would not have it otherwise. I mean that I am content to give what I have given and must always give, and take in payment those crumbs that fall from my mistress' table, the memory of a few kind words, the hope one day in the far undreamed future of a sweet smile or two of recognition, and a little show of thanks for my devotion to her—and Leo.

If that does not constitute true love I do not know what does, and all I have to say is that it is a very bad state of mind for a man on the wrong side of middle age to fall into.

XXVII

WE LEAP

We passed through the caves without trouble, but when we came to the slope of the inverted cone two difficulties stared us in the face. The first of these was the laborious nature of the ascent, and the next the extreme difficulty of finding our way. Indeed, had it not been for the mental notes that I had fortunately taken of the shape of various rocks, &c., I am sure that we never should have managed it at all, but have wandered about in the dreadful womb of the volcano—for I suppose it must once have been something of the sort—until we died of exhaustion and despair. As it was we went wrong several times, and once nearly fell into a huge crack or crevasse. It was terrible work creeping about in the dense gloom and awful stillness from boulder to boulder, and examining it by the feeble light of the lamps to see if I could recognise its shape. We rarely spoke, our hearts were too heavy for speech, we simply stumbled about, falling sometimes and cutting ourselves, in a rather dogged sort of way. The fact was that our spirits were utterly crushed, and we did not greatly care what happened to us. Only we felt bound to try and save our lives whilst we could, and, indeed, a natural instinct prompted us to it. So for some three or four hours, I should think—I cannot tell exactly how long, for we had no watch left that would go— we blundered on. During the last two hours we were completely lost, and I began to fear that we had got in the funnel of some subsidiary cone, when at last I suddenly recognised a very large rock which we had passed in descending but a little way from the top. It is a marvel that I should have recognised it, and, indeed, we had already passed it going at right angles to the proper path, when something about it struck me, and I turned back and examined it in an idle sort of way, and, as it happened, this proved our salvation.

After this we gained the rocky natural stair without much further trouble, and in due course found ourselves back in the little chamber, where the benighted Noot had lived and died.

But now a fresh terror stared us in the face. It may be remembered that, owing to poor Job's fear and awkwardness, the plank upon which we had crossed from the huge spur to the rocking stone had been whirled off into the tremendous gulf below.

How were we to cross without the plank?

There was only one answer—we must try and *jump* it, or else stop there till we starved. The distance in itself was not so very great, between eleven and twelve feet I should think, and I have seen Leo jump over nineteen when he was a young fellow at college; but then, think of the conditions. Two weary, worn-out men, one of them on the wrong side of forty, a rocking stone to take off from, a trembling point of rock some few feet across to land on, and a bottomless gulf to be cleared in a raging gale. It was bad enough, God knows, but when I pointed out these things to Leo, he put the whole matter in a nutshell by replying that, merciless as the choice was, we must choose between the certainty of a lingering death in the chamber and the risk of a swift one in the air. Of course, there was no arguing against this, but one thing was clear, we could not attempt that leap in the dark; the only thing to do was to wait for the ray of light which pierced through the gulf at sunset. How near to or how far from sunset we might be, neither of us had the faintest notion; all we did know was, that when at last the light came it would not endure more than a couple of minutes at the outside, so that we must be prepared to meet it. Accordingly, we made up our minds to creep on to the top of the rocking stone and lie there in readiness. We were the more easily reconciled to this course by the fact that our lamps were once more nearly exhausted—indeed, one had gone out bodily, and the other was jumping up and down as the flame of a lamp does when the oil is done. So, by the aid of its dying light, we hastened to crawl out of the little chamber and clamber up the side of the great stone.

As we did so the light went out.

The difference in our position was a sufficiently remarkable one. Below, in the little chamber, we had only heard the roaring of the gale overhead— here, lying on our faces on the swinging stone, we were exposed to its full force and fury, as the great draught drew first from this direction and then from that, howling against the mighty precipice and through the rocky cliffs like ten thousand despairing souls. We lay there hour after hour in terror and misery of mind, so deep that I will not attempt to describe it, and listened to the wild storm-voices of that Tartarus, as set to the deep undertone of the spur opposite against which the wind hummed like some awful harp, they called to each other from precipice to precipice. No nightmare dreamed by man, no wild invention of the romancer, can ever equal the living horror of that place, and the weird crying of those voices of the night, as we lay, like shipwrecked mariners on a raft, and tossed on a black, unfathomed wilderness of air. Fortunately the temperature was not a low one; indeed, the wind was warm, or we should have perished. Well, we lay and listened, and while we were stretched out upon the rock a thing happened that was so curious and suggestive in itself, though doubtless it was a mere coincidence, that, if anything, it added to, rather than deducted from, the burden on our nerves.

It will be remembered that when Ayesha was standing on the spur, before we crossed to the stone, the wind tore her cloak from her, and whirled it away into the darkness of the gulf, we could not see whither. Well—I hardly like to tell the story; it is so strange. As we lay there upon the rocking-stone, this very cloak came floating out of the black space, like a memory from the dead, and fell on Leo—so that it covered him nearly from head to foot. We could not at first make out what it was, but soon discovered by its feel, and then poor Leo, for the first time, gave way, and I heard him sobbing there upon the stone. No doubt the cloak had been caught upon some pinnacle of the cliff, and was thence blown hither by a chance gust; but still, it was a most curious and touching incident.

Shortly after this, suddenly, without the slightest previous warning, the great red knife of light came stabbing the darkness through and through—struck the swaying stone on which we lay, and rested its sharp point upon the spur opposite.

"Now for it," said Leo, "now or never."

We rose and stretched ourselves, and looked at the cloud-wreaths stained the colour of blood by that red ray as they tore through the sickening depths beneath, and then at the empty space between the swaying stone and the quivering rock, and, in our hearts, despaired, and prepared for death. Surely we could not clear it—desperate though we were.

"Who is to go first?" said I.

"Do you, old fellow," answered Leo. "I will sit upon the other side of the stone to steady it. You must take as much run as you can, and jump high; and God have mercy on us, say I."

I acquiesced with a nod, and then I did a thing I had never done since Leo was a little boy. I turned and put my arm round him, and kissed him on the forehead. It sounds rather French, but as a fact I was taking my last farewell of a man whom I could not have loved more if he had been my own son twice over.

"Good-bye, my boy," I said, "I hope that we shall meet again, wherever it is that we go to."

The fact was I did not expect to live another two minutes.

Next I retreated to the far side of the rock, and waited till one of the chopping gusts of wind got behind me, and then commending my soul to God, I ran the length of the huge stone, some three or four and thirty feet, and sprang wildly out into the dizzy air. Oh! the sickening terrors that I felt as I launched myself at that little point of rock, and the horrible sense of despair that shot through my brain as I realised that I had *jumped short!* But so it was, my feet never touched the point, they went down into space, only my hands and body came in contact with it. I gripped at it with a yell, but one hand slipped, and I swung right round, holding by the other, so that I faced the stone from which I had sprung. Wildly I stretched up with my left hand, and this time managed to grasp a knob of rock, and there I hung in the fierce red light, with thousands of feet of empty air beneath me. My hands were holding to either side of the under part of the spur, so that its point was touching my head. Therefore, even if I could have found the strength I could not pull myself up. The most that I could do would be to hang for about a minute, and then drop down, down into the bottomless pit. If any man can imagine a more hideous position let him speak. All I know is that the torture of that half minute nearly turned my brain. I heard Leo give a cry, and then suddenly saw him in mid air springing up and out like a chamois. It was a splendid leap that he took under the influence of his terror and despair, clearing the horrible gulf as though it were nothing, and landing well on to the rocky point, he threw himself upon his face, to prevent his pitching off it into the depths. I felt the spur above me shake beneath the shock of his impact, and as it did so I saw the huge rocking stone, that had been violently depressed by him as he sprang, fly back when relieved of his weight till, for the first time during all these centuries, it got beyond its balance, and fell with a most awful crash right into the rocky chamber which had once served the philosopher Noot for a hermitage, as I have no doubt, for ever hermetically sealing the passage that leads to the Place of Life with some hundreds of tons of rock.

All this happened in a second, and curiously enough, notwithstanding my terrible position, I noted it involuntarily, as it were. I even remember thinking that no human being would go down that dread path again.

Next instant I felt Leo seize me by the right wrist with both hands. By lying flat upon his stomach on the point of rock he could just reach me.

"You must let go and swing yourself clear," he said, in a calm and collected voice, "and then I will try and pull you up, or we will both go together. Are you ready?"

By way of answer I let go, first with my left hand, and then with the right, and swayed out as a consequence clear of the overshadowing rock, my weight hanging upon Leo's arms. It was a dreadful moment. He was a very powerful man, I knew, but would his strength be equal to lifting me up till I could get a hold on the top of the spur, when owing to his position he had so little purchase?

For a few seconds I swung to and fro, while he gathered himself for the effort, and then I heard his sinews cracking above me, and felt myself lifted up as though I were a little child till I got my left arm round the rock, and my chest was resting on it. The rest was easy; in two or three more seconds I was up, and we were lying panting side by side, trembling like leaves, and with the cold perspiration of terror pouring from our skins.

And then, as before, the light went out like a lamp.

For some half-hour we lay thus without speaking a word, and then at length began to creep along the great spur as best we might in the dense gloom. As we got towards the face of the cliff, however, from which the spur sprung out like a spike from a wall, the light increased, though only a very little, for it was night overhead. After that the gusts of wind decreased, and we got along rather better, and at last reached the mouth of the first cave or tunnel. But now a fresh trouble stared us in the face: our oil was gone, and the lamps were, no doubt, crushed to powder beneath the fallen rocking stone. We were even without a drop of water to stay our thirst, for we had drunk the last in the chamber of Noot. How were we to see to make our way through this last boulder-strewn tunnel?

Clearly all that we could do was to trust to our sense of feeling, and attempt the passage in the dark, so in we crept, fearing that if we delayed to do so our exhaustion would overcome us, and we should probably lie down and die where we were.

Oh, the horrors of that last tunnel! The place was strewn with rocks, and we fell over them, and knocked ourselves up against them till we were bleeding from a score of wounds. Our only guide was the side of the cavern, which we kept touching, and so bewildered did we grow in the darkness that we were several times seized with the terrifying thought that we had turned, and were travelling the wrong way. On we went, feebly, and still more feebly, for hour after hour, stopping every few minutes to rest, for our strength was spent. Once we fell asleep, and, I think, must have slept for some hours, for, when we woke, our limbs were quite stiff, and the blood from our blows and scratches had caked, and was hard and dry upon our skin. Then we dragged ourselves on again, till at last, when despair was entering into our hearts, we once more saw the light of day, and found ourselves outside the tunnel in the rocky fold on the outer surface of the cliff which, it will be remembered, led into it.

It was early morning—that we could tell by the feel of the sweet air and the look of the blessed sky, which we had never hoped to see again. It had, so near as we knew, been an hour after sunset when we entered the tunnel, so it followed that it had taken us the entire night to crawl through that dreadful place.

"One more effort, Leo," I gasped, "and we shall reach the slope where Billali is, if he hasn't gone. Come, don't give way," for he had cast himself upon his face. He got up, and, leaning on each other, we got down that fifty feet or so of cliff—somehow. I have not the least notion how. I only remember that we found ourselves lying in a heap at the bottom, and then once more began to drag ourselves along on our hands and knees towards the grove where *She* had told Billali to wait her re-arrival, for we could not walk another foot. We had not gone fifty yards in this fashion when suddenly one of the mutes emerged from some trees on our left, through which, I presume, he had been taking a morning stroll, and came running up to see what sort of strange animals we were. He stared, and stared, and then held up his hands in horror, and nearly fell to the ground. Next, he started off as hard as he could for the grove some two hundred yards away. No wonder that he was horrified at our appearance, for we must have been a shocking sight. To begin, Leo with his golden curls turned a snowy white, his clothes nearly rent from his body, his worn face and his hands a mass of bruises, cuts, and blood-encrusted filth, was a sufficiently alarming spectacle, as he painfully dragged himself along the ground, and I have no doubt that I was little better. I know that two days afterwards when I looked at my face in some water I scarcely knew myself. I have never been famous for beauty, but there was something beside ugliness stamped upon my features that I have never got rid of until this day, something resembling that wild look with which a startled person wakes from deep sleep more than anything that I can think of. And really it is not to be wondered at. What I do wonder at is that we escaped at all with our reason.

Presently to my intense relief I saw old Billali hurrying towards us, and even then I could scarcely help smiling at the expression of consternation on his dignified countenance.

"Oh, my Baboon! my Baboon!" he cried, "my dear son, is it indeed thou and the Lion? Why, his mane that was ripe as corn is white like the snow. Whence come ye? and where is the Pig, and where too *She-who-must-be-obeyed*?"

"Dead, both dead," I answered; "but ask not questions; help us, and give us food and water, or we too shall die before thine eyes. Seest thou not that our tongues are black for want of water? How can we talk then?"

"Dead!" he gasped, "impossible. *She* who never dies—dead, how can it be?" and then perceiving, I think, that his face was being watched by the mutes who had come running up, he checked himself, and motioned to them to carry us to the camp, which they did.

Fortunately when we arrived some broth was boiling on the fire, and with this Billali fed us, for we were too weak to feed ourselves, thereby I firmly believe saving us from death by exhaustion. Then he bade the mutes wash the blood and grime from us with wet cloths, and after that we were laid down upon piles of aromatic grass, and instantly fell into the dead sleep of absolute exhaustion of mind and body.

(To be concluded in our next)

XXVIII

OVER THE MOUNTAIN

The next thing I recollect is a feeling of the most dreadful stiffness, and a sort of vague idea passing through my half-awakened brain that I was a carpet that had just been beaten. I opened my eyes, and the first thing they fell on was the venerable countenance of our old friend Billali, who was seated by the side of the improvised bed upon which I was sleeping, and thoughtfully stroking his long beard. The sight of him at once brought back to my mind a recollection of all that we had recently passed through, which was accentuated by the vision of poor Leo lying opposite to me, his face knocked almost to a jelly, and his beautiful crowd of curls turned from yellow to white,★ and I shut my eyes again and groaned.

"Thou hast slept long, my Baboon," said old Billali.

"How long, my father?" I asked.

"A round of the sun and a round of the moon, a day and a night hast thou slept, and the Lion also. See, he sleepeth yet."

"Blessed is sleep," I answered, "for it swallows up recollection."

"Tell me," he said, "what hath befallen ye, and what is this strange story of the death of Her who dieth not. Bethink thee, my son: if this be true, then is thy danger and the danger of the Lion very great—nay, almost is the pot red wherewith ye shall be potted, and the stomachs of those who shall eat ye are already hungry for the feast. Knowest thou not that these Amahagger, my children, these dwellers in the caves, hate ye? They hate ye as strangers, they hate ye more because of their brethren whom *She* put to the torture for ye. Assuredly, if once they learn that there is nought to fear from Her, from the terrible One-who-must-be-obeyed, they will slay ye by the pot. But let me hear thy tale, my poor Baboon."

This adjured, I set to work and told him—not everything, indeed, for I did not think it desirable to do so, but sufficient for my purpose, which was to make him understand that *She* was really no more, having fallen into some fire, and, as I put it—for the real thing would have been

---

★ Curiously enough, Leo's hair has lately been to some small extent regaining its colour; that is to say, it is now a yellowish grey, and I am not without hopes that it will in time come quite right.

incomprehensible to him—been burnt up. I also told him some of the horrors we had undergone in effecting our escape, and these produced a great impression on him. But I clearly saw that he did not believe in the report of Ayesha's death. He believed indeed that we thought that she was dead, but his explanation was that it had suited her to disappear for a while. Once, he said, in his father's time, she had done so for ten years, and there was a tradition in the country that many centuries back no one had seen her for a whole generation, when she suddenly re-appeared, and destroyed a woman who had assumed the position of Queen. I said nothing to this, but only shook my head, sadly. Alas! I knew too well that Ayesha would appear no more, at any rate that Billali would never see her.

"And now," concluded Billali, "what wouldst thou do, my Baboon?"

"Nay," I said, "I know not, my father. Can we not escape from this country?"

He shook his head.

"It is very difficult. By Kôr ye cannot pass, for ye would be seen, and as soon as those fierce ones found that ye were alone, well," and he smiled significantly, and made a movement as though he were placing a hat on his head. "But there is a way over the cliff whereof I once spake to ye, where they drive the cattle out to pasture. Then beyond the pastures are three days' journey through the marshes, and after that I know not, but I have heard that seven days' journey from thence is a mighty river, which floweth to the black water. If ye could come thither, perchance ye might escape, but how can ye come thither?"

"Billali," I said, "once, thou knowest, I did save thy life. Now pay back the debt, my father, and save me mine and my friend's, the Lion's. It shall be a pleasant thing for thee to think of when thine hour comes, and something to set in the scale against the evil doing of thy days, if perchance thou hast done any evil. Also, if thou be right, and if *She* doth but hide herself, surely when she comes again she shall reward thee."

"My son the Baboon," answered the old man, "think not that I have an ungrateful heart. Well do I remember how thou didst rescue me when those dogs stood by to see me drown. Measure for measure will I give thee, and if thou canst be saved, surely I will save thee. Listen: by dawn to-morrow be prepared, for litters shall be here to bear ye away across the mountains, and through the marshes beyond. This will I do, saying that it is the word of *She* that it be done, and he who obeyeth not the word of *She* food is he for the hyænas. Then when ye have crossed the marshes, ye must strike with your own hand, so that perchance if good fortune go with ye, ye may live to come to that black water whereof ye told me. And now, see, the Lion wakes, and ye must eat the food I have made ready for ye."

Leo's condition when once he was fairly aroused proved not to be so bad as might have been expected from his appearance, and we both of us managed to eat a hearty meal, which indeed we needed sadly enough. After this we limped down to the spring and bathed, and then came back and slept again till evening, when we once more ate enough for five. Billali was away all that day, no doubt making arrangements about litters and bearers, for we were awakened in the middle of the night by the arrival of a considerable number of men in the little camp.

At dawn the old man himself appeared, and told us that he had by using *She's* dreaded name, though with some difficulty, succeeded in getting the necessary men and two guides to conduct us across the swamps, and that he urged us to start at once, at the same time announcing his intention of accompanying us, so as to protect us against treachery. I was much touched by this act of kindness on the part of that wily old barbarian towards two utterly defenceless strangers. A three—or in his case, for he would have to return, six—days' journey through those deadly swamps was no light undertaking for a man of his age, but he consented to do it cheerfully in order to promote our safety. It shows that even among those dreadful Amahagger—who are certainly with their gloom and their devilish and ferocious rites by far the most terrible savages that I ever heard of—there are people with kindly hearts. Of course self-interest may have had something to do with it. He may have thought that *She* would suddenly reappear and demand an account of us at his hands, but still, allowing for all deductions, it was a great deal more than we could expect under the circumstances, and I can only say that I shall for as long as I live cherish a most affectionate remembrance of my nominal parent, old Billali.

Accordingly, after swallowing some food, we started in the litters, feeling, so far as our bodies went, wonderfully like our old selves after our long rest and sleep. I must leave the condition of our minds to the imagination.

Then came a terrible pull up the cliff. Sometimes the ascent was natural, more often it was a zig-zag roadway cut, no doubt, in the first instance by the old inhabitants of Kôr. The Amahagger say they drive their spare cattle over it once a year to pasture outside; all I know is that those cattle must be uncommonly active on their feet. Of course the litters were useless here, so we had to walk.

By midday, however, we reached the great flat top of that mighty wall of rock, and grand enough the view was from it, with the plain of

Kôr, in the centre of which we could clearly make out the pillared ruins of the Temple of Truth, to the one side, and the boundless and melancholy marsh on the other. This wall of rock, which had no doubt once formed the lip of the crater, was about a mile and a half thick, and still covered with clinkers.[1] Nothing grew there, and the only thing to relieve one's eyes were occasional pools of rain-water (for rain had lately fallen) wherever there was a little hollow. Over the flat crest of this mighty rampart we went, and then came the descent, which if not so difficult a matter as the getting up, was still sufficiently break-neck, and took us till sunset. That night, however, we camped in safety upon the mighty slopes that rolled away to the marsh beneath.

On the following morning, about eleven o'clock, began our dreary journey across those awful seas of swamps which I have already described.

For three whole days, through stench and mire, and the all-prevailing flavour of fever, did our bearers struggle along, till at length we came to open rolling ground quite uncultivated, and mostly treeless, but covered with game of all sorts, which lies beyond that most desolate, and without guides utterly impracticable, district. And here on the following morning we bade farewell, not without some regret, to old Billali, who stroked his white beard, and solemnly blessed us.

"Farewell, my son the Baboon," he said, "and farewell to thee too, oh Lion. I can do no more to help ye. But if ever ye come to your own country, be advised, and venture no more into lands that ye know not, lest ye come back no more, but leave your white bones to mark the limit of your journeyings. Farewell once more; often shall I think of ye, nor wilt thou forget me, my Baboon, for though thy face is ugly thy heart is true." And then he turned and went, and with him went the tall and sullen-looking bearers, and that was the last that we saw of the Amahagger. We watched them winding away with the empty litters like a procession bearing dead men from a battle, till the mists from the marsh gathered round them and hid them, and then, left utterly desolate in the vast wilderness, we turned and gazed round us, and at each other.

Three weeks or so before four men had entered the marshes of Kôr, and now two of us were dead, and the other two had gone through adventures and experiences so strange and terrible that Death himself hath not a more fearful countenance. Three weeks—and only three weeks! Truly time should be measured by events, and not by the lapse of hours. It seemed like thirty years since we saw the last of our whaleboat.

---

[1] Pieces of slag, rock that has been melted and fused.

"We must strike out for the Zambesi, Leo," I said, "but God knows if we shall ever get there."

Leo nodded. He had become very silent of late, and we started with nothing but the clothes we stood in, a compass, our revolvers and express rifles, and about two hundred rounds of ammunition, and so ended the history of our visit to the ruins of mighty Kôr.

As for the adventures that subsequently befell us, strange and varied as they were, I have, after deliberation, determined not to record them here. In these pages I have only tried to give a short and clear account of an occurrence which I believe to be unique, and this I have done, not with a view to immediate publication, but merely to put on paper while they are yet fresh in our memories the details of our journey and its result, which will, I believe, prove interesting to the world if ever we determine to make them public. This, as at present advised, we do not intend should be done during our joint lives.

For the rest, it is of no public interest, resembling as it does the experience of more than one Central African traveller. Suffice it to say, that we did, after incredible hardships and privations, reach the Zambesi, which proved to be about a hundred and seventy miles south of where Billali left us. There we were for six months imprisoned by a savage tribe, who believed us to be supernatural beings, chiefly on account of Leo's youthful face and snow-white hair. From these people we ultimately escaped, and, crossing the Zambesi, wandered off southwards, where, when on the point of starvation, we were sufficiently fortunate to fall in with a half-caste Portuguese elephant-hunter who had followed a troop of elephants farther inland than he had ever been before. This man treated us most hospitably, and ultimately through his assistance we, after innumerable sufferings and adventures, reached Delagoa Bay, more than eighteen months from the day when we emerged from the marshes of Kôr, and the very next day managed to catch one of the Donald Currie boats that run round the Cape to England.[1] Our journey home was a prosperous one, and we set our foot on the quay at Southampton exactly two years from the date of our departure upon our wild and seemingly ridiculous quest, and I now write these last words with Leo leaning over my shoulder in my old room in my college, the very same into which some two-and-twenty years ago my poor friend Vincey came stumbling on the memorable night of his death bearing the iron chest with him.

---

[1] Beginning in 1862, Donald Currie and Company ran mail and passenger steamship service between Britain and South Africa.

Is Leo really a reincarnation of the ancient Kallikrates of whom the writer speaks? Or was Ayesha deceived by some extraordinary racial resemblance? The reader must form his own opinion on this as on many other matters. I have mine, which is that she made no such mistake.

And that is the end of this history so far as it concerns science and the outside world. What its end will be as regards Leo and myself is more than I can guess at. But we feel that is not reached yet. A story that began two thousand years ago may stretch a long way into the dim and distant future.

Often I sit alone at night, staring with the eyes of the mind into the blackness of unborn time, and wondering in what shape and form the drama will be finally developed, and where the scene of its next act will be laid. And when that final development ultimately occurs, as I have no doubt it must and will occur, in obedience to a fate that never swerves and a purpose that cannot be altered, what will be the part played therein by that Egyptian Amenartas, the Princess of the race of the Pharaoh Hakor, for the love of whom the ancient Kallikrates broke his vows to Isis, and, pursued by the inexorable vengeance of the outraged Goddess, fled down the coast of Libya to meet his doom at Kôr.

THE END

Appendix A: Victorian Critical Reception

1. Pall Mall Gazette (4 January 1887)

It is not easy to adjust with precision the praise and dispraise due to Mr. Rider Haggard's new romance. It certainly rises above the commonplace, and it as certainly falls short of excellence. At times we are inclined to think it a very cheap work after all. The materials for such inventions lie at everybody's hand. There is a Dark Continent in which the imagination can expatiate at ease. Ancient and titanic civilizations on the one hand, and picturesque barbarisms on the other, supply hints which may well quicken even a sluggish fantasy. The miracles of science, and the marvels reported from the great debate-able land between science and superstition, incline men to widen indefinitely the bounds of what may be called imaginative belief. We have a Napoleonic contempt for the word "impossible," and are too sceptical to disbelieve anything. For his literary methods, or rather devices, the romancer may go to Edgar Allan Poe, Jules Verne, and other practitioners of the realistic unreal. He must have the pen of a ready descriptive writer, but otherwise he need take no thought for his style. It should be easy then to compound fantastic romances after this recipe; yet if it be so easy, why do not more of us do it? There is an undoubted demand, among old readers as well as young, for well-told tales of the marvellous, and if they were things that "any fellow could write" the cheapness of the process would certainly not deter the average literary artisan from turning them out in quantities. The truth is that, all aids and examples notwithstanding, there goes far more than the average mental power to the composition of a work like "She." It is informed by an energy and intensity of imagination that is not to be had for the asking. The conception, indeed, is so powerful that we rebel with a sense of injury against the many defects of execution. It is as though a subject roughed out by Michael Angelo had been executed with an eye to New Bond-street[1] popularity by Gustave Doré.[2] A style alternatively flat and flamboyant, cheap philosophy, shallow sentiment, and a strain of humour which, though harmless enough in itself, is made by its surroundings to seem frivolous to the verge of vulgarity—these are the faults of Mr. Haggard's work. He has vision and faculty, swiftness and strength; but he lacks distinction of touch in handling a theme which a great artist would have treated not only with distinction but with austerity. If Dante had been accompanied on his tour through the "città

---

[1] A famous shopping area in London.
[2] Gustave Doré (1832-83) was a popular commercial illustrator known for his line engravings of literary scenes and depictions of contemporary London.

dolente"[1] by a special correspondent of the *Daily Telegraph*, the result would have been just such a book as "She." This is a compliment (and we mean it) to the conception; and in the sphere of the "largest circulation" it will doubtless be regarded as no less a compliment to the style....

Mr. Haggard may complain that we do not take his book at his own valuation as a mere "history of adventure." We reply that as a mere history of adventure it would have been better had it been treated more soberly; and further, that no work of art, however modest its pretensions, should show such inequalities of execution. It is because Mr. Haggard has powerfully stimulated our imagination that we lament the frequent torpors of his own.

2. *The Literary World* 35 (7 January 1887)

Mr. Rider Haggard has made for himself a new field in fiction. Leaving microscopic analysis of character and realistic descriptions of every-day life and the fortunes of lovers for others, he places the scene of his stories in the unexplored regions of Africa, and there brings his adventurous modern Englishmen into contact with strange peoples living among the stupendous remains of forgotten civilisations, and still subject to the mysterious spells of antiquity. It is not to be wondered at that a method so novel, and taking so strong a hold on the imagination, should, in *King Solomon's Mines*, have immediately caught the popular fancy, and made the writer's reputation. The book before us displays all the same qualities, and we anticipate for it a similar popularity. There is even more imagination in the later than in the earlier story; it contains scenes of greater sensuous beauty and also of more gruesome horror; but there is this disadvantage in the increased rise of the marvellous that any sense of reality is somewhat blunted, and the thrilling interest of the plot proportionally lessened. With this preface let us enter on Mr. Haggard's fantastic kingdom.

3. *Public Opinion* 51 (14 January 1887)

This work, which appeared originally in the columns of an illustrated contemporary, and has been followed by so many readers with such intense interest from week to week, will add to the already considerable reputation of the author of "King Solomon's Mines." We have found it almost as fascinating as Mr. Stevenson's "Treasure Island," and greater praise than that we can scarcely give it. Few books bolder in conception, more vigorous in treatment, or fresher in fancy, have appeared for a long time, and we are grateful to Mr. Haggard for carrying us on a pinion, swift and strong, far from the world of platitudinous dulness, on which most young writers embark, to a

---

[1] The mournful city (Italian); Dante's name for Hell.

region limited only by his own vivid imagination, where the most inveterate reader of novels cannot guess what surprise awaits him....

Out of a sense of justice to the author we will leave the reader to find out for himself the extraordinary drama that is here transacted, than which we have scarcely met with anything more weird in a long course of promiscuous novel reading. If Flaubert's "Salammbô"[1] came as a surprise to the reading world, Mr. Haggard's book is far more fascinating, and is worth sitting up half the night to finish, even for a reviewer. But it is not given to mortals to reach perfection, and "She" contains some minor defects which are proportionally irritating as they were easy to be avoided. Job, intended to be an amusing serving-man, to lighten the sombre portions of the story, is a bore pure and simple, who detracts from the picturesqueness of the narrative, whilst his death adds nothing to the pathos. Fortunately we have not much of him. Leo Vincey's want of conversational dignity jars on the elevated diction necessary for such a work. Indeed, his "Hang it all" and "I say, old fellow," seem eminently out of place and almost offensive. Ustane, the heroic maid who gives her love to the beautiful youth, and whose fate is so swift and piteous, is admirably suggested. On the extraordinary character of *She* the author has lavished a force of imagination, a dramatic instinct, a poetic insight, and an artistic sense of proportion which are truly admirable, and long after the book is finished this strange, lovely, ruthless creature haunts the imagination, and lingers there amid the stranger creations of fancy. However like Tithonus she "may differ from the kindly race of men,"[2] she is still a woman, only with every feminine quality preternaturally intensified. The grim scenery harmonising with the stupendous events of the story is most artistically described, and could only be adequately illustrated by Gustave Doré. The ruined city of Kôr, the titanic tombs, the roaring winds, the yawning gulfs, the fires, the prodigies, are like pictures dimly seen through a nightmare, and *She* flits through all this land of mystery like a sibyl leading trembling mortals through the portals of gloomy Dis.[3] In conclusion, we trust Mr. Haggard will pardon us if we leave him with a word of advice. We have seen so many reputations of promise fall victims to the necessity of over-production, so many a Pegasus[4] of fiction driven till it is lame, that we trust he at least may escape this fate, and not allow his great success to induce him to set before the public hurried or immature work. If he will devote time and critical labour to it the result will have real, and perhaps enduring, value; but if, on the other hand, he prefer

---

1 A novel (1862) by Gustave Flaubert, concerning Carthage and the Punic Wars. Like *She*, it incorporates archaeological detail, cannibalism, and a central, erotic female figure.

2 Quoting from Tennyson's "Tithonus" (1860), a poem written in the voice of an immortal but aging lover of the goddess of the dawn.

3 The underworld or Hell.

4 Winged horse of Greek mythology, associated with literary inspiration.

quantity to quality and guineas to goodness, in spite of the facility of his imagination and the energy of his style, the result will be disappointing and facile.

4. The Queen: The Lady's Newspaper (15 January 1887)

If we are to believe the story-tellers, there is still a Wonderland in Africa, the dark continent. Dr Mayo's somewhat extravagant tale "Kaloolah,"[1] Mr. Haggard's "King Solomon's Mines," Commander Cameron's "The Queen's Land,"[2] wherein the explorers find the long forgotten Queen of Sheba, and now the present history, in which the heroine is a lady of almost equal length of days, are examples to prove our assertion.... We come to love [Ayesha] ourselves; and as the story moves to an end, with her dreams of a new gift of life for herself and her lover, and a new tenderness awakened by his presence her better womanly nature prevails—she will abandon the evil and cleave to the good. But Destiny is too strong; the new Kallikrates is fated to be the avenger of the old. We shall not tell how; but there comes a day when Holly and Leo have each but a tress of hair to take away as Ayesha's token, and the unfading remembrance of her in their hearts. This is a tale that in the hands of a writer not so able as Mr. Haggard might easily have become absurd; but he has treated it with so much vividness and picturesque power as to invest it with unflagging interest, and given to the mystery a port of philosophic possibility that makes us quite willing to submit to the illusion.

5. The Academy (15 January 1887)

...the more impossible it gets, the better (to my taste) Mr. Haggard does it. The conception of an undying character is older than Herodotus. Wandering Jews, Salathiels,[3] and the like, populate the realms of fiction. But Ayesha—"*She* who is to be obeyed"—does not resemble them. The miracles she can work, as when she lays her hand on her rival's dark hair, and leaves the snow-white score of three fingers on her locks, or when the flames follow and fall with her lowered and lifted arms, are a new kind of miracles. Her despair as she watches by the life-like embalmed corpse of her lover, Kallikrates, dead for two thousand years—moves me like few scenes in fiction. The whole story is an allegory of the immortality of love, which death cannot destroy, nor the force of fire abol-

---

[1] William S. Mayo (1812–95), American novelist who wrote, *Kaloolah: or Journeyings to the Djebel Kumri* (1849), a tale of African adventure.

[2] Verney Lovett Cameron (1844–94), Central African explorer and author, whose novel *The Queen's Land* (1886) concerns a race of Africans descended from the Queen of Sheba.

[3] An allusion to a novel of this name by George Croly (published in 1828) which treats the theme of the Wandering Jew, the legendary figure cursed to live until the Last Judgment for mocking Jesus on his way to the Crucifixion.

ish it. Mr. Haggard's practical knowledge and experience of the savage life and wild lands, his sense of the mystery and charm of ruined civilisations, his appreciation of sport (especially with big game), his astonishing imagination, and a certain *vraisemblance*,[1] which makes the most impossible adventures appear true (to a reader of sympathetic fancy), these are the qualities a man admires in *She*, if he chance to admire it at all. Were one to enumerate the drawbacks to such a reader's enjoyment, it might be said that the humour may not be always to his mind, though it is a foil to the terrible passages. Again, some of the scenes of savagery (as when the pot is made red for the stranger, in a kind of Voudou feast, and as in the scene of the Black Goat) are too awful for many young and old students. Ayesha, moreover, discourses, perhaps, at too great length; but then she had not met educated companions for two thousand years, and was full of suppressed conversation. The style is that of Alan Quatermain,[2] rather than of a Cambridge don, though Holly is such an unusual kind of don that this may be of slight importance. Against all this a reader in tune with the author (for all depends on that) will set the scenes in the sculptured catacombs, and the vision of moonlight in the city of Kôr, the dead satellite shining on a city long dead, and the pathos of Ayesha's last caress. But this, be it reiterated, is the sense of a reviewer attached to the impossible romance, of one who confesses himself incredibilium cupitor,[3] an amateur of savage life, fond of haunting, in fancy, the mysterious homes of ruined races, a believer, too, in the moral of the legend.

Here is a "grown-up" literary estimate of *She*. How it will suit boys experiment must declare. Tried on a youth in the Middle Fifth the experiment answered rarely, bringing peace through the whole day, when every form of sport was impossible, and life appeared to be "drawn blank." Any man who is enough of a boy will want to ask: "How did Ayesha get to Kôr?" and, "What happened afterwards in Thibet?"[4]

6. *The Spectator* (15 January 1887)

Mr. Rider Haggard must have meditated on "that not impossible She"[5] of whom young men are apt to dream, till he determined to write a tale about

---

1   "Verisimilitude" (French).

2   Narrator of Haggard's novel, *King Solomon's Mines* (1885), and hero of *Allan Quatermain* (1887); he also features in a number of Haggard's later works, including *She and Allan* (1921), in which he meets Ayesha.

3   "A lover of the fantastic" (Latin).

4   Haggard answered this last question in a sequel, *Ayesha: The Return of She* (1905), which is set in Tibet.

5   A quotation from Richard Crashaw's poem, "Wishes for the Supposed Mistress" (1646): "Whoe'er she be/ That not impossible She/ That shall command my heart and me." The poem was reprinted in Francis Palgrave's *Golden Treasury* (1861), the most influential Victorian anthology of poetry.

a quite impossible she, by way of driving the other out of his head. His tale is a very stirring and exciting one, and shows remarkable imaginative power, though the present writer admits a dislike to Mr. Rider Haggard's favourite literary method of infusing a great mass of real and vivid experience with a single preternatural element of an absolutely impossible order, by the lurid light of which the realism is thrown into strong relief, and brought out with a Rembrandt-like effect. We cannot help feeling that the author is almost laughing at us beneath his mask of dread, when he discloses how his lovely heroine of two thousand years' experience disappears. To the present writer there is a sense of the ludicrous in the end of "She," that spoiled, instead of concluding with imaginative fitness, the thread of the impossible worked into the substance of this vivid and brilliantly told story. Mr. Haggard's method requires great tact in the use of marvel. If you are telling a fairy-story or tale of pure magic, such tact is needless. But where an imaginative author uses the marvellous within the strictest limits only to bring into relief the most admirable realism, he should be careful so to use it as not to detract from the effect of the whole,—so as not to attenuate the impression produced by the author's minute acquaintance with the scenery and physiognomy of savage African life. Even allowing Mr. Haggard his chosen method, we hold that the *finale* put to the career of his aged though ever youthful beauty is incongruous, and too sensational to blend easily with the main features of the story....

For the rest, nothing can be more spirited than the plot from its opening to its close. The ingenuity of the story which gives rise to the search for Leo Vincey's supposed ancestor is as subtle as ever romancer invented, and from the day when he and his guardian or friend land on the coast of Africa, to the day when the revolving pillar of fire is revealed to him by the all but immortal "She who must be obeyed," the interest of the tale rises higher and higher with every new turn in its course,—while every such turn explains and verifies some enigmatic statement made in that original tradition which started the whole series of adventures. It would be difficult to imagine anything more frightfully graphic than the account of the scene in which the Amahagger try to celebrate their savage rite, without directly disobeying their queen, by putting a red-hot pot on the head of the Mahometan servant who accompanied the white men, except the account of the Amahagger night-dance, lighted by the burning corpses of embalmed ancestors, or the description of the last expedition to the revolving pillar of fire. At every stage of the story we feel persuaded that the author has exhausted his resources, and that the interest must begin to decline. As a matter of fact, this is not the case. At almost every page, the weird interest of the story rises till we come to what we cannot help regarding as the anti-climax of the close....

The poetry which Mr. Haggard puts into the mouth of his strange heroine is hardly less effective than his account of the apparently cold accuracy of her calculations. But he is a little inconsistent, we think, when he makes her, in the last scene, do homage not only to the ecstasy of love, which she had evidently held worthy of worship all through life, but to the majesty of virtue. In every previous scene he had represented her as disbelieving in any absolute law of right and wrong, any fixed standard of virtue and sin; and we see nothing in the happiness of gratified love to convert her to the view which her philosophy of two thousand years seems to have led her to reject. But, as we have said, Mr. Haggard seems to have lost sight to some extent of his own general conception in his picture of the heroine's departure from the scene. Except at that point, this story of imaginative adventure is as brilliant as it is unique. This type of romance is not one that we place very high in the literary scale, but in its kind it could hardly be rivaled.

7. H. Rider Haggard, from a letter to the Editor, *The Spectator* (22 January 1887)

Your reviewer, in his very flattering notice of "She,"[1] takes exception to the manner of Ayesha's end. Looking at the work from his point of view, I agree with him that the method of her death might have been modified in some such way as he suggests. But there is another aspect of the story, which he has overlooked in common with the majority of its reviewers, owing, no doubt, to the failure of my attempt to convey the idea without thrusting it into undue prominence. "She" was not intended to be a story of imaginative adventure only. In the first place, an attempt is made in it to follow the action of the probable effects of immortality working upon the known and ascertained substance of the mortal. This is a subject with a prospective interest for us all. Secondly, the legend is built up upon the hypothesis that deep affection is in itself an immortal thing. Therefore, when Ayesha in the course of ages grows hard, cynical, and regardless of that which stands between her and her ends, her love yet endures, true and holy, changeless amid change. Therefore, too, when at last the reward is in her sight, and passion utterly possesses her, it gives her strength to cast away the evil, and (what your reviewer considers inconsistent with her nature) even to do homage to "the majesty of virtue." For love is to her a saving grace and a gate of redemption, her hardened nature melts in the heats of passion, and, as has happened to many other worldly-minded people, through the sacred agency of love, she once more became (or at the moment imagined that she would become) what she had been before disillusion, disappointment, and two thousand wretched years of loneliness had turned her heart to stone.

Lastly, it occurred to me that in She herself some readers might find a type of the spirit of intellectual Paganism, or perhaps even our own modern

---

[1] See Appendix A.6.

Agnosticism; of the spirit, at any rate, which looks to earth, and earth alone, for its comfort and rewards. All through the book, although Ayesha's wisdom tells her that there is some ultimate fate appointed for a man which is unconnected with the world…, it is to this world only and its passions that she clings. Even in the moment of her awful end, she speaks of a future *earthly* meeting with the lover, whom in the past she had feared to follow into death. When Holly, the Christian, refuses her gift of life, and tells her of his own hopes of immortality, she mocks him. To her, all religion is but "a subtler form of selfishness and terror for the end." In the insolence of her strength and loveliness, she lifts herself up against the Omnipotent. Therefore, at the appointed time she is swept away by It with every circumstance of "shame and hideous mockery." Vengeance, more heavy because more long-delayed, strikes her in her proudest part—her beauty; and in her lover's very presence she is made to learn the thing she really is, and what is the end of earthly wisdom and of the loveliness she prized so highly.

These were some of the points which occurred to me in connection with Ayesha's character. If any reader of the book is but half as much in love with She as I confess to being, he will understand how necessary I thought her fate to the moral, before I could steel myself to bring her to such an end. It appears, however, that I did not make my purpose sufficiently clear. Knowing that allegory if obtrusive is bad art, I was anxious not to bring it too much to the fore, with the result that this side of the story has evidently become almost imperceptible.

8. *Blackwood's Edinburgh Magazine* (February 1887)

Mr. Rider Haggard…. is the new *avatar* of the old story-teller, with a flavour of the nineteenth century and scientific explanation, but at the same time a sturdy and masculine force of invention which disdains these helps even in employing them. 'King Solomon's Mines' was a strong pull upon the wholesome curiosity of the race, and their interest in the wonderful; but 'She' is a stronger…. Mr. Rider Haggard is not an exquisite workman like Mr. [Robert Louis] Stevenson, but he has a great deal of power in his way, and rougher qualities which are more likely, perhaps, to "take the town" than skill more delicate. And then he has a distinct sphere which is his own. He "talks of Africa and golden joys,"[1] with a knowledge and certainty that few possess, and is able to thread an unknown river for us as if it were in all the maps, and make the dismal swamps as recognisable as Princes Street.

There is, inevitably we suppose, a certain amount of resemblance between this wonderful tale and its predecessor. There was a map to guide the investigators in the one case; there is a potsherd with a Greek inscription in the

---

[1] Quoting from Shakespeare, *King Henry IV, Part II*, act v, sc. 3: "I speak of Africa and golden joys."

other. In 'King Solomon's Mines' the motive was stronger, for it was the recovery of hidden treasure and of a kingdom to one of the invaders; but in 'She' it is more romantic, being all mixed with a very weird and uncanny kind of love-making. It is no doubt a sort of resurrection that has taken place in this new writer. The fancy of the public has been lately turned, by one of those impulses which periodically sway human sentiment, to the art of the story-teller, which, perhaps, had fallen a little out of repute, dimmed by the modern art of character-painting and analysis.... The methods of the new *raconteur*[1] are not refined, nor his inspiration of any more ethereal kind than that of mingling experience and invention into a stirring tale. Neither satire nor criticism of life is in the strain. His object is to work in as many marvels as possible, with so many realities as to make the whole look as if it might have been, which is an effort much more difficult than that of the writer who flings himself into the person of his hero, and feels and lives with him. Mr. Rider Haggard has not proved as yet that he has anything that can be called imagination at all; but invention he has of the most robust kind, such as may afford a certain amount of pleasure to everybody who reads, and which probably impresses the masses more than most poetic fancy.

'She' is one of the wildest of prosaic conceptions. She is an enchantress who has established an empire in the interior of Africa, unknown to history or tradition, unsuspected by the geographers, a mysterious region which contains the central fountain, or rather fire, of life, in which having bathed she is immortal—or rather comparatively immortal, for there are limits to all things; and up to the time at which the story begins, this personage has lived and reigned only a trifle over 2000 years. Notwithstanding this respectable period of duration, she is still as full of all the arts of coquetry as if she were a young lady of the nineteenth century....

The journey to the centre of life is attended by horrors which suggest stage carpentry more than anything real, and the plank which is carefully carried all the way to be placed over a gap in a tremendous chasm, where the wind is always raving, and where that prosaic bridge has to be thrown between a spur of unsteady rock and a loggan-stone, has surely been invented with some idea of future use in a pantomime. Only once in the twenty-four hours does a ray of sunshine penetrate the blackness of this too awful gulf, and that moment, of course, has to be taken advantage of for the crossing. We recommend it to the attention of Mr. Irving.[2] It might be wrought up into an unparalleled stage effect: but it is rather a failure in pen and ink. The more fearful and wonderful such circumstances are intended to be, the more absurd

---

[1] A teller of tales.
[2] Henry Irving (1838-1905); leading actor of the day and manager of the Lyceum Theatre in London, famous for staging elaborate, spectacular performances.

is the failure of them. We are, alas! not at all alarmed by the plight of Messrs Holly and Vincey, even when they return alone from their sublime adventure. It excites our interest much more to hear how they are to fare at the hands of their savage escort when they come back without the queen, who alone has kept these savages in order. That commends itself to us as a real danger: the other is mere pasteboard and fireworks.

9. H. Rider Haggard, "About Fiction," *Contemporary Review* 51 (February 1887)

The love of romance is probably coeval with the existence of humanity. So far as we can follow the history of the world we find traces of it and its effects among every people, and those who are acquainted with the habits and ways of thought of savage races will know that it flourishes as strongly in the barbarian as in the cultured breast. In short, it is like the passions, an innate quality of mankind. In modern England this love is not by any means dying out, as must be clear, even to that class of our fellow-countrymen who, we are told, are interested in nothing but politics and religion. A writer in the *Saturday Review* computed not long ago that the yearly output of novels in this country is about eight hundred; and probably he was within the mark. It is to be presumed that all this enormous mass of fiction finds a market of some sort, or it would not be produced. Of course a large quantity of it is brought into the world at the expense of the writer, who guarantees or deposits his thirty or sixty pounds, which in the former case he is certainly called upon to pay, and in the latter he never sees again. But this deducted, a large residue remains, out of which a profit must be made by the publisher, or he would not publish it. Now, most of this crude mass of fiction is worthless. If three-fourths of it were never put into print the world would scarcely lose a single valuable idea, aspiration, or amusement. Many people are of the opinion in their secret hearts that they could, if they thought it worth while to try, write a novel that would be very good indeed, and a large number of people carry this opinion into practice without scruple or remorse. But as a matter of fact, with the exception of perfect sculpture, really good romance writing is perhaps the most difficult art practised by the sons of men. It might even be maintained that none but a great man or woman can produce a *really* great work of fiction. But great men are rare, and great words are rarer still, because all great men do not write. If, however, a person is intellectually a head and shoulders above his or her fellows, that person is *primâ facie* fit and able to write a good work. Even then he or she may not succeed, because in addition to intellectual pre-eminence, a certain literary quality is necessary to the perfect flowering of the brain in books. Perhaps, therefore, the argument would stand better conversely. The writer who can produce a noble and lasting work of art is of necessity a great man, and one who, had fortune opened to him any of the doors that lead to material grandeur and to the busy pomp of power, would have shown that the imagination, the quick sympathy, the insight, the depth of mind, and the sense of order and proportion which went to constitute the writer would have equally constituted the statesman or the general. It is not, of course, argued that only great writers should produce books, because if this was so publishing as a trade would come to an end, and Mudie[1] would be obliged to put up his shutters. Also there exists a large class of people who like to read, and to whom great books would scarcely appeal. Let us imagine the consternation of the ladies of England if they were suddenly forced to an exclusive fare of George Eliot and Thackeray! But it *is* argued that a large proportion of the fictional matter poured from the press into the market is superfluous, and serves no good purpose. On the contrary, it serves several distinctly bad ones. It lowers and vitiates the public taste, and it obscures the true ends of fiction. Also it brings the high and honourable profession of authorship into contempt and disrepute, for the general public, owing perhaps to the comparative poverty of literary men, has never yet quite made up its mind as to the status of their profession. Lastly, this over-production stops the sale of better work without profiting those who are responsible for it.

The publication of inferior fiction can, in short, be of no advantage to any one, except perhaps the proprietors of circulating libraries. To the author himself it must indeed be a source of nothing but misery, bitterness, and disappointment, for only those who have written can know the amount of labour involved in the production of even a bad book. Still, the very fact that people can be found to write and publishers to publish to such an unlimited extent, shows clearly enough the enormous appetite of readers, who are prepared, like a diseased ostrich, to swallow stones, and even carrion, rather than not get their fill of novelties. More and more, as what we call culture spreads, do men and women crave to be taken out of themselves. More and more do they long to be brought face to face with Beauty, and stretch out their arms towards that vision of the Perfect, which we only see in books and dreams. The fact that we, in these latter days, have as it were macadamized all the roads of life does not make the world softer to the feet of those who travel through it. There are now royal roads to everything, lined with staring placards, whereon he who runs may learn the sweet uses of advertisement; but it is dusty work to follow them, and some may think that our ancestors on the whole found their voyaging a shadier and fresher business. However this may be, a weary public calls continually for books, new books to make them forget, to refresh them, to occupy minds jaded with the toil and emptiness and vexation of our competitive existence.

---

[1]   Mudie's Select Library (est. 1842), a very influential for-profit lending library of the Victorian era.

In some ways this demand is no doubt a healthy sign. The intellect of the world must be awakening when it thus cries aloud to be satisfied. Perhaps it is not a good thing to read nothing but three-volumed novels of an inferior order, but it, at any rate, shows the possession of a certain degree of intelligence. For there still exists among us a class of educated people, or rather of people who have had a certain sum of money spent upon their education, who are absolutely incapable of reading *anything*, and who never do read anything, except, perhaps, the reports of famous divorce cases and the spiciest paragraphs in Society papers. It is not their fault; they are often very good people enough in their way; and as they go to church on Sundays, and pay their rates and taxes, the world has no right to complain of them. They are born without intellects, and with undeveloped souls, that is all, and on the whole they find themselves very comfortable in that condition. But this class is getting smaller, and all writers have cause to congratulate themselves on the fact, for the dead wall of crass stupidity is a dreadful thing to face. Those, too, who begin by reading novels may end by reading Milton and Shakespeare. Day by day the mental area open to the operations of the English-speaking writer grows larger. At home the Board schools pour out their thousands every year, many of whom have acquired a taste for reading, which, once it has been born, will, we may be sure, grow apace. Abroad the colonies are filling up with English-speaking people, who, as they grow refined and find leisure to read, will make a considerable call upon the literature of their day. But by far the largest demand for books in the English tongue comes from America, with its reading population of some forty millions. Most of the books patronized by the enormous population are stolen from English authors, who, according to American law, are outcasts, unentitled to that protection to the work of their brains and the labour of their hands which is one of the foundations of common morality. Putting aside this copyright question, however (and, indeed, it is best left undiscussed), there may be noted in passing two curious results which are being brought about in America by this wholesale perusal of English books. The first of these is that the Americans are destroying their own literature, that cannot live in the face of the unfair competition to which it is subjected. It will be noticed that since piracy, to use the politer word, set in with its present severity, America has scarcely produced a writer of the first class—no one, for instance, who can be compared to Poe, or Hawthorne, or Longfellow. It is not, perhaps, too rash a prophecy to say that, if piracy continues, American literature proper will shortly be chiefly represented by the columns of a very enterprising daily press. The second result of the present state of affairs is that the whole of the American population, especially the younger portion of it, must be in a course of thorough impregnation with English ideas and modes of thought as set forth by English writers. We all know the extraordinary effect books read in youth have upon the fresh and imaginative mind. It is not too much to say that many a man's whole life is influenced by some book read in his teens, the very title of which he may have forgotten. Consequently, it would be difficult to overrate the effect that must be from year to year produced upon the national character of America by the constant perusal of books born in England. For it must be remembered that for every reader that a writer of merit finds in England, he will find three in America.

In the face of this constant and ever-growing demand at home and abroad writers of romance must often find themselves questioning their inner consciousness as to what style of art it is best for them to adopt, not only with the view of pleasing their readers, but in the interests of art itself. There are several schools from which they may choose. For instance, there is that followed by the American novelists. These gentlemen, as we know, declare that there are no stories left to be told, and certainly, if it may be said without disrespect to a clever and laborious body of writers, their works go far towards supporting the statement. They have developed a new style of romance. Their heroines are things of silk and cambric, who soliloquize and dissect their petty feelings, and elaborately review the feeble promptings which serve them for passions. Their men—well, they are emasculated specimens of an overwrought age, and, with culture on their lips, and emptiness in their hearts, they dangle round the heroines till their three-volumed fate is accomplished. About their work is an atmosphere like that of the boudoir of a luxurious woman, faint and delicate, and suggesting the essence of white rose. How different is all this to the swiftness, and strength, and directness of the great English writers of the past. Why,

The surge and thunder of the Odyssey[1]

is not more widely separated from the tinkling of modern society verses, than the laboured nothingness of this new American school of fiction from the giant life and vigour of Swift and Fielding, and Thackeray and Hawthorne. Perhaps, however, it is the art of the future, in which case we may hazard a shrewd guess that the literature of past ages will be more largely studied in days to come than it is at present.

Then, to go from Pole to Pole, there is the Naturalistic school, of which Zola[2] is the high priest. Here things are all the other way. Here the chosen function of the writer is to

Paint the mortal shame of nature with the living hues of art.[3]

---

1 From Andrew Lang's "The Odyssey," *The Odyssey of Homer* (1881).
2 Émile Zola (1840-1902), French writer whose novels, such as *Nana* (mentioned below) present lower-class life in Paris with unsparing realism.
3 From Tennyson, "Locksley Hall Sixty Years After" (1886).

Here are no silks and satins to impede our vision of the flesh and blood beneath, and here the scent is patchouli. Lewd, and bold, and bare, living for lust and lusting for this life and its good things, and naught beyond, the heroines of realism dance, with Bacchanalian revellings, across the astonished stage of literature. Whatever there is brutal in humanity—and God knows there is plenty—whatever there is that is carnal and filthy, is here brought into prominence, and thrust before the reader's eyes. But what becomes of the things that are pure and high—of the great aspirations and the lofty hopes and longings, which *do*, after all, play their part in our human economy, and which it is surely the duty of a writer to call attention to and nourish according to his gifts?

Certainly it is to be hoped that this naturalistic school of writing will never take firm root in England, for it is an accursed thing. It is impossible to help wondering if its followers ever reflect upon the mischief that they must do, and, reflecting, do not shrink from the responsibility. To look at the matter from one point of view only, Society has made a rule that for the benefit of the whole community individuals must keep their passions within certain fixed limits, and our social system is so arranged that any transgression of this rule produces mischief of one sort or another, if not actual ruin, to the transgressor. Especially is this so if she be a woman. Now, as it is, human nature is continually fretting against these artificial bounds, and especially among young people it requires considerable fortitude and self-restraint to keep the feet from wandering. We all know, too, how much this sort of indulgence depends upon the imagination, and we all know how easy it is for a powerful writer to excite it in that direction. Indeed, there could be nothing *more* easy to a writer of any strength and vision, especially if he spoke with an air of evil knowledge and intimate authority. There are probably several men in England at this moment who, if they turned their talents to this bad end, could equal, if not outdo, Zola himself, with results that would shortly show themselves in various ways among the population. Sexual passion is the most powerful lever with which to stir the mind of man, for it lies at the root of all things human; and it is impossible to over-estimate the damage that could be worked by a single English or American writer of genius, if he grasped it with a will. "But," say these writers, "our aim is most moral; from Nana and her kith and kin may be gathered many a virtuous lesson and example." Possibly this is so, though as I write the words there rises in my mind a recollection of one or two French books where—but most people have seen such books. Besides, it is not so much a question of the object of the school as of the fact that it continually, and in full and luscious detail, calls attention to erotic matters. Once start the average mind upon this subject, and it will go down the slope of itself. It is useless afterwards to turn round and say that, although you cut loose the cords of decent reticence which bound the fancy, you intended that it should run *uphill* to the white heights of virtue. If the seed of eroticism is sown broadcast its fruit will be according to the nature of the soil it falls on, but fruit it must and will. And however virtuous may be the aims with which they are produced, the publications of the French Naturalistic school are such seed as was sown by that enemy who came in the night season.[1]

In England, to come to the third great school of fiction, we have as yet little or nothing of all this. Here, on the other hand, we are at the mercy of the Young Person, and a dreadful nuisance most of us find her.[2] The present writer is bound to admit that, speaking personally and with humility, he thinks it a little hard that all fiction should be judged by the test as to whether or no it is suitable reading for a girl of sixteen. There are plenty of people who write books for little girls in the schoolroom; let the little girls read them, and leave the works written for men and women to their elders. It may strike the reader as inconsistent, after the remarks made above, that a plea should now be advanced for greater freedom in English literary art. But French naturalism is one thing, and the unreal, namby-pamby nonsense with which the market is flooded here is quite another. Surely there is a middle path! Why do *men* hardly ever read a novel? Because, in ninety-nine cases out of a hundred, it is utterly false as a picture of life; and, failing in that, it certainly does not take ground as a work of high imagination. The ordinary popular English novel represents life as it is considered desirable that schoolgirls should suppose it to be. Consequently it is for the most part rubbish, without a spark of vitality about it, for no novel written on those false lines will live. Also, the system is futile as a means of protection, for the young lady, wearied with the account of how the good girl who jilted the man who loved her when she was told to, married the noble lord, and lived in idleness and luxury ever after, has only to turn to the evening paper to see another picture of existence. Of course, no humble producer of fiction, meant to interest through the exercise of the intelligence rather than through the senses, can hope to compete with the enthralling details of such cases as that of Lord Colin Campbell[3] and Sir Charles Dilke.[4] That is the naturalism of this country, and, like all filth, its popularity is enormous, as will be shown by the fact that the circulation of one evening paper alone was, I believe, increased during the hearing of a recent case by 60,000 copies nightly. Nor would any respectable author wish

---

[1] Alluding to the Biblical parable of the wheat and the tares (Matthew 13).

[2] Alluding to Charles Dickens's novel *Our Mutual Friend* (1865), in which the priggish Mr. Podsnap disapproves of anything that might "bring a blush to the cheek" of a "Young Person."

[3] Lord Colin Campbell (1853-95); son of the Duke of Argyll and Member of Parliament, who divorced acrimoniously and publicly from Lady Campbell in 1886, amidst scandalous accusations of adultery on both sides.

[4] Sir Charles Dilke (1843-1911); Member of Parliament and rising star of the Liberal Party, whose career was ruined when he was cited as an adulterer in the divorce case of Donald Crawford in 1885.

to compete with this. But he ought, subject to proper reservations and restraints, to be allowed to picture life as life is, and men and women as they are. At present, if he attempts to do this, he is denounced as immoral; and perchance the circulating library, which is curiously enough a great power in English literature, suppresses the book in its fear of losing subscriptions. The press, too—the same press that is so active in printing "full and special" reports—is very vigilant in this matter, having the Young Person continually before its eyes. Some time ago one of the London dailies reviewed a batch of eight or nine books. Of these reviews nearly every one was in the main an inquiry into the moral character of the work, judged from the standpoint of the unknown reviewer. Of their literary merits little or nothing was said. Now, the question that naturally arose in the mind of the reader of these notices was—Is the novelist bound to inculcate any particular set of doctrines that may at the moment be favoured by authority? If that is the aim and end of his art, then why is he not paid by the State like any other official? And why should not the principle be carried further? Each religion and every sect of each religion might retain their novelist. So might the Blue Ribbonites,[1] and the Positivists, and the Purity people,[2] and the Social Democrats, and others without end. The results would be most enlivening to the general public. Then, at any rate, the writer would be sure of the approbation of his own masters; as it is, he is at the mercy of every unknown reviewer, some of whom seem to have peculiar views—though, not to make too much of the matter, it must be remembered that the ultimate verdict is with the public.

Surely, what is wanted in English fiction is a higher ideal and more freedom to work it out. It is impossible, or, if not impossible, it requires the very highest genius, such as, perhaps, no writers possess to-day, to build up a really first-class work without the necessary materials in their due proportion. As it is, in this country, while crime may be used to any extent, passion in its fiercer and deeper forms is scarcely available, unless it is made to receive some conventional sanction. For instance, the right of dealing with bigamy is by custom conceded to the writer of romance, because in cases of bigamy vice has received the conventional sanction of marriage. True, the marriage is a mock one, but such as it is, it provides the necessary cloak. But let him beware how he deals with the same subject when the sinner of the piece has not added a sham or bigamous marriage to his evil doings, for the book will in this case be certainly called immoral. English life is surrounded by conventionalism, and English fiction has come to reflect the conventionalism, not the life, and has in consequence, with some notable exceptions, got into a very poor way, both as regards art and interest.

---

1 Members of the Temperance movement, who were given a blue ribbon to wear when they swore to give up alcohol.
2 The Purity movement aimed to eliminate prostitution, adultery, and pornography.

If this moderate and proper freedom is denied to imaginative literature alone among the arts (for, though Mr. Horsley[1] does not approve of it, sculptors may still model from the naked), it seems probable that the usual results will follow. There will be a great reaction, the Young Person will vanish into space and be no more seen, and Naturalism in all its horror will take root among us. At present it is only in the French tongue that people read about the inner mysteries of life in brothels, or follow the interesting study of the passions of senile and worn-out debauchees. By-and-by, if liberty is denied, they will read them in the English. Art in the purity of its idealized truth should resemble some perfect Grecian statue. It should be cold but naked, and looking theron men should be led to think of naught but beauty. Here, however, we attire Art in every sort of dress, some of them suggestive enough in their own way, but for the most part in a pinafore. The difference between literary Art, as the present writer submits it ought to be, and the Naturalistic Art of France is the difference between the Venus of Milo and an obscene photograph taken from life. It seems probable that the English-speaking people will in course of time have to choose between the two.

But however this is — and the writer only submits an opinion — one thing remains clear, fiction à l'Anglaise becomes, from the author's point of view, day by day more difficult to deal with satisfactorily under its present conditions. This age is not a romantic age. Doubtless under the surface human nature is the same to-day as it was in the time of Ramses.[2] Probably, too, the respective volumes of vice and virtue are, taking the altered circumstances into consideration, much as they were then or at any other time. But neither our good nor our evil doing is of an heroic nature, and it is things heroic and their kin and not petty things that best lend themselves to the purposes of the novelist, for by their aid he produces his strongest effects. Besides, if by chance there is a good thing on the market it is snapped up by a hundred eager newspapers, who tell the story, whatever it may be, and turn it inside out, and draw morals from it till the public loathes its sight and sound. Genius, of course, can always find materials wherewith to weave its glowing web. But these remarks, it is scarcely necessary to explain, are not made from that point of view, for only genius can talk of genius with authority, but rather from the humbler standing-ground of the ordinary conscientious labourer in the field of letters, who, loving his art for her own sake, yet earns a living by following her, and is anxious to continue to do so with credit to himself. Let genius, if genius there be, come forward and speak on its own behalf! But if the reader is inclined to doubt the proposition that novel writing is becoming every day

---

[1] John Calcott Horsley (1817-1903); painter and Rector of the Royal Academy, who, in 1885, began a public campaign against the depiction of nudes in works of art.
[2] Ramses II, who ruled Egypt around 1250 BCE.

more difficult and less interesting, let him consult his own mind, and see how many novels prosper among the hundreds that have been published within the last five years, and which deal in any way with every day contemporary life, have excited his profound interest. The present writer can at the moment recall but two—one was called "My Trivial Life and Misfortunes," by an unknown author,[1] and the other, "The Story of an African Farm," by Ralph Iron.[2] But then neither of these books if examined into would be found to be a novel such as the ordinary writer produces once or twice a year. Both of them are written from within, and not from without; both convey the impression of being the outward and visible result of inward personal suffering on the part of the writer, for in each the key-note is a note of pain. Differing widely from the ordinary run of manufactured books, they owe their chief interest to a certain atmosphere of spiritual intensity, which could not in all probability be even approximately reproduced. Another recent work of the same powerful class, though of more painful detail, is called "Mrs. Keith's Crime."[3] It is, however, almost impossible to conceive their respective authors producing a second "Trivial Life and Misfortunes" or a further edition of the crimes of Mrs. Keith. These books were written from the heart. Next time their authors write it will probably be from the head and not from the heart, and they must then come down to the use of the dusty materials which are common to us all.

There is indeed a refuge for the less ambitious among us, and it lies in the paths and calm retreats of pure imagination. Here we may weave our humble tale, and point our harmless moral without being mercilessly bound down to the prose of a somewhat dreary age. Here we may even—if we feel that our wings are strong enough to bear us in that thin air—cross the bounds of the known, and, hanging between earth and heaven, gaze with curious eyes into the great profound beyond. There are still subjects that may be handled *there* if the man can be found bold enough to handle them. And, although some there be who consider this a lower walk in the realms of fiction, and who would probably scorn to become a "mere writer of romances," it may be urged in defence of the school that many of the most lasting triumphs of literary art belong to the producers of purely romantic fiction, witness the "Arabian Nights," "Gulliver's Travels," "The Pilgrim's Progress," "Robinson Crusoe," and other immortal works. If the present writer may be allowed to

---

1   *My Trivial Life and Misfortune: a Gossip with No Plot in Particular* (1883). The author remains unknown, although she refers to herself as "a plain woman." She also wrote *Poor Nellie* (1887) and *Annora* (1915).

2   *The Story of an African Farm* (1883), by Ralph Iron (pseud. for Olive Schreiner [1855-1920]), a feminist or "New Woman" novel set in South Africa, in which the characters struggle against societal expectations.

3   *Mrs. Keith's Crime* (1885), by Lucy Clifford (1846-1929); the novel deals with infanticide.

hazard an opinion, it is that, when Naturalism has had its day, when Mr. Howells[1] ceases to charm, and the Society novel is utterly played out, the kindly race of men in their latter as in their earlier developments will still take pleasure in those works of fancy which appeal, not to a class, or a nation, or even to an age, but to all time and humanity at large.

10. From Augustus M. Moore, "Rider Haggard and 'The New School of Romance,'" *Time: A Monthly Miscellany* (May 1887)

In Mr. Haggard's book I find none of the powerful imagination, the elaborate detail, the vivid English which would entitle his work to be described as a romance. It might be somewhat unfair to demand as much from Mr. Haggard as from Defoe, Swift, Poe, Victor Hugo or Dumas, but surely he and his friends claim for him a place as high as that held by Jules Verne.... Jules Verne's style is not the most perfect, but if Mr. Haggard's could compare with it, I would have nothing to say. As has already been shown, *pace* Mr. Andrew Lang, Mr. Haggard has invented no new story or details.... As to his method of storytelling, it seems to me to be the method of the modern melodrama. Irrelevant incidents are dragged in anyhow and without any apparent reason. They are never, as I have said before, accounted for in any way, and they appear and disappear as conveniently as revolving scenes at Drury Lane or the Adelphi.[2] When Mr. Haggard has tired us out with his "hot potting" scene, Mr. Ludwig Horace Holly shuts his eyes, and "Billali," the stage manager, says, "*Cease!*" and the scene revolves and displays the very pretty and truly pathetic scene of "the little foot" ... When "the little foot" has been safely stowed away in Mr. Holly's "Gladstone bag," the scene changes again, and when Billali has been pulled out of a bog-hole the scene revolves and we arrive on "The Plains of Kôr," and so on and so on till half-past eleven, when the curtain is rung down, and the audience are left wondering at what they have seen and how the principal characters ... will find their way across the plains of Kôr to their lodgings in the Hampstead Road. Indeed, we are left at a loss to know what it is all about, and why it was ever written. There is not one single bit of humanity of any kind in it, and Mr. Leo Vincey and Mr. L. Horace Holly have about as much character as two bundles of Mssrs. Cooper Cooper and Co.'s three-and-sixpenny tea sent by parcels post on receipt of P.O.O.[3] The supernatural element, which is represented by Ayesha, is about as impressive as the singing chambermaid who represents the naughty fairy of a pantomime

---

[1]   William Dean Howells (1837-1920); American novelist and man of letters, champion of Realism in literature.

[2]   Two famous London theatres, known for their spectacular productions.

[3]   Post Office Order, equivalent to a money order; the Postal Order system was established in England in 1881.

in tights and a tow wig, and when she blanches the hair of Ustane by touching her on the head, the reader is forcibly reminded that Bridal Bouquet bloom[1] is warranted not to come off. Mr. Haggard has, however, not been content to try and write a mere fairy tale. He has written to the papers to say that this *bourgeoise* story, which is read and re-read with delight in Bermondsey and Bayswater and Bloomsbury,[2] has a moral. I must confess I should never have done Mr. Haggard the injustice of discovering it if he had not said so, and, even now, I am at a loss to find it. Ayesha, a pantomime fairy, murders Kallikrates the priest and flies to Kôr, where, two thousand years afterwards, she is followed by his descendant Leo Vincey, who means to murder her in return. After cohabiting with Ustane, who takes a fancy to him, Leo deserts her for Ayesha, who falls in love with him, after first toying with his friend Holly. She has displayed her charms to both gentlemen, but, as Mr. Haggard and the divorce court reports would say, "there was nothing wrong" between her and Holly. Indeed, it may be well to use Mr. Haggard's own passionate words:

> Then of a sudden, even as I stretched out my arms to clasp, she straightened herself, and a quick change passed over her. Reaching out her hand she held it over my head, and it seemed to me that something flowed from it that chilled me back to common sense, *and a knowledge of propriety and the domestic virtues!*

Could anything be more utterly banal?

Leo, however, instead of avenging his ancestor, falls in love with *She* (to borrow Mr. Haggard's style for a moment) and is stricken with grief when *her* is consumed by the fire of life. Where is the moral?

The casual reference to Mr. Haggard's style reminds me that I have so far only dealt with the origin of his story and his construction of it. It yet remains to be seen what style of language he employs to compensate for his lack of imagination and deficiency in constructive power, and to raise his book above the level of the penny-dreadful.

Mr. Haggard cannot write English at all. I do not merely refer to his bad grammar, which a boy at a Board School[3] would deserve to be birched for.[4] He cannot construct the most ordinary sentence, and his lack of words raises far more smiles than his jocose references to "Gladstone bags," "Paysandu tongues," "Bryant and May matches," "The Army and Navy Stores," etc.,

---

1   A brand of liquid rouge ("bloom") popular at the time, frequently advertised in the *Graphic*.
2   Residential areas of London.
3   An English elementary school established by a school board.
4   Whipped with a birch stick as punishment.

which are about as appropriate in the tombs of Kôr as would have been the mention of "Day and Martin's blacking" by Dante in the *Inferno*, or of "Pears' soap" by Milton in his *Paradise Lost....*

Short extracts only show vaguely how bad Mr. Haggard's English is. The man, however, who could write "he spoke to She" can have no ear at all. Of course I know that he uses "she" as a proper noun, but that makes no difference at all, and all the underlining in the world will never make "he spoke to She" otherwise than offensive. It is as gross and Mary Janeish as his other expression, "I had not even *got* the heart," etc. and offends the eye and ear. It could only have been written by a man who not only knew nothing, but cared nothing for "English undefiled;" and I am afraid that neither time nor tide nor the wit of all the log-rollers will ever make Mr. Haggard any better than a writer of penny-dreadfuls.

It is a sad thing to own that such a commonplace book as *She*, so full of other men's ideas, and so crammed with tawdry sentiment and bad English should have become the success it has undoubtedly been. It is a bad sign for English literature and English taste, and argues that the English Press which has trumpeted its success must be utterly corrupt, and the people who have listened and believed must be very ignorant and wholly devoid of judgment of any kind. God help English literature when English people lay aside their Waverly novels, and the works of Defoe, Swift, Thackeray, Charlotte Brontë, George Eliot, and even Charles Reade for the penny-dreadfuls of Mr. Haggard and Hugh Conway.[1]

---

[1] Pen name of Frederick John Fargus (1847-85), author of melodramatic fiction, most notably, *Called Back* (1883).

Appendix B: Victorian Archaeology: Mummies and Lost Cities

1. From H.G. Tomkins, *The Great Discovery of Royal Mummies at Deir el-Bahari. A Lecture* (Weston-super-Mare, 1882)

At Thebes the Libyan mountain range on the west of the Nile falls back in broken masses seamed with ravines, one of which is the hot and barren defile pierced with those wonderful subterranean halls and corridors, the "tombs of the kings." A mass of mountain shuts it in, and with its spur forms a great semi-circular sweep open on the south and west to the vast plain of western Thebes. Near the midst runs up in rising terraces against the mountain-side the unique and beautiful edifice, now in ruins, of which we shall soon speak as built by Queen Hatasu.[1] This is called from a Christian building Deir el Bahari (Northern Convent). Less than a hundred yards from Queen Hatasu's temple, cunningly concealed in a narrow valley, was the mouth of a pit leading on to an underground gallery or level about 180 feet long and from six to eight feet high, filled with mummy-cases and the furniture of the tomb. Here M. Emil Brugsch,[2] who had got scent of the treasure and went on behalf of the Government to take possession, was astounded to read on the coffins the names of some of the greatest Pharaohs of all Egyptian history. Some thirty-six mummies were there, the greater part royal, and altogether about six thousand objects of an antiquity dating from about 1700 to 1000 years before Christ. A steamer took them all down the Nile, about 460 miles to the Museum at Bûlak,[3] and as the vessel steamed away it was followed by peasant men and women on both banks wailing aloud and discharging firearms, as at a great funeral.

...

[During the Eighteenth Dynasty,] Thothmes II ... shared the throne with his sister Hatasu, a woman of boundless vigour and ambition, who soon succeeded to undivided sway on the early death of the Pharaoh. This haughty creature assumed the entire symbolism of Pharaonic rule, "for," says Brugsch, "she laid aside her woman's dress, clothed herself in man's attire, and adorned

---

[1] Hatshepsut (c. 1502-1450 BCE; 18th Dynasty), the famous "female Pharaoh" of Egypt.

[2] M. Émile Brugsch (1842-1930); German Egyptologist, assistant director of the museum of antiquities at Cairo. He supervised the discovery and clearing of the royal mummies at Deir el-Bahari.

[3] The collection that grew into the Egyptian Museum in Cairo was, from 1858 to 1889, established in a smaller museum in Boulaq.

herself with the crown and insignia of royalty." She offered the royal sacrifice, commanded her armies in person, and even wore the conventional beard of kings, and was spoken of in lapidary inscriptions as "the lord of the country, the King Ma-ka-râ, he." &c. &c. I bring before you the vigorous profile of this "high and mighty prince," crowned with the helm which the Pharaohs wore in battle, and exceeding even the royal audacity of our Queen Elizabeth. For fifteen years this strange potentate set aside her young brother Thothmes III., and had him brought up in the Delta at Buto, where he imbibed a thorough hatred of his proud sister. She had inhumanly chiselled out her elder brother's name from the inscriptions, and after her time her younger brother dealt even so with her name and titles. But this was a woman of fine genius, and erected some of the most magnificent and artistic buildings in Egypt, and quite the finest obelisks of all. Especially she built against the Libyan range of mountains in Western Thebes a temple of white limestone of unique design, rising in successive terraced courts colonnaded in vast cloisters, and boldly sculptured into the bright-coloured pictures of her pride. The grand memorials here display her expedition to the land of Punt. The Red-sea fleet passed out at the straits of Bab-el-Mandeb, and came to land on the shores of Eastern Africa, the Somali coast, among a highly civilized and wealthy people, as simple-minded as "the blameless Æthiopians" with whom the gods of Olympus would go to dine.[1] The prince of Punt, Pa-rihu by name, with his enormous wife riding on an ass, welcomed these amazing foreigners, and gave them tribute of luxurious wealth. Thirty-one incense-trees were removed in their earth to be transplanted into the gardens of Egypt, whilst prodigious dog-headed baboons calmly climbed or sat in the rigging of the Egyptian ships. Gold, ivory, balsams, giraffes, hunting leopards, greyhounds, apes, and long-tailed monkeys, paint for the eye—all were brought up the Red Sea and across the Nile, "the like of which was never brought to any other king." All of these things the great "woman-king" Hatasu, clad in the leopard-skin mantle of the high-priest, consecrated to Amen, and the young Thothmes III offered incense to the sacred bark of the god, while soldiers with triumphal palm-branches in their hands, and the joyful multitude, joined in jubilant delight. After fifteen years Hatasu felt it needful to join her brother with her on the throne, and in about six years more she died. This illustrious queen, who had a peaceful and prosperous reign, and drew her abundant tribute quietly from Syria, Cush, and far extended sunny lands of wealth, is not to be found among the family group, nor does even an empty mummy-case represent her. Only an inlaid coffer bears her name, containing some doleful object embalmed, supposed to be a human liver. Yet her burial place was near at

---

[1]   Alluding to Homer's *Iliad*, Book I, in which Zeus leads the gods to dine with "the blameless Ethiopians."

hand. Mr. Villiers Stuart[1] writes: "Her vault was a small one, but beautifully painted. In it were found two stone sarcophagi, which were violated and plundered not many years ago. I found a woman's foot there, which may have belonged to the poor queen."[2]

2. "Royal Mummies Recently Unbandaged at the Boulak Museum," *Graphic* 34 (31 July 1886)

[This news article was published in the *Graphic* just a few months before *She* began to appear there in serial form. It was written to accompany images (not reproduced here) of the recently-discovered mummies of Seti I and Ramses II.]

These are engravings from photographs of the mummies of two famous Pharaohs—namely, Seti I., father of Ramses the Great, and Ramses II., called "the Great," the Pharaoh of the Hebrew Oppression. Five years ago, some thirty mummies of ancient Egyptian kings, queens, princes, and princesses were found heaped together at the bottom of a subterraneous, rock-cut sepulchre in the western plain of Thebes. These hidden royalties included nearly all the most famous sovereigns of no less than five Egyptian dynasties; there being, between the most ancient and the most modern among them, an interval of at least seven hundred and fifty years. That is to say, the most ancient Pharaoh there found occupies a place in history dating about a century and a half previous to B.C. 1703, the period assigned to the expulsion of the Hyksos invaders and the end of the War of Independence;[3] while the most modern may be reckoned as having lived and died about B.C. 1110. Transported from Thebes to Cairo, the mummied kings and queens and their belongings now occupy a spacious hall called "The Hall of Royal Mummies," and the strange story of their discovery has been told and retold in all the languages of Europe, and read in every quarter of the globe.

About chronologically midway in the historical period represented within the walls of "The Hall of Royal Mummies," lived, reigned, and died the two famous Pharaohs shown in our illustrations. Seti I.... came to the throne in B.C. 1455.[4]

---

[1] Henry Windsor Villiers-Stuart (1827-95); Member of Parliament and author of several books on Egypt, including *Funeral Tent of an Egyptian Queen* (1882), from which this quotation is taken.

[2] Compare Part 5, Chapter IX: "A Little Foot."

[3] Egypt was ruled for several centuries by these so-called "Shepherd" invaders, during the 15th-17th Dynasties. They were expelled at the beginning of the New Kingdom, around 1540 BCE.

[4] The dates given here have since been revised forward approximately two centuries; Ramses II took the throne around 1250 BCE.

He was the second king of the great Nineteenth Dynasty, and he reigned, at all events *de jure*, for the space of fifty-one years. His son, Ramses II., who *de facto* administered the government for many years before the death of the old king, succeeded to the double crown about 1404, and reigned thenceforth for sixty-seven years. Between them, in short, this father and son ruled the land of Egypt for no less a period than 118 years.

After an undisturbed repose of five years in their glass cases at the Boulak Museum,[1] these two royal mummies, with several of their illustrious companions, have recently been unrolled by Professor Maspero and his assistants.[2] The mummy of Ramses II. was opened on the 3rd day of last June, in the presence of H.H. the Khedive,[3] and the leading members of the diplomatic body, home and foreign. The mummy of Seti I. was unbandaged on the 9th day of the same month.

3. From E.L. Wilson, "Finding Pharaoh," *Century Magazine* 34:1 (May 1887)

[This passage is from a copiously illustrated article on the discovery of the royal mummies at Deir el-Bahari, and their transportation to the Boulaq Museum in Cairo (now part of the Egyptian Museum). In it, the German Egyptologist Émile Brugsch tells the story of his discovery to an American reporter, who has accompanied him to the site.]

Then lighting our torches and stooping low, we proceeded to explore the long passage and the tomb at its terminus. The rough way was scattered with fragments of mummy-cases, shreds of mummy-cloth, bunches of papyrus-plant, lotus flowers, and palm-leaf stalks, while here and there a funeral offering was found. After much stumbling we arrived at the inner chamber where, but a few weeks before, stood or reclined the coffins of so many royal dead....

Seated upon a stone which for centuries had served as the pillow of priest or king while waiting for immortality, Herr Brugsch told me the whole story of his historical "find."

It was a unique interview. It made such an impression upon my mind that I can repeat the story here from memory, though I do not, of course, claim that the report is verbatim.

"Finding Pharaoh was an exciting experience for me," said my companion.

---

[1]   See p. 302, n. 3 (Appendix B.1).

[2]   Gaston Maspero (1846-1916); French Egyptologist, director of antiquities and excavations in Egypt from 1881 until his death.

[3]   Tewfik, ruler of Egypt from 1879 to 1896 under the Turkish Sultan. This was a time of extremely high diplomatic tension between Egypt and Britain, leading to military conflict and British occupation of Cairo by the end of the year.

"It is true, I was armed to the teeth, and my faithful rifle, full of shells, hung over my shoulder; but my assistant from Cairo, Ahmed Effendi Kemal, was the only person with me whom I could trust. Any one of the natives would have killed me willingly, had we been alone, for every one of them knew better than I did that I was about to deprive them of a great source of revenue. But I exposed no sign of fear and proceeded with the work. The well cleared out, I descended and began the exploration of the underground passage.

"Soon we came upon cases of porcelain funeral offerings, metal and alabaster vessels, draperies and trinkets, until, reaching the turn in the passage, a cluster of mummy-cases came into view in such number as to stagger me.

"Collecting my senses, I made the best examination of them I could by the light of my torch, and at once saw that they contained the mummies of royal personages of both sexes; and yet that was not all. Plunging on ahead of my guide, I came to the chamber where we are now seated, and there standing against the walls or here lying on the floor, I found even a greater number of mummy-cases of stupendous size and weight.

"Their gold coverings and their polished surfaces so plainly reflected my own excited visage that it seemed as though I was looking into the faces of my own ancestors. The gilt face on the coffin of Queen Nofretari[1] seemed to smile upon me like an old acquaintance.

"I took in the situation quickly, with a gasp, and hurried to the open air lest I should be overcome and the glorious prize still unrevealed be lost to science.

"It was almost sunset then. Already the odor which arose from the tomb had cajoled a troupe of slinking jackals to the neighborhood, and a howl of hyenas was heard not far distant. A long line of vultures sat upon the highest pinnacles of the cliffs near by, ready for their hateful work.

"The valley was as still as death. Nearly the whole of the night was occupied in hiring men to help remove the precious relics from their hiding-place. There was but little sleep in Luxor that night. Early the next morning three hundred Arabs were employed under my direction—each one a thief. One by one the coffins were hoisted to the surface, were securely sewed up in sail-cloth and matting, and then were carried across the plain of Thebes to the steamers awaiting them at Luxor.

"Two squads of Arabs accompanied each sarcophagus—one to carry it and a second to watch the wily carriers…. Then a third set took up the ancient freight and carried it to the steamers. Slow workers are these Egyptians, but after six days of hard labor under the July sun the work was finished.

"I shall never forget the scenes I witnessed when, standing at the mouth of the shaft, I watched the strange line of helpers while they carried across that historical plain the bodies of the very kings who had constructed the

---

[1] Nefertari (1295-1255 BCE; 19th Dynasty); wife of Ramses II.

temples still standing, and of the very priests who had officiated in them—the Temple of Hatasou nearest; away across from it Qûrneh; further to the right the Ramesseum, where the great granite monolith lies face to the ground; further south Medinet Abou, a long way beyond the Deir-el-Medineh; and there the twin Colossi, or the vocal Memnon and his companion;[1] then, beyond all, some more of the plain, the line of the Nile, and the Arabian hills far to the east and above all; and with all, slowly moving down the cliffs and across the plain, or in the boats crossing the stream, were the sullen laborers carrying their antique burdens.

"As the Red Sea opened and allowed Israel to pass across dry-shod, so opened the silence of the Theban plain, allowed the strange funeral procession to pass,—and then all was hushed again.

"When you go up, you will see it all spread out before you—with the help of a little imagination.

"When we made our departure from Luxor, our late helpers squatted in groups upon the Theban side and silently watched us. The news had been sent down the Nile in advance of us. So, when we passed the towns, the people gathered at the quays and made most frantic demonstrations. The fantasia dancers were holding their wildest orgies here and there; a strange wail went up from the men; the women were screaming and tearing their hair, and the children were so frightened I pitied them.

"A few fanatical dervishes plunged into the river and tried to reach us, but a sight of the rifle drove them back, cursing us as they swam away. At night fires were kindled and guns were fired.

"At last we arrived at Bûlâq, where I soon confirmed my impressions that we had indeed recovered the mummies of the majority of the rulers of Egypt during the eighteenth, nineteenth, twentieth, and twenty-first dynasties, including Ramses II., Ramses III., King Pinotem, the high-priest Nebseni, and Queen Nofretari, all of which you have seen and photographed at Bûlâq, arranged pretty much as I found them in their long-hidden tomb. And thus our Museum became the third and probably the final resting-place of the mummy of the great Pharaoh of the Oppression."

4. From H. Rider Haggard, "Preface" to A. Wilmot, *Monomotapa (Rhodesia), Its Monuments, and its History from the most Ancient Times to the Present Century* (London: T. Fisher Unwin, 1896)

[The Great Zimbabwe ruins were much discussed after the German explorer Karl Mauch rediscovered them in the early 1870s. At the time,

---

[1] These are all ancient Egyptian tombs and monuments in the Valley of the Kings, located on the plain of Thebes.

European archaeologists asserted that they could not have been built by black Africans, but must be the product of an ancient fair-skinned people such as the Phoenicians or Egyptians. This essentially racist proposition has since been struck down, and the ruins have been shown to be the product of a less-ancient native African civilization. When he wrote *She*, Haggard knew of Great Zimbabwe, and likely took the ruins as inspiration for his lost city of Kôr. This later preface essentially restates the European theories, and ends by speculating that "the Anglo-Saxon race" will take up residence there as part of Britain's imperial project.]

Southern and South Central Africa has been named the country without a past. Till within recent years its untravelled expanses were supposed from the beginning to have harboured nothing but wild beasts and black men almost as wild, who for ages without number had pursued their path of destruction as they rolled southward from the human reservoir of the north, each wave of them submerging that which preceded it. Within the last thirty or forty years, however, rumours arose that this was not true, or at least was not all the truth. Baines,[1] and other travelers now dead, reported the existence of great ruins in the territories known as Matabele and Mashona Lands, and on the banks of tributaries of the Zambesi River, which from their construction must have been built by a race of civilised men; and in 1871 Herr Mauch[2] re-discovered the fortress-temple of Zimbabwe, that now, as in the time of the early Portuguese, was said to be nothing less than the site of one of the ancient Ophirs.[3]

It has been left, however, to the Hon. Mr. Wilmot, the author of this book, as a result of his patient searchings of the Vatican and other archives, to show that Zimbabwe was well enough known to the Portuguese between the years 1550 and 1700; that it was the home of the court of the so-called Emperor of Monomotapa; that a Christian Church flourished, or at any rate existed there; and that under the shadow of its ancient walls the proto-martyr of South-eastern Africa, Father Gonsalvo Silveira, of the Society of Jesus, laid down his life in the service of the Faith. Afterwards it would seem that a new incursion of barbarians took place—how many such have these ruins witnessed? Probably these savages were of the Zulu section of the Bantu race; at least they stamped out whatever civilisation, Christian or Mahommedan, still flickered in Monomotapa so completely that even native tradition is silent concerning it, and once more oblivion covered the land and its story.

In 1891, after the occupation of Mashonaland by the Chartered Company

---

1   Thomas Baines (1820-75), explorer and artist who published a series of descriptive narratives about his experiences in southern Africa.

2   Karl Mauch (1837-75), German archaeologist who explored Great Zimbabwe in 1871.

3   Ancient Biblical city to which King Solomon and King David sent for gold; associated with the Queen of Sheba. See also Appendix B.5.

of British South Africa, Mr. Bent,[1] the learned explorer, visited the ruins of Zimbabwe and proved to the satisfaction of most archaeologists that they are undoubtedly of Phoenician[2] origin. There are the massive and familiar Phoenician walls, there the sacred birds, figured, however, not as the dove of Cyprus[3] but as the vulture of her Sidonian[4] representative, Astarte, and there, in plenty, the primitive and unpleasing objects of Nature-worship, which in this shape or that are present wherever the Phoenician reared his shrines. There also stands the great building, half temple, half fortress, containing the sacred cone in its inner court, as at Paphos, Byblos, and Emesus.[5] It is now ascertained moreover that within the walls of this temple men did not only celebrate their cruel and licentious rites, they also carried on their trade of gold-smelting. Here have been found crucibles and moulds for the refined metal and stones upon which it was burnished; indeed, the traveller has but to sift the soil to discover amongst it beads and other objects of pure gold. In a neighboring ruin some two years ago a friend of the present writer ... unearthed, amidst the crumbling bones of men and the barbed arrow-heads of ancient make which in a past age had slain them, no less than six hundred ounces weight of gold, some of it in little flattened nuggets, as it had been beaten from the quartz, some melted together with the brazen vessels which contained it, in the conflagration that destroyed the building, and some in the shape of beads. More recently, as Mr. Wilmot mentions, another discovery of gold has been made, all of it showing traces of the skill of cunning and civilised jewelers, and in several instances ornamented with a deep incised pattern that is new to me. One of the gold beads ... I hold in my hand as I write. Unhappily it cannot tell its story, for if this were possible a most mysterious and fascinating chapter of history would be opened to us, as indeed may still happen should the explorers of the future have the good fortune to discover an undisturbed burying-place of the ancient inhabitants of Monomotapa. But, although such testimony is lacking, the many external evidences to which allusion has been made force the student to conclude, with Mr. Bent and Mr. Wilmot, that these buildings must have been constructed and that the neighboring gold mines were worked by Phoenicians, or by some race intimately connected with them, and impregnated with their ideas of religion and architecture.

---

[1] James Theodore Bent (1852-97), English antiquarian and explorer who wrote *The Ruined Cities of Mashonaland* (1892).

[2] Ancient eastern Mediterranean civilization (c. 1200-900 BCE), famous for seafaring and trading from its principal coastal cities of Tyre and Sidon.

[3] The Greek island of Cyprus is the mythic homeland of Aphrodite, goddess of love, one of whose attributes or symbols is a dove, which features on ancient Cyprian coins.

[4] From Sidon, ancient Phoenician city.

[5] Paphos and Byblos in Cyprus are sites of ancient temples to Astarte. Emesus, or Emesa (present-day Homs), was a Phoenician city known for its great temple to Baal, the sun god.

.... Admitting that the inhabitants of Tyre, Sidon, and Carthage were exclusively seafaring traders, there is nothing to show that upon occasion they may not have penetrated to the interior of the countries which their navies visited, and even have settled there. Gain and slaves were the objects of the voyages of this crafty, heartless, and adventurous race, who were the English of the ancient world without the English honour, and at the ports of Eastern Africa, with which they doubtless trafficked, they must have learned that in the interior gold and slaves were to be won in abundance. It would seem that this temptation of vast profit caused them to break through their rule and march inland. But the distances and dangers of the journey, considerable even in these days, must then have been tremendous. A mere trading expedition was impossible; for it will be remembered that the servants of Solomon could not accomplish their visit to Ophir and return thence with the merchandise which was prepared for them, in a less time than three years. Moreover, as is the case to-day, the development and working of the inland mines by the help of native labour must have necessitated the constant presence and supervision of large numbers of armed and civilised men. It was therefore necessary that these adventurers, sojourning in the midst of barbarous tribes, should build themselves fortresses for their own protection, as it was natural that in their exile they should follow the rites and customs of their fathers. Doubtless in time the race became much mixed, for the women of the community must to a large extent have been supplied from the native peoples; but, as has been said and is amply demonstrated in the following pages, it seems clear that its origin and characteristics were essentially Phoenician.

At what date this Phoenician occupation began, for how many centuries or generations it endured, and when it closed no man can say for certain, and it is probable that no man ever will be able to say. The people came, they occupied and built, they passed away, perhaps in some violent and sudden fashion such as might well have been brought about by a successful insurrection of their slaves, or by the overwhelming incursion of Arabian or more savage races. As Mr. Lang writes—

Into the darkness whence they came,
        They passed, their country knoweth none,
They and their gods without a name
        Partake the same oblivion.
Their work they did, their work is done,
        Whose gold, it may be, shone like fire,
About the brows of Solomon,
        And in the House of God's Desire.

. . . .

The pestilence, the desert spear,
    Smote them: they passed, with none to tell
The names of them who laboured here:
    Stark walls and crumbling crucible,
Strait gates and graves, and ruined well,
    Abide, dumb monuments of old,
We know but that men fought and fell,
    Like us, like us for love of gold.[1]

Of the history of the ancient Zimbabwe and its long-lost wealth and glories we can gather no more than these scanty gleanings. The Arabs appear to have been acquainted with the place, but their geographers and historians tell us little, and it is not until the year 1560, or thereabouts, that, chiefly through the labours of Mr. Wilmot, the silence is broken. At this date, long after the Portuguese occupation of East Africa, Father Silveira, assisted by two colleagues, having successfully converted some minor chiefs in the coast regions, proceeded alone to the court of the Emperor of Momomotapa at Zimbaoe, or Zimbabwe.

What was the condition of this so-called empire, and what the measure of the effective dignity of its emperor, are points rather difficult to determine. The reader will form his own opinion upon them from Mr. Wilmot's pages, but they appear to have been much overrated by mediaeval writers and geographers.

.... Now, after the lapse of another two centuries and a half, that veil has been lifted once more by the bold enterprise of the British South Africa Company, and the crumbling temple of Zimbabwe, the scene of so much forgotten history and of so many unwritten tragedies, by a strange chance has received the bones of the heroic band of Englishmen who fell with Wilson on the banks of the Shangani river.[2] It is legitimate to hope, it seems probable even, that in centuries to come a town will once more nestle beneath these grey and ancient ruins, trading in gold as did that of the Phoenicians, but peopled by men of the Anglo-Saxon race.

---

[1] Quoting stanzas 1 and 3 of the poem, "Zimbabwe," by Andrew Lang (1844-1912), man of letters and close friend of Haggard.

[2] Major Alan Wilson and his troop of men were killed on the banks of the Shangani River by African warriors during the 1893 Matabele War. They were buried in Zimbabwe, but eventually moved to Matapos near the grave of Cecil Rhodes.

5. From James Bryce, "Out of the Darkness—Zimbabwe," *Impressions of South Africa* (London: Macmillan and Co, 1897)

[Bryce's essay offers the European theories about the fair-skinned builders of Great Zimbabwe, and makes an intriguing link to the tomb of Queen Hatshepsut at Deir el-Bahari, where the royal mummies were discovered (see Appendix B.1).]

In very remote times there existed, as is known from the Egyptian monuments, a trade from South-east Africa into the Red Sea. The remarkable sculptures at Deir el-Bahari, near Luxor, dating from the time of Queen Hatasu, sister of the great conqueror Thothmes III. (B.C. 1600?), represent the return of an expedition from a country called Punt, which would appear, from the objects brought back, to have been somewhere on the East African Coast.[1] Much later the Books of Kings (I Kings ix.26-28; x.11,15,22) tells us that Solomon and Hiram of Tyre entered into a sort of joint adventure trade from the Red Sea port of Ezion-geber to a country named Ophir, which produced gold. There are other indications that gold used to come from East Africa, but so far as we know it has never been obtained in quantity from any part of the coast between Mozambique and Cape Guardafui.[2] Thus there are grounds for believing that a traffic between the Red Sea and the coast south of the Zambesi may have existed from very remote times. Of its later existence there is of course no doubt. We know from Arabian sources that in the eighth century an Arab tribe defeated in war established itself on the African coast south of Cape Guardafui, and that from the ninth century onward there was a considerable trade between South-east Africa and the Red Sea ports—a trade which may well have existed long before. And when the Portuguese began to explore the coast in 1496 they found Arab chieftains established at various points along it as far south as Sofala,[3] and found them getting gold from the interior. Three things, therefore, are certain—a trade between South-east Africa and the Red Sea, a certain number of Arabs settled along the edge of the ocean, and an export of gold. Now all over Mashonaland and Matabililand[4] ancient gold-workings have been observed. Some are quite modern,—one can see the wooden supports and the iron tools not yet destroyed by rust,—and it would seem from the accounts of the natives that

---

[1] See Appendix B.1.

[2] The apex of the Horn of Africa, at the tip of Somalia, on the Gulf of Aden.

[3] African province in Mozambique, on the Indian Ocean, located south of the Zambezi river. Its port city (and capital) Beira would have provided landlocked Rhodesia access to sea trading.

[4] Renamed Rhodesia after Cecil Rhodes, the British imperialist and financier; in 1980, following a declaration of independence, the area was renamed Zimbabwe.

the mining went on to some small extent down to sixty years ago, when the Matabili conquered the country. Others, however, are, from the appearance of the ground, obviously much more ancient. I have seen some that must have been centuries old, and have been told of others apparently far older, possibly as old as the buildings at Zimbabwye. I was, moreover, informed by Mr. Cecil Rhodes (who is keenly interested in African archaeology) that he had seen on the high plateau of Inyanga, in eastern Mashonaland, some remarkable circular pits lined with stone, and approached in each case by a narrow subterranean passage, which can best be explained by supposing them to have been receptacles for the confinement of slaves occupied in tilling the soil, as the surrounding country bears marks, in the remains of ancient irrigation channels, of an extensive system of tillage where none now exists. The way in which the stones are laid in these pit-walls is quite unlike any modern Kafir[1] work, and points to the presence of a more advanced race. Putting all these facts together, it has been plausibly argued that at some very distant period men more civilised than the Kafirs came in search of gold into Mashonaland, opened these mines, and obtained from them the gold which found its way to the Red Sea ports, and that the buildings whose ruins we see [i.e., the Great Zimbabwe] were their work. How long ago this happened we cannot tell, but if the strangers came from Arabia they must have done so earlier than the time of Mohammed, for there is nothing of an Islamic character about the ruins or the remains found, and it is just as easy to suppose that they came in the days of Solomon, fifteen centuries before Mohammed. Nor can we guess how they disappeared: whether they were overpowered and exterminated by the Kafirs, or whether ... they were gradually absorbed by the latter, their civilization and religion perishing, although the practice of mining for gold remained. The occasional occurrence among the Kafirs of faces with a cast of features approaching the Semitic has been thought to confirm this notion, though nobody has as yet suggested that we are to look here for the lost Ten Tribes.[2] Whoever these people were, they have long since vanished. The natives seem to have no traditions about the builders of Zimbabwye and the other ancient walls, though they regard the ruins with a certain awe, and fear to approach them at twilight.

It is this mystery which makes these buildings, the solitary archaeological curiosities of South Africa, so impressive. The ruins are not grand, nor are they beautiful; they are simple even to rudeness. It is the loneliness of the landscape in which they stand, and still more the complete darkness which surrounds their

---

[1] Literally, Arabic for "unbeliever"; in South Africa, a disparaging term for black Africans.
[2] The Lost Tribes of northern Israel, expelled from the Holy Land by the Assyrians in the eighth century BCE. There has been much speculation about where they settled and who are their descendants.

origin, their object, and their history, that gives to them their unique interest. Whence came the builders? What tongue did they speak? What religion did they practice? Did they vanish imperceptibly away, or did they fly to the coast, or were they massacred in a rising of their slaves? We do not know; probably we shall never know. We can only say, in the words of the Eastern poet:

They came like water, and like the wind they went.[1]

6. From G. Elliot Smith, "The Mummy of Queen Nsikhonsou," *The Royal Mummies. Catalogue Général des Antiquités Égyptiennes du Musée du Caire* (London, 1912)

[Smith's work is a catalogue, illustrated with copious wonderful photographs, of the royal Egyptian mummies discovered at Deir el-Bahari in 1881-82 and moved to the Museum of Cairo (see Appendix B.1-B.3). During the late-Victorian period, they were enthusiastically studied, catalogued, exhibited, and in many cases (such as this one), unwrapped. Queen Nsikhonsou (known today as Neskhons, wife of Pinudjem II, circa 980 BCE) is one of the best-preserved mummies of the collection. The photo of her mummy is on the cover of this edition.]

61095. The Mummy of Queen Nsikhonsou

This mummy was partially unwrapped by M. Maspero[2] on June 27th, 1886 (*Les Momies royales*, p. 578 and 579), and I completed the process just twenty years later.

This is a typical example of the distinctive technique of embalming of the XXIst and XXIInd Dynasties; but its freedom from the gross distortions of face and members that marked the earlier attempts at packing is perhaps a distinguishing mark of XXIInd Dynasty work.

The neck is stuffed with the cheese-like material in the manner described in the case of Mâkerî's mummy (vide supra).[3]

There is a vertical incision, 0m. 03cent. long, on the antero-lateral aspect of each shoulder … from which a small quantity of packing material was introduced under the skin of a localized area of the extreme upper and lateral part of the chest wall, and also into the arms as far as the wrists. The stuffing consists

---

[1] Alluding to *The Rubiyat of Omar Khayyam*, trans. Edward FitzGerald (1859), number 28: "I came like the Water, and like the Wind I go."

[2] Gaston Maspero (1846-1916), French Egyptologist who became head of the Antiquities Service in Egypt in 1881. Smith's book is based upon Maspero's *Les Momies Royales de Deir-el-Bahari* (Paris, 1889).

[3] "See above" (Latin).

of sawdust; and the moulding of the arms has been skillfully done. The hands are not packed. The arms are placed vertically at the sides of the body; and the fully extended hands are placed alongside the lateral surface of the thighs....

The legs are stuffed in the customary manner. The embalmer introduced his hand into the embalming wound in the left flank and forced the packing-material (in this case a mixture of mud, sawdust and the cheese-like material, to which I have already referred), into each leg. In plate LXXXII the skin on the inner side of the right thigh can be seen to be broken away, so that the packing material is revealed in situ.

The feet are stuffed; but I was unable to determine the spot where the packing material was introduced.

Flowers were wrapped around the great toe of each foot and a flower on a long stalk was placed upon the upper surface of the left foot, and another encircled the left ankle.

The breasts are large and pendulous: but no attempt was made to pack them and restore the form of the bust.

The pudenda were treated in the way that was customary in the XXIst and XXIInd Dynasties: the labia majora were pressed together so as to hide the rima.

The embalming wound is in the situation characteristic of this period: it is a vertical incision passing from the margin of the ribs to within om. 035 mill. of the anterior superior spine of the left ilium. It is visible in plate LXXXII alongside the left elbow.

The embalming wound is om. 125mill. long and gapes to the extent of om. 050mill.

It was covered by a wax plate of the usual form but without the usual eye design. Onion scales were placed upon the surface of the plate.

The body cavity is packed with sawdust.

The skin of the abdomen is loose and pendulous; and the mammillae are large and prominent. These two signs make it certain that Nsikhonsou was parous.[1]

Nsikhonsou is 1m. 615mill. in height. There is nothing to give any definite indication of her age; but she has no grey hairs.

The face is of a graceful, narrow, elliptical form and the light colour of the skin suggests that it must have been very fair originally.

The face is thickly encrusted with powdered resin, and large cakes of resinous material cover the eyes, nostrils and mouth. Underneath the resin shields artificial eyes of stone are found, but the material is badly disintegrated. The ears are pierced and the lobules drawn out into long strings (om. 16cent.)....

The long, dark brown hair hangs down as far as the front of the chest ... There are a few small plaits, but most of the hair consists of simply wavy strands. Most of these have been collected into two large masses, each of which

---

[1] Having brought forth children; Smith suggests that she died in, or soon after, childbirth.

is held together by means of a bandage wound spirally around it. One of these masses is brought down on the side of the neck to the front of the chest.

The hair is thickly strewn with powdered red resin.

The following measurements were made. Those of the head and face are merely estimations, for the thick mass of hair and the encrustations of resin render precise measurements impossible.

[chart of measurements of body parts omitted]

The nose is narrow and aquiline, but not prominent: its profile passes in a straight line into the brow; and there is a sloping forehead, low and receding.

Foot, 0m. 224mill. long and 0m. 065mill. broad.

7. From H. Rider Haggard, "Egypt," *The Days of My Life* (1926)

After 'She' had been fairly launched, … I started, in January 1887, on a journey to Egypt. From a boy ancient Egypt had fascinated me, and I had read everything concerning it on which I could lay my hands. Now I was possessed by a great desire to see it for myself.…

I went to Egypt seeking knowledge and a holiday. The knowledge I acquired, for when the mind is open and desirous, it absorbs things as a dry sponge does water. I had an introduction to Brugsch Bey, who was then, I think, the head of the Boulak Museum. He took me round that heavenly place. He showed me the mummies of Seti, Ramses, and the rest, and oh! with what veneration did I look upon them. He told me, trembling with emotion, of the discovery, then recent, of the great Deir-el-Behari *cache* of Pharaohs and their treasures.[1] He said when he got to the bottom of that well and entered the long passage where for tens of centuries had slept the mighty dead, huddled together there to save them from the wicked hands of robbers or enemies, and by the light of torches had read a few of the names upon the coffins, that he nearly fainted with joy, as well he might. Also he described how, when the royal bodies were borne from this resting-place and shipped for conveyance to Cairo, there to find a new tomb in the glass cases of a museum, the fellaheen women ran along the banks wailing because their ancient kings were being taken from among them. They cast dust upon their hair, still dressed in a hundred plaits, as was that of those far-off mothers of theirs who wailed when these Pharaohs were borne with solemn pomp to the homes they called eternal. Poor kings! who dreamed not of the glass-cases of the Cairo Museum, and the gibes of tourists who find the awful majesty of their withered brows a matter for jests and smiles. Often I wonder how we dare to meddle with these hallowed relics, especially now in my age. Then I did not think so much of it; indeed I have taken a hand at the business myself.

---

[1]   See Appendix B.1.

On that same visit I saw the excavation of some very early burials in the shadow of the pyramids of Ghizeh, so early that the process of mummification was not then practised. The skeletons lay upon their sides in the pre-natal position. The learned gentleman in charge of the excavation read to me the inscription in the little ante-chamber of one of these tombs.

If I remember right, it ran as follows: 'Here A.B. (I forget the name of the deceased), priest of the Pyramid of Khufu, sleeps in Osiris awaiting the resurrection. He passed all his long life in righteousness and peace.'

That, at any rate, was the sense of it, and I bethought me that such an epitaph would have been equally fitting to, let us say, the dean of a cathedral in the present century. Well, perhaps a day will come when Westminster Abbey and our other sacred burying places will be ransacked in like manner, and the relics of *our* kings and great ones exposed in the museum of some race unknown of a different faith to ours. I may add that in Egypt even an identity of faith does not protect the dead, since the Christian bishops, down to those of the eighth or ninth century, have been disinterred, for I have seen many of their broidered vestments in public and private collections. The idea seems to be that if only you have been dead long enough your bones are fair prey. All of which is to me a great argument in favour of cremation.

Still it must be remembered that it is from the Egyptian tombs that we have dug the history of Egypt, which now is better and more certainly known than that of the Middle Ages. Were it not for the burial customs of the old inhabitants of Khem,[1] and their system of the preservation of mortal remains that these might await the resurrection of the body in which they were such firm believers, we should be almost ignorant of the lives of these people. Only ought not the thing to stop somewhere? For my part I should like to see the bodies of the Pharaohs, after they had been reproduced in wax, reverently laid in the chambers and passages of the Great Pyramids and there sealed up for ever, in such a fashion that no future thief could break in and steal.

Dr. Budge[2] told me of a certain tomb which he and his guide were the first to enter since it had been closed, I think about 4000 years before. He said that it was absolutely perfect. There lay the coffin of the lady, there stood the funeral jars of offering, there on the breast was a fan of which the ostrich plumes were turned to feathers of dust. There, too, in the sand of the floor were the footprints of those who had borne the corpse to burial. Those footprints always impressed me very much.

In considering such matters the reader should remember that nothing in the world was so sacred to the old Egyptian as were his corpse and his tomb.

---

[1] Ancient name of Egypt.
[2] E.A. Wallis Budge (1857-1934), archaeologist and writer, later the Curator of Egyptian and Assyrian Antiquities at the British Museum.

In the tomb slept the body, but according to his immemorial faith it did not sleep alone, for with it, watching it eternally, was the Ka or Double, and to it from time to time came this Spirit. This Ka or Double had, so he believed, great powers, and could even wreak vengeance on the disturber of the grave or the thief of the corpse.

From Cairo I proceeded up the Nile, inspecting all the temples and the tombs of the kings at Thebes, to my mind, and so far as my experience goes, the most wondrous tombs in all the world. So, too, thought the tourists of twenty centuries or more ago, for there are writings on the walls recording their admiration and salutations to the ghosts of the dead; and so, too, in all probability will think the tourists of two thousand years hence, for the world can never reproduce such vast and mysterious burying-places, any more than it can reproduce the pyramids.

About eighteen years later I revisited these tombs and found them much easier of access and illuminated with electric light. Somehow in these new conditions they did not produce quite the same effect upon me. When first I was there I remember struggling down one of them—I think it was that of the great Seti—lit by dim torches, and I remember also the millions of bats that must be beaten away. I can see them now, those bats, weaving endless figures in the torchlight, dancers in a ghostly dance. Indeed, afterwards I incarnated them all in the great bat that was a spirit which haunted the pyramid where Cleopatra and her lover, Hamarchis, sought the treasure of the Pharoah, Men-kau-ra.[1] When next I stood in that place I do not recall any bats; I suppose that the electric light had scared them away.

However on that second visit, with Mr. Carter,[2] at that time a superinden-dent of antiquities for this part of Egypt, my companions and I were the first white men, except the discoverer, a Greek gentleman, to enter the burying-place of Nofertari, the favorite or, at least, the head wife of Ramses II. There on the walls were her pictures as fresh as the day they were painted. There she sat playing chess with her royal husband or communing with the gods. But it is too long to describe. The tomb had been plundered in ancient days, probably a couple of thousand years ago. Just before the plunderers entered a flood of water had rushed down it, for when they came the washed paint was still wet, and I could see the prints of their fingers as they supported them-selves on the slope of the incline.

One of my tomb explorations in 1887 nearly proved my last adventure. Opposite Assouan[3] some great caverns had just been discovered. Into one of

---

[1] Haggard refers to his novel, *Cleopatra*, written just after *She* and his subsequent trip to Egypt.

[2] Howard Carter (1873-1939), archaeologist in Egypt, famous for discovering the tomb of King Tutankhamen.

[3] Aswan, city on the Nile at the southern border of ancient Egypt.

these I crept through a little hole, for the sand was almost up to the top of the doorway. I found it full of hundreds of dead, or at least there seemed to be hundred, most of which had evidently been buried without coffins, for they were but skeletons, although mixed up with them was the mummy of a lady and the fragments of her painted mummy case. As I contemplated these gruesome remains in the dim light I began to wonder how it came about that there were so many of them. Then I recollected that about the time of Christ the town, which is now Assouan, had been almost depopulated by a fearful plague, and it occurred to me that doubtless at this time these old burying-places had been reopened and filled up with the victims of the scourge—also that the germ of plague is said to be very long-lived! Incautiously I shouted to my companions who were outside that I was coming out, and set to work to crawl along the hole which led to the doorway. But the echoes of my voice reverberating in that place had caused the sand to begin to pour down between the cracks of the masonry from above, so that the weight of it, falling upon my back, pinned me fast. Like a flash I realised that in another few seconds I too should be buried. Gathering all my strength I made a desperate effort and succeeded in reaching the mouth of the hole just before it was too late, for my friends had wandered off to some distance and were quite unaware of my plight.

Appendix C: Race and Empire

[Haggard's work is better understood in relation to late-Victorian theories of race, which often assume that whites are naturally superior to blacks, and that the Anglo-Saxons are meant to "civilize" the globe. The attitudes of Holly, Leo, and Job towards the Amahagger reflect these assumptions, as does the rule of Ayesha, the white queen, in Africa.]

1. From Robert Knox, M.D., *The Races of Men: A Philosophical Enquiry into the Influence of Race over the Destinies of Nations*, 2nd ed. (London: Henry Renshaw, 1862)

[Knox claims that only white-skinned people can be truly civilized. This type of argument was often used to justify the extension of the British Empire.]

Now this leads the author of this resumé to a question of great difficulty. What is the exact standing of the savage races on the earth? and are there races of men, who by reason of their savage nature can never assume any true civilization? To this class of men seems to him to belong most of the coloured races of men, and even others but slightly tinged. The Moor, or Kabyle, is a true savage; just as he was under the time of Marius and Jugurtha,[1] he is still. Under the Roman empire he became, as it were, highly civilized, and affected to be a Christian! It proved a mere varnish simply skin deep.... The native American race, or races, are still savages, and so are the New Zealanders; the Hottentot and Caffres will remain as they are. Between the true savage and the civilized man there is, as has ever been, an antagonism not to be overcome. Even England, with all her professions of humanity and philanthropy, cannot afford to admit within the pale of society any coloured, that is, savage race; cannot afford to admit any coloured man to the rights of civil and military freedom; in other words, no coloured man can attain in England the full enjoyment of the rights of a citizen. But this is not all. The fall of the Roman empire decided another great question—the question of acclimatization. At one time Southern and Western Europe, and Northern Africa and Western Asia, Syria, to the Euphrates and beyond, were peopled by Roman citizens of the Italian race: now and for many centuries not a vestige of such a race could be pointed out in any of these countries.

---

[1] Jugurtha (160-104 BCE), king of Numidia (in present-day Algeria) under the Roman empire. Marius conquered him in 105 BCE.

It is not merely savage races, properly so called, which seem incapable of civilization; the Oriental races have made no progress since the time of Alexander the Great. The ultimate cause of this, no doubt, is race. One circumstance peculiarly worthy of note is, that from the earliest period of history all their educational institutions were stereotyped, so that all minds ultimately sank to the same level. As a consequence they ever confounded fable with truth, and myths they mistook for history. True science based on an unalterable love of truth they could not comprehend, and thus the *true light* never penetrated the hazy realms of the Oriental mind.

2. From James Hunt, *On the Negro's Place in Nature* (London: Trubner and Co, 1863)

[James Hunt, President of the Anthropological Society of London, read this paper to that Society in 1863. Like Knox (Appendix C.1), he sees whites as inherently superior to blacks, whom he believes can only be "humanised" under European rule.]

The assertion that the negro only requires an opportunity for becoming civilised, is disproved by history. The African race has had the benefit of the Egyptian, Carthaginian, and Roman civilisations, but nowhere did it become civilised. Not only has the Negro race never civilised itself, but it has never accepted any other civilisation. No people have had so much communication with Christian Europeans as the people of Africa, where Christian bishops existed for centuries.* Except some knowledge of metallurgy they possess no art; and their rude laws seem to have been borrowed and changed to suit their peculiar instincts. It is alleged that the Negro only requires education to be equal to the European; but all experiments of this kind have proved that such is not the fact. With the negro, as with some other races of man, it has been found that the children are precocious: but that no advance in education can be made after they arrive at the age of maturity, they still continue, mentally, children. It is apparently of little consequence what amount of education they receive, the same result nearly always follows, the reflective faculties hardly appear to be at all developed. The dark races generally do not accept the civilisation which surrounds them...

The many assumed cases of civilised Negroes generally are not those of pure African blood. In the Southern States of North America, in the West Indies and other places, it has been frequently observed that the Negroes in place of trust have European features, and some writers have supposed that

---

* "It is said that when the Negro has been with other races, he has always been a slave. That is quite true: but why has he been a slave?" [Hunt's note]

these changes have been due to a gradual improvement in the Negro race which is taking place under favourable circumstances.... but we believe such not to be the fact. It is simply the European blood in their veins which renders them fit for places of power, and they often use this power far more cruelly than either of the pure blooded races....

We now know it to be a patent fact that there are races existing which have no history, and that the Negro is one of these races. From the most remote antiquity the Negro race seems to have been what it now is. We may be pretty sure that the Negro race has been without a progressive history; and that Negroes have been for thousands of years the uncivilised race they are at this moment. Egyptian monuments depict them as such, and holding exactly the same position relative to the European....

Some writers have assumed that the Negro has degenerated from some higher form of civilisation, but we see no evidence to support such an assertion. We, however, fully admit that there are found traces of a higher civilisation, especially along the coasts visited, during all ages, by Europeans. The working of metals and imitation of European manufactures also exist in many parts of Africa.

There is good reason to believe that, like all inferior races, there has been little or no migration from Africa since the earliest historical records. The European, for ever restless, has migrated to all parts of the world, and traces of him are to be found in every quarter of the globe. Everywhere we see the European as the conqueror and the dominant race, and no amount of education will ever alter the decrees of Nature's laws....

The general deductions we would desire to make are:—1. That there is as good reason for classifying the Negro as a distinct species from the European, as there is for making the ass a distinct species from the zebra; and if, in classification, we take intelligence into consideration, there is a far greater difference between the Negro and European than between the gorilla and chimpanzee. 2. That the analogies are far more numerous between the Negro and apes, than between the European and apes. 3. That the Negro is inferior intellectually to the European. 4. That the Negro is more humanised when in his natural subordination to the European than under any other circumstances. 5. That the Negro race can only be humanised and civilised by Europeans. 6. That European civilisation is not suited to the Negro's requirements or character.

3. From Charles H. Pearson, *National Life and Character: A Forecast* (London: Macmillan and Co, 1893)

[Considering the history of European settlements in South Africa (and specifically in the Natal), Pearson concludes that the strong British presence has brought "order and peace, industry and trade" to the African natives, who now threaten to displace and absorb the whites because of their great numbers and willingness to work the land.]

The case of Natal[1] is more instructive for what may be expected in Africa generally. Natal was seized by the British in 1842, the Boers[2] who had occupied it, and to whom it was valuable for its sea-board, being a mere handful of men among natives who accepted them for the moment as deliverers from the Zulus. Nevertheless, the number of black inhabitants at that time, though great in comparison with the Dutch, was so inconsiderable as to be only five to the square mile.[*] The new possession offered great advantages of soil and climate. A great deal of it is rich land, and it rises in plateaus from the coast, so that several varieties of temperature may be enjoyed. During the first years of settlement there was no danger from the Zulus, whose warriors had almost been exterminated in Dingan's wars.[3] From time to time assisted immigrants were poured literally in thousands into the country. In 1878-79 the presence of a large British army made the fortunes of contractors and farmers. For years the diamond-fields and gold-diggings of the Orange Free State[4] have reflected prosperity over Natal. Nevertheless, in 1891, nearly fifty years after its first settlement, Natal has only 36,000 Europeans out of 481,000 settlers, the remainder being chiefly Zulus, though partly Hindoos and Chinamen. The lower races have nearly doubled in proportion since 1860, when one-seventh of the population was European. The reasons of this are not far to seek. British rule means order and peace, industry and trade, and the enjoyment of property under fairly equal laws. To the African native the establishment of a colony like Natal is like throwing open the gates of paradise.[†] He streams in, offering his cheap though not very regular labour, and supplying all his own wants at the very smallest expenditure of toil. Where he multiplies, however, the British race begins to consider labour of all but the highest kinds dishonourable, and from the moment that a white population will not work in the fields, on the roads, in the mines, or in factories, its doom is practically sealed. It is limited to supplying employees, merchants, contractors, shopmen, and

---

[*]   "Before the Dutch occupied it, the blacks were only as one to six square miles"— Alyward's *Transvaal*, p. 5. [Pearson's note]

[†]   Although the Dutch rule is far less tender to the natives than the British, the immigration of natives began from the establishment of government by the Dutch in 1839. "In their own expressive way of speaking, they could sleep without fear under the shield of the white man."—Theale's *South African History*, chap. xxxi. [Pearson's note]

---

[1]   British territory in southern Africa.

[2]   Dutch settlers.

[3]   Dingane or Dingaan (1795-1840), after 1828, King of the Zulus; he fought vigorously and unsuccessfully to prevent Dutch settlement in Africa.

[4]   Dutch territory in southern Africa.

foremen to the community. Sooner or later the black race will be educated to a point at which it will demand and receive a share in those employments and in the government.* Whenever that happens, the white race will be either absorbed or disappear. The mass will gradually depart, but a few, who have lost the sense of superiority, will remain, intermarry, and be perpetuated in the persons of a few hundred, or it may be a few thousand, mulattoes and quadroons....

The day will come, and perhaps is not far distant, when the European observer will look round to see the globe girdled with a continuous zone of black and yellow races, no longer too weak for aggression or under tutelage, but independent, or practically so, in government, monopolising the trade of their own regions, and circumscribing the industry of the European; when Chinamen and the nations of Hindostan, the States of Central and South America, by that time predominantly Indian, and it may be African nations of the Congo and the Zambesi, under a dominant caste of foreign rulers, are represented by fleets in the European seas, invited to international conferences, and welcomed as allies in the quarrels of the civilised world. The citizens of these countries will then be taken up into the social relations of the white races, will throng the English turf, or the salons of Paris, and will be admitted to intermarriage. It is idle to say, that if all this should come to pass our pride of place will not be humiliated. We were struggling among ourselves for supremacy in a world we thought of as destined to belong to the Aryan races and to the Christian faith; to the letters and arts and charm of social manners which we have inherited from the best times of the past. We shall wake to find ourselves elbowed and hustled, and perhaps even thrust aside by peoples whom we looked down upon as servile, and thought of as bound always to minister to our needs. The solitary consolation will be, that the changes have been inevitable. It has been our work to organise and create, to carry peace and law and order over the world, that others may enter in and enjoy. Yet in some of us the feeling of caste is so strong that we are not sorry to think we shall have passed away before that day arrives.

4. From Benjamin Kidd, *Social Evolution* (London: Macmillan, 1894)

[Kidd makes the case for benevolent imperialism, suggesting that the Western nations (i.e., the white races) have a responsibility to govern and administer the resources of the rest of the world.]

---

* This is already the case, to some extent, at the Cape. Mr. Theale remarks, that as landholders the Fingoes "are entitled to vote for members of Parliament, and large numbers avail themselves of this privilege."—*South African History*, chap. xxvii. [Pearson's note]

Now it would appear probable that we have, in the present peculiar relation-ship of the Western peoples to the coloured races, the features of a transition of great interest and importance, the nature of which is, as yet, hardly under-stood. It is evident that, despite the greater consideration now shown for the rights of the lower races, there can be no question as to the absolute ascen-dancy in the world to-day of the Western peoples and of Western civiliza-tion. There has been no period in history when this ascendancy has been so unquestionable and so complete as in the time in which we are living. No one can doubt that it is within the power of the leading European peoples of to-day—should they so desire—to parcel out the entire equatorial regions of the earth into a series of satrapies,[1] and to administer their resources, not as in the past by a permanently resident population, but from the temperate regions and under the direction of a relatively small European official popu-lation. And this without any fear of effective resistance from the inhabitants. *Always, however, assuming that there existed a clear call of duty or necessity to provide the moral force necessary for such action.*

It is this last stipulation which it is all-important to remember in any attempt which is made to estimate the probable course of events in the future. For it removes at once the centre of interest and observation to the lands occupied by the European peoples. It is, in short, in the development in progress amongst these peoples, and not in the events taking place to-day in lands occupied by the black and coloured races, that we must seek for the controlling factor in the immediate future of the tropical regions of the world.

Now, stress has been laid in the preceding chapters on the fact that we have in the altruistic development that has been slowly taking place amongst the European peoples the clue to the efficiency of our civilisation. It is this devel-opment—by its influence in breaking down an earlier organisation of soci-ety, and by its tendency to bring, for the first time in the history of the race, all the people into the rivalry of life on a footing of equal opportunity—that has raised our Western civilisation to its present position of ascendancy in the world....We must, therefore, in any attempt to estimate our future relation-ship to the coloured races outside the temperate regions, keep clearly in mind the hitherto supreme importance to the Western peoples of this altruistic development, and, therefore, of the doctrine of the native equality of men which has accompanied it.

Now, there are two great events which will in all probability fill a great part in the history of the twentieth century. The first will be the accom-plishment amongst the Western peoples of the last stage of that process of social development which tends to bring all the people into the rivalry of life on conditions of social equality. The other will be the final filling up by those

---

[1] Imperial provinces or colonies.

peoples of all those tracts in the temperate regions of the earth suitable for permanent occupation. As both these processes tend toward completion it would appear that we must expect our present relationship towards the coloured races occupying territories outside the temperate zones to undergo further development. With the completion of that process of social evolution in which the doctrine of the native equality of man has played so important a part—and, therefore, with the probable modification of that instinct which has hitherto recognised the vital necessity to ourselves of maintaining this doctrine in its most uncompromising form—it seems probable that there must arise a tendency to scrutinize more closely the existing differences between ourselves and the coloured races as regards the qualities contributing to social efficiency; this tendency being accompanied by a disposition to relax our hitherto prevalent opinion that the doctrine of equality requires us to shut our eyes to those differences where political relations are concerned....

It would seem that the solution which must develop itself under pressure of circumstances in the future is, that the European races will gradually come to realise that the tropics must be administered from the temperate regions. There is no insurmountable difficulty in the task. Even now all that is required to ensure its success is a clearly-defined conception of moral necessity. This, it would seem, must come under the conditions referred to, when the energetic races of the world, having completed the colonisation of the temperate regions, are met with the spectacle of the resources of the richest regions of the earth still running largely to waste under inefficient management.... The right of those races to remain in possession will be recognised; but it will be no part of the future conditions of such recognition that they shall be allowed to prevent the utilisation of the immense natural resources which they have in charge. At no remote date, with the means at the disposal of our civilisation, the development of these resources must become one of the most pressing and vital questions engaging the attention of the Western races....

Lastly, it will materially help ... if we are in a position ... to say with greater clarity ... what it is constitutes superiority and inferiority of race. We shall probably have to set aside many of our old ideas on the subject. Neither in respect alone of colour, nor of descent, nor even of possession of high intellectual capacity, can science give us any warrant for speaking as one race as superior to another. The evolution which man is undergoing is, over and above everything else, a social evolution. There is, therefore, but one absolute test of superiority. It is only the race possessing in the highest degree the qualities contributing to social efficiency that can be recognised as having any claim to superiority.

But these qualities are not as a rule of the brilliant order, nor such as strike the imagination. Occupying a high place amongst them are such characteristics as strength and energy of character, humanity, probity and integrity, and simple-minded devotion to conceptions of duty in such circumstances as may arise.

5. From C. De Thierry, *Imperialism* (London: Duckworth, 1898)

[De Thierry celebrates Queen Victoria's rule over the British Empire, and the spirit of imperialism generally. His superlative rhetoric recalls the awe inspired by that other white queen, "She-who-must-be-obeyed."]

But if the Queen is a power abroad, in her own dominions she is a force which it is impossible to over-estimate. Foreigners, indeed, pay her homage; but her own subjects regard her with a devotion whose intensity makes it akin to a passion. In her they recognize the sole remaining Constitutional link between England and her Colonies: the Great White Mother, the fame of whose virtue has won the loyalty of native races as the genius of an Alexander or a Napoleon never could have done. The secret of her unique position is also the secret of the expansion of her Empire; and so there was a peculiar fitness in the honour paid to both as if they were one. Other thrones have been filled by Sovereigns, who were the objects of a people's devotion, who were great and wise rulers, or who were admirable as wife, mother, and queen. But has any previous age been adorned by a Royal Lady who was all these, as well as an empire-builder second to none? Or has Time, since first he knew civilisation on the banks of the Nile, done reverence before to the Head of a State whose personal character linked a heterogeneous people in the bonds of love? It is this supremacy of the moral principle in English rule which gave the Pageant of June[1] its peculiar suggestiveness. It was a triumph—the first since Rome sank, never to rise again, under the weight of barbarian hordes. But it was to the temple of Jehovah the procession went, not to the Temple of Jupiter; its moving spirit was liberty, not despotism; its glory the glory of peace, not of war. Since the wise men saw the star in the East, Christianity has found no nobler expression; and it was in entire harmony with all our ideas of the fitness of things that it should have not only rivalled but surpassed the most imposing triumphs of the Pagan world. Rome was never mistress of territories to be compared to the British Empire, nor able to command the allegiance of races so diverse as those who people it. And it is not in size and variety alone that English dominion is unique. Its crowning glory is its freedom. The Protectorates and the Tributary States, the Crown Colonies and the self-governing Provinces, of which it is constituted, sent princes and nobles, premiers and officers, cavalry and infantry, to swell the triumph of the Queen and the Imperial idea, not in obedience to a command, behind which was the force of victorious legions, but to give expression to their own enthusiastic loyalty. That is to say, the great Imperial spectacle on record has its origin in those silken ties which bind together the various parts of the Empire

---

[1]   The Diamond Jubilee of 1897, celebrating 60 years of Queen Victoria's reign.

represented in it. All the dominant races have raised themselves monuments, but none a monument so noble and inspiring as the English. A world-wide dominion, whose foundations are laid deep in the national character, is an achievement of which the gods themselves might be proud....

English Imperialism ... has an unique character of its own. Behind it is the strength generated by a thousand years of effort, the prodigious forces an unparalleled development of energy has brought into being. It has a great past and a sense of responsibility for the future. It has poetry and romance and richness of setting. Above all, it has a lively appreciation of the claims of kinship, and a deep, if silent, determination to keep for the Anglo-Saxon race whatever the Anglo-Saxon race has won.

Appendix D: The New Woman

[Ayesha's almost-unlimited power in the novel engages contemporary questions involving female authority in the late nineteenth century, when the "New Woman" was the focus of debate. Empowered, modern, no longer submissive to men, she was a figure that inspired both hope and fear, much like "She-who-must-be-obeyed."]

1. From "Beauty is Power" (Anonymous), *Essays in Defence of Women* (London, 1868)

... Beauty is as potent as the sunshine without any human aid, sways our mundane affairs with just as little traceable mechanism or visible attempt as the moon governs the tides, and can no more be commanded than we can count on length of days or can add a cubit to our stature. Its existence is the strongest argument in favour of the terrible doctrine of predestination that we ever heard of. The possession of it unquestionably predestines certain people to the enjoyment of much bliss in this world, and the want of it equally entails upon certain others much private weeping and a fair amount of public gnashing of teeth.... Who leads the way to dessert? The eldest, cleverest, the best, the most industrious? Not in the least—the prettiest. Who sits near to papa, or to the most illustrious stranger present? Little golden curls, we may be sure. Who gets the bigger half of the orange? The most beautiful, just as of old it got the whole of the apple.[1] ... Beauty, once thoroughly alive to its power, is sure to exercise it in some way or other. Hence, from sixteen to eighteen, when Beauty is "kept back," its path is strewn with the bones of smaller and meaner victims, who on the score of clannish feeling ought to have been spared their terrible fate. This is the sickly season, when male cousins are killed off by the dozen, and promotion is fearfully rapid in the family ranks. It is all the fault of the elders, who will not allow the beautiful destroyer at once to arise and go forth and spoil the Egyptians.[2] Beauty cannot help its ravages; and these propitiatory sacrifices of undergraduate relations serve but to whet, and in no degree to glut, its irrepressible appetite for ruin.... Depend upon it that the moorland has been terribly dreary, and the shore preternaturally barren, for more than the poet, all by reason of "Amy, mine no more!"[3] Yet who is going to turn accuser? Beauty, like the king, can do no

---

1 Alluding to the mythic Judgment of Paris, in which Paris gives an apple labeled "For the fairest" to Aphrodite, goddess of love and beauty.

2 Alluding to Exodus 3:22, "spoil" here means to plunder or pillage.

3 Quotation from Tennyson's poem, "Locksley Hall" (1842), in which the speaker laments his faithless beloved, Amy: "O the dreary, dreary moorland! O the barren, barren shore!" (lines 39-40).

wrong.... It, too, has heard of battles and longs to be in the thick of them. And now it is that its marvellous power becomes so manifest. Every field is open to it, and no arena, however professedly exclusive, bars its doors to the intruder. Society lifts up its gates at the approach of Beauty; and Beauty has only to say, "These are in my train," to obtain admission for others who could not possibly obtain it on any other pretence.... It is magical, and may well be spoken of as gifted with a wand. Venus has properly no other title but that of Victrix.[1] When is she ever anything else? Turn from mythology to political economy, and the point for which we contend remains equally clear. What is the definition, in that accurate science, of the value of a thing? Its purchasing power. What is there that Beauty cannot purchase? Let it be born lowly, and it shall order itself a dukedom, and will not improbably get it. Of course, the tone of the market varies from time to time. Mercantile affairs, we all know, are subject to oscillation. But Beauty can always buy something like the thing it wants. If the beautiful beggar-maid cannot always invest in a king, the beautiful *bourgeoise* need never despair, at least, of obtaining some lordling or other. Should Beauty be fairly enough born, but disagreeably poor, Beauty may drive into Lombard-street,[2] or even walk thither, and take her pick of the *jeunesse dorée*[3] of its celebrated bank-parlours. And even if Beauty be born a fool—and ill-natured people pretend that such is often Beauty's fate—its purchasing power is so unlimited that should it, against all probability, condescend to bid for the brains of the most rising middle-aged barrister, of the most eloquent preacher, or of the most promising young diplomat in the service, there will be no manner of difficulty in making it a bargain. Thus its purchasing power would seem to be commensurate with all desirable commodities. But between it and all other things which enjoy purchasing power there is this remarkable difference. In the language of political economy, they are exchanged for the commodity which they command. But Beauty makes no exchange. It buys everything, so to speak, without paying for it. It purchases birth and wealth, and when it has purchased these two excellent things, everybody declares aloud that it is more beautiful than ever.

We must not omit to point out another peculiarity in the power of Beauty, or we might not be thought to have fully demonstrated our case. Beauty is Power in all times and under all circumstances, whereas every other attribute which sophists may pretend to be likewise power can lay claim to be such in a very limited sense, and only under certain favourable conditions. The power of Beauty is unconditioned—it is absolute—it is universal. All other power is, at best, but particular.... But Beauty is power everywhere and always. You may see it interrupt a lecturer, disconcert a preacher, and make an orator forget the thread of his argument. It disturbs the saint at his prayers, the poet at his sonnet,

---

1   "Conqueror" (Latin).
2   Like Wall Street in the United States, the financial center of Victorian London.
3   Literally, "gilded youth" (French); the young and wealthy.

and the accountant labouring at his sum-total.... This deference to Beauty, this slavish submission to it, may be right or may be wrong, but it is universal. If it is not everybody's nature to practise it, all we can say is, that everybody has caught the habit. There is a positive convention in the bowing down before this tremendous visible divinity. It is omnipotent, and as ruthless as Fate.

2. From John Stuart Mill, *The Subjection of Women* (London, 1869)

It cannot be inferred to be impossible that a woman should be a Homer, or an Aristotle, or a Michael Angelo, or a Beethoven, because no woman has yet actually produced works comparable to theirs in any of those lines of excellence. This negative fact at most leaves the question uncertain, and open to a psychological discussion. But it is quite certain that a woman can be a Queen Elizabeth, or a Deborah,[1] or a Joan of Arc, since this is not inference, but fact. Now it is a curious consideration, that the only things which the existing law excludes women from doing, are the things which they have proved they are able to do. There is no law to prevent a woman from having written all the plays of Shakspeare, or composed the operas of Mozart. But Queen Elizabeth or Queen Victoria, had they not inherited the throne, could not have been intrusted with the smallest of the political duties, of which the former showed herself equal to the greatest.... We know how small a number of reigning queens history presents, in comparison with that of kings. Of this smaller number a far larger proportion have shown talents for rule; though many of them have occupied the throne in difficult periods. It is remarkable, too, that they have, in a great number of instances, been distinguished by merits the most opposite to the imaginary and conventional character of women: they have been as much remarked for the firmness and vigour of their rule, as for its intelligence. When, to queens and empresses, we add regents, and viceroys of provinces, the list of women who have been eminent rulers of mankind swells to a great length*....

---

* Especially is this true if we take into consideration Asia as well as Europe. If a Hindoo principality is strongly, vigilantly, and economically governed; if order is preserved without oppression; if cultivation is extending, and the people prosperous, in three cases out of four that principality is under a woman's rule. This fact, to me an entirely unexpected one, I have collected from a long official knowledge of Hindoo governments. There are many such instances: for though, by Hindoo institutions, a woman cannot reign, she is the legal regent of a kingdom during the minority of the heir; and the minorities are frequent, the lives of the male rulers being so often prematurely terminated through the effect of inactivity and sensual excesses. When we consider that these princesses have never been seen in public, have never conversed with any man not of her own family except from behind a curtain, that they do not read, and if they did, there is no book in their languages which can give them the smallest instruction on political affairs; the example they afford of the natural capacity of women for government is striking. [Mill's note]

---

1 Prophet, judge, and leader of Israel in the Old Testament; see Judges 4-5.

Most great queens have been great by their own talents for government, and have been well served precisely for that reason. They retained supreme direction of affairs in their own hands: and if they listened to good advisers, they gave by the fact the strongest proof that their judgment fitted them for dealing with the great questions of government.

Is it reasonable to think that those who are fit for the greater functions of politics, are incapable of qualifying themselves for the less? Is there any reason in the nature of things, that the wives and sisters of princes should, whenever called on, be found as competent as the princes themselves to *their* business, but that the wives and sisters of statesmen, and administrators, and directors of companies, and managers of public institutions, should be unable to do what is done by their brothers and husbands? The real reason is plain enough; it is that princesses, being more raised above the generality of men by their rank than placed below them by their sex, have never been taught that it was improper for them to concern themselves with politics; but have been allowed to feel the liberal interest natural to any cultivated human being, in the great transactions which took place around them, and in which they might be called on to take a part. The ladies of reigning families are the only women who are allowed the same range of interests and freedom of development as men; and it is precisely in their case that there is not found to be any inferiority. Exactly where and in proportion as women's capacities for government have been tried, in that proportion they have been found adequate.

3. From Olive Schreiner, "Three Dreams in a Desert," *Dreams*, 2nd ed. (London: Fisher Unwin, 1891)

[Olive Schreiner was a South African feminist writer whose novel, *The Story of an African Farm*, Haggard admired (see Appendix A.9).]

I saw a desert and I saw a woman coming out of it. And she came to the bank of a dark river; and the bank was steep and high.* And on it an old man met her, who had a long beard; and a stick that curled was in his hand, and on it was written Reason. And he asked her what she wanted; and she said "I am woman; and I am seeking for the land of Freedom."

And he said, "It is before you."

And she said, "I see nothing before me but a dark flowing river, and a bank steep and high, and cuttings here and there with heavy sand in them."

---

* The banks of an African river are sometimes a hundred feet high, and consist of deep shifting sands, through which in the course of ages the river has worn its gigantic bed. [Schreiner's note]

And he said, "And beyond that?"

She said, "I see nothing, but sometimes, when I shade my eyes with my hand, I think I see on the further bank trees and hills, and the sun shining on them!"

He said, "That is the Land of Freedom."

She said, "How am I to get there?"

He said, "There is one way, and one only. Down the banks of Labour, through the water of Suffering. There is no other."

She said, "Is there no bridge?"

He answered, "None."

She said, "Is the water deep?"

He said, "Deep."

She said, "Is the floor worn?"

He said, "It is. Your foot may slip at any time, and you may be lost."

She said, "Have any crossed already?"

He said, "Some have *tried!*"

She said, "Is there a track to show where the best fording is?"

He said, "It has to be made."

She shaded her eyes with her hand; and she said, "I will go."

And he said, "You must take off the clothes you wore in the desert: they are dragged down by them who go into the water so clothed."

And she threw from her gladly the mantle of Ancient-received-opinions she wore, for it was worn full of holes. And she took the girdle from her waist that she had treasured so long, and the moths flew out of it in a cloud. And he said, "Take the shoes of dependence off your feet."

And she stood there naked, but for one white garment that clung close to her.

And he said, "That you may keep. So they wear clothes in the Land of Freedom. In the water it buoys; it always swims."

And I saw on its breast was written Truth; and it was white; the sun had not often shone on it; the other clothes had covered it up. And he said, "Take this stick; hold it fast. In that day when it slips from your hand you are lost. Put it down before you; feel your way: where it cannot find a bottom do not set your foot."

And she said, "I am ready; let me go."

And he said, "No—but stay; what is that—in your breast?"

She was silent.

He said, "Open it, and let me see."

And she opened it. And against her breast was a tiny thing, who drank from it, and the yellow curls above his forehead pressed against it; and his knees were drawn up to her, and he held her breast fast with his hands.

And Reason said, "Who is he, and what is he doing here?"

And she said, "See his little wings—"

And Reason said, "Put him down."

And she said, "He is asleep, and he is drinking! I will carry him to the Land of Freedom. He has been a child so long, so long, I have carried him. In the Land of Freedom he will be a man. We will walk together there, and his great white wings will overshadow me. He has lisped one word only to me in the desert—'Passion!' I have dreamed he might learn to say 'Friendship' in that land."

And Reason said, "Put him down!"

And she said, "I will carry him so—with one arm, and with the other I will fight the water."

He said, "Lay him down on the ground. When you are in the water you will forget to fight, you will think only of him. Lay him down." He said, "He will not die. When he finds you have left him alone he will open his wings and fly. He will be in the Land of Freedom before you. Those who reach the Land of Freedom, the first hand they see stretching down the bank to help them shall be Love's. He will be a man then, not a child. In your breast he cannot thrive; put him down that he may grow."

And she took her bosom from his mouth, and he bit her, so that the blood ran down on the ground. And she laid him down on the earth; and she covered her wound. And she bent and stroked his wings. And I saw the hair on her forehead turned white as snow, as she had changed from youth to age.

And she stood far off on the bank of the river. And she said, "For what do I go to this far land which no one has ever reached? *Oh, I am alone! I am utterly alone!*"

And Reason, that old man, said to her, "Silence! what do you hear?"

And she listened intently, and she said, "I hear a sound of feet, a thousand times ten thousand and thousands of thousands, and they beat this way!"

He said, "They are the feet of those that shall follow you. Lead on! make a track to the water's edge! Where you stand now, the ground will be beaten flat by ten thousand times ten thousand feet." And he said, "Have you seen the locusts how they cross a stream? First one comes down to the water-edge, and it is swept away, and then another comes and then another, and then another, and at last with their bodies piled up a bridge is built and the rest pass over."

She said, "And, of those that come first, some are swept away, and are heard of no more; their bodies do not even build the bridge?"

"And are swept away, and are heard of no more—and what of that?" he said.

"And what of that—" she said.

"They make a track to the water's edge."

"They make a track to the water's edge—." And she said, "Over that bridge which shall be built with our bodies, who will pass?"

He said, "The entire human race."

And the woman grasped her staff.

And I saw her turn down that dark path to the river.

4. From Sarah Grand, "The New Aspect of the Woman Question," *North American Review* 158:448 (March 1894)

It is amusing as well as interesting to note the pause which the new aspect of the woman question has given to the Bawling Brotherhood who have hitherto tried to howl down every attempt on the part of our sex to make the world a pleasanter place to live in. That woman should ape man and desire to change places with him was conceivable to him as he stood on the hearthrug in his lord-and-master-monarch-of-all-I-survey attitude, well inflated with his own conceit; but that she should be content to develop the good material she finds in herself and be only dissatisfied with the poor quality of that which is being offered to her in man, her mate, must appear to him to be a thing as monstrous as it is unaccountable. "If women don't want to be men, what do they want?" asked the Bawling Brotherhood when the first misgiving of truth flashed upon them; and then, to reassure themselves, they pointed to a certain sort of woman in proof of the contention that we were all unsexing ourselves.

It would be as rational for us now to declare that men generally are Bawling Brothers or to adopt the hasty conclusion which makes all men out to be fiends on the one hand and all women fools on the other. We have our Shrieking Sisterhood, as the counterpart of the Bawling Brotherhood. The latter consists of two sorts of men. First of all is he who is satisfied with the cow-kind of woman as being most convenient; it is the threat of any strike among his domestic cattle for more consideration that irritates him into loud and angry protests. The other sort of Bawling Brother is he who is under the influence of the scum of our sex, who knows nothing better than women of that class in and out of society, preys upon them or ruins himself for them, takes his whole tone from them, and judges us all by them. Both the cow-woman and the scum-woman are well within range of the comprehension of the Bawling Brotherhood, but the new woman is a little above him, and he never even thought of looking up to where she has been sitting apart in silent contemplation all these years, thinking and thinking, until at last she solved the problem and proclaimed for herself what was wrong with Home-is-the-Woman's-Sphere, and prescribed the remedy.

What she perceived at the outset was the sudden and violent upheaval of the suffering sex in all parts of the world. Women were awakening from their long apathy, and, as they awoke, like healthy hungry children unable to articulate, they began to whimper for they knew not what. They might have been easily satisfied at that time had not society, like an ill-conditioned and ignorant nurse, instead of finding out what they lacked, shaken them and beaten them and stormed at them until what was once a little wail became convulsive shrieks and roused up the whole human household. Then man, disturbed by the uproar, came upstairs all anger and irritation, and, without waiting to learn what was the matter, added his own old theories to the din, but, finding they did not act rapidly, formed new ones, and made an intolerable nuisance of himself with his opinions and advice. He was in the state of one who cannot comprehend because he has no faculty to perceive the thing in question, and that is why he was so positive. The dimmest perception that you may be mistaken will save you from making an ass of yourself.

We must look upon man's mistakes, however, with some leniency, because we are not blameless in the matter ourselves. We have allowed him to arrange the whole social system and manage or mismanage it all these ages without ever seriously examining his work with a view to considering whether his abilities and his motives were sufficiently good to qualify him for the task. We have listened without a smile to his preachments, about our place in life and all we are good for, on the text that "there is no understanding a woman." We have endured most poignant misery for his sins, and screened him when we should have exposed him and had him punished. We have allowed him to exact all things of us, and have been content to accept the little he grudgingly gave us in return. We have meekly bowed our heads when he called us bad names instead of demanding proofs of the superiority which alone would give him a right to do so. We have listened much edified to man's sermons on the subject of virtue, and have acquiesced uncomplainingly in the convenient arrangement by which this quality has come to be altogether practised for him by us vicariously. We have seen him set up Christ as an example for all men to follow, which argues his belief in the possibility of doing so, and have not only allowed his weakness and hypocrisy in the matter to pass without comment, but, until lately, have not even seen the humor of his pretensions when contrasted with his practices nor held him up to that wholesome ridicule which is a stimulating corrective. Man deprived us of all proper education, and then jeered at us because we had no knowledge. He narrowed our outlook on life so that our view of it should be all distorted, and then declared that our mistaken impression of it proved us to be senseless creatures. He cramped our minds so that there was no room for reason in them, and then made merry at our want of logic. Our divine intuition was not to be controlled by him, but he did his best to damage it by sneering at it as an inferior feminine method of arriving at conclusions; and finally, after having had his own way until he lost his head completely, he set himself up as a sort of a god and required us to worship him, and, to our eternal shame be it said, we did so. The truth has all along been in us, but we have cared more for man than for truth, and so the whole human race has suffered. We have failed of

our effect by neglecting our duty here, and have deserved much of the oblo-
quy that was cast upon us. All that is over now, however, and while on the
one hand man has shrunk to his true proportions in our estimation, we, on
the other, have been expanding to our own; and now we come confidently
forward to maintain, not that this or that was "intended," but that there are
in ourselves, in both sexes, possibilities hitherto suppressed or abused, which,
when properly developed, will supply to either what is lacking in the other.

The man of the future will be better, while the woman will be stronger
and wiser. To bring this about is the whole aim and object of the present
struggle, and with the discovery of the means lies the solution of the Woman
Question. Man, having no conception of himself as imperfect from the
woman's point of view, will find this difficult to understand, but we know his
weakness, and will be patient with him, and help him with his lesson. It is the
woman's place and pride and pleasure to teach the child, and man morally is
in his infancy. There have been times when there was a doubt as to whether
he was to be raised or woman was to be lowered, but we have turned that
corner at last; and now woman holds out a strong hand to the child-man, and
insists, but with infinite tenderness and pity, upon helping him up.

5. From H. Rider Haggard, "A Man's View of Woman," *African Review of Mining, Finance, and Commerce* 4:96 (September 1894)

[Haggard was one of the founding editors of the *African Review*, which
was published weekly in London from 1892 to 1904, and was aimed
specifically at Englishmen with commercial interests in the African
colonies. This essay is a review of Sir Edward Sullivan's book, *Woman:
The Predominant Partner* (London: Longmans, 1894).]

Sir Edward Sullivan, greatly daring, has written a book about woman, or,
rather, the preface to a book, since he explains that were he to write all that
he might, the book would be far too long for the most patient. His book, or
his preface, is learned, witty, and clever. Sir Edward seems to have studied
women even more attentively than most of us mere men. He draws her again
and again from the life, beginning with the era of the nude and antique, and
ending with this of the divided skirt. He deduces her from history; adorns her
from legend; and illustrates her from fable, and he achieves a result interesting and amusing, though perhaps the theme is a little overdone. The subject,
in its nature intoxicating, seems to have carried away Sir Edward Sullivan, till
at times he degenerates or rises to rhapsody. For instance, we are told that
women would make much better bishops than do men, and in woman it
would appear reside every grace, grandeur, beauty, and virtue; qualities that

are sadly wanting in her "subordinate" partner. Perhaps it is so; one is glad to think that it is so; only then the inquirer wonders how it comes about that the ladies do not occupy their proper position at the top of the world's tree, and why they do not hasten to relieve the incompetent male of his somewhat exaggerated share of the world's work. "Be honest for once in your lives," says Sir Edward, speaking in *falsetto*; "acknowledge the truth, that when we women wish it, it is we who are the stronger sex, not you men." So be it. But then, O! women, take the place of the stronger, and leave *us* to cultivate the graces. Again, "whenever they (women) compete with men, they beat them hands down;" and yet again, "in exuberant verbosity men are surpassed by women." Who will question this? One statement may be questioned, however. It is set down that many of our laws, in so far as they affect women, are "abominably unjust, abominably selfish, and abominably cruel." Is this so? The late Lord Justice Bowen,[1] speaking a year or two back at a Royal Academy banquet, said, alluding to the judgment of the Court of Appeal in the famous Jackson case:[2] "We hear much of the wrongs of women, but who dare contemplate her rights as defined by my learned brethren of Appeal?" or words to that effect, and his "selfish and cruel," but not unintelligent, audience laughed and cheered. The other day a man appeared before a certain bench of magistrates and complained that during his temporary absence his wife had sold all his goods and run away. He asked to be informed of the remedy for this matrimonial incident, and it was the duty of that Bench to tell him that he had none. The truth is that Sir Edward Sullivan writes chiefly of a class—the upper class with which he is best acquainted—and forgets that outside of certain minor grievances, many of which may fairly be called sentimental, the amended law of England offers the most ample protection to the female inhabitants of these realms at large. He quotes, indeed, the common instance of child murder, and almost seems to think that, if anybody, the man who is partly responsible for the infant's original life should be hung, and the woman should go free. He says that the mother's agony, shame, and despair are not accurately weighed. Is this a fact? Is it not a fact that the law is invariably strained to the utmost in favour of such unfortunates, and must not the child, the helpless child, who is thus bereft of existence be considered, as well as the trouble and difficulties of the mother? Infanticide, though found convenient by the Chinese, is scarcely a practice to be winked at by us. Moreover, does

1 Charles Synge Christopher Bowen (1835–94), influential English judge who sat on the Queen's Bench and later (during the Jackson case) on the Court of Appeal.

2 A famous civil case (in March 1891) in which a husband (Edmund Jackson) held his wife Emily against her will and she petitioned for her freedom. The English High Court of Justice turned down her request, maintaining the husband's rights, but this decision was overturned in the Court of Appeals. The case has been remembered as an historically important assertion of the personal rights of married women.

not the law, differing from the stern regulation of the Code Napoleon,[1] compel the putative father to contribute to the support of his offspring? "Certainly women should be tried by a jury of women," says our author. Many of us would give a great deal to see the face of the pretty plaintiff in an ordinary breach of promise action when this noble offer was made to her. That of the lady's solicitor would probably be as instructive and entertaining.

With much that Sir Edward says, however, it is easy to agree. That woman is always potentially the noble creature, and often actually so, there can be no doubt. Thus when we imagine perfection in any shape or form we generally imagine it as female—at least men do. Also her variety is pre-eminent; this the novelist knows well. Well he knows the hopeless and baffling sameness of the average educated male of under fifty years of age, and the joy wherewith he turns to pourtray the women folk, no two of whom are the same. Ladies say that this is only because he is a man, and therefore more interested in the opposite sex; but a study of their own work does not reveal a striking mastery of the complexities of nineteenth century male nature—if it has any.

To sum up, it seems to this humble critic that while Sir Edward Sullivan, in the interests of his fair clients, has made capital of many minor sorrows and disabilities, he has scarcely touched upon the real grievance of the British woman of to-day—the grievance of competition and of the over-increasing numbers. Notwithstanding the energetic repudiations of the fact that meet us at every turn, it may be taken for granted that in most cases it is the natural mission of women to marry; that—always in most cases—if they do not marry they become narrowed, live a half life only, and suffer in health of body and of mind. But how can they marry when there are none to marry them, even supposing them to be willing to take the first who offers? If every man in this kingdom were able to support a wife, and should he so inclined, there would still remain nearly a million, yes, ten hundred thousand women, who could not find any sort of husband, and of course the actual figures are far larger. Nor has woman any other resource. Whatever her nature may be, however deep are her maternal and affectionate instincts, without sin and sorrow she may not gratify them except first she pass the lawful gate of holy matrimony. The reasons, under our system—probably the best on the whole, however great the individual suffering it may cause—are sufficiently obvious. Putting aside for a moment the varying laws of religion and morality, virtue and value are still, *au fond*,[2] exchangeable terms, as they have been from the beginning of history, in that to accept in marriage the tarnished is a height of chivalry to which few can rise. Also this highly civilised and very expensive

---

[1]   Napoleon's civil code, which emphasized equality and freedom among adult males but placed women and children in a harshly subordinate position under the law.

[2]   "Fundamentally" (French).

world has enough to do to provide for its legitimate offspring. Nature, in her simplicity, made certain arrangements to meet these difficulties; civilization in its wisdom has altered those arrangements, it is believed for the benefit of society at large. It has laid down new and stricter rules for the game, and, in consequence, too often the individual player must suffer and smile. But how long will these myriad numbered women, who are never allowed any sort of innings, continue to smile and suffer? How long will the dam of custom and training resist these pent-up waters of disappointment and empty loss? And when Nature at last reasserts her sway (if she ever does) what will happen? Will the lonely Rachel[1] of the future always be content to weep in secret for her children that are not, and, without shame, can never be? And when at last she has conquered at the polls, and as a political factor occupies the place that her numbers will give her, what then? Already in the press, in literature, in society appear signs and tokens of an uprising; and though, perhaps fortunately, we of this generation shall not see it, all thinking men must wonder as to its ultimate course and direction. Which will win in the end, primary human impulse or inherited custom and tradition? That is one of the many problems of the unborn twentieth century. Or will the question settle itself in some fashion at present quite unforeseen?

6. From Hugh E.M. Stutfield, "The Psychology of Feminism," *Blackwood's Edinburgh Magazine* (January 1897)

The Soul of Woman, its Sphinx-like ambiguities and complexities, its manifold contradictions, its sorrow and joys, its vagrant fancies and never-to-be-satisfied longings, furnish the literary analyst of these days with inexhaustible material. Above all do the sex-problem novelist and the introspective biographer and essayist revel in the theme. Psychology—word more blessed than Mesopotamia—is their never-ending delight; and modern woman, who, if we may believe those who claim to know most about her, is a sort of walking enigma, is their chief subject of investigation. Her ego, that mysterious entity of which she is now only just becoming conscious, is said to remain a *terra incognita*[2] even to herself; but they are determined to explore its inmost recesses. The pioneers of this formidable undertaking must of necessity be women. Man, great, clumsy, comical creature that he is, knows nothing of the inner springs of the modern Eve's complicated nature. He sees everything in her, we are told, without comprehending anything, and the worst of it is that often he cannot even express his ignorance in good English. Man possesses brute force, woman divine influence, and her nature is in closer relation with

---

[1] See Jeremiah 31:15 and Matthew 2:18.
[2] "Unknown territory" (Latin).

the infinite than the masculine mind.... To be subtle, inscrutable, complex—
irrational possibly, but at any rate incomprehensible—to puzzle the adoring
male, to make him scratch his head in vexation and wonderment as to what
on earth she will do next,—this is the ambition of the latter-day heroine. She
is consumed with a desire for new experiences, new sensations, new objects
in life. Like Evadne in "The Heavenly Twins," she "wants to know";[1] to
penetrate to the core of truth; to dive deep down into the sacred heart of
things, and learn their true sequence and meaning. But in spite of the awakening of her intellect she remains a being of transient impulses and more or
less hysterical emotions. Curiously enough, in all this mystification of hers,
which to the uninitiated appears sheer puzzle-headedness, some weird witch-
ery is supposed to lurk. Her lover, poor fellow, is baffled by her elusive and
contradictory spirit; he understands nothing of the perpetual conflict within
her, the canker of mysterious care that gnaws at her heart, her immense yearn-
ings, and great vague thirst for heaven knows what. The dualism of her nature,
half instinct, half intellect ... is all Greek to him. He endures her tantrums as
best he may, though his simple self would be better mated with an open-
hearted natural woman, who wore her heart upon her sleeve, than with an
animated riddle or an enigma in flounces and furbelows.[2] For, be it understood, love itself fails to unravel the mystery of her being, and Mr. Spooner's
flirtations with Miss Up-to-date in no way give him the key to the feminine
abstraction of which she is the external garniture. And it is good for him that
it should be so, else he, too, might suffer the pangs of disillusionment.
Nowadays, however, the solution of the feminine conundrum is a less hopeless task than formerly for the bewildered and slightly irritated male; and the
present year has given birth to at least two books which throw much light
upon the subject.

Of these the most remarkable in some respects is the "Ascent of Woman"
by Mrs Roy Devereux....[3] It is, to begin with, a distinctly clever book. It
contains much shrewd observation, while the style is polished and epigram-
matic to a fault.... But it is less with the manner than with some of the matter
of these essays that I am now concerned, as much in them will be news to a
great many people. They originally bore the title of "*Dies Dominae*,"[4] and
they are dedicated to "The most dear vision of Her that shall be." Signs, I
think, are not wanting that the *dies dominae* will dawn before very long, and
in that case "She that shall be" will most probably appear as "She-who-must-
be-obeyed." The authoress does not profess to dispel the cloud of mystery

---

1   Alluding to Sarah Grand's New-Woman novel, *The Heavenly Twins* (1893).
2   Trimmings on a lady's dress.
3   *The Ascent of Woman* (1896), a feminist work by Margaret Rose Roy Pember-Devereux.
4   "The Day of the Lord" (Latin).

which envelops her subject, but she does raise for our benefit a corner of the veil which shrouds the Great Arcanum[1] of the feminine soul.... The mission of the authoress (everybody who writes nowadays must have a mission) seems to be to recall to the daughters of Eve that ideal of beauty which she has partially lost. The temple of Aphrodite is now a ruin, says Mrs. Roy Devereux in her grandiloquent way, and the world has long ceased to pour libations to the goddess. But the religion of the woman of the future will be the service of beauty through the medium of comely apparel, and the gospel of the authoress may be termed the Gospel of the Higher Chiffon.

---

[1] The great mystery or secret.

Appendix E: Major Revisions for the First English Edition (1887)

[The following notations record some of the larger and more interesting changes Haggard made when revising the serial version of *She* for publication in novel form. Most of the additions involve transcriptions and elaborations of the material written upon or included with the Sherd of Amenartas. Haggard also added a number of editorial notes, indicated here by asterisks (*), that provide scholarly ballast to the narrative. Note that a great many smaller changes of wording and punctuation are not recorded here.]

Page 42 (part 1)

a Mendesian Prince of the Twenty-ninth Dynasty] a Mendesian pharaoh of the twenty-ninth dynasty, and his grandfather, I believe, was that very Kallikrates mentioned by Herodotus.★ (★ The Kallikrates here referred to by my friend was a Spartan, spoken of by Herodotus (Herod. ix. 72) as being remarkable for his beauty. He fell at the glorious battle of Platæa (22 September 479 BCE), when the Lacedæmonians and Athenians under Pausanias routed the Persians, putting nearly 300,000 of them to the sword. The following is a translation of the passage, "For Kallikrates died out of the battle, he came to the army the most beautiful man of the Greeks of that day—not only of the Lacedæmonians themselves, but of the other Greeks also. He when Pausanias was sacrificing was wounded in the side by an arrow; and then they fought, but on being carried off he regretted his death, and said to Arimnestus, a Platæan, that he did not grieve at dying for Greece, but at not having struck a blow, or, although he desired so to do, performed any deed worthy of himself." This Kallikrates, who appears to have been as brave as he was beautiful, is subsequently mentioned by Herodotus as having been buried among the 'ιέυες (young commanders), apart from the other Spartans and the Helots.—L.H.H.)

Page 60 (part 2)

beautiful Greek of the period it is to have been written of an Egyptian born] very good Greek of the period it is, considering that it came from the pen of an Egyptian born. Here is an exact transcript of it:—

ΑΜΕΝΑΡΤΑΣΤΟΥΒΑΣΙΛΙΚΟΥΓΕΝΟΥΣΤΟΥΑ
ΙΓΥΠΤΙΟΥΗΤΟΥΚΑΛΛΙΚΡΑΤΟΥΣΙΣΙΔΟΣΙΕΡ
ΕΩΣΗΝΟΙΜΕΝΘΕΟΙΤΡΕΦΟΥΣΙΤΑΔΕΔΑΙΜΟ
ΝΙΑΥΓΟΤΑΣΣΕΤΑΙΗΔΗΤΕΛΕΥΤΩΣΑΤΙΣΙΣ
ΘΕΝΕΙΤΩΓΑΙΔΙΕΓΙΣΤΕΛΛΕΙΤΑΔΕΣΥΝΕΦΥΓΟ
ΝΓΑΡΓΟΤΕΕΚΤΗΣΑΙΓΥΠΤΙΑΣΕΓΙΝΕΚΤΑΝΕΒ
ΟΥΜΕΤΑΤΟΥΣΟΥΓΑΤΡΟΣΔΙΑΤΟΝΕΡΩΤΑΤΟ
ΝΕΜΟΝΕΓΙΟΡΚΗΣΑΝΤΟΣΦΥΓΟΝΤΕΣΔΕΓΡΟ
ΣΝΟΤΟΝΔΙΑΓΟΝΤΙΟΙΚΑΙΚΔΜΗΝΑΣΚΑΤΑΤΑ
ΓΑΡΑΘΑΛΑΣΣΙΑΤΗΣΛΙΒΥΗΣΤΑΓΡΟΣΗΛΙΟΥ
ΑΝΑΤΟΛΑΣΓΛΑΝΗΘΕΝΤΕΣΕΝΘΑΓΕΡΓΕΤΡΑ
ΤΙΣΜΕΓΑΛΗΓΛΥΓΤΟΝΟΜΟΙΩΜΑΑΙΘΙΟΓΟΣ
ΚΕΦΑΛΗΣΕΙΤΑΗΜΕΡΑΣΔΑΓΟΣΤΟΜΑΤΟΣΓΟ
ΤΑΜΟΥΜΕΓΑΛΟΥΕΚΓΕΣΟΝΤΕΣΟΙΜΕΝΚΑΤΕ
ΓΟΝΤΙΣΘΗΜΕΝΟΙΔΕΝΟΣΩΙΑΓΕΘΑΝΟΜΕΝΤ
ΕΛΟΣΔΕΥΓΑΓΡΙΩΝΑΝΘΡΩΓΩΝΕΦΕΡΟΜΕΘΑ
ΔΙΑΕΛΕΩΝΤΕΚΑΙΤΕΝΑΓΕΩΝΕΝΘΑΓΕΡΓΤΗΝ
ΩΝΓΛΗΘΟΣΑΓΟΚΡΥΓΤΕΙΤΟΝΟΥΡΑΝΟΝΗΜ
ΕΡΑΣΙΕΩΣΗΛΘΟΜΕΝΕΙΣΚΟΙΛΟΝΤΙΟΡΟΣΕΝ
ΘΑΓΟΤΕΜΕΓΑΛΗΜΕΝΓΟΛΙΣΗΝΑΝΤΡΑΔΕΑΓ
ΕΙΡΟΝΑΗΓΑΓΟΝΔΕΩΣΒΑΣΙΛΕΙΑΝΤΗΝΤΩΝΞ
ΕΝΟΥΣΧΥΤΡΑΙΣΣΤΕΦΑΝΟΥΝΤΩΝΗΤΙΣΜΑΓΕ
ΙΑΜΕΝΕΧΡΗΤΟΕΓΙΣΤΗΜΗΔΕΓΑΝΤΩΝΚΑΙΔ
ΗΚΑΙΚΑΛΛΟΣΚΑΙΡΩΜΗΝΑΓΗΡΩΣΗΝΗΔΕΚΑ
ΛΛΙΚΡΑΤΟΥΣΤΟΥΣΟΥΓΑΤΡΟΣΕΡΑΣΘΕΙΣΑΤ
ΟΜΕΝΓΡΩΤΟΝΣΥΝΟΙΚΕΙΝΕΒΟΥΛΕΤΟΕΜΕΔ
ΕΑΝΕΛΕΙΝΕΓΕΙΤΑΩΣΟΥΚΑΝΕΓΕΙΘΕΝΕΜΕΓΑ
ΡΥΓΕΡΕΦΙΛΕΙΚΑΙΤΗΝΞΕΝΗΝΕΦΟΒΕΙΤΟΑΓΗ
ΓΑΓΕΝΗΜΑΣΥΓΟΜΑΓΕΙΑΣΚΑΘΟΔΟΥΣΣΦΑΛ
ΕΡΑΣΕΝΘΑΤΟΒΑΡΑΘΡΟΝΤΟΜΕΓΑΟΥΚΑΤΑΣ
ΤΟΜΑΕΚΕΙΤΟΟΓΕΡΩΝΟΦΙΛΟΣΟΦΟΣΤΕΘΝΕ
ΩΣΑΦΙΚΟΜΕΝΟΙΣΔΕΔΕΙΞΕΦΩΣΤΟΥΒΙΟΥΕΥ
ΘΥΟΙΟΝΚΙΟΝΑΕΛΙΣΣΟΜΕΝΟΝΦΩΝΗΝΙΕΝΤ
ΑΚΑΘΑΓΕΡΒΡΟΝΤΗΣΕΙΤΑΔΙΑΓΥΡΟΣΒΕΒΗΚ
ΥΙΑΑΒΛΑΒΗΣΚΑΙΕΤΙΚΑΛΛΙΩΝΑΥΤΗΕΑΥΤΗΣ
ΕΞΕΦΑΝΗΕΚΔΕΤΟΥΤΩΝΩΜΟΣΕΚΑΙΤΟΝΣΟ
ΝΓΑΤΕΡΑΑΘΑΝΑΤΟΝΑΓΟΔΕΙΞΕΙΝΕΙΣΥΝΟΙΚ
ΕΙΝΟΙΒΟΥΛΟΙΤΟΕΜΕΔΕΑΝΕΛΕΙΝΟΥΓΑΡΟΥ
ΝΑΥΤΗΑΝΕΛΕΙΝΙΣΧΥΕΝΥΓΟΤΩΝΗΜΕΔΑΓΩ
ΝΗΝΚΑΙΑΥΤΗΕΧΩΜΑΓΕΙΑΣΟΔΟΥΔΕΝΤΙΜΑ

ΛΛΟΝΗΘΕΛΕΤΩΧΕΙΡΕΤΩΝΟΜΜΑΤΩΝΓΡΟΙ
ΣΧΩΝΙΝΑΔΗΤΟΤΗΣΓΥΝΑΙΚΟΣΚΑΛΛΟΣΜΗ
ΟΡΩΗΓΕΙΤΑΟΡΓΙΣΘΕΙΣΑΚΑΤΕΓΟΗΤΕΥΣΕΜ
ΕΝΑΥΤΟΝΑΓΟΛΟΜΕΝΟΝΜΕΝΤΟΙΚΛΑΟΥΣΑ
ΚΑΙΟΔΥΡΟΜΕΝΗΕΚΕΙΘΕΝΑΓΗΝΕΓΚΕΝΕΜΕΔ
ΕΦΟΒΩΙΑΦΗΚΕΝΕΙΣΣΤΟΜΑΤΟΥΜΕΓΑΛΟΥΓ
ΟΤΑΜΟΥΤΟΥΝΑΥΣΙΓΟΡΟΥΓΟΡΡΩΔΕΝΑΥΣΙ
ΝΕΦΩΝΓΕΡΓΛΕΟΥΣΑΕΤΕΚΟΝΣΕΑΓΟΓΛΕΥΣ
ΑΣΑΜΟΛΙΣΓΟΤΕΔΕΥΡΟΑΘΗΝΑΖΕΚΑΤΗΓΑΓ
ΟΜΗΝΣΥΔΕΩΤΙΣΙΣΘΕΝΕΣΩΝΕΓΙΣΤΕΛΛΩΜ
ΗΟΛΙΓΩΡΕΙΔΕΙΓΑΡΤΗΝΓΥΝΑΙΚΑΑΝΑΖΗΤΕΙ
ΝΗΝΓΩΣΤΟΤΟΥΒΙΟΥΜΥΣΤΗΡΙΟΝΑΝΕΥΡΗ
ΣΚΑΙΑΝΑΙΡΕΙΝΗΝΓΟΥΓΑΡΑΣΧΗΔΙΑΤΟΝΣΟ
ΝΓΑΤΕΡΑΚΑΛΛΙΚΡΑΤΗΝΕΙΔΕΦΟΒΟΥΜΕΝΟ
ΣΗΔΙΑΑΛΛΟΤΙΑΥΤΟΣΛΕΙΓΕΙΤΟΥΕΡΓΟΥΓΑ
ΣΙΤΟΙΣΥΣΤΕΡΟΝΑΥΤΟΤΟΥΤΟΕΓΙΣΤΕΛΛΩΕ
ΩΣΓΟΤΕΑΓΑΘΟΣΤΙΣΓΕΝΟΜΕΝΟΣΤΩΓΥΡΙΛ
ΟΥΣΑΣΘΑΙΤΟΛΜΗΣΕΙΚΑΙΤΑΑΡΙΣΤΕΙΑΕΧΩΝ
ΒΑΣΙΛΕΥΣΑΙΤΩΝΑΝΘΡΩΓΩΝΛΓΙΣΤΑΜΕΝΔ
ΗΤΑΤΟΙΑΥΤΑΛΕΓΩΟΜΩΣΔΕΑΑΥΤΗΕΓΝΩΚ
ΑΟΥΚΕΨΕΥΣΑΜΗΝ

For general convenience in reading, I have here accurately transcribed this inscription into the cursive character:—

Ἀμενάρτας, τοῦ βασιλικοῦ γένους τοῦ Αἰγυπ-
τίου, ἡ τοῦ Καλλικράτους Ἴσιδος ἱερέως, ἣν οἱ μὲν
θεοὶ τρέφουσι τὰ δὲ δαιμόνια ὑποτάσσεται, ἤδη τελ-
ευτῶσα Τισισθένει τῷ παιδὶ ἐπιστέλλει τάδε· συνέ-
φυγον γάρ ποτε ἐκ τῆς Αἰγυπτίας ἐπὶ Νεκτανέβου
μετὰ τοῦ σοῦ πατρός, διὰ τὸν ἔρωτα τὸν ἐμὸν ἐπιορ-
κήσαντος. φυγόντες δὲ πρὸς νότον διαπόντιοι καὶ κʹδʹ
μῆνας κατὰ τὰ παραθαλάσσια τῆς Λιβύης τὰ πρὸς
ἡλίου ἀνατολὰς πλανηθέντες, ἔνθαπερ πέτρα τις μεγάλη,
γλυπτὸν ὁμοίωμα Αἰθίοπος κεφαλῆς, εἶτα ἡμέρας δʹ
ἀπὸ στόματος ποταμοῦ μεγάλου ἐκπεσόντες, οἱ μὲν
κατεποντίσθημεν, οἱ δὲ νόσῳ ἀπεθάνομεν· τέλος δὲ
ὑπ᾽ ἀγρίων ἀνθρώπων ἐφερόμεθα διὰ ἑλέων τε καὶ

τεναγέων ἔνθαπερ πτηιῶν πλῆθος ἀποκρύπτει τὸν
οὐρανὸν, ἡμέρας ἱ, ἕως ἤλθομεν εἰς κοῖλόν τι ὄρος, ἔνθα
ποτὲ μεγάλη μὲν πόλις ἦν, ἄντρα δὲ ἀπείρονα· ἤγαγον
δὲ ὡς βασίλειαν τὴν τῶν ξένους χύτραις στεφανούντων,
ἥτις μαγείᾳ μὲν ἐχρῆτο ἐπιστήμῃ δὲ πάντων καὶ δὴ καὶ
κάλλος καὶ ῥώμην ἀγήρως ἦν· ἡ δὲ Καλλικράτους
τοῦ σοῦ πατρὸς ἐρασθεῖσα τὸ μὲν πρῶτον συνοικεῖν
ἐβούλετο ἐμὲ δὲ ἀνελεῖν· ἔπειτα, ὡς οὐκ ἀνέπειθεν,
ἐμὲ γὰρ ὑπερεφίλει καὶ τὴν ξένην ἐφοβεῖτο, ἀπήγαγεν
ἡμᾶς ὑπὸ μαγείας καθ' ὁδοὺς σφαλερὰς ἔνθα τὸ βά-
ραθρον τὸ μέγα, οὗ κατὰ στόμα ἔκειτο ὁ γέρων ὁ
φιλόσοφος τεθνεώς, ἀφικομένοις δ' ἔδειξε φῶς τοῦ
βίου εὐθύ, οἷον κίονα ἑλισσόμενον φωνὴν ἱέντα καθάπερ
βροντῆς, εἶτα διὰ πυρὸς βεβηκυῖα ἀβλαβὴς καὶ ἔτι
καλλίων αὐτὴ ἑαυτῆς ἐξεφάνη. ἐκ δὲ τούτων ὤμοσε
καὶ τὸν σὸν πατέρα ἀθάνατον ἀποδείξειν, εἰ συνοικεῖν
οἱ βούλοιτο ἐμὲ δε ἀνελεῖν, οὐ γὰρ οὖν αὐτὴ ἀνελεῖν
ἴσχυεν ὑπὸ τῶν ἡμεδαπῶν ἦν καὶ αὐτὴ ἔχω μαγείας.
ὁ δ' οὐδέν τι μᾶλλον ἤθελε, τὼ χεῖρε τῶν ὀμμάτων
προίσχων ἵνα δὴ τὸ τῆς γυναικὸς κάλλος μὴ ὁρῴη·
ἔπειτα ὀργισθεῖσα κατεγοήτευσε μὲν αὐτόν, ἀπολόμενον
μέντοι κλάουσα καὶ ὀδυρομένη ἐκεῖθεν ἀπήνεγκεν, ἐμὲ
δὲ φόβῳ ἀφῆκεν εἰς στόμα τοῦ μεγάλου ποταμοῦ
τοῦ ναυσιπόρου, πόρρω δὲ ναυσίν, ἐφ' ὧνπερ πλέουσα
ἔτεκόν σε, ἀποπλεύσασα μόλις ποτὲ δεῦρο Ἀθηνάζε
κατηγαγόμην. σὺ δέ, ὦ Τισίσθενες, ὧν ἐπιστέλλω μὴ
ὀλιγώρει· δεῖ γὰρ τὴν γυναῖκα ἀναζητεῖν ἤν πως τὸ τοῦ
βίου μυστήριον ἀνεύρῃς, καὶ ἀναιρεῖν, ἤν που παρασχῇ,
διὰ τὸν σὸν πατέρα Καλλικράτην. εἰ δὲ φοβούμενος
ἢ διὰ ἄλλο τι αὐτὸς λείπει τοῦ ἔργου, πᾶσι τοῖς
ὕστερον αὐτὸ τοῦτο ἐπιστέλλω, ἕως ποτὲ ἀγαθός τις
γενόμενος τῷ πυρὶ λούσασθαι τολμήσει καὶ τὰ ἀριστεῖα
ἔχων βασιλεῦσαι τῶν ἀνθρώπων· ἄπιστα μὲν δὴ τὰ
τοιαῦτα λέγω, ὅμως δὲ ἃ αὐτὴ ἔγνωκα οὐκ ἐψευσάμην.

Page 60 (part 2)

the cartouche of the original Kallikrates] the cartouche of the original
Kallikrates★ (★ The cartouche, if it be a true cartouche, cannot have been that
of Kallikrates, as Mr. Holly suggests. Kallikrates was a priest and not entitled
to a cartouche, which was the prerogative of Egyptian royalty, though he
might have inscribed his name or title upon an *oval*.—EDITOR.)

Page 61 (part 2)

'I cannot go. To thee, my son Kallikrates.'] 'I could not go. Tisisthenes to his son, Kallikrates.' Here it is in fac-simile with its cursive equivalent:—

ΟΥΚΑΝΔΥΝΑΙΜΗΝΓΟΡΕΥΕϹΘΑΙΤΙϹΙϹΘΕΝΗ
ϹΚΑΛΛΙΚΡΑΤΕΙΤΩΙΓΑΙΔΙ

οὐκ ἂν δυναίμην πορεύεσθαι.
Τισισθένης Καλλικράτει τῷ παιδί.

Page 61 (part 2)

'I started to seek, but the gods were against me. To thee, my son.'] 'I ceased from my going, the gods being against me. Kallikrates to his son.' Here it is also:—

ΤΩΝΘΕΩΝΑΝΤΙΣΤΑΝΤΩΝΕΓΑΥΣΑΜΗΝΤΗΣ
ΓΟΡΕΙΑΣΚΑΛΛΙΚΡΑΤΗΣΤΩΙΓΑΙΔΙ

τῶν θεῶν ἀντιστάντων ἐπαυσάμην τῆς πορείας.
Καλλικράτης τῷ παιδί.

Page 62 (part 2)

the name of a Roman lady.] The name of a Roman lady. The following list, however, comprises all the Latin names upon the sherd:—

C. CAECILIVS VINDEX
M. AIMILIVS VINDEX
SEX. VARIVS. MARVLLVS
Q. SOSIVS PRISCVS SENECIO VINDEX
L. VALERIVS COMINIVS VINDEX
SEX. OTACILIVS. M. F.
L. ATTIVS. VINDEX
MVSSIVS VINDEX
C. FVFIDIVS. C. F. VINDEX
LICINIVS FAVSTVS
LABERIA POMPEIANA CONIVX MACRINI VINDICIS
MANILIA LVCILLA CONIVX MARVLLI VINDICIS

the doggerel couplet.] the doggerel couplet. To the left of this, inscribed in faint blue, were the initials A.V., and after them a date, 1800.

Page 62 (part 2)

the Latin black letter translation of the uncial Greek] the mediæval Latin translation of the uncial Greek of which I shall speak presently. This I also give in full.

Facsimile of Black-Letter Inscription on the Sherd of Amenartas.

Ista religia est valde misticu et myrificb ops qd maiores mei ex Armorica ff Brittania miore secu cōvehebāt et qdm ses elerirs sfper pri meo in manb ferebat qd pfitus illvd destrueret affirmās qd esset ab ipso sathana cōflatb prestigiosa et dyabolica arte qre pter mevs cōfregit illvd ī dvas ptes qs qdm ego Johs de Uiceto salvas servabi et adaptabi sievt apparet die līe pr post fest beate Marie virg anni gre mccccxlv

Page 63 (part 2)

Marie Virginis anni gratie MCCCCXLV."] Marie Virginis anni gratie MCCCCXLV.

Facsimile of the Old English Black-Letter Translation of the above Latin Inscription from the Sherd of Amenartas found inscribed upon a parchment.

Thys rellike ys a ryghte mistycall worke
& a marveylous pe whyche myne aun=
ceteres afore tyme dyd conveighe hider wt pm
ffrom Armoryke whe ys to scien Britayne pe
lesse & a certayne holpe clerke shoulde allweyes
beare my ffadir on honde pt he owghte vttirly
ffor to ffrusshe pe same affirmynge pt pt was
ffourmyd & confflatyd off sathanas hym selffe
by arte magike & dyvellysshe wherefore my
ffadir dyd take pe same & to brast yt yn tweyne
but I Iohn de Uincey dyd save whool pe tweye
ptes therof & topeeeyd pm togydder agayne soe
as yee se on ps deye mondaye next ffolowynge
after pe ffeeste of seynte Marye pe blessed
vyrgyne yn pe yeere of salvacioun ffowertene
hundreth & ffyve & ffowrti.

Page 63 (part 2)

dreamt of in your philosophy, Horatio."] dreamt of in your philosophy,
Horatio." And now there remained but one more document to be examined—namely, the ancient black-letter transcription into mediæval Latin of
the uncial inscription on the sherd. As will be seen, this translation was
executed and subscribed in the year 1495, by a certain "learned man,"
Edmundus de Prato (Edmund Pratt) by name, licentiate in Canon Law, of
Exeter College, Oxford, who had actually been a pupil of Grocyn, the first
scholar who taught Greek in England.★ (★Grocyn, the instructor of Erasmus,
studied Greek under Chalcondylas the Byzantine at Florence, and first
lectured in the Hall of Exeter College, Oxford, in 1491.—EDITOR.) No doubt
on the fame of this new learning reaching his ears, the Vincey of the day,
perhaps that same John de Vincey who years before had saved the relic from
destruction and made the black-letter entry on the sherd in 1445, hurried off
to Oxford to see if perchance it might avail to solve the secret of the mysterious inscription. Nor was he disappointed, for the learned Edmundus was
equal to the task. Indeed his rendering is so excellent an example of mediæval learning and latinity that, even at the risk of sating the learned reader with

too many antiquities, I have made up my mind to give it in fac-simile, together with an expanded version for the benefit of those who find the contractions troublesome. The translation has several peculiarities on which this is not the place to dwell, but I would in passing call the attention of scholars to the passage "duxerunt autem nos ad reginam *advenaslasaniscoronantium*," which strikes me as a delightful rendering of the original,

'ἤγαγον δὲ ὡς βασίλειαν τὴν τῶν ξένους χύτραις στεφανούντων.'

Mediæval Black-Letter Latin Translation of the Uncial Inscription on the Sherd of Amenartas

Amenartas e gen. reg. Egyptii vxor Callicratis sacerdot Isidis quā dei sovēt demonia attēdūt filiol' svo Tisistheni iā moribūda ita mādat: Effugi quōdā ex Egypto regnāte Nectanebo cū patre tvo, ꝓpter mei amorē pejerato. Fvgiētes autē v'sus Notū trans mare et xxiiij mēses p'r litora Libye v'sus Oriētē errans vbi est petra quedā mgna scvlpta instar Ethioꝓ capis, deinde dies iiij ab ost flum mgni eiecti p'tim submersi sumus p'tim morbo mortui sum: in sine autē a fer hōibs portabamur ꝓr palvd et vada. vbi aviu m'titvdo celū obūbrat dies x. donec advenim ad cavū quēdā montē, ubi olim mgna vrbs erat, cauerne quoꝗ imēse: dvxerūt autē nos ad reginā Advenaslasaniscoronātiū que magic vtebair et peritia omniū rer et salte pvlcris et vigore isescibil' erat. Hec mgno patr tui amore ꝓcvlsa p'mū q'dē ei conubiū michi mortē parabat. postea v'ro recvsāte Callicrate amore mei et timore regine affecto nos ꝓr magicā

abduxit p'r vias horribil' vbi est puteus ille
ꝓfūdus, cuius iurta aditū iacebat senioꝛ philo=
sophi cadauer, et aduꝺīctib mōstrauit flamā
Uite erectā, istar columne volutātis, voces
emittēte q̄si tonitrus : tūc ꝑr igne ipetu nociuo
expers trāsit et iā ipa sese formosior visa est.

    Quib faci iūrauit se patrē tuū quoꝗ iūꝰꝛ=
talē ostēsurā esse, si me prius occisa regine
cōtuberniū mallet ; neꝗ enī ipsa me occidere
valuit, ꝓpter nostratū m̄gicā cuius egomet
ꝑtem habeo. Ille vero nichil huius gen̄
maluit, manib̄ ante ocuꝉ passis ne mulieꝛ
formositatē adspiceret : postea eū m̄gica ꝑcussit
arte, at mortuū efferebat īde eū fletib et vagitib,
me ꝑr timorē expulit ad ostiū m̄gni flumiū
veliuoli porro in naue in qua te peperi, uix
post dies huc Athenas inuecta sū. At tu, O
Tisilthen, ne q'd quorū m̄do nauci fac : necesse
enī est mulierē exqvirere si qva Uite mysteriū
ipetres et vīdicare, quātū in te est, patrē tuū
Callicraꝉ in regine morte. Sin timore seu aliꝗ
cavsa rē reliquis īfecta, hoc ipsū oīb posteꝛ
m̄do dū bonus q̄s inueniatur qvi ignis lauacrū
nō ꝑrhorrescet et ꝑtentia digū dōlabiꝉ hōīu.

    Talia dico incredibilia q̄dē at mīe ficta de
reb michi cognitis.

    Hec Grece scripta Latine reddidit vir
doctus Edm̄ds de Prato, in Decretis Li=
cenciatus e Coll. Exon: Oxon: doctissimi
Grocyni quondam e pupillis, Id. Apr. A°.
Dn̄i. MCCCCLXXXXU°.

Expanded Version of the above Mediæval Latin Translation

AMENARTAS, e genere regio Egyptii, uxor Callicratis, sacerdotis Isidis, quam dei fovent demonia attendunt, filiolo suo Tisistheni jam moribunda ita mandat: Effugi quondam ex Egypto, regnante Nectanebo, cum patre tuo, propter mei amorem pejerato. Fugientes autem versus Notum trans mare, et viginti quatuor menses per litora Libye versus Orientem errantes, ubi est petra quedam magna sculpta instar Ethiopis capitis, deinde dies quatuor ab ostio fluminis magni ejecti partim submersi sumus partim morbo mortui sumus: in fine autem a feris hominibus portabamur per paludes et vada, ubi avium multitudo celum obumbrat, dies decem, donec advenimus ad cavum quendam montem, ubi olim magna urbs erat, caverne quoque immense; duxerunt autem nos ad reginam Advenaslasaniscoronantium, que magicâ utebatur et peritiâ omnium rerum, et saltem pulcritudine et vigore insenescibilis erat. Hec magno patris tui amore perculsa, primum quidem ei connubium michi mortem parabat; postea vero, recusante Callicrate, amore mei et timore regine affecto nos per magicam abduxit per vias horribiles ubi est puteus ille profundus, cujus juxta aditum jacebat senioris philosophi cadaver, et advenientibus monstravit flammam Vite erectam, instar columne volutantis, voces emittentem quasi tonitrus: tunc per ignem impetu nocivo expers transiit et jam ipsa sese formosior visa est.

Quibus factis juravit se patrem tuum quoque immortalem ostensuram esse, si me prius occisa regine contubernium mallet; neque enim ipsa me occidere valuit, propter nostratum magicam cujus egomet partem habeo. Ille vero nichil hujus generis malebat, manibus ante oculos passis, ne mulieris formositatem adspiceret: postea illum magica percussit arte, at mortuum efferebat inde cum fletibus et vagitibus, et me per timorem expulit ad ostium magni fluminis, velivoli, porro in nave, in qua te peperi, vix post dies huc Athenas vecta sum. At tu, O Tisisthenes, ne quid quorum mando nauci fac: necesse enim est mulierem exquirere si qua Vite mysterium impetres et vindicare, quantum in te est, patrem tuum Callicratem in regine morte. Sin timore seu aliqua causa rem relinquis infectam, hoc ipsum omnibus posteris mando, dum bonus quis inveniatur qui ignis lavacrum non perhorrescet, et potentia dignus dominabitur hominum.

Talia dico incredibilia quidem at minime ficta de rebus michi cognitis.

Hec Grece scripta Latine reddidit vir doctus Edmundus de Prato, in Descretis Licenciatus, e Collegio Exoniensi Oxoniensi doctissimi Grocyni quondam e pupillis, Idibus Aprilis Anno Domini MCCCCLXXXXV°.

Page 108–109 (part 5)

struggling.... put upon her by Job.] struggling. He fought like a fiend, shrieking in the abandonment of his despair, and notwithstanding the noose round him, and the efforts of the men who held his legs, the advancing wretches were for the moment unable to accomplish their purpose, which, horrible and incredible as it seems, was *to put the red-hot pot upon his head.*

I sprang to my feet with a yell of horror, and drawing my revolver fired it by a sort of instinct straight at the diabolical woman who had been caressing Mahomed, and was now gripping him in her arms. The bullet struck her in the back and killed her, and to this day I am glad that it did, for, as it afterwards transpired, she had availed herself of the anthropophagous customs of the Amahagger to organise the whole thing in revenge of the slight put upon her by Job. She sank down dead, and as she did so, to my terror and dismay, Mahomed, by a superhuman effort, burst from his tormentors, and, springing high into the air, fell dying upon her corpse. The heavy bullet from my pistol had driven through the bodies of both, at once striking down the murderess, and saving her victim from a death a hundred times more horrible. It was an awful and yet a most merciful accident.

Page 146 (part 7)

Arabian am I by my birth.] Arabian am I by my birth, even 'al Arab al Ariba' (an Arab of the Arabs), and of the race of our father Yárab, the son of Kâhtan, for in that fair and ancient city Ozal was I born, in the province of Yaman the Happy. Yet dost thou not speak it as we used to speak. Thy talk doth lack the music of the sweet tongue of the tribes of Hamyar which I was wont to hear. Some of the words too seemed changed, even as among these Amahagger, who have debased and defiled its purity, so that I must speak with them in what is to me another tongue."* (*Yárab the son of Kâhtan, who lived some centuries before the time of Abraham, was the father of the ancient Arabs, and gave its name Araba to the country. In speaking of herself as "al Arab al Ariba," *She* no doubt meant to convey that she was of the true Arab blood as distinguished from the naturalised Arabs, the descendants of Ismael, the son of Abraham and Hagar, who were known as "al Arab al mostárcba." The dialect of the Koreish was usually called the clear or "perspicuous" Arabic, but the Hamaritic dialect approached nearer to the purity of the mother Syriac.—L.H.H.)

Page 156 (Part 7)

she went on, "it must be one like it."] she went on, "it must be one like it, and yet never did I see one like to it, for thereto hung a history, and he who wore it prized it much."* (* I am informed by a renowned and learned Egyptologist, to whom I have submitted this very interesting and beautifully finished scarab, "Suten se Rā," that he has never seen one resembling it.

Although it bears a title frequently given to Egyptian royalty, he is of opinion that it is not necessarily the cartouche of a Pharaoh, on which either the throne or personal name of the monarch is generally inscribed. What the history of this particular scarab may have been we can now, unfortunately, never know, but I have little doubt but that it played some part in the tragic story of the Princess Amenartas and her lover Kallikrates, the forsworn priest of Isis.—EDITOR.)

Page 170 (Part 8)

"My empire is a moral one."] "My empire is of the imagination."

Page 174 (Part 8)

in the tomb with its fathers' bones.] in the tomb with its fathers' bones.★ (★Note: The name of the race Ama-hagger would seem to indicate a curious mingling of races such as might easily have occurred in the neighbourhood of the Zambesi. The prefix "Ama" is common to the Zulu and kindred races, and signifies "people," while "hagger" is an Arabic word meaning a stone.—EDITOR.)

Page 183 (Part 9)

the Man who taught them.] the Man who taught them. Also I told her that among her own people, the Arabs, another prophet, one Mohammed, had arisen and preached a new faith to which many millions of mankind now adhered."

Page 184 (Part 9)

what Ayesha really believed.] what Ayesha *really* believed, and what her philosophy was.

"Well, my Holly," she continued, "and so those people of mine have found a prophet, a false prophet thou sayest, for he is not thine own, and, indeed, I doubt it not. Yet in my day was it otherwise, for then we Arabs had many gods. Allât there was, and Saba, the Host of Heaven, Al Uzza, and Manah the stony one, for whom the blood of victims flowed, and Wadd and Sawâ, and Yaghûth the Lion of the dwellers in Yaman, and Yäûk the Horse of Morad, and Nasr the Eagle of Hamyar; ay, and many more. Oh, the folly of it all, the shame and the pitiful folly! Yet when I rose in wisdom and spoke thereof, surely they would have slain me in the name of their outraged gods. Well, so hath it ever been;—but, my Holly, art thou weary of me already, that thou dost sit so silent? Or dost thou fear lest I should teach thee my philosophy?— for know I have a philosophy. What would a teacher be without her own philosophy? and if thou dost vex me overmuch beware! for I will have thee learn it, and thou shalt be my disciple, and we twain will found a faith that shall swallow up all others."

Page 213 (Part II)

threw off her veil, and broke out] threw off her veil, and broke out, after the ancient and poetic fashion of the dwellers in Arabia,* (* Among the ancient Arabians the power of poetic declamation, either in verse or prose, was held in the highest honour and esteem, and he who excelled in it was known as "Khâteb," or Orator. Every year a general assembly was held at which the rival poets repeated their compositions, when those poems which were judged to be the best were, so soon as the knowledge and the art of writing became general, inscribed on silk in letters of gold, and publicly exhibited, being known as "Al Modhahabât," or golden verses. In the poem given above by Mr. Holly, Ayesha evidently followed the traditional poetic manner of her people, which was to embody their thoughts in a series of somewhat disconnected sentences, each remarkable for its beauty and the grace of its expression.—EDITOR.)

Page 213 (Part II)

exceedingly difficult to render into English.] exceedingly difficult to render into English, and ought by rights to be sung to the music of a cantata, rather than written and read.

Page 215 (Part II)

thou hast not been born again to me.... unkindly soil.] thou hast not been born again to me. Nay, look not so—put away that pale cast of doubt, for oh be sure herein can error find no foothold! Sooner shall the suns forget their course and the swallow miss her nest, than my soul shall swear a lie and be led astray from thee, Kallikrates. Blind me, take away mine eyes, and let the darkness utterly fence me in, and still mine ears would catch the tone of thine unforgotten voice, striking more loud against the portals of my sense than can the call of brazen-throated clarions:—stop up mine hearing also, and let a thousand touch me on the brow, and I would name thee out of all:—yea, rob me of every sense, and see me stand deaf and blind, and dumb, and with nerves that cannot weigh the value of a touch, yet would my spirit leap within me like a quickening child and cry unto my heart, behold Kallikrates! behold, thou watcher, the watches of thy night are ended! behold thou who seekest in the night season, thy morning Star ariseth.

She paused awhile and then continued, "But stay, if thy heart is yet hard-ened against the mighty truth and thou dost require a further pledge of that which thou dost find too deep to understand, even now shall it be given to thee, and to thee also, oh my Holly."

Page 237 (Part 12)

smoulder away for hours.] smoulder away for hours.★ (★ After all we are not much in advance of the Amahagger in these matters. "Mummy," that is pounded ancient Egyptian, is, I believe, a pigment much used by artists, and especially by those of them who direct their talents to the reproduction of the works of the old masters.—EDITOR.)

Works Cited and Recommended Reading

Addy, Shirley M. *Rider Haggard and Egypt*. Accrington, Lancashire: AL Publications, 1998.

Aldiss, Brian W., with David Wingrove. *Trillion Year Spree: The History of Science Fiction*. London: Victor Gollancz, 1986.

Arata, Stephen. *Fictions of Loss in the Victorian Fin de Siècle: Identity and Empire*. Cambridge: Cambridge UP, 1996.

Ardis, Ann L. *New Women, New Novels: Feminism and Early Modernism*. New Brunswick: Rutgers UP, 1990.

Atwood, Margaret. "Superwoman Drawn and Quartered: The Early Forms of *She*." *Second Words: Selected Critical Prose*. Toronto: Anansi, 1982. 35–54.

Brantlinger, Patrick. *Rule of Darkness: British Literature and Imperialism, 1830–1914*. Ithaca: Cornell UP, 1988.

Bunn, David. "Embodying Africa: Woman and Romance in Colonial Fiction." *English in Africa* 15:1 (1988): 1–27.

Chrisman, Laura. *Rereading the Imperial Romance*. Oxford: Clarendon, 2000.

Cohen, Morton. *Rider Haggard: His Life and Works*. London: Hutchinson, 1960.

Ellis, Peter B. *H. Rider Haggard: A Voice from the Infinite*. London: Routledge, 1978.

Etherington, Norman. *Rider Haggard*. Boston: Twayne, 1984.

———. "Rider Haggard, Imperialism, and the Layered Personality." *Victorian Studies* 22 (Autumn 1978): 71–88.

Franklin, J. Jeffrey. "Memory as the Nexus of Identity, Empire and Evolution in George Eliot's *Middlemarch* and H. Rider Haggard's *She*." *Cahiers Victoriens et Edouardians* 53 (2001): 141–68.

Freud, Sigmund. *The Interpretation of Dreams*. ed. James Strachey. London: Allen and Unwin, 1954.

Gilbert, Sandra M., and Susan Gubar. *No Man's Land: The Place of the Woman Writer in the Twentieth Century. Volume 2: Sexchanges*. New Haven: Yale, 1989.

Gold, Barri J. "Embracing the Corpse: Discursive Recycling in H. Rider Haggard's *She*." *English Literature in Transition 1880–1920* 38:3 (1995): 305–27.

Haggard, H. Rider. *Ayesha: The Return of She*. London: Ward Lock, 1905.

———. *The Days of My Life*. 2 vols. London: Longmans, Green, and Co., 1926.

———. *The Annotated* She, ed. Norman Etherington. Bloomington, IN: Indiana UP, 1991.

———. *She and Allan*. London: Hutchinson and Co., 1921.

———. *Wisdom's Daughter: The Life and Love Story of She-Who-Must-Be-Obeyed*. London: Hutchinson and Co., 1923.

Haggard, Lilias R. *The Cloak That I Left: A Biography of the Author Henry Rider Haggard*. London: Hodder and Stoughton, 1951.

Higgins, D.S. *Rider Haggard: The Great Storyteller*. London: Cassell, 1981.

Hinz, Evelyn J. "Rider Haggard's *She*: An Archetypal 'History of Adventure.'" *Studies in the Novel* 4:3 (1972): 417–31.

Katz, Wendy. *Rider Haggard and the Fictions of Empire*. Cambridge: Cambridge UP, 1987.

Low, Ching-Liang G. *White Skins / Black Masks: Representation and Colonialism*. New York: Routledge, 1996.

Malley, Shawn. "'Time Hath No Power Against Identity': Historical Continuity and Archaeological Adventure in H. Rider Haggard's *She*." *English Literature in Transition 1880–1920* 40:3 (1997): 275–97.

Manthorpe, Victoria. *Children of the Empire: The Victorian Haggards*. London: Victor Gollancz, 1996.

McClintock, Anne. *Imperial Leather: Race, Gender and Sexuality in the Colonial Contest*. New York: Routledge, 1995.

Michalski, Robert. "Divine Hunger: Culture and the Commodity in Rider Haggard's *She*." *Journal of Victorian Culture* 1:1 (Spring 1996): 76–97.

Michalson, Karen. *Victorian Fantasy Literature*. Lewiston: Edwin Mellen, 1990.

Michael, Leo. *She: An Allegory of the Church*. New York: Frank Lovell and Co., 1889.

Moss, John G. "Three Motifs in Haggard's *She*." *English Literature in Transition* 16:1 (1973): 27–34.

Munich, Adrienne. *Queen Victoria's Secrets*. New York: Columbia, 1998.

Murphy, Patricia. "The Gendering of History in *She*." *Studies in English Literature 1500–1900* 39:4 (1999): 747–72.

Pearson, Richard. "Archaeology and Gothic Desire: Vitality Beyond the Grave in H. Rider Haggard's Ancient Egypt." *Victorian Gothic*. Ruth Robbins and Julian Wolfreys, eds. New York: Palgrave, 2000. 218–44.

Pocock, Tom. *Rider Haggard and the Lost Empire*. London: Weidenfeld and Nicholson, 1993.

Rickels, Laurence. "Mummy's Curse." *American Journal of Semiotics* 9:4 (1992): 47–58.

Rodgers, Terrence. "Empires of the Imagination: Rider Haggard, Popular Fiction, and Africa." *Writing and Africa*. Mpaliva-Hangson Msiska and Paul Hyland, eds. New York: Longman, 1997. 103–21.

———. "Queer Fascinations: Rider Haggard, Imperial Gothic, and the Orient." *Decadence and Danger: Writing, History, and the Fin de Siècle*. ed. Tracey Hill. Bath: Sulis Press, 1997. 46–63.

———. "Restless Desire: Rider Haggard, Orientalism, and the New Woman." *Women: A Cultural Review* 10:1 (1999): 35–46.

Showalter, Elaine. *Sexual Anarchy: Gender and Culture at the Fin de Siècle*. New York: Viking, 1990.

Stott, Rebecca. "The Dark Continent: Africa as Female Body in Haggard's Adventure Fiction." *Feminist Review* 32 (Summer 1989): 69–89.

UCLA Department of Special Collections. H. Rider Haggard papers. Collection 418.

Whatmore, D.E. *H. Rider Haggard: A Bibliography*. London: Mansell, 1987.